A
BLACK
SOUL

ALSO BY STUART THAMAN

NEF HOUSE PUBLISHING

ISBN: 978-1-948374-16-3

Cover by J Caleb Clark (www.jcalebdesign.com)
Interior layout by Bodie D Dykstra (www.bdbookdesign.com)

A
BLACK
SOUL

FORSAKEN TALENTS
— GRIMDARK LITRPG —

STUART THAMAN

"Get thee hence, thou horrid monster,
To the caverns of the white-bear,
To the deep abyss of serpents,
To the vales, and swamps, and fenlands,
To the ever-silent waters,
To the dead-seas of the Northland.
Get thee hence to Kalma, the god of the tombs."

~The Old Kalevala, compiled by Elias Lönnrot, 1835

CHAPTER 1

I had died before in the game, of course. Back when the servers were fully functional, death had been easy. Everything would go black, it would hurt for a few seconds, and then I would awaken above my respawn unit in my apartment. Sometimes I would have a headache, other times I would feel fine. Mostly, I woke up tired and hungry, eager to get a snack and head back into the game.

When I died in front of King Ahmose II's castle, pinned to the door by five magical arrows, it wasn't anywhere close to the same experience. It was instantly harrowing, and the flood of memories it brought racing to my mind was nearly too much for me to handle. Being dead, I had no escape. I couldn't get the images to stop, couldn't even close my eyes or look away—my only option was to stare in unmoving horror. I didn't know how long my mind could survive.

The first thing I saw was the crushing darkness of absolute void. There was simply nothing. I could think, I knew I could see, but wherever my eyes looked there was just more infinite nothing. The darkness was ceaseless. It felt oppressive on my shoulders, my head, my chest; though it didn't actually bring any pain. Perhaps my physical body did not yet exist. In truth, I wasn't sure if the spell Xollmomath had placed upon me would be successful. Without the respawn mechanic being active in the game, would my soul still be captured and returned to my body?

I had no idea.

The thought of dying for real didn't scare me at all. When it really came down to it, the only thing still fueling me was revenge. I hadn't killed Vic, hadn't even figured out where to look for him, but that was all I had left. My wife was dead. She'd been dead for years. My daughter, Ingrid, was dead as well. My parents had died more than a decade ago when the medicine started running out. I didn't have any brothers or sisters. Everyone I had ever loved was dead.

In the soul-crushing darkness, I wondered if that was even true. Did I love my underlings? Did I love the handful of players who served me at Undercroft Citadel? Maybe. I wasn't sure.

Elyk was too unhinged for me to use that kind of powerful language when describing our relationship. The man was a faithful servant and a powerful warrior, but what we had was more like the standard trappings of friendship and mutual reliance, not love.

Helvegen was really the only one who had ever opened up to me. I felt a connection to her that was different from the others. Did I love her? No. *Could* our friendship turn into something more than it was? Potentially. Perhaps I would come to view her as the sister I never had. I knew she looked at me with admiration—at least that's how I interpreted it— and I also knew that something was missing from my entire life. Ingrid's death had left a massive, painful chasm in my heart that demanded to be filled.

If I would ever find that kind of fulfillment at Undercroft

Citadel—assuming I survived at all—I could not say with certainty.

Staring into the abyss, I felt my emotional pain far stronger than any physical pain the arrows pinning me to the door could ever cause. I had nothing, I loved no one, and I knew it.

The crushing void of infinite darkness seemed to last forever. I had no accurate perception of time, no way of knowing how long I had been caught in the cruel space between life and death, and every second that passed by was nothing short of an eternity.

Finally, something started to change. I couldn't tell what it was at first, just that I was beginning to feel a little different, and then I saw it: the pure black curtain I had been relentlessly gazing into was starting to lift. Shapes were taking form in the darkness, and though they held no meaning that I could discern, they gave me comfort. They were something I could latch onto to anchor me in space and time.

Hours ticked away, and the shapes gradually became clearer and clearer until I could start to assign them names and descriptions based on things I had known in life. Identifying what I saw was kind of like finding constellations in the sky. I had to look both at what was there and what was not there in order to actually see anything, and even then I was still applying a significant amount of my imagination.

As the shapes continued to sharpen in my vision and become more concrete, my terror escalated further. I saw the outline of a woman, one I instantly recognized, and I could not look away. I had no eyelids to close, no neck to turn, and no hands to block my vision. I stared in horror as my wife slowly materialized into view. She was lying down as she had in her final days and weeks, plastic tubing running from a myriad of places on her body to disappear into the void above her head.

Instead of seeing her in the hospital bed where she had

lived out her last several months, I saw her half-covered in inky slime, partially submerged beneath the fetid waters of a rancid swamp. She was looking away from me, or I was simply approaching her from the side, and the water level rose up almost to her head. Her arms and legs stuck up from the black morass as well. They almost resembled fallen, rotten branches that hadn't quite been pulled into the liquid depths of the swamp.

I watched, and my wife was unmoving. She just stared to the side, to my left, and I could not turn my head to see what had so captivated her attention. I wanted to call to her and try to offer her some measure of comfort, but I had no voice. I could not call to her. I could not speak her name, not even a whisper, and she did not turn to see me. She only stared, and I was utterly powerless.

The scene before me eventually cleared enough that I could make out the water in which my wife sat so motionless. Or rather, I could start to see what was underneath the water, and a fresh wave of fear and nauseating helplessness rushed through my consciousness. Just beneath the water's black surface lurked a collection of faces, each of them missing a body.

I instantly recognized the faces. Chief among them was Ingrid, her eyes full of pain and begging me to help. Surrounding her tormented visage were at least two dozen others, and I had killed every single one of them. I recognized faces from the members of the Pyreborn Legion. They wore scowls, staring intently at me from just below the surface of the murky water. The people I had killed in Whitechapel were there as well. Their faces held the same expressions—judging, searching, and finding me unworthy.

In addition to Ingrid and the faces of everyone else I had killed, I saw King Ahmose II's daughter. Her face was next to the decapitated head of Briggan, the paladin I had butchered in the king's castle. Theirs were the only faces showing blood on them. It wasn't overly grotesque, just a faint smattering of red across their flesh, but it was enough for revulsion to consume my consciousness.

My mind floated close enough to the swampy scene for me to smell it. Part of my consciousness regarded the addition of the new sensory information to be a good thing—perhaps some indication that I would soon awaken, but the rest of me dreaded it. If I could smell, I knew my hearing would return as well. I didn't want to hear.

I didn't want to hear my wife's voice asking me to kill her so she wouldn't have to endure another round of chemo or another disfiguring surgery. I didn't want to hear her screams of pain as the doctors performed another spinal tap, her hand desperately crushing mine within its grip.

I didn't want to hear Ingrid crying in pain as magical poison coursed through her body.

More than anything else, I didn't want to hear my daughter's cries as she clung to her mother's body, the droning sound of a flat-lined heart monitor ringing in my ears.

Ever so slowly, my wife's face turned. Little ripples radiated out from her body as she moved, gently obscuring all the faces gathered beneath the surface. My wife faced me, and I saw the right side of her body. It was torn and tattered, the skin hanging loosely from the bone underneath, and her eyes looked sad. She was crying. Everything about her countenance spoke only of fear and pain. Of ruin.

If she could see me—whatever I truly was in that space between life and death—she did not give me any indication.

Her eyes were vacant and soulless. They bored into me, but they were not the eyes of a person with life. They lacked all their former luster and sheen, all their spark . . . they were just as dead as she was.

All I could do was watch. My fear was at its apex, sorrow

the only emotion competing with it, and my mind threatened to slip away. I felt like my only anchor to reality was deteriorating. My mind couldn't handle the images I saw combined with the infinite darkness surrounding me. If I ever awoke back in Wonder, I had no idea if I would be sane.

Perhaps I would never awaken. If I stayed in the space between life and death for eternity, I would lose whatever shreds of my sanity remained. I would lose them quickly, and then none of it would matter. Desperate to cling to whatever sanity remained within the darkest trappings of my mind, I forced myself not to break. I stared at my dead, rotting wife, and I willed myself to survive. I had told her to be strong hundreds of times, and now it was my turn.

Pain shot through the intangible part of space where I imagined my head must have been, and then my sense of touch returned all at once. I could feel the swampy, stagnant water covering my entire body, though I had no physical form to see, not even a reflection coming from the surface.

Sound came next. I heard insects clicking and buzzing in the black void comprising the distance. I could hear the water as it slowly lapped against my dead wife's legs. I heard my breathing as well, which gave me pause, for I could not choose to hold my breath or otherwise control my lungs in any way.

I wished beyond hope that I would not hear anything else. The sounds of the swamp were enough.

Sadly, my hope was poorly placed. My wife, her eyes still looking past me rather than at me, started to speak. Her rotten jaw unhinged at an odd angle, drooping down more on the right than on the left. "You have served Lady Kalma well, Ben Hales, Defender of the Necropolis. You have earned her favor, Ben Hales."

"You'll bring me back to life?" I asked, my voice coming from every bit of air over the swamp at once.

My decaying wife nodded, and her jaw unhinged a little more. "You have been blessed with Lady Kalma's shroud. Such blessings are not offered often or without deep deliberation, and you have earned the fruits of your labor. But do not take your tasks lightly, Ben Hales."

"What does Lady Kalma ask of me?"

"You have taken on her mantle, Ben Hales, and you must stay within Lady Kalma's favor if you are to survive. She demands conquest and more corpses to add to her endless stench. Go and conquer the seven worlds of Wonder. Bring Lady Kalma's abyssal message to all the people of Wonder. Kill any who resist. Proselytize for the true goddess, Ben Hales!" Her voice was animated and powerful, though her body did not move to match her passion.

I didn't really understand exactly what kind of message I was supposed to deliver. As far as I knew, Lady Kalma didn't have shrines or temples like the other gods of Wonder. Hell, I wasn't sure anyone other than those of us who lived at Undercroft Citadel had even heard Lady Kalma's name. Perhaps *that* was the message. I needed to bring back the goddess's name from Wonder's ancient history.

"What would you have me do? Build temples?" I asked.

The dead woman laughed. "Lady Kalma has blessed your necropolis with a chapel. Further her name, and conquer in her stead, Ben Hales. Spread her chapels throughout the land, and Lady Kalma will provide you with infinite reward."

"All I want is another day with my wife . . . with my daughter . . ." I quietly replied.

No matter what the strange images promised me, I knew it wouldn't be possible. The game didn't understand that the respawning module had been corrupted, so it had no way of knowing what death truly meant. Maybe that was for the best. If the AI changed too much in response to the attacks on the servers, the results could be cataclysmic. I shook my head. Or I tried to shake my head, but of course my physical body did not exist, and nothing happened.

"Lady Kalma is a god!" the swamp-covered image of my dead wife cheerfully announced. "Anything you desire can be yours! All she asks is for your service! And your soul!"

Before I had a chance to ask the strange image what exactly she meant, everything returned to black once more. I floated through time and space, through the vast expanse of nothingness that existed between life and death, for what felt like a second lifetime. My brain had no practical way of coping with the trauma of my own death, and my ability to perceive time—or anything else—accurately was beyond destroyed.

Eventually, I felt my real eyes begin to flutter open. They were crusted with blood, and it took a significant effort to pry them open even the tiniest fraction.

I still couldn't see. Even when my eyes were fully open and I was blinking once more in the real world, my vision had not returned. Or . . . was I blind?

When players had obtained resurrection spells before the server corruption, something altogether rare to come by, the mechanic had simply dropped them off in a new version of their body right at the nearest portal. But since the portals were now closed, the magic had decided to return me to my own body, presumably because it could not generate the needed code to produce a new one at any portal.

Everything hurt more than I could process. My senses were overloaded beyond reason, and for a long moment I simply hung on the wooden door and struggled to get my body once more under my control. It took a concerted effort, but I eventually managed to rein in enough of my consciousness to get my eyes and ears working once more.

I could hear the sounds of people coming from behind me, from the throne room. Their voices sounded sad. What exactly had happened? The last thing I remembered . . . was an arrow slicing through my right arm and holding it against the wood of the door.

But before that . . . things were fuzzy. I blinked several times, and the castle bailey in front of me started to come into focus. I must have bled from my scalp at some point, because everything was coated in a red tint that reminded me of blood. As I looked out at the bailey, the events leading up to my death started to come back to me in bits and pieces. I remembered fighting Kevin, one of the most powerful rangers in all of Echelon, but . . . I couldn't remember where my armor had gone. Had the guild looted my corpse? If they had taken the armor, I didn't have a chance. Undercroft Citadel would fall.

No, the memory of taking off my armor started coming back, and I knew I had given it to my party before I had died. *Always thinking ahead.*

The door I was pinned to started to move. Someone was pushing it outward.

I hung my head back down and pretended to be dead. It didn't take much effort to affect the ruse, covered in blood and mired in pain as I was.

Whoever it was that came out was female; I could tell by her voice, and she cursed me. She was crying, and it felt like she even spit on my legs, probably standing with her hands on her hips and shaking her head. "You fucking bastard," she sobbed. "You didn't have to kill Ophelia, you jackass. She was just a girl! Barely old enough to play the game!"

The woman spit on me again. I thought back to my own dead wife and child. There was no sympathy in my heart. Not a single drop. Whoever the woman was, she would know more pain before I was truly gone from the game. Her first taste of loss was nothing.

I opened my eyes.

CHAPTER 2

The woman screamed. The noise that left her mouth was truly blood-curdling, a piercing wail that would have been more natural had it come from a banshee in a dungeon instead of a player standing in a muddy bailey.

The scream was so loud that I knew whoever else was inside the keep must have heard. I didn't have much time.

Summoning all of my strength—and wishing for the added physical bonus offered by my gauntlets—I wrenched my left arm from the door. The arrow was still lodged through the meat of my bicep, but I didn't care. I was alive, and Lady Kalma was sustaining me.

I pulled my right arm free, and then the weight of my body broke the two magical arrows in my legs to send me tumbling to the ground. I caught myself before the woman could hope to run, terrified as she was, and then I stood.

The woman was middle-aged and short, and I towered over her cowering frame. She continued to wail at the top of her lungs. The name hovering above her head had a title behind it. She was the Queen of Echelon. Ophelia had been her daughter.

With a blood-soaked arm, I reached out and grabbed her by the front of her tunic. She scratched weakly at my arm, but my iron grip prevailed. When she was close enough to taste my breath, I unleashed *A Feast of Spores* into her mouth, and her screams quickly devolved into rough wheezing and panicked coughs.

I followed my first talent activation with *Malignant Putrescence*, my most recent skill acquisition. Magic surged through my veins and out of my palm. In the space of a heartbeat, a poisonous sack appeared under the flesh of the queen's neck, throbbing and moving with her own pulse. Her neck would explode in three minutes, and I only hoped she would be surrounded by guards when it happened.

"Do not worry," I told her as she struggled for air. "You'll see your precious daughter soon enough."

With my free hand, I reached for the bottom of her throat and began clawing at her skin. Despite the woman's age, she had not played much of the game itself, and her level was even lower than mine. My higher physical stat made tearing out her esophagus with my fingers a relatively easy task—easier than doing it on Earth would have been, at least. Luckily, whatever poison my magic had implanted in her body didn't come spilling out all over my arm.

Her wailing came to an abrupt halt, and I threw her corpse aside without another thought.

I needed to get home. I remembered the general layout of the castle's kitchen, barracks, and the stables, and I ran across the bailey for the door that would eventually lead beyond the castle walls. Behind me, I could hear footsteps pounding on the bloody marble of the keep's main entryway. When someone finally burst through the doors, I was already beyond their view, back once more in the barracks.

It didn't take me long to follow the hideous trail of blood

and butchery all the way from the barracks to the grazing pasture outside the castle walls. All the guards on the other side of the wall were no doubt tending to the new horror I had left for them, and no one pursued me beyond the city. I was free at last. Alive and free.

◄◆►

By the time I arrived within view of Undercroft Citadel a few hours later, my unholy endurance was nearly expended. The adrenaline that had kept my legs pumping had expired. I still had two broken arrows lodged in my thighs and another in my gut, and I had to assume that the only reason I had even been able to move was a result of Lady Kalma's powerful shroud ensuring that I returned to life.

The top of the wall was alive with activity; zombies and warlocks were patrolling on high alert, and I saw a pair of gargoyles circling above them as well. Almost at once, the complement of lookouts patrolling the perimeter saw me approaching, though I couldn't tell if they recognized who I was or not. I waved, and the effort of raising my arm above my head brought so much pain that I nearly passed out.

I fell to my knees. When the front gate started swinging outward a few seconds later, I smiled. Helvegen was leading the charge, with several others behind her and what appeared to be a pair of winged gargoyles.

I didn't have enough strength to greet my party. I closed my eyes and let them get to work. A potion was roughly forced down my throat, and then two heavy claws dug into my shoulders. Another set wrapped around my ankles. Then I was aloft, flying back to the necropolis with the magical effects of a healing potion starting to calm my tormented mind.

I awoke some time later, and I could see a faint purple light through my eyelids. I was in my room. Bandages covered almost every inch of my body, and my muscles creaked and groaned when I tried in vain to sit up.

"You need more rest," a woman's voice said from my left. It was Helvegen.

"Praise Lady Kalma, he lives!" Xia added from somewhere else in the room.

Their voices felt too loud inside my head, reminding me of the hangover I had dealt with after the Dark Revelry.

"Be quiet, I . . . need to sleep more," I said. Someone's hands gently brushed against my forehead, and then another glass bottle was pushed up to my lips. I greedily drank the healing potion before letting my head collapse back down to my pillows, my eyes shut tight against the world.

Before I drifted off to sleep once more, I mentally commanded my room to bring down the temperature. I thought I could hear a few murmurs of surprise from around my bed when the cool air started moving. A few moments later, I was asleep.

When I awoke again, my body felt relatively normal. I was able to move my head and neck without too much pain, and even my back was starting to feel better. The second healing potion had been stronger than the first. My eyes fluttered open, and I saw no one else in the room. The gentle breeze from the room's magical cooling system felt great on my sore chest. The bandages covering my wounds were no longer soaked in blood, and I knew that I was out of the woods. I would survive.

At least for the time being.

There was still so much work to be done. I had pissed off the royal family—what was left of it—and I had no doubt that

Echelon would be moving against Undercroft Citadel before long. They would hire the Resurrection guild as well, and that fight would be a difficult one to win. I could practically feel our luck running out with every passing second. That sinking sensation in the pit of my stomach didn't go away.

When I finally stood from my bed and raised the lights, I figured it was sometime in the late afternoon. I immediately noticed a new pair of guards stationed outside my door. They were stone gargoyles, and they perched completely motionless to either side of my room's entrance. Unless I had mentally commanded them in my sleep, I had not given the statues any orders to guard my room. I also didn't think anyone else in Undercroft Citadel had the ability to mentally communicate with the various pieces of the necropolis. Perhaps I was wrong. I'd have to ask Xollmomath and Xia about it later.

I stretched, and a few icy fingers of pain lanced through my upper thighs. For the first time since returning home, I decided to look underneath the bandages and see what kind of damage had been done. Before the server corruption, taking huge hits had never really meant much in terms of scarring or long-term disfigurement. Healing potions didn't do anything to fix cosmetic damage, but every time a player logged out of the game and went home, the scars they had acquired in Wonder disappeared. Without a working portal to exit, I had to live with my skin, as flayed as it had surely become.

Hesitantly, I peeled back a few layers of the bandage around my right thigh. My fears were correct. The skin had been destroyed, and the accelerated healing process granted by potions meant that a large, red scar that looked like a misshapen star had already formed. I pushed down gently on the top of the bandages on my left leg, and I felt a similar lump of scar tissue there as well. Oh well. I wasn't terribly concerned.

The scars my wife had sustained from all of her surgeries had been far worse, and I'd never stopped loving her.

After a few more stretches, I opened the door to the necropolis and stepped out into the afternoon light. Almost at once, my stomach started churning. I was about thirty feet above the ground—a full thirty feet higher than I should have been. When I had left Undercroft Citadel for Echelon, my room had been on the ground floor of the necropolis, not towering three stories in the air. At least the magic controlling the necropolis had seen fit to build a staircase down to the ground so I wouldn't need to fly back and forth with gargoyles every time I needed to sleep or grab something from my room.

The staircase itself was a sight to behold just as much as the view was. The stairs were made of obsidian, glistening and reflective under the sunlight, and they flared outward like something from a history textbook about the baroque era. Every five or so stairs were marked by stone animals, though not more gargoyles. The new guardians were kind of like trilobites, some sort of heavily armored insect or crustacean with ten legs and four antennae. They each stood about two feet tall, the antennae sticking up from their heads half as long as their bodies.

I mentally commanded one of the creatures to come to my side. It moved at once, eager to obey my silent instructions, and rolled into a little ball like a pill bug. Using two of its legs to propel itself, it rolled up the staircase to my feet where it unfurled and stood strangely bipedal before me. Somehow, I felt like the stone insect was attempting to stand at attention and that being on two legs was not its preferred stance.

You can relax, I told the bug. It dropped back down to all ten legs, its armored carapace expertly concealing the rest of its body. I held out my arm and then commanded the creature to scurry up to my palm, which it readily obeyed. Before it reached my hand, I had to set it back down once more as it was simply too heavy for me to lift. The small statue must have weighed at least a hundred pounds.

Without anything else for me to learn about the critter, I let it return to its place at the side of the stairs and revert back to its non-animated form.

Then came the somewhat arduous trek down to ground level. My legs burned with every step, struggling to support my body weight as I descended. I could have summoned a gargoyle to fly me down, but I wanted to get used to walking unaided as soon as I could. My sore, battered legs needed the brief spurt of exercise.

The first floor of the necropolis was far larger than it used to be. The workshop had been sublimated into the new ground level, improved as well, and it was now abutting several other freshly minted rooms. The first one closest to the staircase turned out to be an armory. Racks of spears, breastplates, and helmets lined the walls. The gear wasn't anything exceptional by any means, but it would be more than adequate to give to the zombie soldiers and send them into battle. The room also had a few practice dummies and a couple bins full of scrap.

Next to the armory was a barracks not unlike the one my party had been inside just yesterday . . . or . . . I didn't actually know how long I had spent recovering. It felt like yesterday, but it could have been last week. I'd have to ask.

The barracks had ten sets of bunks, each with three beds, and a set of cabinets lining the back wall. Our undead soldiers didn't need to sleep, but I imagined someday having an army of both NPCs and players to fill the barracks, and the first one would only be one of many. I would command thousands, and Echelon would crumble beneath my boot heels.

Next to the barracks was a small stable with six stalls and

a little paddock in front of it. Sadly, while there were buckets hanging from the side of each stall, we had no horses. That was something we could figure out later.

The final room on the bottom floor of the necropolis was our new chapel. Inspecting the bone-covered doors, I thought that perhaps calling it an ossuary might have been a better designation. The entire section of the necropolis around the chapel was constructed from thin white bones and bleached skulls. They weren't human—not all of them— but the skeletons of all sorts of wild beasts. The skulls right above the doorway were mostly from imps, though the one in the very center was most definitely a human. I wondered for a moment if it was *my* skull. I had died, after all, and it wouldn't surprise me if Lady Kalma had taken a macabre memento. Perhaps she had replaced the skull around my brain with something else entirely.

I silently willed the chapel's bone doors to open, and they obeyed my command. Dark, swirling energy scattered out from the inside of the chapel. It was a mix of black shadow, deep purple shimmer, and wisps of grey that reminded me of smoke. More bones made up the interior walls. I walked into the gloom and mentally told the lights to come on, but nothing happened. There were no magical crystals on the ceiling to control the atmosphere, so I just left the doors open to see by what little sunlight managed to penetrate the darkness.

The chapel wasn't very large. There were no pews or benches for parishioners to sit on and watch a service, and I got the idea that traditional church customs were far from the norm for Lady Kalma's followers. Against the far wall opposite the door stood a horizontal altar. It was the only object in the room not made from bones. I looked above it, and a smile broke out across my face. There was a bone knife dangling from a hook right above the table. The table was meant for sacrifice. I practically jumped with excitement at the thought of what garish rewards we might reap with the right offerings.

Seeing the sacrificial altar reminded me that we had succeeded in our quest. We had claimed the scarab for ourselves, and that meant Xollmomath could reassemble his master's ancient relic. I had looted some other artifacts as well, and I hoped my warlocks had made good use of them. As I thought about restoring the Founder's Stake, a new quest notification scrolled across the bottom of my vision:

System Notification: New Event! The forces of Undercroft Citadel have recovered a mighty relic once thought lost to the ages. If the relic is restored, untold effects may begin to spread across the land, placing all of Echelon in danger. King Ahmose II has called upon all loyal subjects to rid the land of Undercroft Citadel!

"Well . . ." I muttered. I read the notification twice to make sure I didn't miss anything. We had been upgraded from a dungeon to a raid. Everyone loyal to Echelon had officially been recruited to slay us. I figured we had at least a few days, perhaps a week, before anyone from the city would risk moving against us. But it wouldn't be a single guild at our gates, and they wouldn't be poorly prepared. The king would organize a real raid, maybe hundreds of players, and they would be ready for the challenge. I thought of Kevin and the Resurrection guild. In all likelihood, they would lead the charge.

I needed to know exactly what Xollmomath could do with the scarab. I found him near the front gate commanding our charnel golem as an excavator to help Geirr, our resident engineer, with the new trap he had built. Everyone seemed to be in good spirits to see me up and about.

"Welcome back to Undercroft Citadel, Master," Xollmomath said when he caught sight of my approach.

I grasped him by the forearm and smiled. "Good to be with you once more," I said. I couldn't simply ask the bald necromancer about the system notification since he was an

NPC and would not have received it, but I could instantly tell that he knew why I had come to him.

"You did well returning the scarab," he stated.

"What exactly does it do?"

The man rubbed a calloused hand over his hairless head, his red eyes boring into me. "The Founder's Stake was my first master's weapon. He stole magic from the very center of the world, the knowledge of life and death itself, and trapped it inside the wood. With the Founder's Stake in his hand, my master was able to conquer city after city, laying waste to their populations and bringing forth armies of the undead to serve as his slaves."

Death, destruction, eternal servitude—I could only imagine what kind of spells the Stake would unlock. Of course, Xollmomath wouldn't be able to tell me in explicit terms, but the way he described it was clear enough. I also got the idea that the Founder's Stake allowed the wielder to make new necromancers as well. That could certainly be useful. I'd never heard of player characters in Wonder becoming class trainers before. Being able to bestow classes on more players would give me a monumental advantage.

"Alright, so how do we reforge it or put it back together?" I asked. The ancient item was almost entirely wood, so I wasn't sure if Geirr would be able to figure it out or not.

Xollmomath shook his head, his dark eyes cast down. "Reassembling the Founder's Stake will be an easy task. All that is required is for the fragments to be near enough to each other, and the powerful magic within will bind itself, becoming whole once more. But it is not so easy, Defender of the Necropolis."

Of course it wouldn't be that simple. If restoring the relic was just a matter of tossing the parts onto a table, Xollmomath would have done it by now.

"The Stake will require sustenance," the necromancer

explained. "The spirit within the scarab has slumbered for many centuries, and it shall be in need of flesh to consume the moment it awakens. You must be prepared with a sacrifice."

"Could we just sacrifice one of the zombies? We have plenty of them. We might as well, right?" I figured burning through another mindless undead soldier couldn't hurt, and it actually felt like something a necromancer's trapped spirit would appreciate.

Sadly, Xollmomath's face darkened with worry. "No, Ben Hales, a soulless monster will not suffice. You must make a proper sacrifice—something you hold dear and do not want to lose—but something that must be destroyed. If you do not shed worthy blood, the Founder's Stake will claim your own."

"What did your old master sacrifice when made the Stake in the first place?" I asked. Restoring the artifact was starting to sound more and more difficult.

"My master had a mighty necropolis, a proper fortress of darkness that rose up to the clouds. His city covered miles. There was nothing within a thousand miles that could rival the strength or size of his kingdom. With such power came many other benefits, and my master kept a harem of thirty slaves, each one a wife, and each one very much loved. My master had them brought to his chapel one at a time where he plunged the Founder's Stake through their hearts. When it was finished, the blood was drained from their corpses, and their empty bodies were burned." I felt the necromancer's fathomless eyes boring into my very soul. The weight of his words was almost too much for me to fully comprehend, and mention of the harem brought flashbacks of my wife's funeral to the forefront of my mind.

"What . . . did he do with the blood?" I asked, though I wasn't sure I was prepared for an answer.

Xollmomath's dark countenance took on a sinister grin.

"My master had it collected in two great porcelain tanks. When he finally conquered the largest kingdom in the land, the city that once stood where Olympia City now stands, he drowned the royal family in the blood of his wives. The children went first while the king and queen watched, and then they went into the tanks as well. When it was finished, the two porcelain vats were buried beneath the castle in Olympia City, sealed forever."

"And was all that required just to be able to use the Founder's Stake in battle?" I went on. It seemed like a hell of a lot of work just to get a weapon and go on a campaign across the land.

"Only the sacrifice is required," Xollmomath explained. "Once the Stake has been sated, you will be free to use it as you please. Drowning your enemies in blood and burying them beneath the ground is not something the Stake demands of the one who wields it."

That was a relief, if only for the fact that putting together such a morbid ritual would take years to plan. Still, I wasn't exactly sure what I would do about a sacrifice. I couldn't just grab some hapless NPC from Riverside and cut out their heart. That would never be good enough to satisfy the kind of evil Xollmomath had described.

I thanked the necromancer for his help, then climbed up to the top of the gatehouse to watch Geirr work as I mulled over everything I had learned. The engineer was about forty yards from the gate, working alongside the charnel golem, and getting his floating trap fixed into the ground. Depending on how quickly he could build a second one, I really wanted to see a demonstration. The whole contraption sounded ridiculous.

Eventually, my thoughts still muddled with a myriad of different thoughts regarding the Founder's Stake, Geirr came over to the gatehouse to take a break.

"Hey," I said, welcoming him beside me on the wooden decking.

The engineer stopped for a moment, his eyes searching something on my face, then shook his head. "Glad to see you back . . . You, uh, you don't have a mirror, do you?"

I instinctively reached up to my face, but I felt nothing out of the ordinary. No lumps, bumps, or anything besides a little bit of scraping that had almost fully healed. "What is it?" I asked.

Geirr sat down next to me and sighed. "Looks like a scar coming on. Something black working up the side of your face. Have Xia or the herbalist take a look at it. One of them would probably know what it is."

"Shit. How bad is it?"

"Nothing much. It just kind of looks like a little black worm stuck in your skin." Geirr touched a spot on my neck and then traced it up to the bottom of my jawline. "Not too big. Not yet, at least."

"I wonder why Xollmomath didn't say anything about it," I said. I had talked to the necromancer for a good amount of time, and he had never bothered to mention my new little addition.

"Heh, he's probably seen so much corruption in his life that something small doesn't even register." Geirr pulled a waterskin from a pocket and took a long drink. He was sweating from all his work, though he looked like he enjoyed it quite a bit.

"How long have I been out?" I asked.

"It's been three days since you stumbled up to the front gate," Geirr answered. "Honestly, I still don't know how the hell you were alive. The way my sister talks about it, you took on an entire high-level guild all on your own. No way you could have killed them all, right? Or is it true?"

His eyes were wide like a kid meeting his favorite celebrity.

"No, whatever Helvegen or Elyk have said about what happened, I didn't win. Resurrection, one of the biggest guilds in Echelon, showed up to defend the keep. I let them kill me."

Geirr's eyes screwed up in confusion. "But . . ."

"Lady Kalma brought me back," I said with a laugh. "Xollmomath had cast some kind of shroud on my body. It was just a one-time thing, though. No immortality."

"Damn. That would have been nice."

"Yeah. So I didn't kill a whole guild by myself. I just died and convinced them to leave my body alone, mutilated as it was."

Geirr joined my subtle laughter. "To hear my sister tell the story, you'd think you were a god. She says you basically sacked the entire castle, left nothing but corpses behind, and then you went off solo to slaughter the rest of the city. Ha, the way she talked about it and how she was worried sick when you didn't wake up, I think she's got a little something for you, if you don't mind me saying."

"Not at all, Geirr. I appreciate the honesty." In truth, it was exceedingly satisfying to just sit down and talk to someone without ordering them around or going over official business. I liked getting to have a genuine conversation.

"You should talk to Hel. I know she's been missing you, and she was more than concerned. And don't worry at all about me. If you want to date my sister or . . . whatever, just don't worry about me. I'm here for the long run." The man's voice awkwardly trailed off, and he looked away, clearly embarrassed.

I clapped him on the shoulder. "Hey, I was married back on Earth. My wife might have died, but I'm still married to her, you know? But I'll at least go let Hel know I'm alive and walking around."

Geirr was clearly relieved, though the awkward air hanging between us didn't fully dissipate. I decided to let him get back to his work and left the gatehouse roof with a smile on my face—my scarred face, I realized, though I didn't really care. I had a few other small scars in various places, and I had never been too concerned with physical appearance in the first place.

I found Helvegen in the new and expanded workshop on the first floor of the necropolis. She was helping Kulgun, our alchemist, with a few glass beakers. I stood to the side of the doorway and watched her for a few moments, wondering if there was any chance that I could come to think of a woman the way Geirr had suggested I think of Helvegen. The woman was attractive, that much was clear for anyone to see, but all I saw was my wife when I closed my eyes and let my mind drift to more carnal places.

The woman saw me a few seconds later and broke my contemplation. "You're awake!" she gasped. She set down the beaker she was holding and ran to me, wrapping me in her arms and nearly knocking me to the ground. My legs were too weak to fully support the both of us. Realizing that I was about to fall, Helvegen let go of me at once, and her face filled with concern. "I'm so sorry!" she said.

"Ha, you're fine," I told her. "I'm just glad you made it back alive."

"You're glad that *I'm* alive?" she gaped.

"I'm glad we're *all* alive." The mere fact that we had raided the king's castle and sacked the royal archive without losing a single player was nothing short of a miracle. A single warlock, some zombies, and the truthbreaker paladin were welcome prices to pay for all we had gained. Losing Elyk, Helvegen, or Xia would have been disastrous.

The woman hugged me again, that time showing a little more restraint and a little less enthusiasm. When she finally let go, I saw what it was Geirr had been describing. The way her eyes filled with longing when she looked into mine told me everything.

I kept her at arm's length. "I know we brought back a little more from the archive. What all did we get? Anything good?" I figured that changing the subject would be a decent way to let her down easy or at least divert her attention.

My question worked, and Helvegen excitedly bounded back into the workshop to collect a few things and show me what we had taken. "Here, this recipe is the best one," she said, showing me an alchemical formula with an accompanying schematic.

I didn't understand any of it. My craftsmanship skill was still woefully low, and I had never watched any of the professional crafters on the streams. "What's it make?" I asked.

"An enchanter's potion," she answered with a huge smile.

That was something I recognized. Enchanter's potions were hard to come by, and I guessed the material components involved would be hard to acquire as well, but having the recipe and a skilled alchemist on hand to make them would be wildly useful. The potions basically accelerated the work of a high-level enchanter or wizard.

The brew could be applied to items to add magical properties to them. The strength of the enchantment depended on the potency and purity of the mixture, though even small augments were usually helpful. Even better, the enchantment wasn't random like other effects in Wonder. It would be something related to whatever item was the target. For instance, soaking a warhammer in an enchanter's potion could never give a buff to slashing damage or increase the wielder's trade skill. The most likely result would be something to either buff an element or the efficacy of the hammer's attacks. In the end, every enchanter's potion was a roll of the dice, but it had only the slightest chance of abject failure.

"How quickly does Kulgun think we can start making potions?" I asked. I was practically salivating at the idea of adding enchantments to all the gear we had. Elyk needed magical

enhancement badly, and I knew whatever an enchanter's potion would give to his scythe would have to be amazing.

At my question, Helvegen seemed to deflate a little. "We
need more plants from the herbalist. Her grove is up and
running, but it will be at least a week before she has anything
ready to use, and the first few batches of herbs won't be very
good. She needs more experience."

Our herbalist was probably our most important asset, at
least for the time being. The armory and workshop were both
nice, though with all my legendary gear, outfitting soldiers
wasn't nearly as pressing a concern as brewing potions and
pushing our magic to new heights. That's where the herbalist
would come in. Higher levels and more talents would mean
not only better plants growing in the grove, but it would also
bring higher yields and faster growth rates.

I silently wondered if there was some way to easily start
power-leveling the NPC. Training to fight would be the
quickest way to gain primary stats, but we would have to
make up too much ground before her physical stat surpassed
her cunning in order to increase her level. Perhaps if we had
a chess board or some other mentally stimulating puzzles,
it could work. The herbalist could farm during the day, and
at night she could play mind games against the warlocks. I'd
heard of other players taking a similar route. It only worked
at low level, but that's what we had. Unfortunately, I didn't
want to pull Geirr away from his other tasks just to fashion a
game board and some pieces.

"Hopefully the herbalist levels up quickly. We need those
potions," I said, shaking the chess idea from my head. Maybe
I could come up with something else later.

Helvegen returned the recipe to its place and then showed
me a pair of small glass vials, each one about half full with a
foamy, purple liquid. "We stole these as well, two giant slay-
ing potions, and they're really high tier. If we ever need to

fight something larger than our own charnel golem, they'll come in handy."

"Not bad," I said with a nod. "Anything else in the lock box we took? And what about those trinkets I grabbed?"

The painter reached under her shirt and brought out a small locket. It was silver and square-shaped. It didn't look expensive, but it glowed with the tell-tale sign of magic. Rather than reading the item's stats in my vision and stealing Helvegen's enthusiasm, I asked her what it did.

"It actually increases my influence score and gives me a new passive that lets me get along better with the NPCs, especially when I have to order them around." Her eyes drifted downward as she finished the explanation, and the edges of her smile started to fade. "Here, you can have it. You have more influence than me already, so you should take it," she said.

I pushed the locket back to her. "No, you keep it. I'll make you my manager. I'd rather not have to visit every single place in Undercroft Citadel every single morning, so just telling you the plan for each day actually makes my life a lot easier. How does that sound?"

Once more, Helvegen beamed. She tucked the small charm back under her shirt and brushed a few loose strands of hair back behind her ear. "That's *perfect!*" she said.

"Just make sure you find me after breakfast each day, and if I'm not around, use your best judgment. Keep things running at full speed around here."

She went back to one of the workshop shelves and grabbed a bundle of bright red cloth. It was the banner I had stolen from the Pyreborn Legion and given to Xia for enchantment. From what I could tell, it was finally finished.

"Here's your new cape," Helvegen happily announced. "Try it on."

I took it from her and held it out in front of me, finding

the black spider jewels that served as the clasps. The spiders were designed to latch onto the pauldrons of my armor, so I couldn't easily wear it as a traveling cloak. That was fine by me. Focusing my vision, I pulled up the stats:

The Black Goblin's Restless Vengeance: Gravlox, an ancient goblin shaman, had two small spiderlings crafted by a renowned scrimshander. Now affixed to a cloak, the spider relics can be called upon to summon an image of the mighty goblin to fight for the wearer, casting shamanistic magic for several minutes.

If my understanding was correct, the cloak itself wasn't actually enchanted. The two spider likenesses contained all the item's power, and they were certainly impressive. "How did Xia make it?" I asked in wonder.

"She was able to use some of the smaller relics you had stolen from the archive, and Xollmomath granted her a bit of magic from all the histories he knows. Do you like it?" She was waiting for my approval, despite not being the one who had actually made the cloak.

"I love it," I told her, and she beamed once more. It would make a fine addition to my already insanely powerful raiment.

Beyond the cloak's magic, I loved the color. It was the same shade of red as the dress I had bought for Ingrid. It would be a proper token to carry into battle, a constant reminder of why I was risking my life and leaving behind a bloody path of ruin.

I gave Helvegen one last heartfelt hug before turning to leave the workshop to find Elyk, the next underling on my list.

Helvegen stopped me before I left the building. "I won't let you down," she said with confidence. "If there's ever anything you need, just let me know. I'm here to help, Ben."

If she had somehow become a little too devoted to the cause, so be it. In fact, I rather enjoyed her enthusiasm. Undercroft Citadel was a bleak and dour place by its very nature.

Perhaps the painter's high spirits and overflowing morale would help everyone else give a little more each day. At the very least, having Helvegen as my unfailing manager would free me up to do whatever else needed to be done.

My next task of the day was to visit Elyk. I found him outside the walls training with a couple of the warlocks. The NPCs were casting spells at him, and the harvester was dodging back and forth in full armor. If he couldn't dodge a particular attack, he would duck his head behind the small buckler we had stolen and deflect the magic. The warlocks weren't casting their most powerful spells by any means, but it was still an impressive display—and I knew he was scooping up experience points with every dodge, training both his physical and cunning stats.

I watched for a time from the wall, and eventually he grew too tired and had to stop. When he did, I called him over to my side. "Thanks for bringing back the armor," I said. "Had we lost it, we would have lost everything."

Elyk nodded, then pulled the stopper from a waterskin and took a long drink. He was covered in sweat and a few minor burn marks from some of the warlock spells. "I killed a few more guards with your sword on the way out. I couldn't imagine what it would be like to wear the full armor set and charge into battle. You must feel invincible."

"Ha, I sort of do, but not always. And especially not now that I've used up my shroud. That ranger and his guild—I used to watch them on the streams before I started playing every single day. Even with my armor, I'd never be able to fight him. He's too strong." The idea of going against Kevin once more in single combat was terrifying. Even if I could get close enough to hit him with Infernum, my legendary sword, I doubted it would do much good. His magical wards and protections were beyond anything I had ever encountered.

"We need him on our side. You've seen him more than

I have; any chance he'd join us with the right motivation?" Elyk asked.

"I'm not sure what it would take. Guys like that are loyal to Echelon. He's played since the portals first went online, so he's given several years of his life to the king. But I like what you're thinking. An ally like Resurrection would more than double our strength." I thought it over in my head, trying to remember if Kevin had any particular vice or weakness that we would be able to exploit, but I came up with nothing.

Elyk seemed a little lost in thought himself. Finally, he took another drink and then rubbed a sleeve of his tunic across his forehead. "Maybe he has a relative stuck in the game, someone we could hold hostage. It might be worth checking out."

"I don't think so," I said with a half-hearted laugh. "If we went after him like that, he'd take it personally. Then his whole guild would come burn Undercroft Citadel to the ground. We need something else. Maybe magic."

"Right. I bet if anyone knows how to subjugate an entire guild at once, it would be Xollmomath. That guy's terrifying." Elyk gave me a nod before adjusting his buckler and stepping back out to face the warlocks.

I watched for another few minutes as I pondered the possibility of recruiting Resurrection as an ally, though no new ideas leapt into my head. In any event, we would need to be *a lot* stronger before we took on a quest of that proportion. It would have to wait. I watched Elyk train a little longer before heading back to my room.

I was already feeling tired as I walked back to the necropolis. I knew it was just fatigue from . . . whatever it was that Lady Kalma had actually done to my body . . . and I wanted to go to sleep. Tomorrow, I would feel better and be strong enough to start taking on more tasks.

CHAPTER 3

I awoke the next day feeling a lot better. My arms and legs were still tired, but they didn't outright hurt like they had yesterday. That was a fantastic improvement.

I figured the time was a little before noon, and everyone was up and at their tasks before I emerged into the sunlight. Thankfully, the ground had dried a good bit since the rain, so my boots didn't stick to the mud. Even though my necropolis was essentially made of bones and exuded pure evil, I didn't like things getting needlessly dirty. Tracking mud through our apartment in Atlanta had gotten Ingrid in trouble more than once when she was younger.

Around the fire where everyone took their meals, I noticed we had a few new barrels of fresh water and a rack of smoked fish that hadn't been there before. That meant a new shipment of food had come in from Riverside.

I found Helvegen working with the herbalist NPC in our little patch of farmland. They had dug a shallow irrigation canal from the farm plot to the moat, though there still weren't more than a couple inches of water there, so the canal was dry for the time being. "Hey," I called, grabbing the woman's attention. "Did everything go well with the food delivery? No incidents?"

Helvegen smiled and brushed some of the dirt from her pants. "I took care of it all," she said proudly.

"Excellent." Having a manager to run the more tedious parts of Undercroft Citadel would certainly be useful. I was already sold on the idea.

"Would you like a progress report on the rest of the citadel's activities?" she asked.

I couldn't imagine that much had changed since yesterday, so I politely declined her offer. I felt like the president getting a national security briefing from my closest advisors. It was a nice feeling to command so much respect and authority. When I had managed an entire office at the Ministry of Health back on Earth, I had commanded similar respect, though it was never exactly genuine. I had lived as a cog inside the merciless machine of bureaucracy, and I had had more than a few detractors. Of all the people who had hated me, Vic had practically been their leader, my eternal nemesis. Just like he was now. Some things never changed.

"I need to go visit Tendershoot Mine today, and I'd appreciate if you went with me to see how things are going," I told my personal assistant. Helvegen was starting to remind me of the secretary I had employed back at the ministry, though she lacked a digital notebook strapped to her forearm and a headset resting around her neck. She did, however, have a few squares of parchment folded up and sticking out of the top of her belt along with a charcoal pencil.

Helvegen readily agreed, and I stepped back inside the necropolis to grab Infernum before heading out beyond the walls.

We left through the main gate and started circling back to the direction of the mine. "Any ideas how we could fill the moat?" I asked. We walked next to the ditch the charnel golem had constructed, and while it was still an impressive structure, it was woefully far from what it needed to be to actually keep people out.

Helvegen thought for a moment with her hand on her chin. She took out some of her notes, read a few lines, then returned them to her belt. "Kulgun doesn't know any alchemical methods of collecting or producing massive amounts of water," she answered. "Perhaps there is some other warlock magic that might be able to fill the moat. I'll talk to the conjuror this afternoon and find out."

"Perfect. And it doesn't even have to be water. Maybe the warlocks can cook up some nasty magic for it. When we get back from the mine, see what you can come up with. I'd like to get the moat filled in this week." I thought of shadowy black tentacles of magic reaching out of the moat like an evil, sentient rift. Something like that would certainly fit in with the overall aesthetic of Undercroft Citadel, and I had to imagine that Lady Kalma would approve, were she here to see it.

"I'll see to it today," Helvegen said.

We started walking away from the walls, and I was pleased to note that the tracks our NPCs were laying had come quite a long way since I had last checked on them. "Wow, the miners have been busy," I remarked. The iron cart tracks only needed another two or three hundred yards to reach the wall. That was certainly impressive.

"I've had the workers taking extra shifts since the moment I returned from Echelon," Helvegen happily announced.

"You know, if you worked for me back on Earth, I'd offer you raise," I said. The woman's forethought and tenacity were things I really valued.

"More than anything else, I knew we would need more raw materials coming into the workshop and the forge. When you didn't return right away, I started getting everyone ready to fight. Enhancing the defenses is a top priority," she explained.

We reached the end of the track, and four NPCs from Riverside were busy laying more lengths of track and hammering them into the ground. They reminded me of pictures I had seen in history texts when I was in college. They just needed some overalls and old-fashioned hats, and they would fit right into the nineteenth century age of expansion when all the captains of industry had sent rail tracks from coast to coast. I wondered how many of those old railway lines still existed, now submerged under hundreds of feet of ocean water. There must be millions of pounds of steel and iron rusting beneath the ocean waves along with everything else the sea had claimed.

Stealing my focus back to Wonder, one of the NPC workers came up to us and offered a polite bow. "If you are going to the mine, would you like to ride there instead of walk, masters?" the woman offered.

The group of workers had a small minecart full of supplies nearby, and the front of it had a heavy rope where it could be pulled along the tracks. "No thanks," I said. "I could use the walk. My legs are a bit sore, and they need the exercise."

The NPC dutifully bowed again before returning to her labor. It was backbreaking work to drive rail spikes into the hard ground and set the tracks. I called up the worker's stats and confirmed my hope that the woman had added to her physical stat. She was level twelve, already fairly high for a classless peon, with a physical stat not far from my own. Her craftsmanship was also high, though I suspected that doing the same repetitive task over and over wouldn't keep yielding a benefit to that category for very long. Still, when the next fight came, I could give our laborers swords and send them to the front lines as an effective peasant militia. That much in physical meant that even though the woman wouldn't know how to fight, she'd still be able to crack a few skulls.

"We should rotate the laborers out every few days to train with Xollmomath," I told Helvegen as we kept walking down the tracks toward the mine entrance. "They're strong, and if we need them, I'd like to know that they're at least moderately competent in a fight."

Helvegen took out her notes once more and jotted down a few lines. "I'll make a different work schedule for them right away. When they're not in the mine, I can have the warlocks take over to train their physical stats as well."

"Yeah, that's what I want. We have to make sure everyone is getting at least a little bit of cross training. You never know when we'll need certain NPCs to take on different roles." We arrived at the mine entrance, and two NPCs were there working the small forge. They had a pile of iron ore along with a few bits and pieces of other metals lying in a wooden crate, and two fresh ingots of different sizes were sitting in another box waiting to go to Geirr at the workshop.

"How much have you harvested?" Helvegen began, ready once more to record the progress of every single worker in Undercroft Citadel.

The NPC wiped his brow and counted some of the materials. "We sent six ingots earlier, five of iron and one brass. There's a lot of exposed ore down where the previous miners had left, so getting it out of the rock is easy. Once that vein is finished, it'll take a lot more time to bring the raw ore up to the surface. Even though we don't have too many miners, we're working quickly."

I gave the man a pat on the back and thanked him for the progress he was making. He seemed genuinely appreciative, though I didn't know how loyal the AI would make him after only a few days of servitude.

Once Helvegen had the mine's progress and resources

catalogued, I turned our sights farther north. "Alright, we need to know exactly what's out there. I have a rough idea of the landscape from watching streams and playing a little bit before the server crash, but almost anything could have changed. If we're going to keep expanding Undercroft Citadel, we have to know what kind of territory surrounds us. Ready for a little exploring?"

Instead of the smile I expected, Helvegen looked a little worried. "You didn't bring your armor," she said.

I wrapped my fingers around Infernum's hilt on my left hip. "We aren't trying to fight anything today," I explained. "We just need to do a little scouting. The moment we see something we can't handle, we head back to the base. And besides, if I go down, you're more than capable of running things on your own, right?"

Helvegen's expression soured even more. "But—"

"Lighten up!" I interrupted with a laugh. "We aren't going to fight. We'll be fine. Come on, let's go."

Finally, the painter seemed to grasp exactly what it was we were setting out to do, though I did hear the mumblings of further protest under her breath.

It was kind of nice having someone who feared for my safety like Helvegen did. Even long before my wife died, no one had paid any attention to my wellbeing at all. All the focus had been on her—her treatments, her doctor visits, her medications—and rightfully so. If I had died in a car accident on my way to visit her, the focus still would have been on the next round of chemotherapy or the next surgery, not planning my funeral. After she had finally lost her battle, the general atmosphere hadn't changed. For the most part, Ingrid had been too young to worry. On top of that, it wasn't like working at the Ministry of Health was a particularly dangerous job. I wasn't a police officer heading out on patrol or a relief worker bringing supplies to any of the radiated zones.

Now I was the leader of a powerful dungeon, and I had people looking to me for direction every single day. If I died, there would be serious consequences. Knowing that Helvegen was worried about me venturing outside the walls without my armor brought a smile to my face.

We marched along in silence, neither of us keen on small talk, until we saw the first vestiges of something other than grassy plains. The land became much wetter beneath our feet, and large willow trees jutted up with increasing regularity.

A ways into the marshy trees, we saw a building. A tower rose above the willows, and it was flanked on either side by a long stone wall about eight feet high. It looked like the corner of a keep half submerged beneath the swamp. Judging by the amount of vines and creepers crawling up the sides, it hadn't been maintained in years.

I batted away a mosquito trying to land on my arm. Undeterred, the insect flew around my head until I lost sight of it. I felt a sting on the back of my neck a few moments later and grimaced. I hated insects. Giant spider dungeon bosses were one thing, but natural insects that were nothing more than annoying always got on my nerves. Killing them didn't even yield experience points.

Helvegen and I approached the tower head on, cautious but not overly concerned. All we could hear were the sounds of the marsh. When we were right up against the tower, I reached up to the bottom of a windowsill and started hauling myself out of the murky water. The tower and walls had sunk just low enough so that what had once been a high first-story window was now only a few inches above my head.

I pulled my head up to the bottom of the arrow slit and peered inside. Everything was dark and musty. Without a torch, I couldn't hope to see much beyond my own face. I drew Infernum as gingerly and quietly as I could and then held it up behind me, a little bit to the side so that it wouldn't be in full view of the window. When I willed it to life, I saw that the tower was abandoned. It held a crumbled assortment of stone and wood resting among at least a foot of smelly, fetid water. There were no windows on the other side of the wall to tell me what else might be there.

I dropped back down into the marsh with a splash. "Just old debris inside," I said. "Let's keep looking around."

Helvegen had her paper out and was writing down the location of the ruined keep. When she finished, we began walking east next to the sunken wall toward the next tower.

About halfway to the northeast corner, I heard a voice. It sounded vaguely human, though I couldn't tell for sure.

I held up a hand, though I didn't need to—Helvegen stood as still as the wall, her eyes betraying a little bit of fear.

"We're just looking, remember?" I whispered.

About thirty feet ahead was a fallen willow tree resting against the side of the wall. It extended far enough up the stones to serve as a decent ladder. I clambered up the wet, moss-covered tree and balanced at the top of the ruined wall.

In the small keep's battered, debris-strewn courtyard sat a dozen or so human captives. Two of them were players with names floating above their heads: a level fifteen warrior and a level twelve wizard. Their hands were bound behind their backs, and they looked terrified. Off in one corner—what looked like it had been a stable at some point—was a heap of remains. Whatever captured the humans had been eating them.

I didn't have to wait long to see what it was. A noisy band of orcs, each of them ponderously large at over seven feet tall and with sagging, unclothed bellies, marched in through what remained of the keep's gate. They were cheering and waving weapons around above their heads like they had just come from a successful raid. The humans awaiting their deaths had probably lived in a nearby village, and the orcs had likely taken them the previous night. None of the captives looked like they had been beaten or otherwise physically harmed, leading me to think they had only just begun their ordeal.

As I watched from my position on the top of the sinking wall, one of the human captives noticed me. His eyes went wide, and I shook my head, holding a finger over my lips. Luckily, the prisoner didn't make a noise. He looked a little relieved, and then he turned his head back toward the ground and pretended I wasn't even there.

I dropped down from the wall with a splash. "A band of orcs with some prisoners," I told Helvegen. "Maybe twenty orcs, probably ten humans left. Two of them are players."

"What do you want to do?" the woman quietly asked.

I knew what she was thinking. I had told her we wouldn't fight, and that was certainly my intention. Without my armor, it wasn't worth the risk. On the other hand, rescuing the villagers could lead to a massive reward. If their homes were destroyed, I could offer each of them a place in Undercroft Citadel where they would have food, shelter, and a backbreaking job mining ore out of the ground. Both players were classes that would be useful as well. A warrior wasn't terribly exciting, but a wizard would be more than useful for our ranks.

"We need more information," Helvegen said after she had a moment to think it over.

I agreed. We didn't know where the humans were from, how far away their homes were, or if there were any more left. For all we knew, we could charge in to save them only to be attacked from the rear as their own villagers came storming up from behind to take us unawares. Making matters worse was the issue of time. If we went back to the citadel to gear up and get more people, we ran the chance that the entire human group would be killed before we returned. The two players alone were a prize worth the risk of fighting.

"Come on, let's find a better spot to watch things. Then if we go in, we're not doing it blind," I whispered.

Helvegen shook her head, but she followed me none-theless. I led her along the wall to the next guard tower, one with a gaping hole where a catapult shot had torn through many years ago. The hole was large enough for us to slosh through, the water coming up over our boots and dripping nasty, foul-smelling slime down onto our toes.

From the inside of the northeast tower, we had two op-tions. A partially disintegrated staircase went up to our right, and a short door missing most of its planks exited into the courtyard to our left. Without knowing where the stairs would lead, we didn't have much of a choice. "Once we come out of the door, the orcs will see us. We won't have much time," I said quietly.

"Do you intend to fight them all?" Helvegen asked.

I had to stop and think before answering. Outside, a dis-tinctly human scream cut through the buzzing sound of swamp insects. It carried on, wailing at full volume, until it abruptly stopped. "If we can save the two players, I don't mind leaving the NPCs behind. But we could use the labor-ers for the mine. Our first priority should be killing every single orc."

Helvegen nodded and took a few deep breaths. "When-ever you're ready."

Honestly, I didn't *feel* ready. My arms and legs were still a little sore, and without my armor, I didn't know what was going to happen. In my mind, I saw it playing out rather sim-ply. I'd charge forward, cut down two or three of the lum-bering orcs before they had the chance to fully react, and then Helvegen would cast a spell to make them see all sorts of armies and other monstrosities bearing down upon them. The orc tribe would turn tail and run, and we'd have a brand new wizard ready to serve Undercroft Citadel.

Of course, the way I saw it in my mind was far from how things began. I charged out of the ruined tower with a war-cry, Helvegen close behind me, and sliced through the first orc's midsections. Blood and fire flew everywhere. Orc innards splattered the ground, floating atop the swampy water like bits of morbid cereal in a bowl.

Chaos erupted everywhere. I pushed through the muck toward the next closest orc while simultaneously flinging my shadow pet at a third, buying myself enough room to properly maneuver Infernum before more of the grey-skinned beasts could figure out what was happening.

Two more orcs fell before me, and then I heard Helvegen shouting. I turned to see her, but she wasn't yet engaged in melee.

"My magic doesn't work on them!" she called to me.

I should have known the orcs wouldn't care what the painter made them see. They were bloodthirsty brutes, only barely intelligent. That was going to be an issue.

The rest of the orc tribe had finally gotten their bearings. They ran toward me like giant bipedal animals, saliva running from their mouths and incoherent grunts rising up from between their stubby tusks. I cut down another, and then I had to backpedal. In the swampy, uneven marsh, I held every disadvantage. The orcs knew the land, and their footing never faltered. They had probably been born in the swamps, lived their entire lives there, and I had so little experience that I could barely hope to maintain my balance enough to stay on my feet.

Two heavy orc hands came rushing at my torso, one from either side. I slashed down on the first hand, severing it cleanly at the wrist, and the second caught me in the kidney. I flew sideways and lost my balance. Infernum sizzled as I dragged it through the water, desperately using it like a cane to keep from falling flat on my back.

My shadow pet drained another hit of my stamina, and I had to release it. I needed every ounce of energy I could muster if I was going to survive.

Looking for an answer, I summoned my character sheet to the bottom of my vision and quickly flipped through all of my talents. A huge grey foot stomped down toward my head. I activated *Forsaken Barrier* at the last possible moment, and the spell jolted me through space in the blink of an eye. The illusion it left behind was convincing. The big orc howled in victory when his foot smashed through an intangible skull, and then Infernum cleaved him apart at the shoulders.

A heavy club came rocketing in for my back. I could hear the speed of it cutting the air, and I knew that a single solid hit would probably be enough to lay me low. I still had enough endurance left to activate *Forsaken Barrier* at least one more time, but there were more than a dozen orcs left in the swamp. I couldn't keep it up forever.

Then I saw my answer staring me in the face from my character sheet. The orcs were sheer physical, nothing but mindless brutes who knew how to brawl and could do little else. The simple fact that one of them had genuinely thought it had killed me when it had stomped through my illusion was testament to how little cunning the creatures possessed.

I planted my feet and activated *Visage of the Dark One*. Translucent black wings dripping ethereal magic sprouted from my shoulder blades, and a swirl of green magic suddenly danced in the air in front of me. I had no way of knowing for sure, but the heat around the front of my face gave me the impression that my eyes were glowing with power. "Stop!" I commanded, holding out a hand directly in front of the orc's chest.

To my utter shock, the creature stopped moving. It stared dumbfounded, its mouth still open and its hands still wrapped around a primitive club.

The green magic surrounding my torso leapt outward and wove a delicate pattern through the remaining orcs, stupefying each one in turn. Their collective cunning score was so low that I had effectively ensnared each and every one of them in a mental trap from which they could not escape.

"Throw down your weapons!" I shouted.

At once, the grey-skinned orcs obeyed. They tossed their clubs and axes into the water at their feet without a single inkling of dissension.

I turned to Helvegen with a smile plastered across my face. "I think we just got ourselves a tribe of orcs," I said.

Your Influence skill has increased to 26!

Looking back to the orc right in front of me, my magical wings still gently fluttering above the water, I issued another command. "Show me your leader!"

The orc obeyed, dipping its head and moving in front of a female orc. The tall creature was bedecked in a leather skirt and matching vest, though the garments did little to conceal her impressive mass, nor did they look to be useful in combat. Various bones and other trinkets dangled from the female orc's clothing, and they swayed back and forth as she moved, clicking into each other like a child's noisemaker.

"You! Bow before me!" I bellowed.

Moving slowly like a landslide cascading into the swamp, the orc woman dropped down to her knees and bowed her head.

I had no idea if the orcs spoke any language or not. On the streams, orc encounters had always been rather one-sided, involving far more violence than diplomacy. Still, I had to try. "What is your name?" I demanded.

"Ugg'chugg," the orc replied, her voice as slow and heavy as her movements.

"Ugg'chugg . . . you belong to me now. Do you understand? I am your new master!" I twirled Infernum at my side for a bit of theatrics. Behind the orc, the human prisoners had amassed into one thick knot of panic, pressed up as tightly against the fortress wall as possible.

The orc female looked defiant. "No one is chieftain except me!" she shouted. Her breath was putrid and hot on my face.

I waved her back with my sword. Even on her knees, the orc was still about an inch taller than me. "You will remain chieftain, Ugg'chugg, but I am your master. You obey my orders and help my people, or I'll kill every single one of your tribe. Is that clear?"

The orc seemed to think it over for a moment, if indeed she was capable of such complex cognition, before lumbering back to her feet. I didn't know if the orc standing once more meant she was about to attack me or pledge her loyalty. The situation felt like it could go either way.

Thankfully, Ugg'chugg didn't reach down into the swamp to retrieve her war club. She slammed a meaty hand on my shoulder, nearly knocking me down in the process, and then offered a toothy, rotten grin. "If you and yours are killing humans, the mighty Half Goat clan has no problem serving a new master."

The 'Half Goat' moniker sounded oddly familiar—maybe I had read about it on the forums or in a book, I couldn't remember—though it didn't matter in the end. The orcs would be a fine asset to Undercroft Citadel. I just didn't want them living within the confines of the walls on account of the stench. I also wasn't sure how much food they would need or what it would look like.

I returned the woman's strong shoulder pat, stretching up on my toes in the muck to reach her, but I was still too short. All I managed to do was awkwardly grab at the top of Ugg'chugg's vest. Thankfully, she got the idea. We had made a pact. "Let's get these captives back to my necropolis. I'm eager to show you around and see where everyone will fit in."

The orc's toothy grin widened, and she finally reclaimed her crude weapon from the slime beneath the murky water. Before I could ask what she was doing, Ugg'chugg whirled on the tied captives and bashed the brains from the nearest one. The humans shrieked and tried to scramble away, but there was nowhere left for them to go.

At their chieftain's command, the rest of the surviving orcs turned on their prisoners, smashing them to pieces with their clubs and axes.

I ran as fast as I could through the swampy muck for the wizard. He was the only one I cared to save. I reached him just a moment before one of the orcs did, knocking aside a huge grey hand with the flat of my blade. The orc looked upset, but it soon found solace in the guts of another human captive, and it lost interest in the wizard altogether.

"Come with me if you want to live," I told the player. The name floating above his head was Karlo. The man nodded, his eyes so wide they looked like they might fall out of his head, but he scrambled along as quickly as he could. I led him back to where Helvegen was waiting.

The screams began to dwindle as the human livestock was reduced to nothing more than butchered meat. Some of the orcs had already begun to indulge in their feast, not bothering to build another fire to cook the bloody body parts, and I had to turn away from the scene.

Helvegen took a knife from her belt and cut the man's wrist ties. "We need to run!" Karlo said urgently. "We can escape while they're busy . . . with my friends." The horror in his eyes spoke volumes.

I shook my head. "We aren't going to run," I told him.

Karlo's knees buckled, and he lost his balance. Helvegen lifted him roughly by the shoulders until he regained his footing.

"The orcs are mine," I said flatly. "They're going to serve

me at Undercroft Citadel, and you are as well. Unless, of course, you'd rather join your fellow villagers over there being torn to bits and eaten. Your choice."

The wizard's eyes darted back and forth between me and the orc tribe. From the corner of my vision, I saw the man's hands starting to move in a specific kind of pattern reminiscent of spell casting. I didn't wait for him to finish whatever spell he was about to unleash. Without my armor, I couldn't be sure that the spell wouldn't kill me outright, so I swung Infernum as hard as I could for the wizard's waist. My sword bit into the flesh of his thigh and then cleaved through the bone underneath, and the man's spell died on his fingertips.

Karlo gurgled out a few incomprehensible last words as he died.

"So much for our wizard," Helvegen said.

I shook the corpse off the end of my blade and turned back to watch the last of the slaughter. The orcs were making a sport of it, tossing a pair of the still-living humans back and forth and taking turns bashing them with their clubs. "They'll make fine soldiers, but I don't want them inside the walls ever," I casually remarked. "If they get ahold of our zombies, they'd probably tear them to shreds. We can't let them destroy everything we've worked so hard to build."

"Where do want to keep them? I don't know if orcs build towns and cities like humans. I don't think so." Helvegen looked mildly alarmed as she watched the last few prisoners expire, the final one pulled apart with an orc holding her legs and another holding her arms. A few months ago, the sight of such horror would have churned my stomach and forced me to look away. Now . . . I didn't care. That was life. Well, it was death—and I was certainly no stranger to it.

"We'll figure out what their chieftain needs to keep them happy and obedient, and then we can set them up with some land around the mine tracks coming into Undercroft Citadel," I answered.

Helvegen liked the idea. "They can guard the shipments coming in," she reasoned.

"Exactly. We'll use them as a buffer outside the walls. And we only have NPCs working the tracks right now, so if one of them happens to go missing every now and then to sate an orc's belly, I honestly don't care. That's the price we pay for protection. Also, make a note to have Xollmomath and Elyk test the brutes tomorrow. I need a clear picture of their combat capabilities. I know they're strong, but the leader is a shaman as well. Hopefully they can fight."

When the orcs were finished with their gruesome meal, I instructed their chieftain to gather whatever supplies they had and follow us back to the citadel. As it turned out, they didn't own too many worldly possessions. The orc clan numbered seventeen after I had cut down a fair number of them at the beginning of the battle. Their leader was a level twelve shaman, and all the others had the rather generic raider class which meant they would have talents relating to pillaging, plundering, and otherwise sacking enemy developments. Combined with their brute strength and overwhelming size, the tribe was already more than powerful enough to raze a settlement the size of Riverside. When the final battle with Echelon came to fruition, letting the orcs loose in the middle of the town square was going to be a fun thing to watch. They'd bring terror and destruction no matter where I dropped them off.

Helvegen and I spent the rest of the afternoon getting the Half Goat clan settled into a spot about half way between Undercroft Citadel and the mine entrance. I had to tell them each more than once that they would incur my wrath if they went around eating the other workers. The only thing the orcs seemed to respect was power, and Infernum certainly delivered that in spades. Hopefully the clan would follow my orders and I wouldn't have to come back and kill them all. I used *Visage of the Dark One* again to ensure that my various rules about orc behavior had made an impact beyond their dense skulls before heading back to the necropolis and some much-needed rest.

I climbed the stairs to my room and mentally commanded the lights to come on. Everything was bathed in a soft purple glow. I hung Infernum on the wall peg next to my legendary armor, and when I turned around, Helvegen was standing in the entryway looking sheepish.

"Hey, what's up?" I said. I had expected her to be spending more time managing the rest of Undercroft Citadel in my stead, so I was surprised to see her. At least her lack of urgency told me that nothing was on fire and there was no army about to knock down our walls.

"Um," she began, shifting from foot to foot.

I sat down on the edge of my bed, exhausted from the day's work, and gave her a look that I thought prompted her to go on. When she still didn't say anything, I stood up and walked over to her. "What's on your mind?"

She paused again, then turned back toward the staircase. "Nothing, I just had some ideas for a few new buildings. I'll tell you tomorrow. Good night!"

Helvegen scampered down the stairs and was out of sight, clearly embarrassed.

Whatever it was could clearly wait until the morning, and I just wanted to get some rest. I commanded the lights to dim so that they were barely visible and climbed under my sheets. Once the magical air conditioning was blowing a gentle breeze of chilled air, I fell asleep.

CHAPTER 4

Much to my surprise, Elyk woke me up the next morning with a few hard knocks on my door. I answered it once I was dressed and little less sleepy, and the harvester was standing there in full battle gear with a cup in his hand.

"Two things," he said before I could greet him. "Well, actually three. First, no invasion or anything, so don't freak out. I know it's early." Behind him, the sun was about three quarters of the way above the horizon, so early was correct. "The second thing you're going to like. I hope." He handed me the wooden cup. A brown liquid filled the inside, and I easily recognized the scent. I'd know it anywhere.

"You made coffee?" I brought the cup to my lips and tilted it back for a taste before I thought to ask if the man had brought it for me.

Elyk laughed. "The herbalist knows a few spells that she can weave into the soil. We have two mature, bean-yielding coffee bushes down in the farm. Kulgun roasted a few handfuls in front of the forge. The whole workshop smells like coffee now. It isn't much, but I figured you would want some."

"You're right. It's perfect. The coffee houses in Echelon were always so expensive, and I had been saving every bit of gold I could get to buy Ingrid a pass, so I've actually never had coffee grown in Wonder before." I took a small drink, and it tasted great. It was dark and rich, and it reminded me for some reason of a gentlemanly library or bookstore, maybe a cigar shop.

I drank more from the cup, then remembered Elyk had three things to tell me. "What's next on the list?" I asked.

Elyk let out a sigh. "Alright, maybe four things. Maybe I'm not so good at math. But Helvegen got drunk last night and kind of trashed her place. She's passed out in the barracks room now on one of the cots. If there was something she needed to do today, I'd be happy to give her the day off. And . . . uh, she talks a lot when she's drunk. I'll leave it at that."

My coffee cup was already starting to run low. I mulled over the information as I sipped, completely unsure what it was I needed to do with a drunken subordinate. If I was being honest, I didn't really care. If she wanted to have a day off, all she needed to do was ask.

"The fourth thing," Elyk went on, "you'll need to come handle yourself. One of the warlocks on guard duty last night caught someone trying to scale the outer wall. The rope they had brought wasn't long enough to get them all the way up from the bottom of the moat, so they didn't get in."

That piqued my interest greatly. "Take me to him. And next time, you don't have to wait until morning to tell me about an intruder." I finished the coffee and returned the cup to Elyk, then grabbed my gauntlets and sword from the armor rack. Wearing all of my armor would certainly be the smartest choice, but in a hurry the gauntlets made the most sense. Especially for an interrogation. If I needed to punch the truth out of someone, having the physical score of someone fifteen levels higher than me would be useful.

I followed Elyk down the stairs and past a few of the old Whitechapel buildings to a small house we hadn't yet fully demolished. A pair of warlocks stood guard outside, and Xollmomath was there as well.

"One more thing," Elyk said before we opened the door and entered. "He's pretty young, probably only got into the game a few days or weeks before everything went to hell."

I nodded and entered the house, a gauntleted hand resting on the hilt of my sword. The kid was nothing more than that: a kid. His hands were tied behind his back to one of the house's foundational beams, and he wore two black eyes to complement his ligatures.

The captive barely acknowledged me. He tilted his head up slightly, but that was it.

"What's your name?" I started. I figured being personable would be a better approach than just reading his name from the letters floating above his head.

He didn't respond. I figured he was probably sixteen or seventeen, terrified out of his mind, and fully expected to die rather soon.

"Any chance you tell me your name?" There wasn't enough room in the small house for me to pace back and forth like a proper tyrant interrogating a captive, so I stood in front of him and tried to look at least a little inviting. "You were caught trying to climb the walls. I have to assume that you knew where you were going and what you were doing. Everyone in Echelon has read the system notifications about Undercroft Citadel. We aren't the good guys here. And judging by the fact that you didn't bring an army with you, I'd say you weren't looking to take us out and claim the king's reward for yourself. So what is it? Are you here to join?"

The boy, Peter was his name, finally met my eyes. He was level eight and classless. "I guess . . ." he muttered.

"What the hell kind of answer is that? You guess you would

break into a heavily guarded citadel of evil and . . . what? Everything would just work out in the end?" I knew the kid was scared, but his answer didn't even make sense. None of it did.

Peter squirmed a little against his bindings.

I decided to alter my approach. "You know, I don't really have time for you. There's a necromancer outside who turns corpses into zombie soldiers to fight my battles. I'm very tempted to give him your body and let him get to work."

Peter looked at me with tears in his eyes. "I'm sorry," he weakly muttered. "I shouldn't have left the city. I thought . . . maybe I could join you guys and level up. Ever since the server crashed, no one is running raids or even taking the riskier quests. I'm so fucking bored!"

I couldn't help but laugh. The prospect of Echelon being strangled by its own fear was ridiculous. Of course they would be. They were helpless maggots all begging to have their hands held by the king and be told what to do. They couldn't think for themselves.

"You think you would fit in here?" I demanded of the boy.

He cowered away from the thunder in my voice. "Y-yes . . ." he stuttered, casting his eyes toward the ground once more.

"Well you're wrong. Cowards belong in Echelon, not here." I drew Infernum and willed it to life.

The boy started screaming. He turned his head so far to the side to try to get away that I could hear his neck pop.

I emerged from the house a few seconds later with my sword once more on my side. "You don't need our zombies to have heads, right?" I asked Xollmomath.

The ancient necromancer grinned. "A headless body shall suffice, master," he answered.

"Good." I left the man to his unholy task and silently willed a gargoyle to come get me. I could have easily walked back to the necropolis, but I wanted to go up to the top and take in all the sights once more. I needed to go over the defenses and check out the information on my character sheet. Managing the overall picture from a place where I could actually *see* the overall picture felt like a fine choice.

I landed on the roof and angled myself away from the rising sun before calling up Undercroft Citadel's information.

Undercroft Citadel (Dungeon)

Commander: Ben Hales (Influence: 36)

Bosses: Xia (Warlock), Helvegen (Painter), Xollmomath (Necromancer), Elyk (Harvester), Ugg'chugg (Shaman)

Resources: Moderate stockpiles of food and lumber, moderate stockpiles of weapons, minor stockpiles of wealth (gems), no stockpiles of exotic goods or artifacts, moderate stockpiles of crafting resources

Military Strength: 3 warlocks, 13 zombies, 1 charnel golem, 16 orc raiders

Specialists: 1 engineer, 1 alchemist, 1 herbalist, 1 hospitaler

Defensive Structures: Reinforced wooden wall enhanced with fear glyphs (detonating corpses), minor defensive wards, minor physical traps (punji pits), small guard tower, necropolis, moat, 5 stone gargoyles, 6 stone pillar bugs

Active Production Facilities: 2 forges, 2 crafting benches, 1 engineering bench, 1 alchemy bench, 1 herbalist grove, 1 bone chapel

I still couldn't believe how light our losses had been during our incursion into Echelon. We could have lost it all. And knowing a name for the trilobite guardians watching over the staircase to the second floor of the necropolis was nice. 'Pillar bugs' was an interesting way to describe then. Then again, they did look a bit like pillars with the way they stood at attention on either side of the staircase, though they weren't holding up any roof.

From my elevated position far above the rest of the buildings, I could finally see the work crew laying down tracks. They had progressed quite far since yesterday. To the side of the track, I saw that the orcs had lent their considerable strength to the effort as well, likely hurrying along the development by accelerating the rate at which iron could be dragged from the forge to the track. Hopefully they would take to their new task and at least be content living in the shadow of my empire. They were, after all, one of the evil races of Wonder. They'd probably love the chance to smash some shiny knights off their horses and eat their insides. If everything went according to plan, I would give them the opportunity to do some killing before long.

The orc tribe had also started constructing some crude huts on either side of the iron tracks. I wasn't sure if they had gotten the wood and other materials from our stores or if they had brought them along from the swamp, but it didn't matter. Either way, they would need some sort of shelter if they were going to have the closest settlement to my walls.

In the long run, I knew we needed more than one tribe to act as a buffer. The orcs were just a start. Whatever we managed to subjugate next, I only hoped they would be more hygienic and less refractory. Whatever our next allies would be, we needed them to bring some horses with them as well. We still had an empty stable waiting for mounts. Riding into battle next to the orc tribe would be a sight to behold.

I allowed myself to lean back a little and enjoy Undercroft Citadel's prosperity. We still weren't nearly strong enough to take on Resurrection by ourselves, but we were getting closer every single day. Once the guild fell, there wouldn't be much between us and Echelon. The city would burn, and I would watch smoke tarnish the clouds for days.

On the ground, I saw Helvegen slowly exit the barracks with a hand pressed against her forehead. She looked miserable. I had no idea what had driven her to drink, and Elyk's vague message about her left me wondering. Ever the dutiful worker, Helvegen had her notes in her hand before long, and I watched as she made her first rounds between the production buildings.

When she finished checking numbers, I decided to have a gargoyle fly me down to see what exactly it was she had been trying to tell me last night—presumably what had driven her to drink as well.

She seemed surprised when she saw me, maybe a little flustered. "Hi," she awkwardly started. "How's your morning?"

Well, I butchered a kid before dawn . . . "Hey, I . . . uh, what were you going to say last night? I'm sorry I kind of fell asleep on you before you told me."

The woman's cheeks flushed with red, and she looked away. "It was nothing," she said. "Just a stupid idea that probably wouldn't work."

I knew she wasn't telling me what was really on her mind. I searched my own thoughts to try and figure out what it was, but nothing struck me as the source of her consternation. Perhaps she was upset about the raid through King Ahmose II's keep. But she'd never shied away from combat and slaughter before, so that didn't feel right. I knew she had been upset when I sacrificed myself, and from what Geirr said she was perhaps a little drawn to my authority and leadership, but again, those weren't adequate reasons for her to hide something from me.

Then my mind went down a darker path. Perhaps she had done something. She had made a mistake, and she either felt too guilty to tell me outright or she was stalling for time to try to fix it. I tried to remember if anything was wrong with the necropolis. My sword and armor, the most important possessions in all of Undercroft Citadel, were right where they belonged. The rest of the NPCs were all accounted for as well, or I would have noticed something different on the information pane.

I looked Helvegen in the eyes and decided to be blunt. "You can tell me anything," I explained. "I don't care if you think an idea won't work. If it has merit, it might be worth trying. And if there's anything else weighing on your mind, you can tell me about it. We have to be able to trust each other. Keeping secrets doesn't build a whole lot of trust."

The woman turned her gaze away. "It was nothing," she said again. "I . . . I don't know. I was thinking about building a bathhouse or something similar. We haven't been able to leave and take a shower in a couple weeks now. But we don't have a source of water."

The moment she started speaking was the same moment I knew she was lying to me. She used the bathhouse idea as a cover to deflect my questioning from what was really tumbling around between her ears. Whatever it was, she wasn't ready to come forward with it, so I let it drop. "You know, a bathhouse wouldn't be a terrible idea. We're still working on getting enough water to fill the moat, but after that, I wouldn't mind getting a bathhouse up and running. We certainly need it."

Helvegen nodded and turned, scurrying off without another word on the subject. The actual bathhouse idea wasn't a bad one, either. Especially as we continued to grow, we would need more general sanitation and hygiene facilities just like any city would have. I lifted the edge of my shirt up to my nose and confirmed my suspicions about my own smell. It had been weeks since I had bathed.

I filed the idea in the back of my mind for later exploration and went to visit Geirr in the workshop. We hadn't used the floating trap yet, and a demonstration would be excellent. I wanted to know the trap's capabilities and how many more of them we could create in the next few days.

The burly smith was busy working on a second trap when I entered, and he was happy to see me. "Think we could see a demonstration today?" I asked. "We also need to try and fix the water issue with the moat. Honestly, I have no idea how we're going to fill it. Talk to the conjuror this afternoon and see if the two of you could come up with something. Kulgun didn't know any alchemical methods that might help."

"I think I can manage both," the smith answered. "A demonstration would be rather entertaining. And if you want some spikes in the bottom of the moat, it wouldn't take me long to make them."

"We might as well go with spikes for the time being. If we can fill it with water or magic, that would be great. If not, there's nothing we can do." The amount of materials in the workshop had grown significantly in a short time, and I was happy with how much we had. We were close to needing another engineer if we were going to keep up with the influx of ore from the mine. That gave me an idea. "Actually, you keep working on the complex projects like the traps. I'll see if one of our new orc friends could swing a hammer and make some spikes."

"Good idea," Geirr said.

"How about a trap demonstration around noon? Will that work?" I asked.

Geirr rubbed a hand through the stubble on his chin. "What kind of target do you have in mind?"

I hadn't thought that far. "Well . . . I'm not sure. Do we have anything that would work?" I should have saved the kid from earlier instead of handing him over to Xollmomath to join our zombie ranks. Seeing the trap in action against a living target would give the most meaningful results. Oh well. The opportunity had passed. We could use zombies, but I felt like they would fall apart when the hit the ground, and it wasn't worth sacrificing even a single fighter.

"I'll see if Kulgun can get something together that vaguely resembles a man. We'll have it ready to go in front of the main gate at noon," the engineer finally said when he realized that I wasn't coming up with any more ideas.

"Works for me," I told him. "I'll go see if any of the orcs have decent craftsmanship. I can get a couple of them making spikes for the moat."

I left the workshop in the direction of the tracks coming from Tendershoot Mine. In two more days, the rail line connecting us to the ore would be complete. The NPCs had cut a square window of sorts into the side of the wall right where the tracks would come through. A pair of the workers were busy with hammers and nails making a short bridge to carry the supplies over the empty moat.

"We'll need a way to protect the track entrance from any incoming invaders," I told the pair. They were covered in sweat and the veins on their arms stood out in the sun. The laborers had been working hard. Laying railroad track was no easy task.

"We could build a door," one of the peons suggested.

The idea wasn't a terrible one, and it might have some possibilities. Still, something about a door didn't seem quite right. "If we're pushing the cart all the way down the tracks, a door will either slow things down too much or else the momentum of the cart will just smash right through. Whoever is pulling the cart won't be able to stop it."

The NPC stood and slid his hammer through a loop on his pants, staring at the hole in the wall and scratching his sweaty head.

"What if we built a lever farther out and tied a rope to it? We could tie the other end to the back of a vertically sliding door, and then as the cart comes down the tracks, there could be a hook on the front to catch the rope and pull open the door before it arrives. It would also help slow the cart before it gets into the forge and hits the backstop." I saw it all coming together neatly in my mind, and the game AI rewarded me with an increase to my craftsmanship skill as well.

"I think I could make that," the NPC replied.

"Good. Give it a try. If it doesn't work, we'll think of something else." I gave the overworked man a friendly pat on the shoulder and left for the orcs.

The Half Goats had constructed a row of three large tents about half way down the tracks that were basically nothing more than dead trees driven into the ground with a few lengths of cloth stretched between them. The cloth ceilings reminded me of the robes and other clothing the human captives had been wearing in the swamp. I suspected that was exactly where the orcs had gotten the materials.

I found Ugg'chugg pretty easily since she seemed to be the only female creature in the tribe. She was busy directing a few other orcs in the construction of something else, though the ramshackle building was too far from complete for me to be able to know what it was.

"How are things going for the clan?" I asked by way of greeting.

The towering orc turned to regard me with a sneer. Despite her menacing facial expression, she didn't come off as overtly aggressive. I figured the scowl was just how she usually carried herself. "This spot is not great for orcs," she practically shouted. Bits of gristle flew from her mouth.

"You're more accustomed to the swamp?" I asked.

Ugg'chugg nodded, and the little bones sewn into her clothes rattled.

"Unfortunately, the swamp is too far away. I need to keep you close if you're going to serve Undercroft Citadel," I stated. I also wanted them nearby in case they decided to get hostile and attack, though I still had confidence that my influence was strong enough to keep them on a tight leash. The mere fact that I was standing before the entire clan with only my sword and my gauntlets and they weren't attacking was testament enough to the orcs' loyalty.

Allaying my fears, Ugg'chugg smiled a little. "The Half Goats like swamps, but we are no strangers to the plains. We will make a fort, and we will ring it with human skulls!"

"Ha, you're going to fit right in with that kind of decor." I looked past her to the orcs working on the new building, and a few of them seemed like they knew what they were doing with their crude tools. "I have another task for the mighty Half Goat Clan, if you have the time," I said.

Ugg'chugg liked the flattery, and her weak smile grew into a genuine grin. "Half Goats will serve the master," she replied.

"Great. There's a good amount of iron coming down the tracks here. Take some of the next shipment and see if your best craftsman can build me some spikes. We need to line the bottom of the moat with them, so the spikes need to be . . . about as tall as you are. Does that make sense?" I had no idea how intelligent the orcs were, so the chance of them fully understanding the task was completely up in the air.

The shaman didn't waste any time. She summoned one of the workers from the current project, an orc named 'Brain-Eater,' and immediately sent him to the rudimentary forge right outside Tendershoot Mine to get started. I liked that kind of work ethic. The orcs were smelly and altogether disgusting, but they would be useful.

I spent a little more time with the Half Goat Clan trying to become a more familiar face to them before heading back to the necropolis and Geirr's trap demonstration. Word of the display had spread through Undercroft Citadel, and just about everyone was gathered at the main gate to witness the event. I climbed up to the top of the gatehouse and stood at the rail next to Elyk and Xia.

Geirr, Kulgun, and Helvegen were out on the road getting everything ready. They had sloppily thrown together a scarecrow-esque dummy roughly the size of a person for our target. The dummy sat atop an even cruder horse made from old wooden planks that had been salvaged from one of the few remaining Whitechapel houses. The whole thing looked more like a child's toy than a military device, though I figured it wouldn't be long before it was shattered across the ground anyway.

When everything was in order, Geirr turned back to the gatehouse with a hand over his eyes to block the sun. I gave him a thumbs up.

Geirr and the others ran back to the gatehouse dragging a long rope behind them. They gave it a pull, and the wooden horseman jerked a few feet forward, tipping onto its nose, and the trap rocketed up from the ground like a huge set of metal jaws. The initial force of the clamping jaws was enough to break the target into timbers. Even without the alchemical reaction I knew was coming, the trap was more than effective.

Everyone waited in silence for the second stage. It took a few seconds, and then a sharp hissing sound emanated from the trap. It reminded me of helium being filled into a balloon.

After about five seconds of hissing, the trap rattled in the ground, shaking a few splintered planks loose of its leather straps, and then it started rising into the air with its prey still held tightly in its jaws. I watched in awe as the device climbed. It gained more and more altitude until it was about twice as high above the ground as the roof of my necropolis. The hissing stopped, and the trap hung at its apex, suspended in the air for a split second before wrenching itself open a few feet.

What was left of the target dummy rained down a few feet ahead of the trap itself. The whole assembly crashed into the hard-packed road with a loud, metallic bang. I was the first one to start clapping, but everyone else joined in at once.

Geirr wore the biggest smile I had ever seen on him, and

he turned to offer the three of us on the top of the gatehouse a bow.

"Well done, good sir," I called to him. "Now make me a hundred more!"

With a field of floating bear traps surrounding the walls, we would be impenetrable. It wouldn't matter how many knights and raiders and wizards came to siege Undercroft Citadel. Echelon and Resurrection could send every player they had, and we would kill them all.

The rest of the audience offered Geirr their admiration before returning to their tasks. I stayed behind, eager to learn more about the trap. As I watched Geirr and Helvegen inspect the metal frame, a new idea crept into my mind.

With enough of the alchemical liquid and gas sacks, we could fly.

As far as I knew, no one in Wonder had ever successfully achieved flight. Especially in the early days of the game, a few guilds had built ornithopters and other gliders, but the AI strictly forbade that kind of advanced tech. Anything seen as too modern or too powerful for Wonder's medieval setting wasn't simply deleted from the system . . . no, the game developers had created a much more interesting method of limiting technological achievements. Whenever a guild managed to develop something that shouldn't exist, the game generated something much more powerful to come and destroy it.

I remembered a guild from Arcturus, the capital city with its portal located in downtown Caracas, that had built a pair of functioning ornithopters. Everyone on the forums had watched them achieve flight, soaring over the cliffs and waterfalls that surrounded their jungle city, and the internet had basically exploded with ideas. Gunpowder, cannons, combustion engines, even lasers and other cutting-edge technology had been the talk of the forums. The plans had been so ambitious that it seemed Wonder would eventually surpass Earth in technological prowess.

The day after Wonder's first flight test had been just as interesting as the test itself. System notifications spread through everyone in Arcturus. A new enemy was coming, and the city needed to mobilize for war. About a week later, an army of trolls was seen on the horizon. The beasts were taller than the city's walls, and they had brought siege engines with them as well. For a month, the jungle outside Arcturus was practically a sea of leathery hides and swinging trebuchets.

It didn't take long for everyone watching on the forums to realize where the trolls were targeting. They bombarded the guild halls with an absolute armageddon of rocks and flaming pitch. By the end of the siege, most of Arcturus had been reduced to rubble. The last thing anyone online had heard of the guild was that they were fleeing the city with their contraptions, heading as far from other players as possible to an unexplored continent. They posted their final message on one of the Arcturus forum boards, gave a general indication of their destination, and were never heard from or seen again. The entire guild simply dropped off the streams.

Of course, everyone had their theories about what happened. I agreed with the most popular one: the guild had ventured into the wilderness to test their flying machines again, and without an entire city of players to protect them, the AI had slaughtered them all. When they respawned, they had disbanded their guild altogether, probably too embarrassed and traumatized to try again.

Over the years since the Siege of Arcturus, other guilds had dabbled with other advanced technology, and they had all met similar fates, albeit not quite as dramatic. The typical game response was to spawn a few extremely high-level creatures and sack the offending guild. The troll army, according to the online theories, had been overkill designed to send a clear message to every single player.

Watching Geirr reset the air sacks and check his metal frame, I wondered if we hadn't stumbled upon a loop-hole. The alchemical recipe for the gas had come from a game-generated loot box, after all. It was something that was meant to be found, not advanced tech brought in from the outside world. Or maybe the server corruption had led to new exceptions in the long-standing rules—I would never be sure.

It would be risky, but developing a flying ship would give Undercroft Citadel an unparalleled advantage.

I practically salivated at the idea.

CHAPTER 5

E veryone woke up the next day in good spirits. Geirr's impressive demonstration had lifted the general morale, giving us all a fresh burst of hope that we could survive the next few weeks. In my own mind, the specter of Resurrection invading Undercroft Citadel still festered like a rotten tooth.

I pushed thoughts of the guild out of my mind and opened the door to my room. Sitting at the top of the stairs was a neat wooden tray with a cup of coffee and a hard biscuit. As a follower of Lady Kalma, I didn't need to eat, but I appreciated the gesture. And no matter what kind of buffs Lady Kalma saw fit to bestow upon me, I didn't think I would ever turn down fresh coffee.

I sat at the top of the stairs to enjoy my sparse breakfast between the statuesque pillar bugs. Watching my growing empire from above was quickly becoming one of my regular activities. It was nice to get a top-down view of how things were progressing. Besides the view, I felt like everyone else had a clearly defined role to perform. We had a few craftsman working at their stations, Xollmomath and Xia training the warlocks, and Elyk leveling up his physical stat alongside the laborers in Tendershoot Mine. I didn't have anything specific that needed my personal presence to accomplish.

Under normal circumstances, I probably would have spent the day exploring Echelon, talking to NPCs and other players about the lore and what was going on, and maybe completing a few smaller quests. If Ingrid had been by my side, we probably would have hunted down a low-level dungeon to complete a quest or two.

My most pressing tasks at the moment were all out of my reach. I needed to figure out a proper sacrifice to restore the Founder's Stake, and the only other major issue was an impending invasion. I didn't honestly know where to begin procuring an appropriate sacrifice, and getting ready for the forces of Echelon to come seeking revenge was more than a one-man task.

I watched a couple NPCs working on the short bridge for the rail track to go over the moat and got an idea. The orcs had raided a village before Helvegen and I found them. Perhaps paying a visit to that village would prove useful.

I grabbed my armor and sword from my room and headed outside the walls, confident that everything would continue like clockwork in my absence.

The structure the orcs were building was starting to resemble an animal pen, though it was far from completed. Ugg'chugg was back in her supervisory position ordering around a different set of orcs than yesterday. I assumed the crafters were off at the forge in front of the mine working on the spikes for our pit.

"The master has returned," Ugg'chugg stated upon my arrival.

I offered her a slight bow like she had given to me. "I have a few questions for the leader of the mighty Half Goat orcs." She looked curious. "Where did you get all those humans in the swamp? Where was their village, and how much of it is still standing? Did you raze all the buildings?"

Ugg'chugg showed me her toothy, rancid grin. "The human scum chased us out of our fort in the swamp. They burned our huts and threw all of our food into the murky waters. Slug-Crusher followed them back to their town, and then we captured them to replace our food stores, but there are still many humans living in their village."

"Do you think Slug-Crusher would be able to guide me to their village? I'd like to pay them a visit," I said.

"Slug-Crusher!" the shaman yelled, waving for one of the nearby orcs to join us. The raider came lumbering over, a war club in his hand that probably weighed as much as I did. "Take our master to the puny human settlement. And bring back more meat for the clan!"

"I don't know how much more meat we'll be getting, but I would like to see the village with my own eyes," I explained.

Ugg'chugg was taken aback. "No meat?" she questioned.

"Well, I don't know. I'm just not making any promises." The orc clan *did* need a steady source of food. If they kept eating from our stores without bringing in anything extra, we would run out of food before long. The tall, massive orcs each ate three or four times the average human . . . of course, that was only when they weren't eating actual humans.

Slug-Crusher grabbed a few pieces of loose-fitting leather armor before we set out. He wasn't a talkative orc as we hiked along the tracks and back toward the swampland, and that was fine with me. Honestly, Slug-Crusher didn't strike me as the most intelligent member of the orc clan. He didn't have much competition among his brethren, and he was still one of the dumber members of his clan.

Despite Slug-Crusher's dimwittedness, he still knew where to find the human settlement. The village was along the edge of the swamp lands. The ruined keep where I had found the orcs had very likely been the house of whatever lord used to rule over the town in days past.

The two of us crouched among a dense patch of reeds on the side of a road and watched the villagers going about their business. Most of them were humans, though we did see a handful of NPC elves as well. After a few minutes, a player stepped out of one of the buildings. He was wearing decent armor and carried two axes at his sides, somewhat unusual weapons for a level fifteen druid. From a distance, he struck me as a capable player.

I wouldn't mind adding a druid to the ranks of my underlings. I watched the player for a few more minutes, Slug-Crusher moving nervously back and forth beside me in the reeds, until the druid disappeared into another building with a few NPCs.

"Go back to the clan," I told my orc companion. I didn't want him stirring up trouble, and his low cunning meant he would probably botch whatever tasks I gave him.

Slug-Crusher grunted and turned back the way we had come. When he was gone, I emerged from the reeds and brushed some of the slimy muck from my legendary boots. I held my helmet at my side and kept Infernum sheathed, strolling into the village without any semblance of malice at all. To my knowledge, none of the villagers suspected a thing about my involvement with their missing comrades, and I wanted to keep it that way.

The first building along the side of the small village road was a tannery. The shop was small, and it didn't look like there was much of interest inside, so I passed it by. Next to the tannery stood a garden shop with a few patrons inside browsing between rows of flowers and other potted plants. Some of the flora would no doubt be useful to Kulgun and our herbalist, and I made a mental note to grab a few things if I ended up sacking the town. For now, I just wanted to check things out.

A little of the destruction caused by the orcs was visible on the north side of the village. A handful of buildings had been burned to the ground.

In addition to about three dozen houses, the town also contained a ceramics dealer, two pubs, a small forge, a quaint botanical garden at the edge of the swamp, and a large lumber mill turning felled logs into worked planks for construction. The lumber mill would be a welcome addition to Undercroft Citadel, though the village was too far from our walls. Sending troops to process wood and haul it back every day would be an arduous task—and it would leave us understaffed for entire days at a time.

Moving the lumber mill would also be too difficult to be worth it. It would take weeks, and that wouldn't solve the problem of our relative lack of wood at Undercroft Citadel. Whitechapel had been built on a grassy plain, not in a forest, so getting enough material to use the mill would be impossible.

A single raid on the village might be our best course of action. We could sack the town, loot all the stores and the lumber mill, and then just haul all of the stolen goods back home. I knew it would work. It would, however, make another long-term enemy. We already had at least two of those.

"Whoa, never seen a deathbringer before. How'd you get that class?" someone asked from behind.

I turned and saw the druid standing behind me. I hadn't noticed his approach. "Yeah, I did a pretty strange quest, and a necromancer trainer gave me a new class. It was pretty unexpected."

The druid's name was Kingsley, and the color of the font above his head was one I didn't recognize. I figured he was loyal to the village we were in, and that was a good thing. At least he wasn't beholden to Echelon.

"Your title, Defender of the Necropolis," he said, taking a hesitant step backward. "You're *the* Ben Hales, right?"

I smiled and tried to put him at ease. "Yeah, but don't worry. I'm just here checking things out. Undercroft Citadel is a little ways south, and I like to know what all is around."

Kingsley shook his head. "Damn, I thought that was a lot farther away. When the servers crashed, I had been doing quests out here with a couple buddies. I haven't been near Echelon in months. I figured the city would have devolved into chaos. All those people panicking at the same time—it must have been anarchy."

"Honestly, it wasn't too bad. Most people are just too scared to go outside now. They stopped doing quests and stopped running through dungeons," I explained.

"Everyone except you, it seems." The druid held himself on guard, tense and worried, his eyes shifting around and checking all the shadows for an ambush.

"Hey man, I'm not here for a fight," I said. I let him get a good look at my armor. "If I was, you'd probably be dead already. I don't really mess around."

Kingsley nodded, though he was still clearly nervous. "Alright. I just . . . I can't imagine why anyone would want to kill players for real. That's . . . murder . . . no offense."

As quickly as the guy spoke, his face turned bright red and he knew he had made a mistake. I held up my hands and laughed a little, trying to put him at ease. No matter what he thought of me, I still didn't want to kill him. Besides, he was right. I was a murderer. "Right when everything happened, a warlord named Vic sent someone to kill my daughter. It was only her second day in the game."

Kingsley's eyes showed his sympathy. "Sorry to hear that, man. My two friends were captured by a group of orcs a couple days ago. We're trying to get a group together to go rescue them. The village put up a reward of fifty gold, and I'm sure they'd cut you in if you wanted to go along."

I shook my head and looked away. "No thanks. Now that I have a dungeon to manage, quests like that don't hold a lot of interest for me."

"Yeah, I get it," Kingsley went on. "You're probably raiding dragon lairs and sieging castles."

"You know, if you want to join us, I would be willing to consider it. We need strong willed players who aren't afraid of dragon lairs and sieging castles. Judging by your armor, you've taken on a few quests that were beyond your level." I extended a hand toward the druid in hopes that he would shake it and accept my offer, but he didn't. He just kept looking off in the distance, probably wondering where his friends had gone.

Once it was apparent that the druid wasn't that interested, I started walking away, leaving him in the middle of the dirt road with his thoughts. On some level, I kind of felt bad for the man. His friends were dead, of course. Torn apart in the swamp and eaten by orcs. If Kingsley had been any kind of threat to me or Undercroft Citadel, he would have met a similar fate, carved into pieces by Infernum. Something about the druid made me like him, though. I wanted him to serve the necropolis—I just wasn't sure how I would be able to convince him to join. Not yet.

I still needed to figure out a way to get lumber from the mill as well. Subjugating the small village would be easy enough. I could kill their mayor and install myself as the new leader, demanding payments of fealty just like Riverside. One thing would make it difficult, however. The village—I still didn't know the name—was too far away to be under the close watch of Undercroft Citadel. Riverside was only a few hours' walk. Coming here to manage the village would take a full day. Perhaps a trade agreement would be more effective.

I found the village municipal building, a long, single-story structure with a sign over the entrance identifying the village as Tall Timbers. I pushed open the door, and a circle of NPCs inside turned at once to see who was interrupting them. Apparently, they had been in the middle of an important meeting, probably putting together the group to go and rescue their missing villagers.

The elf in the middle of the meeting stood from his wooden stool and swallowed hard. He no doubt knew what 'Defender of the Necropolis' meant, and he could see it right after my name. "What do you want?" the elf demanded, showing a little more bravery than I had expected from him.

I put on a friendly smile and tried to ease the tension I had created. "Sorry to interrupt your meeting. I've never been here before and just wandered in. I spoke to Kingsley outside, and he mentioned that your village was having a problem with some orcs. Is that true?" I finally had the seeds of an idea taking hold in my mind and knew how I could secure lumber for the citadel.

The elf swallowed again. The other members of the meeting—village elders or councilors, I figured—were slowly reaching for their weapons like they thought I couldn't see them. If it came to it, I knew without a doubt that I could slaughter each and every one of them without taking as much as a scratch on my armor. Judging by the overly nervous expressions on the NPCs, they knew it as well.

"You can sit back down," I said calmly, trying not to look too imposing. "If you have a few moments, I'd love to talk about the orcs."

The elf nodded, but he didn't retake his seat. "Alright. If you want to talk about orcs, let's talk about orcs. They raided Tall Timbers six days ago and took many of our residents. The clan has been a plague upon our people for years. It is time they were exterminated."

"Yes, the Half Goat Clan, if I'm not mistaken," I explained. "I am familiar with them. I've come to propose a deal, if you don't mind making one."

The elf looked intrigued, cautious as he was. "Go on," he said.

I had them right where I wanted them. "I can, shall we say, *convince* the Half Goat Clan to leave Tall Timbers alone and vacate the swampland for good. In exchange, my settlement needs lumber. You happen to have a rather nice lumber mill right here in town."

The mayor rubbed a hand across his pointed chin. I decided to give them a little privacy to discuss the matter, so I busied myself looking out the window. I could still hear their hushed debate, but at least I was giving them the semblance of a private conversation.

After a few moments, the mayor cleared his throat to get my attention. "How will you take care of the orcs?" the elf asked.

I slowly drew Infernum from its sheath, making more than one of the town councilors scoot back in fear, and willed it to life with my mind. Flames leapt up from the blade, casting everyone in an orange glow. One of the older councilors yelped in fear.

With a smile, I extinguished the flames and returned Infernum to my side. "It will take a lot more than a single orc tribe to stop me."

The elvish mayor slowly nodded. I could see a bit of sweat coating his smooth brow. "If you can take care of the orcs for us, we'll agree to sell you lumber at a fair price. Does that sound agreeable?"

"Certainly. And don't get your hopes up when it comes to rescuing the lost villagers. Orcs are known to eat people, so if they've been gone for more than a couple days, they're probably all dead," I said.

The mayor hung his head. "We're aware of the severity of the situation. There might not be any hope left for our people, though we must try."

"I understand. I'll get rid of the orcs, and if any of your residents are alive, I'll bring them back. Do we have a deal?" I asked.

After another few minutes of discussion among the councilors, they agreed to my proposal.

"One more thing," I added. "I want Kingsley, the druid I met outside, to be the one bringing lumber to Undercroft Citadel every week. He will deliver the lumber to the me, and I'll give him payment."

The elf mayor looked to his advisors, and none of them said a word. "Alright. If Kingsley agrees, he will be your point of contact with Tall Timbers. Now go take care of our orc problem. Bring back proof."

I nodded and left the town hall. The ruined fortress where the orcs had devoured their captives wasn't that far away, and I had a general idea of which direction to go. After about an hour trudging through the muddy swamp, I found the ruins once more. Everything was more or less as I had left it. A handful of dead orc corpses were scattered near one tower and the wall, and the ravaged pieces of countless humans bobbed slowly on the surface of the murky water.

I collected a pair of human hands and tied them to my belt as proof of the villagers' demise, then set about cutting the head from one of the dead orcs. Everything smelled horrible. The swamp itself had an unpleasant stench, and the plethora of old carcasses made it that much worse. It was hard not to gag as I finished removing an orc head from its neck.

When it was finished, I started the long walk back to Tall Timbers. I took it slower than I could have, leisurely working

my way through the insect-ridden swamp just to make sure
that the amount of time I was gone would be believable.

I reached the outskirts of the small town, and I could immediately tell that something was wrong. More people were
in the streets, and all of them were armed. They were trying to look casual and not arouse suspicion, but it was far
too obvious. I knew they were waiting for me. The moment
I stepped into the village, I'd be attacked by at least twenty
NPCs. Curiously, I didn't see Kingsley among all the people
in the street. Perhaps he knew better than to challenge me. If
the man was smart, he'd stay away.

I sighed and readjusted the orc head balanced over my
shoulder. I carried it by its stringy black hair, and the severed neck was dripping a constant stream of ooze down the
back of my breastplate. A few of the villagers clearly watched
me as I stepped onto the main road only a few hundred feet
from the small town hall. I gave the nearest man a smirk and
pushed past him, the orc head sliding a little from my shoulder to thud into his side as I went.

The NPC turned as I walked by, and I could hear him fiddling with a weapon at his waist. Before I reached the door to
the town hall, it swung open. The elf mayor stepped outside
and held up a hand.

I tossed the orc head to his feet, and a splatter of sticky
blood landed on his shoes.

"I took care of the orc tribe," I announced. "They won't
bother you ever again. Unfortunately, all of your villagers
were already dead when I found them this afternoon."

I untied the hands from my belt and threw them next to
the orc head.

Unnerved and horrified, the elf used his foot to push away
the severed head. "All of our citizens were . . . dead?" he cau-
tiously asked.

A few of the braver members of the village had come

closer and were looking at the gruesome display with their hands on their weapons, no doubt ready to attack me should their mayor give the word.

"The orcs had eaten them. They're rather fond of human meat, I suppose. But the orc head should be proof enough of their demise. I didn't bring the thing here for fun." I looked around at the others getting closer and closer, and each of them seemed to shrink away a little under my gaze. They showed more courage than I had originally thought them capable of.

After another tense moment, the elf relaxed a little. "It is lumber you want? And how much? We should make our deal, and then you can be off."

I liked his idea. The sooner I could leave, the less chance there was of a slaughter. Killing everyone in Tall Timbers wouldn't do me any favors. "I want a cart full of processed lumber every single week. The first three will be payment for taking care of the orc tribe, and then I'll start sending either gold or a single gemstone after each new cart. And I want that druid personally bringing the lumber each week. Do we have a deal?"

The elf spoke a few lines to one of his advisors, and they both nodded. "Only the first two shipments for free," he tentatively countered.

"Fine." Honestly, I didn't particularly care what the price was going to be or how many carts we would actually have to pay for. We needed the finished goods to keep expanding our territory, and gold was something that we would very likely have a lot of once the mine was fully operational. I was essentially buying labor at the lumber mill, and that was worth a lot more than I was offering.

With the deal settled, a notification scrolled through the bottom of my vision telling me my trade skill had increased to ten.

The elf stuck out his hand, and I shook it before turning to leave. None of the villagers drew their weapons as I walked away from the town hall.

At the edge of Tall Timbers, Kingsley came out from a copse of trees looking nervous. "Why do you want me to be the one to deliver the lumber?" he asked without any greeting or other small talk.

I kept walking back toward home, and the druid matched my pace, which I found a little surprising. "I trust you more than an NPC," I told him honestly. "I'd rather know that the chances of being tricked or sabotaged in any way are low."

"You don't think I would move against you? I'm . . . I'm not like you. I'm not evil. You kill people. I don't," Kingsley said.

"You have more to lose than any NPC would ever understand. You've already lost your friends, and you don't want to join them. And you know I could kill you easily. Beyond that, you know I wouldn't hesitate."

The druid was silent for a long time as we walked, lost in contemplation with his eyes locked on the ground. Finally, when we were at least half way back to Undercroft Citadel, he spoke again. "Did you actually kill the orcs?" he asked.

"No," I answered. "I killed a handful of them a day ago, but the tribe works for me now. And your friends, along with the rest of the villagers, *were* eaten by the orcs."

Kingsley nodded, and his breath hitched in his throat like he was holding back a sob. "Alright. I believe you. I'll make sure you get plenty of lumber every week. You won't come back to wipe out Tall Timbers, will you?"

"Keep the lumber supply flowing, and you have nothing to worry about. And if anyone else comes to Tall Timbers looking to start trouble—orcs, elves, players—come find me. I'll kill them all and raise their corpses as zombies for my army," I said.

The druid stopped walking and let out a sigh. "I don't

think you're going to kill me," he said quietly. "I'll have lumber for you tomorrow. I know how to get the rest of the way there."

"You'll come across a mine entrance with a track before you reach Undercroft. Just leave the lumber there, and my people will load it up on the track and bring it inside. After the first two shipments, your payment will be there waiting for you to pick up. And if you ever get tired of being an errand boy for Tall Timbers, talk to me. I could use a druid." I contemplated thanking the man for his help, but he wasn't exactly volunteering.

We parted ways, and I returned to Undercroft Citadel pretty happy with the progress I had made. The lumber would certainly be useful. The orcs needed more than a collection of poorly made huts, and our walls were still woefully thin and short.

The sun was starting to set, and I mentally called to one of my gargoyles to get me from outside the wall rather than walking all the way around to the front gate. I flew to the top of the necropolis and sat down to observe my growing empire and plan my next move. All in all, we had most of what we needed. Our alchemy and engineering capabilities were moving along well, we had a steady source of income and raw materials from the mine, our herbalist would be producing useful plants in good quantity soon enough, and now we had scheduled lumbered deliveries to go along with the food from Riverside. Everything was coming along nicely.

Our next task made me more than a little nervous.

It was time to start making a serious effort toward finding Vic. He was from Olympia City, the capital that correlated to the portal not far from Oslo in the real world. In Wonder, Olympia City and Echelon were exactly a thousand miles apart. The seven capital cities, each in their own distinct region with natural barriers of water running between them, formed a circle kind of like a pinwheel. The capital cities sat close to the inside portion of the overall pinwheel formation while the rest of the massive regions spread out until they wrapped around Wonder's spherical curvature and reached other regions.

Helvegen and Geirr had both entered the game through the portal in Oslo. They had been to Olympia City, and that meant they had more knowledge of the area than anyone else.

I commanded my gargoyle pet to fly me back to my room and then sent it off in search of the painter. The two of them arrived at the grand staircase leading to my chambers a few moments later.

Helvegen looked nervous at first, but I waved away her trepidation with a smile and an invitation to join me inside.

CHAPTER 6

I explained our new lumber supply arrangement before asking about Olympia City. Helvegen was happy to record the information, dutifully writing it all down in her notes. More and more I was growing both accustomed to and appreciative of her services as a manager.

I knew the woman wasn't keen on discussing too many details of her past, but they inevitably bubbled up to the surface as we talked about her first couple days inside Wonder.

"Olympia City is far different than Echelon," Helvegen explained. "Everything is themed and designed differently. I was on the run when I went through the portal in Oslo, so I hadn't taken any time to research. I jumped in, and everything was so drastically different that I thought I was going to get sick."

Right when the game first released and the portals went online, tons of players had been so overwhelmed by the sheer magnitude of Wonder that they had reported getting nauseous. So many people had gotten sick that it was like a new disease was running its course through all the populations of

Earth. "What kind of city is it? What's the architecture like?" I asked.

Helvegen smiled as she remembered. "Everything is Eastern. The city is run by a shogun and a council of warlords, and each warlord has their own prefecture. There are eight different prefectures, and you have to have special passes to enter and exit each one."

"You didn't have one of those passes though, right?" I asked.

She shook her head. "Not right when I went through. But the central part of the city is free to access. I think the developers set it up that way on purpose so that the player base wouldn't get frustrated and leave for a different portal in another city."

"How'd you get a pass? How much do they cost?" The idea of taxing the citizens for moving between the various sectors of the city was so different than what I was used to. Echelon had taxes, of course, but they only applied to sales within the city walls and people living there long-term. By Earth standards, the taxes were so low they might as well not have existed. Even when compared to the taxes of other cities in Wonder, Echelon was still a cheap place to live.

"I stole a pass," Helvegen said with a grin. "It wasn't too hard to lift one from a careless drunk at a sake house. Getting a calligrapher to wash the ink off the original and replace it was much more difficult."

"How long did you stay in Olympia City?" I asked.

"Only until I could get out. I was being hunted, but it was early enough in the history of Wonder that no one understood jurisdiction," she explained. "The police chasing us took a few days to even come through the portal, and by then I was well hidden. Geirr and I waited for about week as we gathered enough supplies for a trip, and then we left. It was a long journey to the coast, and then we bought passage on the cheapest ship we could find and came here."

It was good to know that when we finally marched to Olympia City, whenever that would be, Helvegen wouldn't be a wanted woman. None of the eight warlords controlling the city would have a score to settle with her. Hopefully none of that had changed, though the odds that it had would be slim.

"How much of the landscape between Echelon and Olympia City do you remember? Do you think you could lead us there when the time comes?" In my mind, I had grand visions of an entire army marching across the world. We had siege engines and miles of supply train stretching out behind us. In the air, Geirr had a dozen or more flying machines held aloft with chemically fueled air sacks. Xoll-momath and Elyk both led the army from the front on the backs of huge destriers, streaming red banners flying from their shoulders.

A glorious vision indeed.

"I think I could," Helvegen answered, though she wasn't confident. "There might be a better way. Getting a wizard to teleport you to Olympia City wouldn't be impossible."

I had mulled over the exact same possibility before. "It would take an extremely high-level wizard to teleport me that far. And I'll need to send more than just myself. At the very least, we'll need the two of us, Elyk, Xia, Xollmomath, and fifty or more NPCs. When the time comes, we're going to war. It won't be a quick jaunt through the night for a handful of murders. It will be an onslaught."

"Teleporting an army has never been done before," she said quietly.

We were sitting on the chairs in front of the main part of my room, and I scooted mine a little closer to hers, grabbing one of her hands. "If we keep working hard and never let down our guard, we'll have an army. And I want you playing an integral role every step of the way."

Helvegen blushed, but she didn't pull away. "I was always . . . Well, back on Earth I was a fuck up. I never did anything right. The worst part is that I know it was all my fault. I made bad choices." She hung her head, avoiding my gaze, and I could tell there was so much more she was holding back.

I felt sorry for her. The woman carried the weight of so much carnage and destruction. Every single day she spent at Undercroft Citadel only added to that moral burden. For a moment, I thought about telling her to leave and to return to Echelon, to live a life free from evil and killing. But I couldn't just let her walk out and never return. I needed her here. Beyond that, she was in too deep. Resurrection would probably kill her on sight if they saw her waltzing through the city streets.

"You always have a home here with me," I said, telling her what she needed to hear rather than what I was thinking.

She nodded and fought back a sob.

I remembered what Elyk had said about her talking a lot when she had gotten drunk, so I decided to try and broach the subject one last time. If she still resisted, I'd let it drop. "You know you can tell me whatever is on your mind, right?" I started.

A single tear escaped down her cheek. She didn't say anything.

"I know there's something bothering you," I went on. "If you need to tell me something, you can. I'll help you if I know how. Whatever it is, you can move past it. You might just need a little help."

Through the rest of the night, Helvegen never told me what it was that bothered her. We spent a few hours sitting in the entryway to my room talking about the days before

Wonder when the world had made a little more sense. Before Helvegen was wanted by all the governments of Europe for terrorism. Back when I had family. I used a gargoyle to summon one of the warlocks from the barracks sometime past midnight and sent the man to get a bottle of wine from the storehouse. The bottle he brought back was homemade barleywine, rather poor quality, but it helped ease the mood nonetheless.

Both of us were still sober when we left the chairs in the entryway and found our way into my chambers. Wrapped in the memories of better lives and the comfort of each other's arms, we simply drifted off to sleep under the cool purple glow of magic crystals.

Morning came, and I was instantly filled with regret. My head pounded from the cheap, awful barleywine, and what thoughts I managed to cobble together into coherent ideas all revolved around my wife. If I was anything, I was loyal to her. And I was *still* loyal to her.

"Nothing happened . . ." I muttered to myself, gently extricating myself from the sheets. As I moved, Helvegen's long hair brushed against my shoulder, and she reached out a hand toward my chest. I slipped away a moment before she could pull me back and made my way outside, eager to get some coffee and clear my head.

What *had* happened? Physically speaking, nothing. All we had done was fallen asleep side by side. It had felt romantic in the moment, but now it only felt like betrayal. If I was starting to feel anything deeper than friendship for Helvegen . . . no, I wasn't. We were friends, and she had needed someone to talk to in order to cope with her past. That was all.

"Nothing happened," I repeated to the early morning air. We had talked so long that I had barely gotten any sleep.

The door opened behind me, and then Helvegen nearly

ran down the stone steps, never looking back to even say good morning.

I sighed. She had heard me mindlessly talking to myself. Clearly, Helvegen didn't share my sentiment. Very slowly, all the pieces started coming together. It was still a theory, but it made sense. The woman, for whatever reason, thought of me as more than just a friend. She had probably said as much to Elyk when she had gotten drunk, and that was what she had been hiding last night as well. Falling asleep together was probably far more meaningful for her than it had been for me, and then I'd crushed it. Now she was gone. If she left Undercroft Citadel altogether—something I considered unlikely—I would let her go.

I shook my head and cursed my stupidity. Letting the promise of coffee wait, I went back inside and got ready for the day. I wasn't sure if it would be best to let the woman go or to track her down and apologize. I decided that finding Elyk first and talking to him would be a decent course of action.

The harvester, wearing full armor and ready for another long day of training, was at the herbalist's grove with a mug of coffee in his hand. I joined him and poured my own mug, taking in the stiff morning breeze and the hearty scent of the fresh coffee wafting through the air.

"Morning," Elyk said, tipping his head.

"Hey." I took a few sips of my coffee and leaned against the side of the wall.

"Need me for something today, boss?" Elyk asked. He sounded hopeful, like it had been too long since he had fought and he longed for more carnage.

His offer gave me an idea. "Yeah, actually," I answered. "But that's not why I'm here now. You said Helvegen told you something the other day when she had a run at the liquor stock. She's acting strange this morning. Any chance you could clue me in?"

Elyk shook his head and let out a heavy sigh. He was more serious than I had been expecting, and his demeanor caught me off guard. "I don't know, man. If I were you, I'd leave it alone. She'll talk when you're both ready."

I didn't really know what to think. I had expected Elyk to readily tell me all about how Helvegen had fallen in love with me and told him her darkest secrets. Maybe my assessment of the entire situation was wrong. It was starting to feel like it.

Without any other ideas about what it was she didn't want me to know, all I could do was let it drop. If she wanted to tell me eventually, she would. "Alright, thanks," I said. "You're a good friend. I appreciate you not telling me. It isn't my place to pry."

Elyk finished his coffee with a smile. "No problem. Not sure you want to know in any case."

I pushed the cryptic words from my thoughts and started putting together a plan for the day. "Yeah, whatever it is, it can wait. But for today, what do you think about a little reconnaissance mission back to Echelon?"

His grin grew wider with anticipation. "Hell yeah," he said.

"Good. We need information. We're getting stronger every single day, but that doesn't mean we're immune to an attack. We need to know what's out there and what's coming to kill us. If we can get some information, it'll give us a needed advantage. I want to leave soon. Anyone else you want to take along?" I finished my own cup of coffee and returned it to its shelf for an NPC to take care of later.

"Well, Helvegen would be the smartest choice," the man answered. "Being able to change what people see could come in handy."

"Yeah, let's not take her today. Just . . . not a good time."

"Then Xia," Elyk said with confidence.

The warlock was my choice as well. "Alright. Go find her

and meet me at the gate in a few minutes. Tell her to dress for a battle, just in case."

Elyk nodded and left in the direction of the necropolis.

Infiltrating Echelon was going to be difficult. Especially so soon after we had sacked the keep, the whole city would be on high alert. No matter the risk, we needed information. We had to know when the next attack would occur, and we had to know what kind of force was coming against us. The sinking feeling in my gut told me I wouldn't like the answer.

CHAPTER 7

The three of us approached Echelon in full war attire. I had my set of legendary gear along with a few other things Geirr and Kulgun had made. My blood-red cloak was fastened to my pauldrons by black spider gems, giving me even more power than I had wielded on my last trip to the city.

Xia and Elyk strode at my sides. The warlock wore a heavy robe reinforced with horizontal bands of hardened leather, a tight arming cap on her head, and steel-plated boots. At her waist she carried two short swords and a trio of enchanted wands, ready to unleash all kinds of destruction should it come to that. Elyk clanked along in a heavy set of steel. He wore metal boots salvaged from a dead member of the Pyreborn Legion, a breastplate Geirr had fashioned for him, and matching gauntlets and helm. The only part of him not covered in thick plates were his upper legs. He needed mobility more than anything, so he opted to forgo more traditional tassets. He had his magical buckler strapped to his left forearm, and his huge scythe was resting in a baldric on his back.

We approached the city from the north, and that meant we were standing in the middle of the battlefield where Vic and his goons had mounted their ill-fated attack. Raids like his had been somewhat commonplace back before the server corruption. Bloodthirsty warlords would attack cities they had no chance of taking just for the experience gain. Now . . . everything was eerily quiet. The silence was unsettling, and it let my memories of the fight run unchecked through my mind. I knew the exact location where Ingrid and I had been cut down. I had to pull my eyes from the spot and consciously bring myself back into the present.

It was still before noon. The whole city was neatly contained within its walls. No wagons rumbled down the road to the gatehouse, and none of the smaller doors along the wall were propped open as they used to be. Along the top battlements, a handful of soldiers marched back and forth with halberds in their hands. They wore wide-brimmed steel helmets and bright blue tabards over their armor. From the way they carried themselves, I got the impression that they were a lot tougher than the average city guard.

"King Ahmose II has beefed up his security since our previous visit," I said quietly. We were crouched down in a divot left behind from the earlier battle, using the broken remains of a ballista for cover. I guessed we were about thirty yards from where I had died before.

"What's the plan?" Elyk asked.

The pattern the guards were taking around the walls was coordinated and well-timed. They had put thought into their movements, and they left no apparent holes in their coverage. Sneaking up on the gatehouse and slipping inside undetected would be impossible.

"Any sort of distraction would put the city on even higher alert. I don't think it's worth the risk," I said. We could use Xia's magic to make a big fireball or explosion somewhere and then make a run for it. It wouldn't work, and it was the only idea that came to mind.

"Too bad your gargoyles can't leave the necropolis," Elyk added.

Xia looked hopeful. "Perhaps I can get us through," she said. "It might be painful, but I think I can do the trick."

A painful option with a chance of failure sounded exactly like something Lady Kalma would enjoy. "Perfect. Let's do it."

"Close your eyes," the warlock told us. Elyk took his weapon from his back and tightened his grip around the haft.

"Wha—"

The ground beneath my feet lurched, and then I was hovering above it for a split second. All at once, every inch of my skin became painfully hot. It felt like I was stuck in the center of a fireball hurtling toward the city walls. I opened my eyes for a split second and confirmed that I actually was in the center of a fireball. All three of us were.

We rocketed through the air like a comet and slammed into the parapet with a shower of quickly-dissolving flames and sparks. Xia's aim had been spot on. We collided with one of the patrolling guards, setting him on fire and breaking more than a few of his bones. The man let out a shrill, abbreviated shriek right before Xia's dagger ended his life.

While certainly an effective method of transport, our fiery arrival on the top of the wall was less than stealthy. The nearest guard came running—shouting at the top of his lungs all the while—and I scrambled to my feet, sprinting to meet him. He had a snarl on his face and a spear raised high, ready to impale me before I ever got close enough to draw my sword.

The guard stabbed out with his spear, and a blast of fiery magic slammed into his chest at the same time, knocking him back and burning the hair from his face and arms. The man's breastplate absorbed the brunt of the spell, but the force imparted on his chest was enough to send him over the inside lip of the wall. He plummeted to the ground and landed with a heavy crack, his cries of alarm suddenly silenced.

Two more guards were already springing into action. One of them was rushing toward us while the second ran for a guardhouse, no doubt heading for a bell or some other way to alert the town. I couldn't let that happen. I knew Elyk and Xia would be more than capable of handling a single city guard NPC, so I took off after the soldier heading into the guardhouse.

He beat me to the small building, but I wasn't far behind. The guardhouse was just one small room with a staircase going to the upper battlements on my right and a rack of spears on the left. The center of the room was dominated by a large wooden wheel that could raise and lower the portcullis. I didn't see the guard, so I made a hard right for the stairs.

The man's spear was lying on the ground, haphazardly discarded, and the guard was waving a black flag side to side as hard as he could.

I drew Infernum and willed it to life in an instant. The NPC saw me coming, and he tried to angle away to give himself another second or two of life, but that was all he got. I cleaved him in half where he stood. His bloody legs remained upright for some awful reason, and I gave them a sharp kick to knock them over. Apparently, the guard wasn't fully dead despite being shorn apart at the waist. He sputtered out a few breaths, his eyes wild and darting in every direction.

Ignoring the dying man, I grabbed his black banner and held it to Infernum's blade, easily reducing the fine material to ash in a few seconds.

I watched the city from the elevated view of the guardhouse for a few moments, holding my breath and waiting for an army of guards and players to come storming through the streets to answer the guard's signal. No army came to meet us. A few of the nearest civilians—thankfully all NPCs—were running away toward houses and other buildings, obviously terrified.

Some of the NPCs might still raise the alarm, but they were too few in number for me to worry about them. I didn't want to waste any time getting the information we had come to collect.

Back out on the lower battlements, Elyk and Xia had made quick work of the one remaining guard. He was lying face down on the stone, his flesh still smoldering, and one of his arms was missing.

"Ready?" I asked.

Both of them nodded. We found a staircase a little way down the wall and quickly descended. The section of town we were in was mostly residential with only a few businesses and public buildings scattered between all the houses. My heavy boots planted solidly on the ground, I heard the sounds of a few panicked Echelon citizens coming from inside the nearest building. They were scared, but they hadn't raised any kind of alarm. I moved past the small house without giving them another thought. We came up behind a building that faced one of the main thoroughfares on the other side, and it had a glass window on the rear wall where I could peer through. The view was hazy, but I saw two large desks in the center of a single room. A player sat at one of the desks across from an NPC in similar fashion to how business was conducted at the counting houses spread throughout the city, but the building was certainly too small to be a counting house. "Go around the side. I want to know what I'm looking at," I whispered to Elyk.

The harvester gave a grim nod and departed. He came back only a moment later. "Sign out front says legal services.

Must be one of the lawyers sent by Wonder after the server crashes," he reported.

That was interesting. I remembered the system messages in the first hours and days after the crash talking about legal representatives coming to each capital city to talk to people, but I had never given it much consideration. What could a stuffy lawyer trapped in a game possibly do for me? And anyone representing the corporation would have had to be already inside when everything happened. They wouldn't be outsiders, and that meant they weren't likely to have any new information. Still, my curiosity was thoroughly piqued.

"We need to listen in," I said. The walls of the building were thick, and we couldn't hear a word of the conversation going on inside. That explained why the lawyer and his client hadn't run upon hearing our rather loud arrival. They might have even had a magical means of silencing the room already in place.

"If you need answers, I know how we can get them," Elyk stated with a sinister grin. He held himself up with his scythe like a weary boatman come to collect the dead.

I knew exactly what Elyk had in mind, and his method wasn't exactly going to get us anywhere. Busting through the front door and taking the lawyer hostage was plan B.

"Not yet," I said. "I'd like to hear what that player is talking about first."

Xia began moving toward the corner of the small building and started a spell. A few seconds later, she had conjured a small floating eye in the air right above her fingertips. The disembodied organ dripped putrid blood onto the ground from a seemingly endless supply, its goopy sclera shifting and oozing with even the slightest movement. "One of the zombies back at Undercroft Citadel just lost both of its eyes," the warlock said.

The singular eye floating above the woman's fingers was

probably about four times the size of a normal human eye, and I didn't have any idea where the extra mass had come from. "We need to listen to them, not just see them," I told her.

"The Eye of the Necropolis carries all of your senses with it, Master," Xia answered.

"Oh." That would be useful. "Alright, let's do it."

Xia turned to Elyk. "Get on the roof and start prying up shingles. It doesn't need much room, just enough to get inside."

The harvester nodded and began to climb.

Then Xia turned to me, and I knew whatever I had to do to bond my senses to the eyeball wasn't going to be pleasant. "You need to merge with the Eye," she stated, instantly confirming my suspicion.

"How?"

She moved closer, pushing the hovering eyeball closer to me. "Slide your face into it, and then I'll do the rest."

I took a deep breath to steady myself and closed my eyes. In my mind, all I saw was Ingrid's lifeless body in the middle of the street and Vic's goon running away at full speed. *Everything I do is for you, Ingrid.* I pushed forward, and a wave of sticky viscera cascaded over my face. It felt like sticking my head into a water balloon, except the balloon was filled with guts and putrid slop instead of cool, refreshing water.

Xia moved and positioned the Eye of the Necropolis until it was fully seated over my entire head. Inside the sticky membrane, I couldn't breathe. Panic started to set in at the edges of my awareness, but then Xia ripped the magical abomination away from my body before I had enough time to truly be afraid.

As the Eye of the Necropolis was wrenched from my flesh, I felt all of my senses fleeing with it. My sight came to me from the disjointed perspective of the hovering orb, and it was joined by my hearing, touch, smell, and even my balance.

Everything about it was profoundly wrong.

I watched from the Eye as my physical body collapsed to the ground. I couldn't send any signals to my legs—the Eye had no nervous system connected to my own spine—and it felt like watching my own death.

In horror, I realized that I *could* have just witnessed my own death. I didn't know the details of the abominable spell. It could have actually killed me, transporting my senses into the sickening eyeball forever. Of course, Xia wouldn't understand the finality of it all. She didn't know that death was now real, so her lack of telling me made sense.

All I could do was hope that whenever the spell ended, I would return to my body and my armor and be whole once more.

"Shingle's up," I heard from somewhere above me.

I turned my consciousness toward the noise, and I overshot the distance, swiveling almost uncontrollably through the air like a spinning top with too much momentum. I finally got myself to stop rotating, and the nauseating, overwhelming sensation of being detached from my own body made me want to vomit.

I heard the telltale gurgle of someone retching. I turned again, and I saw my own body coughing up a brown spew of vomit underneath my helmet.

My physical body would suffocate if I wasn't moved. Thankfully, Xia knelt down and removed my helmet, freeing my mouth from the watery contents of my stomach. Since I hadn't truly eaten a full day's worth of food in weeks, there wasn't much to expel other than partially digested coffee. The mixture of smells—the sting of stomach acid, old coffee, and a little bit of blood—stung my senses. It seemed that however the Eye of the Necropolis actually processed the olfactory sense was more acute than what my physical body was capable of.

I shuddered, and my floating body swerved violently in midair. Existing inside the Eye of the Necropolis would take a long time to get used to.

I willed my new physical body upward through the air and overshot the roof by about ten feet. I came back down, overshot the roof in the opposite direction, and then finally got to the right height to approach the shingle.

Elyk gave my body a little nudge in the proper direction, and I floated toward the gap in the roof. Sadly, the hole wasn't large enough for me to get through without squeezing. Forcing my eyeball body through the opening produced another torrent of unique, indescribable sensations. I felt every inch of the shingles as they scraped some of the goop from my body, pinching and scratching at my enormous sclera. Some of the damage also seemed to affect my vision. It was like my whole body was surrounded by a continuous layer of cornea, and I was foolishly battering it with old shingles.

When I finally popped through the gap to the other side, I was surrounded by new sights and smells. The small attic had no floor, so I could see through to the main room below, though a few rodents had taken up residence in the crisscrossing beams that held up the roof, and their pungent droppings assaulted my olfactory sense just as much as my own vomit had.

I rotated to get a better view of the scene. If I had been capable of gasping, I would have. The player's name floating above his head was one I recognized all too well: Madrid Bonebreaker. He had reached level twenty-seven since last I had seen him, but I didn't really care much about that.

He was the one who had killed Ingrid. I still had his poisoned dagger stored safely back at Undercroft Citadel.

Every ounce of my body wanted to charge down and slaughter him where he sat, but of course, I could not. I was just a floating eyeball, and I had come for information, not to kill. Not yet.

I waited and listened from the attic.

"How can you be sure?" Madrid asked. He wore a full set of heavy armor, and it looked both effective and expensive.

The lawyer was dressed more appropriately for his profession in a brocade outfit set with gold and emerald accents. "Trust me here," he answered. "Our legal team is the best in the world. When the portals come back online, and they *will* be fully restored, nothing you've done inside the game will follow you. Our terms-of-service agreement is ironclad, and we already have declaratory judgments from almost every major world government."

Was he talking about Ingrid? Did Madrid fear some sort of legal consequence for killing my daughter? I had no way of knowing. What I did *know was that legal troubles were the last thing he needed to fear.*

"But when is everything going to go back to normal?" he demanded, his Spanish accent making him a little hard to understand.

Or maybe my rage at seeing him again was distracting me. No, it wasn't rage. It was bloodlust. A thousand different images and scenarios flashed through my mind. In every single one of them, Madrid was dead with his own dagger sticking out of his chest.

The lawyer shook his head. He had long brown hair pulled into a ponytail and tied with twine. "Our technical teams are working on it as hard as they can. I can't tell you everything, but here's what I've been authorized to disclose: communication with the developers on the outside is working normally as of a few days ago. That system has been repaired. The first attack, however, was not the only one. A small group of militants hit a couple of our other buildings, even after we sent heightened security teams to protect them. About half of the assailants are in custody. We think they were trying to crash the entire game. With the body reconstitution modules corrupted, bringing down the game would simply . . . kill everyone still inside. All at once." The man snapped his fingers to illustrate his point, and I felt another shudder travel through my spherical body.

Madrid ran a hand through his shaggy hair. His helmet was sitting on the floor at his feet. "Who was behind it? Who wants to kill what, half the population of the Earth?"

"That kind of information hasn't been passed to me or any other lawyer in Wonder," the man answered.

Pushing back his chair to leave, Madrid shook the attorney's hand. "Well, I—"

The spell containing my consciousness within the Eye of the Necropolis ended. My real eyes opened, and I found myself sitting upright in my armor, leaning against the back of the small building. Returning to my normal body was almost as jarring as the trip through the floating eye had been.

I pushed down a fresh wave of nausea and stood, fixing my helmet back on my head.

"What did you—"

I cut off Xia before she could finish. "Let's go. The guy in there talking to the lawyer—he's the one who killed Ingrid. I want him alive."

Elyk's eyes went wide. "Vic?" he asked.

"Not Vic. One of his lackeys."

The harvester nodded, and a familiar smile returned to his face. "We'll bring him back alive, you got that right." He paused for a moment. "You going to be alright?"

We shared a nod, and then the three of us ran around the side of the building. Out front, two more people had lined up to get their turn talking to the lawyer. They were nervous and constantly shifting from one foot to the other, and each of them was fully armored. Most interesting was the color in which their names were listed above their heads. They were both allied with Vic. I didn't recognize them, but I knew at once that they recognized me.

The man closest to me was a level twenty-three raider. He drew a wide-bladed scimitar from his waist and swung hard. Infernum was up to meet his blade in a flash.

"Take them alive!" I growled at the same time I parried. The more prisoners I captured the better.

The raider I was fighting activated two talents in rapid succession. The first one augmented his strength, though with my legendary gauntlets, I still had the superior physical stat. The second talent produced a ring of crackling lightning around his head like a halo. I guessed that it would shock me if I hit him, but again, my legendary armor was no doubt far better than anything he could cast.

I pushed through the man's scimitar and quickly turned his attack into a staggering, off-balance parry. He shifted his feet backward, and I swung with both hands on Infernum's hilt, aiming my blade for his crossguard. I could have angled differently and very likely cut off his head. When Infernum landed on his sword's crossguard, I heard the metal shear apart. I hadn't cut clean through it, but the curved blade was now twisted at an awkward angle. I struck again before the raider could take another step in retreat, and the blade clattered to the street.

After each strike, the man's lightning halo fired down on me, rattling my teeth but not causing any further damage.

To my left, Elyk was spinning and whirling with his scythe, battering an armored woman like a storm pounding hail against a statue. Whatever magic was protecting her was strong. At the same time, Xia launched a pair of fiery bolts at the woman's feet. The combined onslaught herded her toward the building across the street from the lawyer's office.

The door to my right burst open, and Madrid came charging into the fray. I didn't have time to deal with him right away—I needed to either beat the raider in front of me into submission or knock him out. No matter what, no one could escape.

I swung again for the raider's chest, and Infernum clacked against his breastplate. As I had anticipated, his lightning halo shot back, zapping my arms with energy that rippled up through my muscles and made me clench my teeth. It hurt, but the pain was gone just as quickly as it had arrived.

I had to pull back my strike lest I risk tearing apart the raider's armor. If possible, I wanted to steal as much of his equipment as I could.

The man rocked backward, and I kept up the attack, hitting him two more times around his shoulders. On the third strike, he lost his footing and collapsed to the ground. Hopefully, his heavy armor would mean he wouldn't be able to get back on his feet quickly.

My spaulder rang with the sound of a strike. I turned to see Madrid bringing back his weapon for another hit. He wore his helmet, so I couldn't see his eyes. I didn't know if he recognized me or not.

He struck again, his sword clanging down hard on my shoulder, and the weapon cracked against the armor's bladebreaker. Without missing a beat, he threw down his broken hilt and drew a second blade from his belt. Growling, Madrid came at me again.

I parried his first strike and slammed back at him again, pivoting my sword past his own weapon to hit him in the face with Infernum's hilt. The force of the blow pushed him backward but didn't knock him down. When he reset his footing, the raider activated a talent that washed his weapon with red magic. He swung for my chest, and he was too quick for my own reflexes. I took the full force of the attack on my chest. My breastplate fired back, throwing a wide spray of flame over Madrid's armored arms.

Both of us fell back a step. He had hit me hard, but my armor was stronger than his strike. The fire from my breastplate had clearly done its work. Madrid was reeling, barely keeping his grip on his weapon. He staggered and started clutching at his belt, his scalloped gauntlets making his fingers clumsy. Whatever he was trying to get from his belt, I knew that I didn't want him to get it.

I slashed down hard at his hand—and Infernum took it off. I hadn't meant to hurt him so badly.

Glancing quickly to both sides, I made sure Xia and Elyk had everything else handled. Both of them had easily overcome the other two members of Vic's band, though Elyk had enough blood splattered across him that I wasn't sure if his opponent was still alive. "Get them back to the wall. Hurry, we need to get out of here." The more we fought, the more we risked raising an alarm throughout the whole city.

I didn't wait for either of them to respond before moving on Madrid. Infernum ignited in flame as I clanked to my knees on the street. Madrid was screaming. He had activated another talent, a bit of magic that was slowly healing him, but the trauma of watching his own hand hit the ground had done too much damage to his psyche. He was clawing at the ground, trying to pull his body away, and splattering the street with more and more blood with every ragged yell.

I grabbed his arm and held his bloody stump in my lap. With Infernum's flames dancing in my face, I pressed the flat of the blade to his amputated wrist and held it there.

Madrid's screams escalated. Down the street, a trio of city guards had arrived with their halberds and short swords ready. They watched in horror, but they didn't advance.

"Want me to handle them?" I heard from over my right shoulder.

Elyk was standing there, a bloody, unconscious woman lying on the street a few paces behind him, and he had his scythe in his hands.

I pointed down the street. "Meet us back at Undercroft. We'll handle the captives."

The harvester nodded and took off at once. I didn't wait to see what would happen with the guards. If I knew Elyk, the NPCs would all be dead in a few moments. What I didn't know was how many others they had alerted. If Resurrection was sending a contingent to investigate all the commotion, Elyk might die.

With Xia's help, we dragged two unconscious members of Vic's band back behind the lawyer's office—the attorney himself was cowering within, the table turned on its side to help bar the door—and then I went back for Madrid.

"You," I said, capturing his attention. "On your feet."

The man shook his head and tried once more to scoot away. "Please . . ." he sobbed.

I cuffed him across the side of his helmet with my fist. He didn't feel it much on account of his armor, so I ripped the helmet from his face and tossed it to Xia, then slugged him again. His nose broke. More and more blood flowed down to mix with all the rest of it already staining the stones.

"One more chance. On your feet," I commanded. I activated *Visage of the Dark One*, using the strength of Lady Kalma's presence to control him. Slowly, still clearly in debilitating shock, Madrid started crawling toward me.

He wasn't moving quickly enough. Elyk hit the guards at the end of the street, commencing another all-out battle that would be sure to alert more of the city. I grabbed Madrid under his arm—the one that still had a hand—and hauled him to his feet. I pushed him in the back to get him moving. Finally, he seemed to get the idea.

Once more behind the lawyer's office, I had to take rapid

stock of our situation. We had two captives, a raider and an arcanist, plus Madrid.

"We can only carry two," I said.

Xia knew exactly what we needed to do. She grabbed the female arcanist and hauled her to her feet, already moving back toward the wall.

I sheathed Infernum and knelt down in front of the battered, barely conscious raider. I breathed *A Feast of Spores* into his face and then activated *Malignant Putrescence*, shooting a vile sack of poison from my palm into his neck.

He would die in minutes, maybe less.

With only one captive left to worry about, I summoned my shadow pet and mentally ordered it to help carry Madrid's weight. Casting so many spells in such rapid succession was starting to seriously tax my lifeforce. I just needed to get Madrid outside the walls before the tax on my body got to be too much.

Xia and I, our pair of prisoners in tow, reached the base of the wall a few moments later. Since I was no longer in combat, my legguards didn't maintain my stamina, and sweat was running down my face to soak the cloth gambeson under my armor.

For better or worse, my physical stamina received a huge boost only a moment later when Xia blasted through the nearest sally port. Two members of Resurrection were galloping past the door on the other side at the same moment Xia's magic blasted it apart. They both whirled, swinging their horses hard in our direction, magic flickering around their bodies.

I dismissed my shadow pet and let Madrid slump to the ground. Xia cast aside her own prisoner and pulled a wand from her belt, setting her feet. She was in front of me, and there wasn't much room underneath the tight stone archway for us to switch positions.

If we ran back the way we had come, we'd probably escape. The riders wouldn't be able to fit through the sally port on horseback, so we'd have a slight advantage.

I gritted my teeth and drew Infernum from my side. Running wasn't an option. I looked back over my shoulder toward the lawyer's office, and my helm let me see Elyk's outline still battling on the street. All I could really tell was that he hadn't fallen and was still engaged.

Xia used one of her wands, unleashing a swirling bolt of magic that caught one of the oncoming horses in the rear flank where it was unprotected by barding. We had about five seconds before the two riders reached us. The first one, a woman dressed in black leather from head to toe, was a level thirty rogue. Her partner, another woman sitting tall on a glistening blue roan, was a level thirty-one arcanist.

Both of our enemies' classes were based on cunning. That meant I had no chance to dominate them like I had done with Madrid. We had to stand our ground and fight, and it was going to be the hardest battle of my life.

CHAPTER 8

For a moment, the archway we were trapped inside worked to our advantage. Xia backed away from the exit a step, reaching for a second wand from her belt.

The rogue turned her mount about five feet before crashing into the stone wall and threw a handful of metal darts right for Xia's chest. Behind the warlock, I couldn't see if any of them hit her, but she yelled in pain, and I had to assume the worst. To her credit, Xia didn't falter. She aimed her second wand and let loose, hitting the rogue in the chest as she dismounted.

I hated being stuck just a foot or two away from the action. Before I could figure out a way to get past Xia without smashing her against the wall, the arcanist was upon us. Shimmering orbs of magic flashed in her hands and rocketed toward us. The first was a deep blue color, spinning rapidly through the air, and about the size of my head. Xia met it with a blast of her own magic, fortunately deflecting the orb into the ceiling.

When the magic exploded, it coated the stones above our heads with a slick sheen of pulsing, brilliantly bright ice.

Even without touching it I could tell that there was more magic in the attack than ordinary frost. The ceiling basically thrummed with pent-up magic, ready to explode the moment we touched it.

The arcanist's second orb of magic hit Xia's arms as she tried to defend her face from the onslaught. She shrieked and fell backward, all of her weight landing on my breastplate. Moving quickly, I dragged her out of the sally port and out of my way. She was badly hurt, with huge strands of crackling magic clinging to her arms and wracking her body with pain. It looked like an octopus made entirely of magic was trying to suck the flesh from her bones with its tentacles.

I didn't have time to help her. Xia was a powerful warlock, capable of fending for herself in almost any circumstance, and she had at least one of Kulgun's healing potions with her as well. Thinking of the potion reminded me of the frost resist potion I carried on my own belt. As I charged out of the sally port with Infernum held in one hand before me, I used my left fist to smash the frost resistance potion against my armor. Breaking it over steel wouldn't be as effective as drinking it, but I didn't care. It would help.

My hasty decision proved immediately fruitful. The arcanist hit me with another frost bomb spell as soon as I emerged from the sally port. It shattered against my armor, almost completely negated by the potion. My breastplate fired a short gout of flame into the air in response, countering the rest of the spell.

The arcanist, still about twenty feet away, turned her horse to increase the distance. I spun on my heels to the right, looking for the rogue who I knew would be closer, but I saw no one. The leather-clad woman was gone.

Then a huge concussive force slammed into my back. I fell to the ground, pain shooting through my body. Whatever had hit me in the back had been insanely powerful. I knew it was the rogue. The class had tons of bonuses to damage when attacking a target from behind, and I had to assume the woman had done exactly that. While I had been focused on the arcanist, she had scaled the wall around the sally port to come at me from an unexpected direction.

I rolled to my back as quickly as I could, and I was only a split second ahead of a strike that would have easily ended my life. The woman's dagger clanged off my helmet, the blade maybe half an inch too thick to fit through the nasal opening on my armor.

Your Fortune skill has increased to 11!

I had to move quickly. With my massive strength, I was able to easily throw the rogue off my chest, though I lost my grip on Infernum in the process and only managed to get back to my knees. I activated the magic in my cloak. Unlike my deathbringer spells, summoning Gravlox from *The Black Goblin's Restless Vengeance* didn't tax my lifeforce. The creature instantly materialized a few feet to my right. He was short and stout, about half as tall as I was, and made completely from black glass.

The rogue launched a shuriken at the same time I summoned the creature, and I thanked my lucky stars again as it missed my chest by a few inches. The woman had been momentarily distracted by the goblin's appearance, and her concentration had faltered.

I got to my feet and scooped up Infernum from the ground. As I charged forward, the rogue's body shifted in the light, and she sprinted away at an impossible speed. I had seen a few rogues on different streams online, and I recognized a lot of their talents by sight. The one the woman had just activated was *Cheetah's Stance*, a lasting buff that made her legs so fast that it was hard to see where she was going.

I swung Infernum in a wide arc in front of me. I hit only air, but that had been my goal. With the rogue's enhanced speed, she could have already circled me for another back-stab, and I just needed to keep her at bay.

"Kill them!" I yelled to my new minion, hoping I wouldn't need to give the glassy creature any more command than that.

The diminutive shaman began casting its own magic, wrenching up big sections of the ground in an apparent effort to trap the sprinting rogue. It was too slow to catch the speedy woman, and the dislodged boulders spiked out of the ground behind her. Still, the magic left a distinct trail for me to follow, letting me at least try to anticipate where the rogue would run next.

I moved to my right and swung again. I connected with something, but it wasn't the rogue. Infernum slammed into a vertical sheet of stone that appeared in the thin air—arcanist magic. Against a lesser blade, the magic would have been devastating. My weapon would have shattered in my hand. As it was, Infernum slammed through the stone and dissipated the wall in a single strike, though it did send a massive wave of pain rattling up my arms.

I charged forward, still following the trail of stone brought forth by the goblin, and lunged. That time I hit her. She came out of her blurred sprint in a roll, sprawling across the ground with a yelp. It looked like Infernum had clipped one of her heels. That would slow her for a bit.

I pressed onward, hoping to bring Infernum down on the rogue's spine, and I was caught again by the arcanist's magic. Bright chains of magic wrapped around my ankles, holding me in place. Even through my armor, I could feel their heat.

Luckily, the little goblin creature I had summoned from my cloak was still free to do as it pleased. A huge chunk of stone dislodged from the ground beneath the scrambling rogue. The woman hadn't expected the sudden shift in her footing, and I had to assume she had already expended any balance talents she might have had. The ground wrenched again. A deep chasm appeared not far from the rogue's grasping hands.

If I could get to her before she regained her feet, I'd easily cut her in half. No matter how much effort I poured into my legs, the magical chains holding them in place were too much. I turned and chopped with Infernum, and the chain around my left leg broke free. Another swing freed my right leg. At the same time I broke away from the magic, another bolt of magic slammed into my breastplate. Whatever it was, my armor fully negated the attack, and I didn't feel a thing.

I stomped forward, implacable despite the arcanist's incoming attacks, and reached the rogue. She was on her knees, heavily wounded with one of her boots leaking so much blood that it was a wonder she could move at all.

The rogue was close enough to touch. She tried to pull herself away, but the broken and jagged ground blocked her right, and the freshly made chasm blocked her left. I kicked her injured foot, and a pitiful scream left the rogue's mouth. I kicked her again, my steel boot crunching into her bones and pushing her toward the chasm.

Screaming about twenty yards away from me, the arcanist was still throwing every magical element she could right at my chest. I smiled as my impressive armor negated it all. In the midst of the chaos, Xia had returned to the sally port, and she was launching her own assault toward the arcanist, splitting the woman's attention.

I kicked the rogue again, and her screams ceased to have beginnings or ends. They had melded into one prolonged wail. Her torso was hanging over the edge of the chasm in front of her. The hole in the ground wasn't terribly deep, only about ten feet, but it would do the job.

I moved around to the rogue's front, and—much to her credit—she tried one last time to defend herself, meekly swinging a dagger for my toes. The blade glanced off my boot and left her hand. I reached down and used my boosted strength to lift the woman to her knees at the very edge of the chasm.

"Ple—"

Her pitiful beg reverted to her previous screaming as I pushed her over the edge. She fell into the bottom of the chasm with a sickening crunch. Her leather armor was thin and designed to stop slashing attacks, not huge amounts of concussive force. Still, she clung to life.

I turned to the shadowy goblin I had summoned and caught its attention. "Bury her!" I commanded with a voice like thunder.

The magical beast turned both of its hands so that its palms faced the sky, and then it clenched its fingers. The two sides of the chasm closed like a bear trap. The rogue's screams stopped.

Exhausted and out of options, the arcanist stopped casting spells. She was already badly wounded as well, having taken a huge blast of Xia's fire on her back just a moment before.

I mentally dismissed my goblin pet and stalked over to the arcanist, Infernum hanging loosely in my grip.

"Xia, what do you think?" I asked, never taking my eyes from the arcanist.

The warlock was panting and clutching her side, though she looked to have recovered at least enough to keep fighting. "She'd be useful," Xia answered. "We should take her to see Xollmomath."

I agreed. I grabbed the arcanist's neck and lifted her to her feet, pulling her in close to my helmet. "You want to live?" I asked.

The arcanist—the text floating above her head told me her name was Alyssa—fought back a sob and nodded.

I activated *Visage of the Dark One*, and leathery black wings of shadow sprouted from the back of my armor. My eyes glowed with green fire behind my helmet. I lifted the arcanist a little higher off the ground. "If you want to live, you have to serve. At first hint of dissension, I won't hesitate to kill you. And it won't be easy. It won't be quick."

Alyssa nodded again, and I released my grip. She gasped for air as she fell to the ground. Nearby, the pair of horses the women had been riding were pawing nervously at the ground, unsure if they should stay near their one remaining master or flee the battleground. I left the arcanist to gather them up, and when I turned back with two sets of reins in my hands, I noticed that Alyssa's name had changed colors. She had switched her allegiance from Resurrection and Echelon to Undercroft Citadel. Her name appeared in blood red, the same terrifying shade as Xollmomath's eyes.

Using the magic of my helmet, I scanned the inside of the city for any sign of Elyk. The helm gave me sight of him anywhere within fifty yards, but he didn't show up in my vision. He was either dead or too far away. In either case, we needed to leave. Our time in Echelon had been more than fruitful, and I didn't want to run into any more members of Resurrection before we had some time to rest and recover.

I handed the horses over to Xia and went back through the sally port. Xia's prisoner was gone. I didn't care. We had traded one arcanist for another, and that was good enough for me.

Much to my satisfaction, Madrid was still exactly where I had left him, full of pain and barely clinging to life. The thought of him dying before we had a chance to . . . have a little fun at his expense . . . briefly crossed my mind. Losing him on the way back to the citadel was an unacceptable outcome.

I grabbed a healing potion from my belt and pulled out the stopper. Delirious, Madrid had no idea who I was or why I was even helping him, and he drank the potion like a man handed a waterskin in the middle of a sand dune. A little mental clarity returned to him, and his eyes went wide. Before he had the chance to do anything I didn't want him to do, I slammed a gauntlet into his temple and knocked him out.

Xia and I loaded Madrid's unconscious body onto the back of the rogue's horse and let Alyssa ride her own back to Undercroft Citadel. The atmosphere between the four of us was more than tense. The arcanist was no doubt wondering when she would be butchered like her friend, and Xia and I were both thinking of Elyk lost somewhere behind the walls. I had to trust that the harvester could handle himself and at least stay alive—but even if he got himself killed, we had captured a living member of Vic's band.

We had gotten so much closer to finding Vic.

When our little band arrived back at Undercroft Citadel, Xollmomath was waiting at the gatehouse to greet us.

"We need somewhere to keep a prisoner," I called up to the ancient necromancer.

The man's red eyes searched us all, and a grin spread across his lips. "Bring your prisoner to the ossuary. I shall meet you there," he replied.

A pair of warlocks opened the gates, and we led our horses and prisoner through. Helvegen was waiting on the other side, and I saw her quickly counting the number of us who had returned.

"Where's Elyk?" she asked, her face downcast.

"Still in Echelon," I said. "We caught the attention of a group of guards, and he went off to handle it." I motioned to the horses. "When we left the city, Resurrection was on patrol. We captured one, but we didn't want to hang around for more to show up."

Helvegen took the reins of both horses. Madrid was still precariously balanced across the back of one of them, and Alyssa had dropped down to stand at my side. "Who's the dead guy?" Hel asked, nodding toward Madrid.

"He's the one who killed Ingrid," I stated.

"Oh."

Helvegen took a step back to avoid having the man fall on her feet as I pushed him off his horse. He landed hard—still unconscious—and it sounded like he broke a wrist. "Take the rest of his armor off and see what Geirr can do with it. Then we'll reconvene at the chapel with Xollmomath."

Alyssa stepped forward and offered a slight nod of deference. "What will you have of me?" she asked.

In all honesty, I didn't have a good answer. I didn't trust her enough to simply turn her loose inside the walls. Normally, Elyk would be the one to handle someone like her. If anyone could strike fear in the woman and secure her loyalty, it was our harvester. Sadly, I didn't have that luxury at the moment.

"Come with me to the chapel," I told her.

Madrid's armor was stripped from his body until the man was just wearing a thin cotton shirt and matching undergarments. By the time we got him to the bone chapel, he was starting to come around, though Xollmomath had enough rope to tie him down in front of the altar. The necromancer tightened the ropes, and Madrid's breathing became shallow and strained.

Xia knelt down and slapped the man's face a few times to get him awake.

"Where am I?" he asked, his eyes only half open.

"Xia, Alyssa, you two stay here with me. Xollmomath, you can go back to your duties. If we need you, I'll send someone,"

I said to the others. Then I turned my attention back to our prisoner. "You work for Vic Fuentes. The day the servers collapsed and death became permanent, you killed my daughter. Now you're in Undercroft Citadel, my fortress. You're going to die here, but probably not for some time."

Madrid hung his head as far as the ropes around his chest would allow. He didn't say anything.

I paced in front of him as the weight of his situation sank in. I wanted him to understand exactly how much shit he was in and how horrible his life was about to become.

Finally, Madrid lifted his head a little and spoke. "I'm sorry, man. I didn't know she'd die. We were just playing the game, you know? Harmless . . ."

I continued my pacing. "That's not going to save you," I said quietly.

Madrid let out a heavy sigh and squirmed a little against his bindings.

"Xia, how long can you maintain The Eye of the Necropolis?" I asked. The first fragment of what would very likely become months of torture was starting to materialize in my mind.

"In here, probably ten minutes," the warlock said with a smile.

I nodded. "Good. Cast it on him." I pointed to Madrid, and the man's eyes went wild. He sucked in a breath, and then the throbbing, gooey eyeball appeared around his head. Xia crouched next to him and placed her hands on either side of the eye before pulling it free. Madrid slumped over further, his consciousness now contained in the floating eyeball.

I reached out with my gauntlet and took hold of the floating eye. It squirmed beneath my touch, struggling in vain to break free from my grasp and rocket out of the small room. On the ground, Madrid's body was motionless, though I knew from experience what he was going through.

I gave the eyeball a vertical spin. It rotated half a dozen times before I stopped it with the flat of my hand. Madrid vomited onto his chest. I started spinning the eye horizontally, speeding it on its axis as quickly as I could. When I took my hand away, it remained where it was like a child's top spinning on a table. I watched as the eye completed a hundred rotations in the space of a few seconds. Finally, after more than a minute had elapsed, I summoned every ounce of strength my physical stat could command and punched the eye, sending it flying into the back wall of the ossuary where it exploded in a rain of sticky sclera and other unidentifiable fluids.

Madrid's consciousness returned to him with a start, and another wave of pungent vomit escaped his mouth. "No . . . p-please," he begged. The bloody stump where I had amputated and then cauterized his hand had started oozing puss. If I wasn't careful, there was always a chance he would get an infection and die. I'd worry about that another day.

It was getting late, and I was tired. "Xia, bring two warlocks and the charnel golem to keep watch over our prisoner. If he escapes, bring him down and secure him, but *do not kill him*. Understood?"

The woman dutifully bowed and left the chapel.

Alyssa still hadn't said anything. For the first time, I got a decent look at her. She was tall, right around my height, and sported a bluish tint to her hair that I liked. Then I noticed her pointed ears, each pierced probably half a dozen times. "You're an elf?" I asked, though I knew it was obvious.

The woman nodded. "I changed a few months ago. Always wanted to play an elf," she quietly answered.

Being an elf meant she would have different talent options available to her as she leveled. She would have an affinity for nature and ancient lore, and that meant her choice of class was a little odd. The lack of synergy between her class and race was probably the reason the fight outside Echelon had not gone much worse.

I turned back to regard Madrid one final time. "Be ready for tomorrow," I told him evenly. "You're going to tell me all about Vic and the rest of your group. If I don't like your answers, I'm going to cut off your other hand. Hell, I might do that just for fun. But I highly recommend that you tell the truth."

I left with Alyssa in tow before Madrid could collect his ruined thoughts enough to respond.

We went to the workshop on the other side of the necropolis. "Everyone here has a job," I explained. "Being an elf and an arcanist, would you prefer to work with our herbalist or our alchemist?"

The blue-haired woman was quiet for a moment. "I was a scout for Resurrection. My . . ." She choked back a sob. "My sister and I served as outriders. We scouted dungeons or other guilds and gathered information. I'm fairly adept with potions as most elves are, but I never focused on it much. My craftsmanship is still only sixteen."

"Alright, thanks for telling me. For now, I'll have you work alongside Kulgun and Geirr at the alchemy station." I opened the door to the workshop and ushered her inside.

"What are you working on right now?" she asked.

"I want as many healing potions as we can get. Madrid is going to need them," I said.

Outside the workshop, Helvegen had returned from the stables. "The horses are good for tonight, but we'll need more food coming in if we're going to feed them and our two new mouths."

She was right, of course, though we didn't have too many options just yet.

"We'll figure it out in the morning," I said. "The herbalist is working on farms, but they won't be producing anything to eat for weeks. That's a long-term plan. Let me sleep on it and see if I can come up with any ideas."

Helvegen nodded and looked down her list of items from the day's work. "The cart tracks from the mine to the forge have been finished and are operational. We should have carts of ore flowing into Undercroft by tomorrow. The orcs also ate one of the NPC miners, so I told them to replace the miner with a worker of their own, which they didn't seem to mind."

"Ha, that's rough." I wiped a bit of sweat from my brow with the back of my hand. "If they keep eating NPCs, I'll kill a few of them and make an example. Keep me posted."

"Geirr should have two floating traps ready to be deployed around the perimeter by tomorrow afternoon, and work has begun on spikes for the moat. Also, the conjuror thinks he can fill the moat with stinging darkness if we give him enough magical power to consume. The magic won't do much damage to any invaders, but it will hide the spikes and it won't need to ever be refreshed. Should I have him begin gathering strength from the magical components we have not yet used?" Helvegen had her papers in hand like a clipboard, a thin ink pen in her hand. She was the perfect image of a secretary.

"Yeah, get it started. Spikes all the way around and fill it with shadows. I like it," I said. "We'll work on food tomorrow. Come get me an hour or so after dawn. And bring some coffee."

Helvegen nodded and left in the direction of the barracks.

I climbed the steps to my bedroom and mentally commanded a pair of gargoyles at the same time. I had them fly in a tight circle above the chapel just in case Madrid figured out a way past the guards we had already positioned to watch over him. I also told the gargoyles to watch for Alyssa and capture her should she make a similar attempt. I didn't know if the stone watchmen would actually be strong enough to bring her in, but they'd at least cause enough commotion to alert the rest of Undercroft Citadel. She wouldn't be escaping anytime soon.

I lay down in my bed and commanded the necropolis to turn on the air conditioning. The cool breeze kicked on, and another idea crossed my mind. If I could control the temperature in my room, why not throughout the rest of the citadel? I mentally commanded the temperature in the chapel to increase. Though I couldn't feel it from my room, I could sense the necropolis following my command. I pushed the temperature up another few notches toward a hundred degrees before settling in beneath my covers to sleep.

Tomorrow would be a big day. I would learn where Vic and his band were hiding, how many people he had under his command, what kind of defenses they employed, and so much more.

CHAPTER 9

I woke up a little after dawn with Helvegen's gentle touch on my shoulder, and the rest of Undercroft Citadel was in the midst of beginning the day's work. I watched them moving around from my stairs as I drank my morning coffee and mentally prepared for the interrogation.

As I was about three quarters through my coffee, I saw Helvegen come running my direction from the area of the workshop around the side of the necropolis. She looked panicked. I immediately finished my coffee and turned back to my room to grab Infernum and my armor, ready to charge into battle if need be.

Helvegen reached the top of the steps as I was beginning to strap on my gauntlets. "The arcanist is missing," she said all at once.

My heart sank. I knew it was my fault. I hadn't taken enough precautionary measures to ensure the woman would remain loyal, and she was too high level for *Corpse Stench's Presence* to keep her in line. She could resist the magic—and all she had to do was wait for her more powerful magic to refresh in order to teleport away.

"Did she hurt anyone?" I asked.

Helvegen shook her head. "She blinked outside the walls. Kulgun heard the spells, but it was too late. She could be anywhere by now."

"Shit!" I slammed my fist down on top of the small counter that held the rest of my armor, and it buckled slightly beneath the strength of my gauntlets. "Get Xia and Xollmomath. Bring them to the throne room."

Helvegen flew back down the steps to carry out her task. I finished putting on my armor and made my own way to the throne room, trying to come up with some sort of plan. Had Alyssa seen too much of the inner workings? I didn't know. She certainly had information, that much was clear. If she took what she knew back to Resurrection, things were about to get a lot harder for us—the guild had a slew of artificers, alchemists, engineers, smiths, and other craftsmanship specialists who could make specific gear for their fighters before raids. If Alyssa told them exactly how many warlocks we had, the state of our zombie army, what kind of defenses we had erected . . . Resurrection would be able to plan the *perfect* raid. We wouldn't stand a chance.

Xia and Xollmomath arrived with Helvegen in the throne room a minute or so later. All three of them wore grim expressions.

"Before we figure out the arcanist, has there been any word from Elyk?" I started.

"Not yet," Helvegen answered.

That wasn't good news. If we were going to hunt an arcanist, I wanted my top general at my side. "Alright. How do we find the arcanist?" I asked, looking to the ancient, red-eyed necromancer standing in front of me. "Any ideas?"

Everyone was quiet. It seemed that none of them had any brilliant ideas that would quickly solve our dilemma.

Finally, Xia was the first to offer up some advice. "She

wasn't a strong enough arcanist to have gone very far. The blink spell requires extensive training. Once she got beyond the walls, she had to go on foot. Both horses are still in the stable, so she's not moving quickly."

"I should have cut off both her feet . . ." I said to myself. "Helvegen, go outside and ask the orcs if they saw anything. The obvious direction for her to be moving would be back toward Echelon, but she has to know that's where we would look first. Maybe she went the opposite direction to throw us off. That would put her in view of the orcs."

The painter offered a curt nod and left.

"Xollmomath," I went on, fixing the necromancer with my gaze. "Do you have any spells that can scry the woman's location? Any magic that can find her quickly?"

He shook his head. "I am not a wizard, though perhaps there is another way. If we send the undead out to look for her, my magic is strong enough to see through their eyes and infuse them with speed. Our zombies could scout in every direction at once. It would add haste to the task, Master."

"Any other ideas?" I asked Xia directly. I wasn't keen on sending out the majority of our defenses if we didn't have to.

"I'll take one of the horses. The conjuror can ride the other. I'll ride toward Echelon. Send the conjuror in the opposite direction. We can at least cover more ground," the warlock answered.

I sighed and readjusted the weight of my armor across my shoulders. "Fine. We'll do it. Without potions, the woman shouldn't have the full use of her magic yet. She should still be exhausted from the fight yesterday, and blinking more than once will have come close to draining her. If you think you can incapacitate her and bring her back, do it. Do not engage her if you don't have confidence that you will win. She might have tricks up her sleeve that we don't know about. Go!"

Xia broke for the stables, and Xollmomath left the throne room as well to organize the zombies.

I was alone on my bone chair, and it felt like the world was slipping away around me.

Undercroft Citadel was powerful. We had sacked the king's keep and built a small army. None of that mattered against a fully prepared guild like Resurrection. I imagined Kevin leading the charge, magical auras of protection swirling around his body and arrows like thunderbolts rocketing into our walls. When we had taken down the Pyreborn Legion, things had been different. Their highest level players had been in the twenties, not the seventies. Xollmomath wouldn't be able to crush the entire Resurrection guild with a single spell.

My head spinning with grim ideas, I stepped outside the throne room and commanded one of the gargoyles to fly me over to the section of the wall closest to the orc encampment. I met Helvegen there, and she finally had a bit of good news.

"One of the orcs saw Alyssa outside the walls. She blinked in this direction, opposite of Echelon like you said. The orc chased her down, but she killed him. Burnt him to a husk with fire." Helvegen's report was excellent news. We had a good direction to start looking.

"Send out the orcs in groups of three. Don't let them get too near Echelon, but get them looking. Tell them I'll let them eat the woman if they find her. That should pique their interest," I said.

She left to go talk to the orcs, and I commanded my gargoyle chauffeur to take me to the top of the necropolis. When we landed, I had a great view beyond the walls. Our zombies were sprinting out in a radial pattern, their black forms powered by extra magic from Xollmomath. In the distance, I saw Xia riding hard on horseback. I glanced down below to make sure the chapel was still guarded. Two warlocks stood sentinel to either side, and the charnel golem looked like a sleeping dog in front of the door.

With everyone running out to find Alyssa, all I had to do was wait. When we found her . . . perhaps Xollmomath could convert her into a powerful, mindless undead like he had done with the paladin we had slaughtered.

Our first word of good news came an hour or so after noon. We hadn't seen Alyssa, but Helvegen reported that a trio of orcs had paid another visit to Tall Timbers. In addition to snatching up an NPC snack, they had seen enough unusual activity to pique my interest. Apparently, the village was on high alert. At the very least, that meant they knew something. Perhaps they were only worried about the orcs I had sent to investigate, but either way it was worth checking out.

I kept the rest of the scouting team deployed and gathered a small force to go investigate Tall Timbers. Helvegen and I stood in front of eight orcs clad for battle. The tall, vicious creatures were eager for a slaughter. Ugg'chugg assured me that her clan would not wantonly murder and eat all the humans the moment we arrived, though I still had some reservations. More gravely, we were leaving Undercroft Citadel as close to undefended as possible.

A few warlocks and the charnel golem were staying behind with Xollmomath, but that was basically it. We needed to move quickly.

Luckily, the orcs were insanely fast when the prospect of a fresh meal motivated their legs, and two of the larger warriors even offered to carry Helvegen and me. I was hesitant to climb up the back of an orc, but it got us to Tall Timbers in less than an hour. I couldn't argue with results.

From the edge of the swampy reeds that marked the village's farthest boundaries, we could tell things were different. We didn't see any patrolling sentries or new battlements constructed to ward off an attack—in fact, we didn't see anyone. Tall Timbers had enough NPC residents that we should have at least heard them going about their day harvesting and processing lumber. The silence was telling.

We crept through the muddy swamp toward the buildings and finally saw the first signs of defense. Two archers, both NPCs, were perched atop a roof along the main road running through the center of the village. They were sitting on the roof's apex back to back, their eyes scanning the swamp. Knowing the orcs' lack of stealth, they'd see us in no time.

"Hel, can you make them see something?" I quietly asked.

She brushed a bit of vegetation from her boots. "What do you have in mind?"

"I don't know. We need to see exactly what they're afraid of. It might not even be related to us, you know?" The possibilities were endless. For all we knew, another orc clan could have just attacked, and the citizens of Tall Timbers were holed up in their homes praying not to die.

Or they could be harboring a fugitive arcanist and scared out of their minds.

Helvegen thought for a moment and then cast, thrusting her palm outward in the direction of the archers. Her wispy magic wrapped itself around the NPCs like a ghostly hug, and both of them quickly turned in the opposite direction. Whatever they saw made them so terrified that one of them actually fumbled his bow for a few seconds, nearly losing his balance on the roof in the process.

"Go now," Helvegen whispered to the rest of the group.

We ran through the reeds to the back of a large building that would hide all ten of us from the archers' view. If my memory was correct, the building we were hiding behind was the main lumber processing center where they turned felled trees into squared beams. The building should have been noisy with the sounds of NPCs and saws and other machinery, but it was just as quiet as the rest of the village. Another sign that something was going on.

I turned to Ugg'chugg. "Do you have any spells that can detect the presence of magic?" I asked. The huge orc was a shaman, and the class was a bit like a magical toolbox, capable of learning all sorts of different talents from the earth-rending destruction of the shadowy goblin I could summon to much more pleasant and mundane abilities like detecting magic.

Ugg'chugg scratched at what looked like a cancerous tumor on her neck. "I can find magics," she finally said. Despite our obvious need for stealth, her voice was deep and rumbling and not the least bit quiet.

She knelt down and placed both of her hands into the muck at our feet. After a few seconds, a glimmer of forest-green magic spread out from her fingers and worked its way underneath the nearby buildings.

We waited as her spell spread out beneath Tall Timbers. After a minute or so, we heard a commotion coming from one of the buildings adjacent to the archer post.

"Two magics," the orc shaman stated proudly. "I tickled them. One is strong, but the other is puny."

Helvegen and I shared a knowing look. "Sounds like the arcanist might be here," I said.

We heard a door opening and several people rushing out into the street, sounds of panic in their voices.

"Let me go first," I told my underlings. "I don't want to spook them into an all-out battle right away. If you hear me yell, come running out and ready to kill. Understood?"

Helvegen and Ugg'chugg both nodded. The other orcs didn't really seem too concerned with anything I had to say.

I straightened my back and kicked off some of the green slime clinging to my greaves. With my head held high, I strode around the side of the building.

As expected, the center of the street was full of commotion. Kingsley was standing in front of a door like a bouncer, the two archers on the roof to his left. A handful of NPCs were spread out through the street with swords and shields held in their hands. All of them were clearly terrified and unprepared.

I took a few steps toward them, and their little circle of defenders pulled back into a knot in front of the door. I held up my hands, Infernum still sheathed at my side. "No need to worry," I announced. "I'm not here for a fight." I didn't see the mayor anywhere among the defenders. The town hall was a few buildings deeper into the village, and I figured he was hiding there. Then I remembered that the mayor had been an elf, and I wondered if Alyssa knew any of the NPCs in Tall Timbers. It would make sense. Echelon wasn't known for having a lot of elves like some of the other cities in Wonder, so Tall Timbers was probably the closest elven haven for a hundred miles.

"What do you want?" Kingsley, the only player in the street other than myself, called to me.

I kept my hands up in surrender. "I'm just looking for someone. A friend of mine . . . went out on a scouting mission this morning, and we expected to have her back by now. I was wondering if anyone around here saw her. She's an elf. Blue hair, fairly attractive—you'd remember seeing her if she passed through."

The two archers gave away the answer at once. They glanced at each other, and both of them tensed. To his credit, Kingsley held his facial expression and didn't give away nearly as much. "We haven't seen her in Tall Timbers," the druid called back.

"I see," I replied, walking up to the edge of the defensive circle. "You know that lying to me has dire consequences, yes?"

The druid swallowed hard. "We haven't seen her. Maybe some of the orcs got to her. There are several clans living in the swamps. I suggest you check with them."

"Oh, don't worry about that. I have my people—well, my undead—searching all over the place. I'm sure she'll turn up somewhere," I said.

Some of the guards seemed to relax a little.

"I do have one other question," I went on. I was standing right in front of the nearest NPC, close enough to cut him in half with Infernum without taking another step. "You see, there's some powerful magic coming from behind that door, and I'd very much like to know what it is. Care to enlighten me?"

The druid's eyes darted all around. "Just . . . some magic I was working on. A batch of potions."

I stifled a laugh. As far as I was concerned, we had found the arcanist. I just didn't know why the druid would risk his life to protect her. The only reason I could come up with was that the elves all knew each other, and Kingsley felt like he owed some duty of loyalty to Alyssa. He had probably agreed to hide her until she could recover enough mana to keep blinking away.

"A new batch of potions sounds interesting. I'm sure you wouldn't mind if I took a quick peek, right? I have a potion master at Undercroft Citadel, and I know he'd be very eager to lend a hand." I tried to take a step past the NPC, but he shifted to block my path.

"I . . . I can't let you do that," the druid said. Sweat had beaded up on his forehead like he was sitting in a sauna. To his credit, it *was* hot, but I still had to laugh.

"One chance," I stated. "Bring Alyssa out and give her to me, or I'll just kill my way through your pathetic little guards here and take her. Either way, I get the arcanist. The only choice is if you're alive at the end of the day or not."

An arrow clanked off my armor. It hit me somewhere on my left side, and it didn't even leave a scratch in the gold and red enamel.

The terror on Kingsley's face grew tenfold.

To the druid's left, a shaky archer—so dumbfounded and thoroughly horrified by my impenetrable strength—abandoned his post. He stood and tried to run, but he lost his footing on the steep roof and came crashing to the ground in a heap of arms and legs.

No one else spoke or made a move. Everyone was waiting to see what I would do.

I drew Infernum slowly, letting the metal ring as I brought it forth, and gripped it with both hands. Faster than the guard in front of me could react, I cut him in half at the waist. His blood splattered onto the thick cloth armor of the man behind him, and then all hell broke loose.

"Now!" I yelled at the top of my lungs, taking another swing at the same time. Helvegen and the orcs came charging into the street.

I took at least half a dozen hits on my armor all at once, though not a single one of them made it through. I knocked two more guards out of my way. Kingsley stood in front of the door like a statue, his terror competing with his resolve to dominate his face. As I was about to bring Infernum down on his head, he summoned a shield of swirling earth and stone to form a tight shell around his body. Infernum cracked off a floating piece of stone, and my arms jerked back from the force. All around me, the NPC guards were quickly being torn apart. Fire from my breastplate had ravaged more than one of them, and the orcs were making quick work of the others.

In the midst of so much chaos, I lost sight of the druid.

His swirling barrier of dirt and stone remained in front of the door without him behind it. I searched to either side of the small building as quickly as I could, but I didn't see him. He must have gone into the building itself, likely preparing a more effective defense with the elf inside.

I tried to cleave through the stone barrier one more time, but I was worried about the rocks I was hitting nicking Infernum's pristine edge. Dulling the blade on armor and bone was one thing—a necessary evil—but needlessly sacrificing it on a magical barrier wasn't worth the cost.

I stalked to the side of the building and willed my sword to life. Fire leapt up its length, the heat a familiar comfort along my arms. The wood on the side of the building was old and covered in moss. I tested it once with my hand, and it felt almost squishy beneath my touch. The building probably hadn't been updated or reinforced a single time since Wonder had come online.

My first strike tore a gash in the wall about two feet long and three inches wide. I swung Infernum again, and more wood went flying. After ten strikes, the hole I had made in the side of the building was large enough for me to enter. The inside was dominated by a straw mattress and the other expected furnishings of a sparsely appointed house. I stepped over a ruined, smoldering cabinet and stood in the very center.

Kingsley was cowering against the back wall, magic still thrumming in his hands. Behind him, the blue-haired elf was preparing a spell.

Clearly the druid had some attachment to the arcanist. Whatever it was, he was willing to die for her. I was eager to give him the opportunity.

I launched my shadow pet into the druid's face, eliciting a series of shouts from the man, and charged at the arcanist. She vanished at the last possible moment. Infernum crashed down on the house's rear wall. The damage I had done to the structure itself was starting to make it lean to my right.

I didn't have enough space to pull my sword back and re-set for another strike, so I simply whirled and slammed the hilt into the back of the druid's head. My considerable physical stat came close to crushing his skull. The man was out of the fight, at least for now, so I mentally redirected my shadow pet to a new task: find the arcanist.

The shifting, translucent creature wormed out of the small hole I had carved in the back of the house, and I bashed my way through behind it using my gauntlets. The house lurched again, and it started falling apart at the corners.

I emerged into Tall Timbers once more, Infernum in my hand. My shadow monster raced to my left. I followed it deeper into the village, checking once to make sure the orcs were busy feasting on a new buffet of fresh NPC corpses, and waved for Helvegen to come along. She saw and came running after me, and we both chased the shadow pet down Tall Timbers' main boulevard.

I caught a glimpse of the arcanist turning to run behind another building. Helvegen and I followed, turning left to stay on the same line as the elf, just two buildings away.

Alyssa turned and fired a torrent of magic from her palms. The spells she cast were a mixture of black, boiling tar and jolting electricity. I managed to dodge about a quarter of it, but the rest slimed its way over my armor like a wave of nasty sludge from a ruptured sewer.

The blast didn't hurt. What it did do, however, was *much* worse.

The magic was eating through my armor. It was siz-zling and corroding, burning my armor with the gentle hiss of acid. I dropped to the ground at once, thankful that the dirt was close enough the swamp to still be wet, and rolled. I ripped my gauntlets from my arms as quickly as I could, eager to save them from the caustic tar, and then used my bare fingers to start scraping the sludge from my breastplate.

Burning pain enveloped my hands. It felt like I had reached into a furnace and wrapped my fingers around a hot coal. Still, I couldn't stop. Even if I lost both of my hands, it would be worth it to save my legendary breastplate. As I flailed and rolled to try and get all the insidious tar from my armor, I summoned my character sheet to my vision to watch the entries for my breastplate and gauntlets. If the tooltips on my sheet vanished, I'd know I had lost the armor—and would likely be killed by the arcanist.

Miraculously, the armor entries didn't fade away. They stayed right where they belonged. Finally, I felt like I had removed all the tar from the steel protecting my body, and I struggled to my knees. About ten feet away, Helvegen was launching spell after spell at the arcanist. The blue-haired elf was firing back, and my painter was quickly tiring. Every dodge was slower than the previous one, and she was taking damage.

I got back to my feet and found Infernum in the muck not far away. I scooped it up and charged toward the arcanist. She hit me in the chest with a bolt of electricity that was strong enough to penetrate through my weakened armor and rattle my chest with pain. I gritted my teeth and kept going. I still had a good amount of talents to use. At first, I had planned on trying to dominate and enslave the arcanist for the good of Undercroft Citadel, but now I just wanted her to die. I could bring her corpse back to Xollmomath and use her that way.

My shadow pet was nowhere to be found. I figured the elf had blasted it to pieces as I flopped around in the mud. Thankfully, Alyssa couldn't hope to take on both Helvegen's mind-altering magic and me at the same time. I reached her before she could start running once more. With both hands,

I swung Infernum and connected with her shoulder—but my blade refused to cleave off her arm as I had expected.

I hadn't retrieved my gauntlets, so my physical stat was back to an average twenty-nine. Whatever magical wards were protecting the woman's body were strong enough to resist my unbuffed strike.

I pressed onward, swinging again and vomiting forth a cloud of spores from my mouth. The elf faltered, and Infernum caught her torso and spun her around, finally drawing a bit of blood in the process. For the first time since the fight began, I heard the elf scream.

Helvegen sent more magic into her, landing a direct hit on her head, and I swung down like a lumberjack about to split a log. My sword lodged six inches deep into the elf's back, knocking her down into the muck.

I fell on her, landing with my armored knee on top of her spine, and grabbed her blue hair in my bare, charred hand. Pain practically consumed my body. I could still feel the violent, tingling effects of the lightning that hit me in the chest, and my hands hurt more than I could describe.

Gritting my teeth through the pain, I slammed Alyssa's head into the muddy ground. I hit her over and over, savagely mashing her into the mud, dirt, and stones beneath us. The area around the elf's head was turning crimson with blood. She kept yelling—or trying to yell—but never had enough of a reprieve to do anything more than gasp and spit between hits.

Finally, the woman's fighting spirit broke. She stopped resisting my grip, and she went limp beneath my knee, though she was still conscious.

As much as I wanted to assimilate the elf into Undercroft Citadel, I knew that I couldn't. I would never be able to trust her again. I laced my fingers through the back of her blue hair and got a firm grasp on her head. Using my body weight to keep her pinned, I pushed her head down into the wet, bloody mud until it covered her mouth and her nose. She kicked, but all the strength was gone from her legs.

After a few quiet minutes, Alyssa was dead. Helvegen had organized the orc clan into ranks on the street awaiting my command. I stood and brushed some of the grime from my armor, then found my gauntlets a few feet away in the mud. When they were once more securely strapped to my forearms, I walked back into the center of the main street to take stock of my victory.

The NPC guards had barely even put up a fight. Only one of the orcs had been injured, and the wound was far from life-threatening.

A bit of commotion caught my attention. The orcs had dug through the building I had ruined and brought out the druid, and he was still somehow alive. One of his legs was badly broken, and he had burns running the entire length of the left side of his body.

Kingsley was barely conscious enough to whimper.

I pointed to the nearest group of orcs. "Get the arcanist's body. Don't eat it, just bring it back to Undercroft Citadel with us. Bring the druid as well. Take them both to Xollmomath," I commanded sternly, my voice leaving no room for disobedience.

"What do you want to do with the rest of Tall Timbers?" Helvegen asked once Kingsley and Alyssa had both been secured across the shoulders of a pair of orcs.

"Keep the lumber mill intact. Organize a group to come back here tomorrow and loot anything of value you can find. Then burn it to the ground," I answered.

Your Cunning skill has increased to 27!

CHAPTER 10

I spent the next morning going over Undercroft Citadel's progress with Geirr. The man was making significant progress. He had also enlisted the occasional help of a few orcs who had some craftsmanship skill, and that made his work go a lot quicker.

The two of us stood outside the southern wall inspecting the moat. The conjuror warlock had taken the handful of small artifacts I had stolen from the Echelon archives and consumed their magic, using it to fuel his spells. Geirr and I were perched at the edge of a swirling moat of darkness. The warlock and a crew of four orcs were working about fifty yards down the wall to our left. The warlock directed his crew, and when they were done installing huge timber spikes in the bottom of the moat, the conjuror would consume a magical relic and use it to create a pool of shimmering darkness. The shadows writhed and turned on themselves, an ever-shifting river of void.

If any of our enemies set foot in the moat and survived the spikes, the black tentacles of magic would hold them down and rip them apart, though Xollmomath had said the primary effect would not be purely physical—the tentacles attacked the mind even more than the body. To get a good idea of exactly how it all worked, I had arranged for a little demonstration.

Behind us, the charnel golem stood at attention with Madrid in its bone pincers. I signaled to the beast, and it lumbered to the edge of the moat with all the grace of an elephant. "Throw him in, but make sure he doesn't just get impaled on the spikes and die. A single spike through a leg will suffice," I commanded.

Madrid was too weak to scream. He whimpered as the bone golem moved him in its grasp, but he did not yell out. He had lost a lot of blood, and that sapped his strength. On top of all the physical trauma, I hadn't yet fed him, though I had a plan for that as well. He would eat tonight, but he wouldn't enjoy it.

The charnel golem angled Madrid's body for the edge of the dark moat and threw him in. He landed perfectly, a thick wooden stake blasting through the meat of his left leg right above the knee. The stakes had all been made from fresh logs from Tall Timbers, and they were so thick that the one Madrid landed on nearly severed his entire leg from his body.

I watched with morbid curiosity.

Though the man had been too weak to scream before, he suddenly found his strength. Perhaps he activated a talent. He crawled away from the spike, cutting and ripping his flesh even more, and left behind his leg on the other side of the stake. Blood poured from the wound like a fountain. In a few minutes, he would bleed out and die.

I pulled two large healing potions from my belt and handed them to Geirr. "Force them down his throat," I said.

The engineer took them with a nod and then began down the steep slope that would take him to the bottom of the moat. He was an ally of Undercroft Citadel, so the grasping tendrils of pure shadow didn't attack him, letting him get right next to the dying Madrid without injury. He grabbed a handful of the raider's hair and jammed the opening of one healing potion into his mouth. I could hear the man's teeth click against the glass.

When both potions had been forced down Madrid's throat, the bleeding from his amputation slowed to something he could survive. The potions had been Kulgun's two strongest creations to date. Using them on a prisoner wasn't the smartest decision—but I didn't care. I couldn't let Madrid die. Not yet.

I signaled for the charnel golem to lower one of its appendages for Geirr to use as a ladder. The engineer climbed back to my side, and I dismissed him to continue overseeing the rest of the moat construction. He looked relieved to be allowed to leave.

In the pit, Madrid had reduced his screaming back to dull whimpers as the healing potions did their work. His skin was knitting back together over the new stump that now matched his missing hand. A few feet away from him, the tentacles had wrapped themselves around Madrid's severed leg and pulled it into the deepest part of the moat, losing it in the shadows. The slow magic was coming back to claim a larger prize, and I was eager to watch it work.

Black fingers coiled around Madrid's chest. They pulled him deeper into the black morass, and the man's screams were renewed with full strength. He bellowed into the morning sky, begging to be killed.

I lay down on the edge of the moat, my hands forming a pillow behind my head, and smiled as I listened. Xollmomath had assured me that the conjuror's tentacles would not be fatal on their own. When he had commanded a different citadel in the game's ancient history, he had used a similar moat. The necromancer told me of an attack he had repelled with his former master. An army of thousands had come to destroy his home, and they had brought over a hundred paladins with them. The holy attackers had built a collection of siege towers to go over the moat, and Xollmomath had taken two of them down with a series of ballista shots. When the battle had concluded and the defenders had won, they found scores of paladins dead in the moat. Almost all of them had died of self-inflicted wounds. Even men as holy and righteous as trained paladins had not been mentally strong enough to withstand the horrors they endured in the moat.

I laughed as I thought of the story, wishing I could have been at the powerful necromancer's side to witness such a slaughter. Somewhere in the midst of the cruel shadows, Madrid's screams were starting to become muffled. He was so deep in the moat that I could no longer see him, and it sounded like the shadows themselves—incorporeal as they were—actually deadened the sounds coming from within their tangled mass.

I lay on the side of the moat and thought of home. Before the medicine shortages and the early part of the famines, I had taken my wife on a short vacation to one of the few beaches near Atlanta. Most of the shoreline was dominated by ruined cities and other debris that made swimming dangerous, but a few places had been cleared, dredged, and turned into tourist attractions for those who could afford to visit. I had just gotten my management job with the government, and we spent my signing bonus relaxing at a resort for three days. The place where we stayed had all sorts of add-on activities we could have bought, but all we wanted to do was forget about life for a while.

I remembered looking out from our small veranda and seeing my wife sunning herself on the sand. The sun was brutally hot, and she couldn't stay out for too long, but in those few hours each morning before it got too hot, she was at peace. I stood at the railing with a cup of coffee and a cigar and admired her. I had bought her a new swimsuit for the trip, and she looked damned good in it. I didn't care about the small collection of scars on the center of her chest. She'd had two surgeries to treat her cancer, and we were still optimistic.

Staring up into the sky next to my moat of spikes and darkness, I tried to remember what that kind of optimism felt like. It had been so long since I'd felt it.

I wasn't sure I remembered. Things like optimism and hope were too far away. They were foreign concepts now, remnants of someone else's life that I had no right to claim.

Instead of hope or optimism or any other uplifting emotion, I found a measure of solitude as I listened to the deadened sounds of Madrid's screams. I closed my eyes and felt the heat of the morning on my face. With the quiet, calming monotony of a condemned man's screams for a soundtrack, I drifted to sleep.

A hand on my shoulder gently shook me awake. I opened my eyes to see Helvegen kneeling next to me, a smile on her face. I was also smiling. I hadn't slept so well since . . . actually, it had been so long that I wasn't sure. I squinted and blocked out the sun with a hand, then pushed myself up to a sitting position with my legs hanging over the side of the moat. It looked like it was a few hours after noon.

Surprisingly, Helvegen sat down next to me. "Sorry to wake you up," she said quietly.

I realized that Madrid's screams had either grown too soft to hear or had stopped altogether. The moat was peaceful. "Don't worry about it," I said. "What's going on?"

She leaned a little closer to me, our shoulders touching.

"Xollmomath finished converting the two newest members of our family. I figured you would want to know."

"Excellent. Kingsley and Alyssa have joined the ranks. What can they do?" I let out a sigh and allowed my head to fall on Helvegen's shoulder. Getting good news from my citadel manager was a great addition to an already fantastic day.

Helvegen didn't pull away from my touch. "The elf is still an arcanist, just an undead one, and she'll be loyal for the rest of her days. No more running away. Xollmomath said her magic will be a little different, more focused on necrotic spells rather than elemental, but she can still blink, and that's the most useful thing she has. Kingsley is a little different. Undead can't be druids, apparently. The magic doesn't work together."

"Oh? I was looking forward to having a druid on staff," I said.

"Ha, he's still sort of a druid, I guess. Xollmomath doesn't have a name for the class. He said he's never resurrected an undead druid before, so he didn't know what to call him. He's already been rather useful, though. I set him to work summoning vines and thorns to serve as armor for the zombie soldiers, and it works really well," Helvegen explained.

"That sounds awesome. I need to see it!" I said, a stupid grin plastered to my face.

Helvegen shared my enthusiasm. "Now that he's working for us, there's a lot more he can do. He can help the herbalist with our food production, and he's already been able to summon a handful of undead ravens to serve as advance scouts and lookouts. Kingsley might be the best addition to Undercroft Citadel that we've ever had."

I couldn't agree more. "Let's go see these zombies and take a look around town. I'd like to get our next projects underway." I stood and offered a hand to Helvegen. She took it and pulled herself up as well.

I pointed to the charnel golem still standing guard about ten feet away. "Get our prisoner and return him to the chapel," I commanded.

"Prisoner?" Hel asked.

The charnel golem lumbered into the shadowy moat and disappeared among the stakes and tentacles.

"I brought Madrid out here for a little test. I don't think he liked it," I answered. We waited for a few moments until the beast emerged and pulled itself up the side of the moat. The golem had retrieved a now unconscious Madrid along with his severed leg.

"He's not going to last a whole lot longer," Hel said.

The man had clawed out one of his eyes in the pit. His only remaining hand was covered in dried blood up to his elbow. I thought about taking his last eye, but I figured that could wait until he had recovered. I wanted him to *appreciate* the gesture as much as possible. "I forced a couple healing potions down his throat," I explained as we walked back to the gate, the lumbering golem following behind like a pet dog.

Helvegen hesitated before speaking. "We'll need those potions ourselves eventually . . ."

"Oh, I know. There's only so much I can cut off the man before there's nothing left. We'll keep our own potion supply stocked, but Madrid is certainly going to be needing more as the weeks go by," I said.

The woman only shook her head. What I was doing wasn't efficient. I knew that. I just . . . I just didn't care. I would do anything to make Madrid suffer.

The two of us walked to the necropolis, and I stood for a moment staring at the pinnacle so far above me. It was truly magnificent to behold. Everything about the structure inspired awe. The guardian insect-statue hybrids standing watch on the stairs reminded me of old Roman columns leading to a library or a temple. Not far from the stairs, the gruesome doors of the ossuary were another wonder of their own. It was all so beautiful—and it was all mine.

I looked at Helvegen next to me, and she was smiling. If I wanted her as well, I knew I could have her. Everything inside my walls belonged to me. Soon, Echelon would bow as well.

"We need to keep building up our defenses," I said.

Dutifully, Helvegen took out her pen and notes.

"Resurrection is the last real threat inside Echelon. Once the guild has been destroyed, we'll march on the city itself and take it for our own." I imagined our grand war machine rolling through the streets of the city and bringing it down brick by brick.

"Will you move your headquarters to the castle?" Helvegen asked.

I shook my head, still imagining the bloody conquest. "No. We'll loot what we can, and then we'll raze it. Every building. And anyone left in the city by the time we arrive will join the ranks of the undead. We'll build a true army."

"When do you plan on asking the prisoner about Vic's location?" Helvegen had lowered her notes and was looking toward the chapel door, a grim expression on her face. In front of the room, the charnel golem writhed slowly as it stood sentinel, its bones making a constant hum of clacking and clicking.

"Soon," I said. "After what he experienced today, I doubt he'll be much use. I'll let him recover a little, then I'll see about what he knows. Speaking of which, let's go find Xollmomath."

As I was about to turn for the training grounds where the ancient necromancer was working with a couple of the warlocks, a handful of my new zombie soldiers walked by. I commanded them to halt for inspection, and they stood at once. The creatures were fascinatingly grotesque. Their flesh had mostly rotted and fallen from their bones. Where their skeletal structures were exposed, wrapping vines covered in thorns now protected them. Between the thorns were flower blossoms and little green pustules—a stark juxtaposition against the ugly horror of the undead.

Overall, the zombies appeared much stronger than before. Their arms and legs were all botanically enhanced, and they'd certainly hold up a lot longer in combat. On top of their toughness, I had the sneaking suspicion that the green pustules growing on the vines were poisonous. It felt like something Lady Kalma would enjoy. I tested my theory and squeezed one of the pustules between my thumb and forefinger. It popped, and a little spore cloud floated out of it.

I felt the magical attack attempting to wear down my stamina and energy, but it didn't work against *Kalma's Forbearance*. The passive ability prevented the necrotic magic from doing anything more than give me the slight sensation that I was under attack.

Happy with the progress my new necro-botanist was already making, I dismissed the group of undead and made my way with Helvegen to the necromancer. Xollmomath was using a short staff to draw designs in a patch of dirt. I assumed the figures were related to the protective wards and traps the warlocks were capable of creating, and he was teaching them new ones to add to their repertoire.

"How fares your day, Master?" the red-eyed man said without turning to see my approach. His uncanny awareness of my arrival made the hairs on the back of my neck stand on end.

"I have a question for you," I said.

The man turned and fixed me with his inscrutable gaze. "Oh?"

"I get the feeling that you can delve into someone's mind. Is that correct?" I asked.

The corners of Xollmomath's lips curled slightly. "Yes, though I was never a true commander of mental invasion. My own master hundreds of years ago had made it his specialty. With a wave of his hand, he could pull your darkest secrets from your eyes."

I wasn't exactly sure what he meant by pulling secrets from someone's eyes. Knowing him, it was literal. The secrets would come gushing out, and the person's eyes would fall to the ground as well.

"What would it take for you to be able to invade our prisoner's mind?" I asked, a plan easily coming together.

Xollmomath's red eyes flashed. "I suspect I will never be able to fully enter a mind separate from my own as my former master did. However, bring me a strong enough relic, and I will find what it is you need to know."

"That's perfect." I wracked my mind for an idea as to what we could use. The strongest magic in Undercroft Citadel was in my sword and armor. Even for the location of Vic's hideout, I wouldn't give it up. But . . .

I turned to Helvegen with a smile. "The gem we got from the king's messenger. Get it." She left at once.

"Do what you can with the gemstone Helvegen is going to bring you. Don't try anything on the prisoner just yet. His mind is . . . a little fragmented right now. Give him a day to recover, but do it tomorrow. Force a healing potion down his throat if you need to get him conscious. Understand?" I liked the way everything was coming together. If the gemstone was strong enough—and communicating with the dead *had* to be some extremely high-level magic—Xollmomath would be able to get our secrets in no time.

The necromancer bowed his head slightly and returned to his trainees without another word on the matter.

◄◆►

By the time I went to sleep for the night, we had made excellent progress. Geirr and Kulgun were busy making the floating traps that would become the bulk of our defenses, and Kingsley had used his druidic abilities to enhance all of the undead soldiers. He was going to move on to the undead bombs we had chained to the outer wall tomorrow.

The elf was still a bit of a mystery to me. Being undead, communication was difficult. The zombies didn't speak. They understood speech and followed commands, but that was all. I couldn't just ask the arcanist what she could do and get a list of abilities in return. It was more guess and check with her.

Asking the elf to blink had yielded no results, but I had expected that. Blinking even short distances required a massive expenditure of mana, and hers had not yet recovered. She had primarily served Resurrection as a scout, so I figured she would be able to cast spells like *Far Sight* and other vision-enhancing boons. I had given her the task of night lookout with one of the warlock patrols until I could figure out a better way to use her abilities. Depending on what her craftsmanship skill was like in life, I could perhaps give her to the workshop to make magical items.

Thinking about the elf when she had been alive gave me another thought. When I killed a player and had Xollmomath resurrect them as an undead, what happened to their consciousness? The perfect loyalty exhibited by my zombies told me their former consciousness was obliterated. Perhaps that wasn't exactly correct. The more I thought about it, the more I realized I had no idea how to even go about discovering the answer.

I lay in my sheets and imagined what it would be like to be undead. Could they think at all? Chances were good that once a player died, that was it, and it didn't matter what happened to their body after their life was gone. I hoped that was the case. I didn't want to torture Kingsley or Alyssa. Neither of them deserved it.

If I could somehow turn Madrid and Vic into perfectly loyal zombies that retained their consciousness and didn't actually die, that would be a plan worth exploring. I smiled as I thought about how I would use such an ability. I would turn them both into undead and then simply build an underground box for them. As zombies, the game didn't require them to eat or drink or sleep to survive. They were perpetual in that regard. If I buried a zombie in a box and simply told it to remain still, it would. It would stand without moving for eternity.

A knock on my door stole me from my thoughts, and I sat up against my headboard. "Come in," I called, mentally commanding the lights in my room to come up enough for me to be able to see who it was.

As I suspected, Helvegen tentatively crept into the room's small foyer. "I hope you weren't asleep yet," she said quietly.

"Not at all," I answered. "What's on your mind?"

"I just . . . I noticed you were happy today. It . . . was nice to see," she said.

I closed my eyes for a moment and remembered the warmth of the sunlight on my body on the edge of the moat. "I think you're right," I told her. "Today was a good day. If we can get some secrets from our prisoner, tomorrow will be an even better day."

Helvegen stayed in the entryway, her eyes locked on the floor. "When you find Vic and kill him, what will you do then?"

I could tell from her voice that she had been afraid to ask the question. If I was being honest with myself, I didn't know the answer. "I'm not sure," I said. "Maybe build a little cabin somewhere and settle down, raise some kids, that sort of thing. Ha."

Helvegen laughed as well. "And if the portals ever come back online and we can go back to the real world?"

That was something I hadn't thought about before. "I have no idea. Tracking down the bastards who attacked the game servers might not be a bad place to start. They're all guilty. Not as much as Vic and Madrid, but they're still at least partly responsible for Ingrid's death."

The pleasant atmosphere in the room instantly soured. I mentally commanded the purple crystals above me to dim the lights and bring down the temperature a little more, my mood essentially destroyed by the thought of Ingrid's death.

Helvegen didn't say anything as she left and closed the door behind her.

CHAPTER 11

Three days passed in relative peace. Things around Undercroft Citadel were quiet. Our defenses continued to grow in both quality and quantity, and seeing the finished spike moat covered in magical shadows was uplifting. Our food supply remained steady now that we had both an herbalist and a necro-botanist on staff to help things grow.

As the citadel continued to progress toward something permanent and sustainable, I made daily trips to visit my prisoner. Xollmomath had evaluated him two days ago to see if his mind was ready to have its secrets expunged, but he had declared Madrid too unstable. Today he was supposedly ready. According to the necromancer, we could cast the spell any time we wanted. All I had to do was give the signal.

I had the interrogation scheduled for dusk. In the meantime, another development required much more of my attention.

Elyk had sent a message the night before. It hadn't come from him personally, but rather a wounded and haggard NPC woman barely clinging to life who had approached our gates. She had a bit of paper clutched in her grasp that read, 'Tomorrow morning, north gate, the crops are ready for harvest.'

My overly cautious mind warned me against a trap—as did both Helvegen and Xia—but I had to think that the reference to a harvest was something from Elyk. He had probably used a coded message just in case his messenger had decided to defect back to Echelon and run right to Resurrection. That was my take on it, at least. As it turned out, the woman had been too wounded to give us anything more than the simple paper message and a few words about a group waiting for us somewhere. Xollmomath added her to the ranks of my undead army.

I stood in a halo of pre-dawn light just outside the walls and the moat. Geirr and Kulgun had installed two floating traps, one on either side of the gate, the day before. Helvegen and Xia stood at my sides, and we were taking a small contingent of warlocks and zombies with us as well. I had considered also bringing the orcs, but the prospect of Elyk having prisoners meant I would need to worry about those prisoners being eaten on the way back, and I felt like it would be too much of a hassle.

Our party set out from the gate on foot, eager to finally find Elyk and bring him home. Next to me, Helvegen didn't say much. I could tell there was still a lot on her mind, and she had been somewhat distant over the past two days. I think something I had said had shifted her mood. I was happy to be on a quest to take my mind from it all.

Once we left sight of Undercroft Citadel, I sent Helvegen ahead to scout for us in case we were about to run into an ambush. At the very least, she would hopefully be able to cast a paint on anyone thinking to catch us unaware. About two hours into our trek, she came running back with a smile on her sweat-covered face.

"What is it?" I called when she was in earshot. Everyone picked up the pace to meet her halfway.

"I found him," she said, her hands on her knees to recover her breath.

I let her have a few minutes before asking her to go on.

"North of the gate," she explained. "Elyk's holed up with some others in what's left of a small outpost. They're fighting. I—" she stopped again to take another deep breath, "—I don't know which side is winning."

"Who are they fighting?" I demanded. If it was the guild, Elyk was as good as dead.

Again, Helvegen needed a moment before speaking. "Not Resurrection," she said, much to everyone's relief. "Basically everyone *but* them."

"What does that mean? The king?" I waved for everyone to start moving again. We had to relieve Elyk as quickly as possible.

Hel nodded. "Not the king personally, but all his best guards. They have others, too. More guilds, just not Resurrection. If we come in from behind, we can crush them all."

Xia stepped up next to us and placed a hand on Helvegen's chest. A soft glow of dark, ominous magic seeped out of her palm and into the painter's body. When the spell was complete, Helvegen's endurance had recovered. "Alright, lead us there. Let's go!"

We all jogged after Hel, and I sorely wished I had brought a horse. My own endurance had grown monumentally since I had been training in my armor, but it was still an absolute pain in the ass. Fortunately, I knew my strength wouldn't break once we got into the battle. The magic in my legguards would keep me going forever so long as I had an opponent trying to kill me.

The outpost we found was a small collection of three buildings meant to guard the road north of Echelon as it wound through the valleys and forests and plains that would eventually take it all the way to the coast and the huge port city perched on the shoreline. The central building was the only one made of stone. It had a two-story tower in the center and small ramparts like wings stretching out for about ten feet to either side. Behind it was a pair of wooden buildings that likely housed the garrison's supplies and sleeping quarters. One of the wooden structures was engulfed in flames, and the other had taken some damage as well, though from what I wasn't sure.

I was only able to find meager cover for my party as we assessed the battle. We were crouched among a small stand of scraggly trees that barely did anything to hide us from the attackers. Luckily, no one was bothering to watch the rear approach. Between us and the outpost were three distinct groups. The main body of soldiers, probably forty or so armored men and women, flew Echelons colors. They had a handful of high-level knights on horseback directing the action.

Their left flank was comprised of a guild I didn't recognize whose colors were orange and black. Most of them appeared to be casters, but I wouldn't be able to tell for sure until we got closer. On the right side of the knights was basically a militia. They didn't have any banners, and they appeared poorly armed and armored.

"You're sure Elyk is the one defending the outpost?" I asked.

Helvegen nodded. "I caught a glimpse of someone using a scythe. I didn't stay long enough to confirm it, though. It . . . could be anyone. I'm sorry." She looked crestfallen.

"Chances are better than not that it's him," I said. "Now we just need a plan. Xia, think you can at least pull the attention of the casters?"

"A few fireballs should get them looking our way," the warlock answered with a devious grin.

"Good. I'll take the zombies right up the middle and hit the knights. Hel, you go—" The loud thrum of a ballista cut off my words. The bolt slammed into the top floor of the tower, hitting the central window with a resounding crack. The militia on the right flank started scrambling to reload the device. "Hel, go for the ballista crew. They aren't really soldiers. Give them something to fear and see if you can break their ranks."

In front of the tower, the thin line of fighters protecting the outpost was clearly faltering. They couldn't hold their own for much longer, especially against a ballista. And if the knights charged, they'd break the line for sure. Sadly, we didn't have any elevation at our little copse of trees, so I couldn't see who it was defending the tower. If Elyk was there, I had no idea. Perhaps he was already dead.

Either way, I was eager for a fight. It had been a long time since I had leveled. I needed to get into the thick of things and start killing. Infernum was hungry for blood.

We didn't wait a second longer. Xia took off to the left, Helvegen broke right, and I led the zombies right up the middle with my flaming sword directing the charge.

The first knight heard me coming about a second before I swung down on his back and basically split him in half. He fell from his panicked horse in a mess of blood, fire, and rent armor. The rest of the knights turned and started to scream, shouting new orders to their troops and kicking their horses. About half of them were moving away, the other half coming for me.

I held my ground in the center as the zombies flooded through the ranks of Echelon city guards. The unmounted soldiers were all NPCs, and they were clearly unnerved by the sudden attack. Vine-strengthened arms started raking through them, bashing against their armor and pulling them to the ground. I stood with Infernum at the ready and awaited the first mounted player. He came at me with a long sword, swinging down from his horse in a wide arc, but his height played against him. I ducked the majority of the blow so that his sword clanged off the back of my breastplate without doing any damage. Fire leapt from my armor, and I swung hard for the horse's legs, severing two of them in a torrent of blood.

The knight was ready for my attack. He jumped from the top of his horse, and his sword came down on the top of my helmet. Though my armor prevented the blade from cutting my head in half, the noise the strike produced was deafening. It rang and echoed inside my skull, making me clench my eyes. Another powerful strike landed on my back, tearing away a bit of my red cloak. In front of me, maybe about ten steps away, another knight was charging forward with a lance leveled at my chest. My armor was extraordinarily good, but I didn't think it would survive a hit like that. The first knight was still behind me, hacking at my back and shoulders, and I crumpled down to my knees with Infernum in front of me like a cane—an effective ruse.

Just as I planned it, the knight behind me was too focused on finishing his kill to see his comrade charging in. I rolled to my side at the last possible moment, and the charging knight's lance skewered his ally. The man was fully impaled, the lance's point pinning his corpse to the ground like a banner. I picked myself up off the ground and kept moving forward. There were still a bunch of knights left, though all of them in the thick of the fight with the zombies had gotten off their horses.

I stalked toward the nearest knight, a level twenty-four player, and swung for his head with a horizontal strike. Infernum cracked through his gorget and decapitated him, throwing fire and blood all over a pair of his closest allies. Another knight wrapped a gauntleted hand around my shoulder and yanked me back, probably trying to throw me to the ground and finish me off with a simple stab through my helmet. I let him grapple me, getting close enough to his face to see his eyes, then let loose *A Feast of Spores* directly into his mouth.

As the man choked and coughed, I threw him to the side and sent my shadow pet after him, confident that he would not get back up to join the fight any time soon.

I was finally close enough to the tower to see the defenders holding the line. They were almost all players, but none of them were human. They were gnomes, and a few of the short creatures were mounted atop steam-powered boars with fiery, spikey tusks. I had never seen such creations before, and I knew they had to have originally come from one of the other provinces in Wonder.

A huge hit from behind knocked me forward, and I fell into the gnomish line. Luckily, the gnomes recognized me as one of their saviors and pulled me quickly to safety. It took me a moment to get my bearings and shake the concussive force of the blow from my mind, and then I was on my feet again.

A horse from one of the knights was panicking and trying to run away, but it had nowhere to go trapped between the gnomes and the stone building they were defending. I grabbed its reins and yanked down on them, pulling it close so I could get a foot in a stirrup. It took me two tries to pull myself on the beast's back, but I made it.

From atop my new steed, I could finally see the battle in full. The gnomes had rallied and were holding the line, though all of my zombies had already been killed. They had taken down all but two of the knights in the center of the battle, leaving the others in bloody tangles of rotting flesh, flaying vines, and rabid bite marks. Helvegen had successfully routed the militia all on her own. I had no idea what she had made them see, but it had worked. The untrained soldiers had abandoned their ballista and gone running back in the direction of Echelon. I could ride out to chase them down, but I'd never get every single one of them, so I let them go.

On the opposite side of the battle, now on my right, Xia was actively retreating. A few smoldering craters remained in the center of the group of casters, and a few of them were dead. The rest had turned and were furiously casting at the warlock. Xia was a higher level than all of them, but she couldn't hold off the onslaught forever.

I looked up to the tower, and a bit of red cloth caught my eye. Then Elyk appeared at the broken window. He was covered in blood from head to toe, but he wore a smile nonetheless.

I pointed to Xia and the battle with the casters. "We have to save her!" I yelled.

Elyk nodded and jumped, landing with a thud next to me. I reached out a hand to pull him on the back of the horse. "Good to see you again, my friend," I said.

He gave me a strong pat on the shoulder. "Let's go slaughter some mages," he loudly declared.

I kicked the horse in the direction of the fight and leaned to my left, tightening my grip on Infernum. I could feel Elyk readying his scythe on the right side of our charging warhorse.

The first trio of casters we hit erupted in torn body parts. They had been protected by enchantments, most of them frost-based, but we cleaved right through them without slowing.

Your Physical skill has increased to 30!

Congratulations! You have increased to level 15!

I pushed the notification from my vision and pulled back my sword to get ready for another attack. My shadow pet had finished its grim work with the knights and had come to the casters for more blood, and it pulled another stream of energy from my body as it darted in front of my horse.

We continued to rampage through the line of mages, wizards, arcanists, shaman, and other spell-slinging casters. They were all talented in their classes and had prepared defensive wards around them, but none of them had adequate protection against Infernum or Elyk's swinging scythe. We were relentless as we cleaved through their ranks. Elyk activated a series of talents that made his scythe move so fast I was worried he would cut me in half just as he did the others. Some of the defensive enchantments I swung into were strong enough to hurt, and by the time we reached Xia on the other side of the battle, I was covered in a myriad of different elemental attacks that had left me scorched, rattled by electricity, frost burned, and soaking wet. Elyk's buckler had nullified all but the most powerful magical attacks, and he had come through nearly unscathed.

I dismissed my shadow pet and jumped from the horse to land beside Xia. Only a handful of attackers were left, and they were all trying desperately to flee as the militia had done. "You alright?" I asked the warlock. She was panting, but she looked unharmed.

Xia nodded. "I'll be fine," she answered. "Just a few hits and a damned rattling headache."

Elyk found the reins and wheeled the horse around, kicking it back toward the fleeing enemies to continue his brutal charge. I spotted Helvegen in the midst of all the bodies, and Xia and I ran to her. She had taken a wicked hit on her shoulder that had her bleeding profusely and barely able to stand. By the looks of it, she had already consumed her own health potion, so I grabbed one from my own belt and handed it over to her. Once she emptied the vial, her wound stopped spewing blood, and a little bit of color returned to her complexion.

One of the diminutive gnomes atop a mechanical boar came trotting through the corpses and waved. I'd never noticed before that gnomes only had four fingers on each hand. The player's name was Spark, and he was a fourteenth level inventor. I had to assume that anyone changing their race to gnome—an unusual choice for any combat class—was pretty seriously invested in the role play and crafting aspects of Wonder. That whole side of the game had always been fascinating to me. I had never wanted to assume a different identity myself, but I admired the people who were able to do it well. Players like that had always brought the game to life.

"You're from Undercroft Citadel, aren't you?" Spark said without a shred of fear in his voice.

I waved back to him. "Yeah. I'm Ben. I run things at Undercroft. What are you guys doing with Elyk?" I couldn't imagine how my harvester had managed to get an entire guild of gnomes to ally with him. It didn't strike me as a likely match.

The gnome smiled. His small head was bald like Xollmomath's save for a pair of dark tufts around his ears. In all honesty, gnomes were probably the ugliest humanoid class a player could choose to take. "I represent the Gnomish Inventors' League," Spark happily announced, offering a short bow at the waist. "Unfortunately, since the portal in the center of Echelon stopped working, there hasn't been a market for the League's services. Without a vibrant market, my guild has nothing productive to do. Your lieutenant believes you might have steady work for us. We were on our way out of the city when the guards attacked."

Something about the gnome's story didn't really make sense to me. If the guild aligned with someone evil like me, they wouldn't be frequently returning to Echelon to spend their money. "I'm not sure about work . . . or rather, I'm not sure what good any payment will do you. I trust that you know about Undercroft Citadel either from Elyk or from all the notifications. If you work for me, you won't be welcome in the city. The gold wouldn't do you much good."

Spark waved away my concerns and maintained his grin. "We . . . heh, we'll work for a share of loot and plunder. We had a few ongoing projects back in Echelon that weren't exactly *approved* by those in power. I don't think you'd mind if we started looking into things again."

His explanation sounded plausible enough. If the guild needed a place to carry out some unsavory experiments, I could certainly provide it. I extended a hand, and the pale, four-fingered gnome shook it. "Agreed," I said. "You can help my own engineer and alchemist set up a better workshop. Help with some of their tasks, and I don't care what else you do as long as it doesn't get in the way or get any of my people killed."

The little gnome looked delighted. He ran back to the rest of his guildmates, and Elyk returned from slaughtering the last few stragglers from the battle. He was covered in gore from head to toe. "Thanks for saving my ass," he said.

"Anytime. How did you—"

"No time for stories. Resurrection will be on our asses any minute. I killed a couple of them, and they were almost ready to march. We have to go. Now!" Elyk led Xia and me back toward the small outpost while shouting orders to the gnomes. The guild—apparently completely fine obeying Elyk's commands—sprang into action.

Curiously, an old man appeared at the broken window on the second floor of the tower. He had a long beard that flowed down to his waist, and he was wearing a simple outfit of tattered, torn sackcloth. The name floating above his head was Ministrel, and he was a level thirty-four wizard.

Elyk beckoned to the man, and the wizard took a nonchalant step out of the broken tower. Instead of falling the fifteen or so feet to the ground, he slowly levitated to the grass in front of me, his hawkish features vacant and expressionless like the entire battle was nothing but a mild inconvenience to his afternoon napping.

The harvester took a moment from his command of the gnomes to make an introduction. "I did a little prison breaking yesterday," he began. "This old guy used to be the leader of the Gnomish Inventors' League. His name's Ministrel. He might be the oldest player in Wonder."

"Not exactly a ringing endorsement." I reached out a hand to welcome the old man to the fold, but he absent-mindedly turned away from me and began scratching the side of his chest.

I decided to talk to the strange wizard later. If Resurrection was hot on Elyk's heels, we needed to move. The gnomes had gone into the last somewhat undamaged building of the outpost and were retrieving several carts full of tools and supplies along with half a dozen horses to pull them. I helped them hook everything up, and we were on our way back to Undercroft Citadel in a few minutes.

At the front of our column, I pulled my mount alongside Elyk to finally figure out what had happened in the time he had been gone. One of the gnomes had graciously given me her steam-powered boar, and the rattling, jolting contraption made me nervous. "So, how'd you find these guys?" I asked once I had a better grip on the light reins that came with the boar.

"After I killed the guards back in Echelon, I just started running. I was hurt, and I needed somewhere to hide. I tried every door I could, but everyone in Echelon had heard the fight, so the doors were all barred. Finally, I busted in on an inventors' guild meeting," Elyk explained.

I raised an eyebrow. "And they just immediately said they wanted to join the bad guys?"

"Ha, not exactly," he went on. "It took a bit of effort on my part just to get them not to throw me back out on the street. As it turned out, we were in positions to help each other. They're inventors and tinkerers, not fighters, and they needed a fighter. Once I agreed to spring the old man from a dungeon, they turned out to be a lot more cooperative. And getting them to come back with us was easy. Apparently, there are a lot more people in Echelon who think like us than you would imagine."

"What's with the geriatric wizard?" I asked. I looked over my shoulder, and I saw Ministrel coming along at the back of our column, though he wasn't riding a mount or sitting in one of the carts full of supplies. Instead, he floated about three or four feet above the ground. Nothing about his movement was fluid, however. He was jerking forward in halting spurts like some invisible slave was trying to push him along and struggling from the effort.

Elyk sighed and glanced behind us as well. "I don't really know. I guess he was their leader back in his younger years, but I couldn't get them to say much other than they wanted him safe."

"And couldn't he just teleport us all back to Undercroft?" I asked. I had seen high level wizards cast such teleportation spells on the streams. I knew it took a huge amount of mana and concentration, but it would still be a lot faster than riding.

Elyk shook his head. "He . . . uh, doesn't really listen to anything I say. Sometimes he's there inside that skull of his. Other times I feel like he's a million miles away."

"Hopefully he turns out to be useful." I didn't like the prospect of a demented old man wandering around Undercroft Citadel with a litany of extremely powerful abilities.

About a mile from the gate, the undead elf and one of the warlock cultists met us on the road. Alyssa, the blue-haired elf who had once been rather beautiful and striking, now wore a thousand-yard stare and had twisting vines crawling all over her body. Next to her, the warlock was clearly terrified, moving his weight from foot to foot and anxious for us to get closer.

"What is it?" I yelled once we were in earshot.

The warlock ran forward and starting spewing information. "About an hour ago, maybe an hour and a half, the elf started pointing toward Echelon. She just started pointing. Xollmomath sent me and the charnel golem to see what was happening. Resurrection is coming from the south. They left Echelon, and they've gathered outside the city. They're probably already marching!"

A grave air of despair sank over me. It was finally happening. Elyk's warning only a short time before had certainly been intense, but now it was *real*. "How many do they have? What kind of troops?" I demanded, kicking my mechanical boar back up to speed and waving for the warlock to run alongside me.

Sadly, the NPC didn't know for sure. If he had gotten close enough to the guild to see all their classes, he would have been killed. "Maybe fifty guild members, I don't know," he said between breaths. "Probably another two or three hundred others. They have cavalry, siege engines, everything."

I reached down and grabbed the warlock by the back of his robes and roughly hoisted him onto the boar behind me, thankful for the huge bonus to physical that my gauntlets gave. I shouted to the elf to run back to Undercroft, and then I pushed my boar as hard as it would go. Everyone in the column behind me didn't need any orders. They moved as quickly as they could without losing the gear, but they were still painfully slow.

We got to Undercroft, and I went straight for my necropolis. From the stairs, I could see almost all of the small town within the walls, and I called out for everyone to gather, mentally commanding a pair of my gargoyles to go and retrieve the orcs by the mine as well. We needed all hands on deck.

As the final group of orcs lumbered through camp to take their place among my assembled forces, I saw the first enemy crest the horizon. A single horse and rider appeared. They stood motionless for a few seconds like a statue misplaced in an empty field, and then the horizon turned dark with a multitude of enemies.

CHAPTER 12

From the time we saw the very first enemy cresting the horizon to the beginning of the actual battle was about an hour. Xollmomath and I gave out orders to everyone in Undercroft Citadel, organizing our defenses as best we could. We got an unexpected break when the necromancer discovered that he could—for a very limited time—directly take control of Alyssa in order to make use of her scouting abilities. Xollmomath was able to give us a clear picture of the forces coming to our gate. Unfortunately, that picture was a grim one.

Resurrection numbered about a hundred members. Most of them were in the low twenties and thirties, probably newer recruits. The core of the guild was made up of Kevin and the rest of the guild's main raiding team. Those ten would be extremely difficult to kill. Our only sliver of hope against them was that almost all of their game experience was against scripted dungeons and not other players. It was little consolation.

In front of Resurrection was a veritable horde of minions. Xollmomath guessed their number to be around five hundred. They were from all different guilds and even other city allegiances. It seemed that quite a few people cared enough about the evil growing in their midst to risk their lives in order to excise it. It made sense. We were growing strong, and that meant no one was safe.

My heart sank when Xollmomath told me not a single one of the attackers was from Vic's group of raiders. We wouldn't be that lucky.

Once they were all assembled about a hundred yards from our wall, the militia began wheeling two great war engines to their front lines. They had a catapult and a siege tower, and from my position atop the necropolis, I could see a couple dozen ladders among them as well. The siege tower would have to be our first priority. Our attackers knew it, and they had cast enough protective wards around the structure to make it glow and shimmer in the afternoon sunlight.

"Xia! How far can you throw a fireball?" I called down to the lone warlock stationed below me on the stairs. She had her own pair of gargoyle escorts to fly her around as needed behind our walls.

"Not that far!" she called back.

"Damn." We needed to take out the siege tower before it got to the moat or we'd be screwed. Our small force could hold the wall for a decent amount of time against the militia, but once they broke through the lines, I didn't think we would last more than a few minutes. There were just so *many* of them.

Time to pick a new talent for hitting level fifteen. As always, I had three options, one for each primary stat:

Become Colossal (Physical): Calling upon Lady Kalma's imperious strength, the deathbringer grows in stature to fully represent the true strength of an unholy goddess. The amount of growth is proportional to the number of corpses surrounding the deathbringer, and the spell lasts as long as killing continues. Active, consumes minor energy.

Shrouded Miasma (Cunning): The deathbringer buries a vile rune below the ground. With a thought, the rune begins emanating noxious gas into the air, channeling the deathbringer's lifeforce in order to pump more and more poison into the atmosphere. Active, consumes moderate energy.

A Voice Among the Dead (Influence): When the deathbringer takes a life, the voice of the slain can be hastily captured and stored indefinitely for later use. Passive.

None of the three options jumped out at me as obvious choices. The physical and cunning choices were clearly the most combat-oriented and would very likely come in handy in the impending battle. I thought about it a bit longer, then focused on *Shrouded Miasma* and unlocked the skill. If I got the chance to bury a rune underneath the battlefield, it could be wildly effective against so many enemies. Of course, it would very likely be just as effective against my allies as well. So be it.

As I watched from on high, two squads of ladder-carrying militiamen broke away from the main group of enemies in opposite directions.

The battle was beginning.

One of the groups went in the direction of the gatehouse while the other was running toward the north end of Undercroft Citadel where the orcs were stationed to defend their own territory and the mine tracks. Honestly, I felt sorry for the expeditionary forces. I knew whoever was in charge of the assault was using the expendable fighters as fodder to test our defenses, and I also knew it wouldn't end well for them.

From my perch, I watched the northern group approach the shadow moat. They had about twenty or so, and all but one of them was an NPC. I had to assume the player was their leader. He stood behind the others barking commands, and the NPCs began levelling their ladders across the moat toward my walls. Two ladders clanged down on the top of the wooden wall, and a pair of NPCs started climbing. When they were about half way across, the shadows reached up and grabbed them, pulling them down into the inky darkness like tendrils of an octopus wrapping around a fish. A few screams came up from the moat, but they were short-lived. Two more NPCs began tentatively climbing across the ladders, and the human commander ordered the rest of his group to start attacking the shadowy rift with spears and swords.

I gave a hand command to Xia, and she sent one of the stone isopods that normally guarded the staircase out toward the north wall.

About twenty seconds later, the tribe of orcs came lumbering around the wall with heavy clubs, smashing into the NPCs with wild abandon. In no time at all, the group attacking the northern wall was scattered and routed. Half of them were dead, either pulled into the shadows never to be seen again or else they had their heads smashed in by orcish clubs. Much to my delight, the orcs actually obeyed the most important of my commands and refrained from eating any of the bodies. Instead, they hurled the corpses over the wall so that Xollmomath could raise them as undead.

Near the gatehouse, the charnel golem and a single warlock managed to turn back the ladder crew, though they produced only a pair of corpses to be converted before the group retreated. The first test was already concluded. Whoever was in charge of the attack knew that we meant business. Undercroft Citadel would not simply roll over and die.

A few tenuous minutes crept by. The forces outside our walls were regrouping and shifting positions. Then, all at once, the entire mass of enemies began moving. Three groups were pushing toward the walls while two other groups moved the siege engines closer. From the bulk of the movement, I knew they weren't going to test us again. They were throwing everything they had at us.

Behind the main attack force, two groups of cavalry split off in opposite directions to flank us. Before I could issue another command, the battle commenced in full. My warlocks launched magic from the walls, and the enemy spellcasters fought back with everything they had, throwing fire, lightning, and all kinds of other magic while constantly casting protective wards over their own troops. The sound of it all was deafening.

I mentally commanded my gargoyles to fly me toward the wall opposite of the siege tower's lumbering advance. One of the cavalry groups was attacking from that direction, and our defenses there were poor relative to the other sections of the wall. I landed on the top of the wall and grabbed on with my gauntlets, using my huge physical stat to keep myself from falling with virtually no effort.

No one in the cavalry group had any ladders or anything else to cross the moat. What they did have, much to my dismay, was a pair of wizards. Both of the players began casting at once. The first, a lightly armored wizard wearing a feathered hat, started raining down frost and ice from the sky as though a blizzard had just formed directly over the wall. The second wizard stayed further back, and I could tell whatever he was doing was going to be bad.

I quickly commanded my gargoyles to fly me in his direction. I drew Infernum and willed it to life, steeling my nerves for the slaughter ahead. Right as I landed, a huge wave of force shot from the wizard's hands and crashed into the wall, blowing bits of wood and rope in every direction. The battle had only just begun, and they had already blown a hole in the wall. Still, they didn't have an easy way to cross the moat just yet.

I swung down with all my weight behind Infernum and smashed into a series of glowing protective wards surrounding the wizard. The man shrieked, but my blade didn't touch his skin. From the corner of my vision I saw a handful of zombies come rushing out of the wall and into the moat. They were the new *recruits* recently raised from Echelon's militia. Thankfully, they pulled a good amount of the cavalry's attention away from me so I wasn't immediately trampled into the ground.

The wizard tried to turn his horse and gallop away, but his wards didn't stop my hand from wrapping around his ankle. I pulled hard, and the man shrieked again, tumbling from his saddle. I stabbed down, and again my blade was stopped just short of flesh. With a grunt, I stomped on the wizard's throat, and his screams came to an abrupt halt.

All around me, the mounted horses were running every direction in an absolute panic. There was no leader among them, and my own troops were nothing but mindless undead clawing up from the moat to bite and tear at whatever they could reach. Everything devolved into pure chaos. I swung left and right with my flaming sword, cleaving through human and equine legs with impunity, and the corpses began to mount. It didn't take long before I was standing amidst a field of death with only a handful of the attacking cavalry still alive. All of them were fleeing back toward the bulk of the army.

I made sure the last few soldiers were dead, then grabbed hold of one of my zombies by a vine that was growing out of its chest. I pulled the creature close and gave it a command. "Tell Xollmomath to get here quickly. I want undead horses with undead riders. Get to it!"

I pushed the creature roughly through the moat and then commanded my gargoyles to take me back to the top of the necropolis. I alighted at the summit and immediately scanned the battlefield. The gate had held, though it had taken a lot of damage. Xia and the warlocks were still there slinging fireballs and desperately countering all the magic raining in. Luckily, we hadn't yet been breached. Both of the floating traps positioned on either side of the main approach had been triggered as well, and the bloody remnants of two horsemen served as a grim reminder of what our defenses could accomplish. If only we had more traps . . .

As the battle at the gate was winding down, the next phase was already well underway. The rest of the army was slowly marching forward and wheeling their siege engines into range. The catapult was setting up about sixty yards from the wall. On the left flank, a knot of soldiers with shields and pavises were pushing up around their tower. At least two magic users were channeling their spells into the tower and the soldiers guarding it as well. We wouldn't be able to blast it down with warlock magic from range.

The group of enemies kept creeping closer and closer, and the seed of a plan formed in my head. I ran to Xollmomath, interrupting his ceaseless conversions of corpses into fighters, and grabbed his attention. "Make me harder to see!" I shouted. "I need some stealth!"

The red-eyed necromancer fixed his inscrutable gaze on me and nodded. "Get the painter," he stated evenly.

I stepped over a fresh corpse the orcs had dragged inside the walls and ran to the guard tower where Helvegen was stationed. I called her to my side, and together we raced back to Xollmomath. The conjuror was there as well. He looked out of breath and badly injured from the fight at the gate. His shoulder was oozing more blood than he could sustain. He was also missing his healing potion, telling me that he had either consumed it already or lost it in the fight. I thought about handing him my own, but we had precious few left to expend. The conjuror would have to pull through on his own.

"Get your gargoyles," the ancient necromancer said. I closed my eyes and summoned a pair of gargoyles. They hovered on their noisy stone wings about five feet above my head. Xollmomath then turned to the conjuror. "Whatever your most powerful demon is, call it forth and bind it. Send it to our enemies' center." The warlock offered a strained bow before moving as quickly as he could toward the wall.

Helvegen's turn was next. "When the demon arrives on our plane, copy it. Make them see as many demons as you can. Fill their vision with the horrors of the underworld," Xollmomath commanded. The woman silently nodded. Her leather armor was splattered with blood, though her resolve looked solid as steel.

Then the necromancer fixed his gaze on me once more. "You wish to appear unnoticed in the midst of the enemy?" he asked.

I had no idea how he was going to do it, but that was exactly what I needed to try out my new talent. "Do it," I told him.

Strangely, Xollmomath shook his head. "Not yet. Now we must wait for the demon. Without a distraction, you will be seen." The necromancer led Helvegen and me to the wall closest to where the siege tower was approaching. We pulled ourselves up by the ropes binding the logs together in order to see the battlefield. The creaking, wheeled machinery was almost in range. We had about thirty seconds before it would be close enough to lower its drawbridge and send soldiers flooding into Undercroft Citadel.

About ten feet down the wall from me stood the conjuror. He was sheathed in dark, swirling magic, and a glowing symbol had sprung to life on the ground beneath his feet. On his face he wore a twisted and tormented expression. It looked like someone—or perhaps some*thing*—was causing him great pain. The man screamed out, and I guessed that I was right. Whatever demon he was summoning was torturing him in the process.

Finally, the warlock collapsed to the ground, and the rune of summoning glowing in the dirt flared once before fading away altogether.

No demon emerged on the other side of the walls to slay our enemies.

The siege tower stopped its advance, and I could hear the sound of our impending doom in the form of creaking chains and cheering soldiers.

"Hurry up!" I screamed. On the other side of the wall, a few of the attackers had gotten too close to the shadow moat, and the tentacles were raking across them, though the men had apparently figured out some way to resist being pulled into the depths altogether. The heavy drawbridge, shrouded in magical protections, began to lower. It was at least ten feet wide and would accommodate four or five enemy fighters abreast. I took another look at our defenses and felt despair. I hadn't yet committed Elyk or his guild of gnomes to the fight—they were my last reserves.

I reignited Infernum and dropped down from the wall to get ready for the first wave of invaders. In the back of my mind, I was bracing myself for death. If we were overrun, I would ensure that my last action involved a certain dagger and a certain prisoner locked away in my bone chapel. But Vic would still be alive . . .

A hideous roar cut through my thoughts and ripped my attention back to the battlefield. My head snapped to the right in the direction of the noise, and I saw that the conjuror had been reduced to little more than a scattered handful of ashes and charred bone fragments. Where the man had collapsed there now stood a demon the likes of which I had never seen. It stood probably twenty feet tall and vaguely resembled a bipedal beetle with a shiny black carapace and a monstrous mandible just above its four segmented arms.

A notification flashed across the bottom of my vision

removing the conjuror from Undercroft Citadel's defenses and adding whatever the hell the demon was to our ranks. At the same time, I felt a wave of unrelenting fear pass through my mind. The creature had an active aura, and simply being the master of the dungeon didn't make me immune to it. Every fiber of my being urged me to run, to put as much distance between myself and the beetle as possible.

I turned and fled. I sprinted back toward the stairs that would take me to the top of the necropolis, thinking of nothing but those terrible, clacking jaws rending me in half. I reached the fourth stair, and my body was suddenly caught in suspension and lifted from the ground. I turned in the air, not of my own accord but as a result of magic, and saw Xollmomath with both hands above his head, his robe falling off his shoulders to reveal his pale, emaciated body. With one hand, the necromancer pulled me away from the necropolis and toward the battle. With the other, Xollmomath was channeling some sort of magical force into the beetle.

The demon absorbed the energy it was receiving and charged. It crashed through the wooden wall with all the decorum of an incensed bull, flinging beams, tentacles from the moat, and a few of our zombies in every possible direction. When it stampeded into the enemy lines, men died. Scores of them.

Helvegen started throwing magic toward the soldiers on the opposite side of the siege tower. The men and women preparing themselves to charge across the drawbridge and invade broke ranks. Their own wizards and mages were hurling magic back at a furious pace, but nothing could stem the tide of so much indomitable fear.

Xollmomath found my eyes for a split second and nodded. I catapulted over the shattered wall on wings of magic and darkness. I landed somewhere in the midst of the fleeing, disorganized army, slamming into the ground like a meteor. I had no doubt that without my legendary armor, I would have been crushed by the impact and immediately killed. As it was, it took me a few breaths to regain enough of my senses to even stand. Everywhere I looked, the battlefield was in chaos. Soldiers were fleeing, shouting commands and orders that went unfollowed, and wrestling over their fallen comrades in their haste to escape.

Unfortunately, despite all the terror, only one of the demons that the army could see was actually tangible. It cut a deep swath of destruction through their ranks, but it was still only a single combatant. The fleeing men would soon be out of the aura's reach, and then they would rally and renew their attack. If I was going to act, I had to do it fast.

I knelt down and dug my left fist through the churned soil, casting *Shrouded Miasma* at the same time. A small seed the shape and size of an acorn seeped out of my hand and through my gauntlet, burying itself in the ground. It took a huge piece of my lifeforce with it. When I pulled back my hand, I couldn't even tell anything was there. I stood to run back to my allies, and a fleeing warrior slammed into my back. He was so confused with terror that he didn't try to fight me, and I could have easily cut him down. Instead, I grabbed his breastplate and pulled him in close, activating *Malignant Putrescence* before shoving him away in the direction of his army.

I ran back toward Undercroft Citadel, giving the beetle demon a wide berth, and stopped just short of the moat. The hole the demon had blasted through our wall was too wide to defend from the inside. We wouldn't get an accurate view of the army as it approached, and now we had to defend the back of the siege tower rather than the front of it. "Hel! Stay at the wall!" I yelled. "Xollmomath! Get the reserves and bring them out. Form a ring around the siege tower!"

As I caught my breath and watched as the beetle continued

its rampage, our reserve forces came pouring out of the breach to form a semi-circle outside the wall around the base of the siege tower. The war engine was still so heavily enchanted with defensive wards that burning it with warlock magic would take far too much time and mana to be worth the effort.

Once we had our defenses properly assembled, I took stock of our position and knew our line had to hold. Xia and the charnel golem were stationed at the gate, and the orcs and gargoyles had command of everything on the opposite side of the walls. I stood with Elyk and the mounted gnomes as the last and only line of defense.

All too late, I realized the glaring error in my strategy: the catapult began firing again. Its crew had recovered from Helvegen's psychological assault. A boulder weighing a hundred pounds or more came flying in low right for our line. The crew was smart and was aiming short of their own siege tower. The gnomes tried to scatter before the boulder landed, but one of them was caught by it and instantly slaughtered. There wasn't enough left of the poor bastard to turn his corpse into a fresh zombie. More hits like that and we wouldn't have a line left to hold.

"Elyk!" I found the harvester in the chaotic disarray that had become our line and pulled him with me to the edge of the moat shielded from the catapult by the siege tower. "Take half the gnomes. Go hit the catapult or we're all dead. Killing the crew won't be enough to stop it. You have to disable it entirely. Cut the ropes and take it apart. Go!"

Elyk nodded and left at once, grabbing a steam-powered boar and rounding up a handful of the gnomes for what would likely be a suicide mission.

If only we had working ballista, we could return fire from afar . . . I had ordered the workshop to finish our pair of floating traps and to help with the spikes in the moat, and now I wished we had finished even a single ballista. But I couldn't focus on mistakes.

The beetle demon had finally gone down. It had killed a vast number of the army, but there were still over a hundred soldiers left, and we hadn't yet seen a single member of Resurrection's core raid team. Worse yet, Kevin was still out there—and he was the strongest player in all of Echelon. If we managed to break the army, we would still have to face the guild.

I watched Elyk and four mounted gnomes charging for the catapult team. The invading army wasn't stupid by any means, and they had surrounded the catapult with a ring of defenders. I knew without a doubt that every one of the four gnomes wouldn't be coming back. They were essentially fodder, a quartet of acceptable losses, hopefully ensuring that the harvester made it to his target and could render the catapult useless.

Elyk's team crashed into the enemy, and another huge boulder came sailing in at our line. At the same time, the main army started advancing again. They had shifted their position slightly and now marched more from my right but were still aiming to reclaim their siege tower.

When the army crossed over the seed I planted, I started channeling my lifeforce. I pumped everything I could into the spell. All at once, it felt like every ounce of blood in my body was being sucked toward some unseen magnet buried deep within the bedrock of the world. The heat and energy drained from my face, and it was hard to focus my vision on the approaching army. Luckily, the poison seeping out of the rune in the battlefield was little more than a faint mist, and the soldiers didn't notice it at first. With so much dust, mud, and blood being thrown around by their armored heels, it was all but impossible to detect floating in the air.

I pumped more and more of my lifeforce into the spell.

The blood drained from my head, and my senses dulled to a vague throb that felt hundreds of miles away. At some point, I collapsed to my knees. Then I fell over completely. I was only minutely aware of whatever action was taking place around me. People were moving, and I thought they were panicked, but I had no way of knowing for sure. Anything I saw with my eyes couldn't be trusted. Everything had basically been reduced to varying shades of red and black anyway.

Once the blood was gone, pain replaced it in my veins. It started like a small pinprick at the very top of my skull and quickly blossomed into a crippling blanket that covered every inch of my skin. It hurt so much that all I wanted to do was scratch and claw until the skin was gone, but I couldn't move. I convulsed, the muscles of my back squeezing tight, and felt a new wave of rattling pain joining its relentless brethren.

Someone pressed a glass vial to my lips. They were screaming, though about what I did not know. Perhaps enemies had flooded through the breach. Maybe they were all dead.

The healing potion brought a radiant bath of cooling that instantly started waging a war against the pain in my nerves. It was a large potion, one of Kulgun's most potent brews, and I felt a few moments of clarity before its effects ended as I continued punishing my body to embolden the spell.

"More . . ." I choked out, just barely catching a glimpse of our attackers from my position curled up in the middle of the broken wall. "More . . . potions . . ."

A few seconds later came another wave of relief. Three more potions were forced down my throat in rapid succession by a set of hands with only nine fingers. In my brief spurts of focus, I could see that she was crying. My own hands looked sunken and paper thin. They looked like the hands of a grandfather, not a middle-aged guy in the prime of his life.

My head lolled to the side, and I finally got a clear view of the destruction my spell had wrought. Everywhere—practically a sea of moving figures—men and women were dying. Their deaths were painful. Merciless. They choked on poison gas, and they died.

Notifications scrolled across the bottom of my vision faster than my addled mind could keep up with them. *Shrouded Miasma* was rooted in cunning, and when I finally caught up to the rapid notifications, my cunning score had reached thirty-five—meaning my level had increased from fifteen to seventeen as well. I didn't have time to pick new talents, so I just focused on the spell as much as I could.

I kept urging the last remnants of my life into *Shrouded Miasma*. I felt the power of the magic thrumming beneath its mask of pain, and I knew I didn't have much left to give. Finally, my spirit gave out, and I went limp on the dirt.

Helvegen's hands wrapped under my pauldrons, and she started dragging me away from the breach. Above us, the sky had darkened with enemy magic, and bolts of lightning were striking everything in sight. At least a pair of our buildings were on fire. The warlocks had magic to try and counter the storm, but they had nothing in their arsenals that would help extinguish the fires.

"Get . . . the orcs . . . the shaman," I said weakly as Helvegen dropped me off on the first stone step leading up to my throne room. A blast of magical lightning slammed the stairs next to me, missing me by only a few feet but rendering my ears temporarily useless. Had the bolt been a real one from nature and not a conjured fragment of magic, I guessed that it would have killed me instantly, arcing from the stairs through my armor to turn off my brain like a switch.

I propped myself up on my elbows and managed to tilt my head enough to see the battlefield through the massive hole in our wall. The great bulk of Echelon's army was dead. Perhaps twenty or thirty of the soldiers, the ones lucky enough to have been on the fringes and far away from the rune, were still alive. Behind them, the Resurrection raid team had formed a semi-circle that was rather slowly moving forward. I imagined it had been one of their spellcasters who had summoned the lightning storm, and they were forming a defensive ring to protect the magic.

In the middle of the field that now looked more like an upturned graveyard than anything else, Elyk was doing what he did best. His small shield had rendered him immune to my poison, and he was out there with his scythe . . . *harvesting*. I shuddered to think of the sheer carnage the man was capable of generating.

A handful of orcs came into my view from the northern section of Undercroft Citadel, their leader and Helvegen among them. I tried to indicate toward the shaman with a nod, but my strength gave out once more, and I had to rely on the painter to figure out what I had intended to command them. Luckily, she didn't have any trouble setting the shaman to summoning rain and ordering the others to begin tearing down the structures already on fire so that the flames could not spread as easily.

In that moment, I could only tenuously grasp how important the woman was to our survival. She worked with the furor of someone who knew her life depended on her efficacy. When she happened to glance at me, all I could see in her eyes was pain. She pitied me, or at least pitied my situation. Then, when her tasks took her vision elsewhere, her countenance would return to one of hardened resolve, filling me with pride. Recruiting the woman to Undercroft Citadel had been the best move I had ever made.

Panting, I struggled to get my knees under my torso. It felt like it took forever just to kneel, and then trying to stand required a herculean effort I wasn't yet ready to give. I mentally summoned one of the statue guardians along the staircase to help me, and the creature eagerly obeyed. It used its many legs to support the weight of my armor, making my task of standing exceedingly less difficult.

I mentally commanded a gargoyle to come down from the air and latch onto my pauldrons. The animated stone creature lifted me a few feet off the ground to ease the burden on my legs of keeping my head aloft, and then the two of us flew forward to get a clearer look at the battle. Elyk had finished off all of the survivors from the poison gas. Only a few of the many figures scattered along the ground were moving, but none of them were in fighting condition. The catapult had also been rendered useless and thrown on its side, though not a single one of the gnomes that had ridden out with the harvester had survived. We only had a handful of the strange humanoids left.

The Resurrection raid team had waded through the corpses to a point roughly in their center. They were spreading out on their mounts.

"Xoll," I called weakly, mentally commanding the gargoyle to lower me down to the necromancer's earshot. "Start converting the dead. Bring them back. Bring them *all* back."

I had grand visions of an army of the undead rising to their feet all around the guild, tearing them to shreds with their hands and teeth, but I didn't know how much more power was left in Xollmomath's tank. All I could do was hope for the best.

"Excuse me . . ." a soft, uncertain voice came from somewhere behind me. I commanded my gargoyle to turn me around. The old wizard who had come with the gnomes was standing near the steps of the necropolis in his tattered robe.

I prompted him with a stare.

"I . . . perhaps I might be of some assistance . . ." the old man continued.

I waved my hand in the direction of the approaching raid party. "By all means, Ministrel," I said. If the old man wanted to try his hand at the guild, I wasn't going to stop him. If he managed to kill even a single one, his life wouldn't be lost in vain.

The man hobbled over to the breach and stood next to the necromancer who was deep in concentration bringing hundreds of zombies to our cause. "You know, I wasn't always called Ministrel. In fact, I had many names once. Many faces, yes."

The old man was rambling. He was senile, and he'd come out from wherever he was hiding to throw his life away in a fit of dementia.

"When I first came to Wonder, they called me a doctor. Doctor Hubert Malbec, but that was before the experiments . . . before the gnomes," he carried on, his calm face looking at nothing in particular.

"Whoever you are, if you're going to help us keep Undercroft Citadel, you better get to it," I called. The strength of my voice was finally returning, though I still felt extremely light-headed and knew that without the gargoyle I would not be able to stand.

The wizard fished for something from within the folds of his tattered clothes. While he was digging around, an arrow of pure magic rocketed in from the approaching guild members, on a path to blow the poor wizard's head to bits. It had been shot by Kevin, the highest-level ranger in Echelon, and I recognized the dark magic from my own encounter. When it was maybe six inches from Ministrel's skull, it simply stopped. The arrow refused to move. Then, inexplicably, the arrow faded away with a small puff of smoke.

My respect for the rambling wizard grew immensely in the space of a heartbeat.

"Alright. Do what you can, old man. We'll support you,"

I stated. My gargoyle taxi lowered me back down below the wall to keep me out of Kevin's keen sight. A few feet to my left, the air around the old wizard began to shimmer with power.

The man—Ministrel, or whatever his name truly was—started to laugh.

CHAPTER 13

I knew I was too spent to fight. I had just enough energy left to defend myself for maybe a minute, certainly no longer than that. My enchanted greaves ensured that my legs never tired from combat, but they did nothing to ease the toll that *Shrouded Miasma* had taken on my body. Every muscle—every inch of my skin—ached. I mentally commanded a gargoyle to fly me over to the staircase so I could watch what was happening from an elevated position.

The lines on both sides had essentially reformed. Elyk had returned to our side of the moat along with the four remaining gnomes. He held the gap in the wall alongside Helvegen and Xia. Throughout the interior of Undercroft Citadel, the orcs were working furiously to extinguish fires. I knew we had lost more than a handful of buildings. Even the workshop had burned, though I felt like enough of it still remained that we could save it and rebuild. If we survived until tomorrow, the damage report would be staggering.

Xollmomath had both of his hands on the ground and the hood of his robe pulled over his bald head. He was pumping magic into the slain army at our doorstep, and some of the closest corpses had already begun to stir.

The most staggering observation I made was in the number of allies I *didn't* see. The charnel golem was nowhere to be found. Kulgun and Geirr were both gone, though I had ordered them to stay out of the fighting anyway, so their absence didn't mean their deaths. Unless they had been hiding in one of the buildings that had caught fire . . . The area behind the necropolis where the hospitaler and the herbalist had set up a small triage was still intact, though the vast majority of our casualties thus far had been too obliterated to try and save, so their makeshift battlefield hospital remained vacant.

As I surveyed my domain, I spotted Alyssa and Kingsley walking together in a trance-like state toward the western wall where the gatehouse stood. They had known each other in life, so perhaps some vestiges of their consciousnesses drew them to one another. Whatever they were doing, it sadly did not look useful to the war effort. They were just walking side by side like old friends. Though they didn't speak or otherwise visibly communicate, of course. Out in the field, ten mounted players were about half way through the field of their fallen brethren. If seeing so much death up close and personal had any effect on their psyches, they didn't let it show. Not a single one of them turned back in favor of survival. Perhaps their confidence was so well-founded that they simply knew they would prevail. Honestly, I didn't blame them. They were a raid team. They had spent hundreds of hours playing Wonder together, slaughtering their way through dungeons and castles and bringing back some of the best loot the game had to offer. Not only would they be more than formidable as individuals, but fighting together they would no doubt be more than the sum of their parts.

"Xia!" I called down to the waiting warlock. She was still

the second-highest level character in all of Undercroft Citadel, so if we were going to have any chance at all, she would play an integral role in the upcoming fight. "Save your energy, but test their defenses. Hit them with something they might not expect. Just a single spell."

The woman nodded and turned back to face the attackers. She put her hands together like someone mashing up dough for a pastry, then loosed a spell almost vertically above the riders' heads. It wasn't a gout of flame or some other typical warlock magic comprised of darkness and evil, but rather a rainbow of shifting colors that lit up the battlefield like a firework. The magic spread out like a hand with a dozen fingers—then shattered with a brilliant cascade of light about thirty feet before it hit the guild.

Xia looked up to me with a grimace. "Strong countermagic," she called. "It didn't even get near them."

My heart sank through my chest. Magic was virtually all we had. If they could so fully resist whatever it was Xia had cast at them, I had little hope that anything else we cobbled together would be effective.

In the back of my mind, thoughts of retreat crept into my strategy. We hadn't planned to leave Undercroft Citadel. When the battle had begun—when my bravado had been at its peak—I had harbored grand notions of going down with the ship. If we lost, I would sink a dagger through what was left of Madrid and then die with at least half of my goal accomplished. Now, dazed from exhaustion and staring my own death in the face, I was having second thoughts.

I needed to dig deeper. My well of hatred and evil had not yet run dry. No, it was limitless. It *had* to be.

I thought of everything I had lost. I remembered my wife's final days of suffering and anguish, lying motionless in a hospital bed and connected to more tubes and monitors than I could count. She had begged for it all to end, but the doctors had prolonged her life for five more excruciating months of fruitless radiation and debilitating chemotherapy. I remembered her vomiting blood during her treatments and crying . . . always so much crying.

Suddenly, I knew what I had to do.

Xollmomath had a way to make me stronger, a way to make me strong *enough*. All I needed to get things started was a sacrifice. Until now, I had falsely believed that I didn't love anything enough to create a proper offering to Lady Kalma, but I was wrong. There were still two things I loved. Exactly two.

Moving with newfound determination, I stalked down the steps to the bald necromancer hunched over in the dirt and pulled back his hood. He didn't move or break his concentration.

"What are you doing?" Xia asked, grabbing my arm. I brushed aside her touch.

"Xollmomath, get up," I commanded.

The man cocked his head and fixed me with a single blood-red eye. "I am only half finished," he said past gritted teeth.

"Half is still two hundred undead. That's good enough." I yanked him up by his robe, and the man staggered to his feet, his dour expression now one of bewilderment.

"What are you—"

"Get the Founder's Stake. We're remaking it. Now!"

Xollmomath didn't move, so I slapped him hard across his face. For a split second, I thought he might kill me where he stood, but he did not. Instead, his eyes bored into my soul. "Meet me in the ossuary. And take off your armor."

"Elyk!" I yelled, though the harvester was only a few feet away. "Help me get out of my armor. Put it on and fight. Hold the wall as long as you can, then hold the necropolis. If it comes to it, fight up the stairs to the throne room. Let them believe I'm inside."

The man didn't ask any questions. He helped me undo all the leather bindings keeping my legendary armor fixed to my body, and when it was finished, I handed him Infernum as well.

Outside the wall, Xollmomath had bought us some time. The legion of undead soldiers had started to rise, and the guild had no choice but to stop and slaughter them. Kevin and his guildmates wouldn't really have much of a challenge cutting through all two hundred of them, but it would take them at least a couple minutes, maybe more.

"Hel, get the dagger I keep in my room and meet me in the chapel," I said. The woman's eyes spoke volumes. She had been terrified before, but her previous fear paled in comparison to what she felt now.

Xia and the rest of the remaining warlocks started battering the oncoming guild with spells, hopefully buying me more precious seconds, and I stalked toward the chapel.

I stood in front of the stone altar in the ossuary wearing nothing but my pants and boots. Xollmomath was on the other side of the altar preparing the Founder's Stake with a reverence I had never before seen from the ancient necromancer. Helvegen arrived a few seconds later with the *Masterwork Dagger of Searing Pain* in her hand. She gingerly offered it to me on the palm of her hand. I took it and watched the vile poison encased in its glass hilt like a connoisseur about to sample a fine wine. Then I whirled and sank the blade into Madrid's collarbone.

"Unchain this piece of trash and drag him outside," I commanded the painter. "When he's dead, and I don't think it will take long, give his body to the orcs. Tell them to eat. Just save the dagger. Take it back to my room. There will still be a single charge left."

The woman nodded and got to work, her expression still showing nothing but fear.

"It is time," Xollmomath stated a few moments later.

I waited until the two of us were alone inside the ossuary and the door was shut before climbing atop the altar. The stone was cold against my back and made me shiver.

"Your sacrifice, Master?" the ancient being asked. He stood over me, and his red eyes narrowed with judgment.

"You still have the gemstone from the king, right?"

He pulled the small gem from a pocket in his robe and held it between two long, hairless fingers.

"Good. I want you to take . . ." A wracking sputter of fought-back tears made my words catch in my throat. I tried to cling to my composure, but I couldn't. Feeling all the brutal pain that had consumed my life for so long, I cried. I *really* cried. "Take my memories. Rip them out like you were going to do to Madrid. Go into my mind and take all the memories of my wife. It shouldn't be hard to figure out who she is. If you can, leave one. I'd like to remember the day my daughter was born. You can take every other memory you find with her. That's my sacrifice."

Xollmomath didn't blink. His blood-red eyes stared at me from above, and I couldn't look back. I had to turn my head. I gripped the sides of the stone altar as hard as I could. Outside, I could hear the battle raging at the wall. Magical explosions were going off so close that the necropolis itself was shaking with each thunderous blast. Beneath the explosions was a chorus of screams muffled by the heavy ossuary doors.

"Do it."

Searing pain ripped through the center of my chest. I felt the tip of the Founder's Stake break through my back and hit stone.

Everything ended.

CHAPTER 14

Dying before the server crashes meant a quick, ethereal trip back to my apartment. Sometimes I would wake up with a headache or sore muscles—nothing too bad by any means. When I died pinned to the door of the king's castle, that had brought a world of misery and tormenting vision, though of what I couldn't quite remember. All I could remember was that it had been miserable. Whatever I had seen . . . was lost somewhere.

My current death—my sacrifice—was different. I had sacrificed myself on Lady Kalma's altar. I remembered the sounds of war raging all around me, and Xollmomath staring into my eyes with his soulless red orbs. Then . . . darkness. Cold and dark. It felt like I had been buried under a thousand feet of snow and ice. Or perhaps I was on some freezing moon devoid of all warmth and light. Wherever I had gone, I was out of the mayhem and chaos surrounding Undercroft Citadel.

Had we prevailed in the battle? I couldn't remember.

But no, if we had won, why was I dead? I would still be alive if we had won.

No . . . I had sacrificed myself on the Founder's Stake. That meant I had given up something. What had I lost? Helvegen? It didn't make much sense. I knew I didn't love her. Xollmomath had been pretty clear on the importance of losing something I loved, or at least something extremely important.

I just couldn't remem—

The darkness faded. Or rather the darkness began to lighten, to transform into something different, something with form and value. Something I could see.

I was kneeling on a stone floor inside a hall. The room was lit by torches to either side, and the flagstone floor beneath my skin was rough and cold. I moved my head to the side, and I saw what was holding the torches. They were bones, human forearms and hands bolted to the walls. They were bones, but they were moving. The finger bones readjusted their grips. The forearms flexed and moved with unseen muscle.

Something inside me was afraid to look up. I felt like I was in a throne room, prostrate before Lady Kalma herself, and I wasn't sure what horror awaited my vision.

A female voice broke the heavy silence in the air. "*Surman suuhun*," it said, low and raspy and grating against my ears.

The words brought a faint recollection. When I had first earned my class, Xollmomath had given the term 'death-bringer' another name in a different language. He said Lady Kalma had called him *Surma*. I looked up from my knees, and there in front of me, sitting upon a throne of bleached bones and stretched human leather, was Lady Kalma herself. I didn't need any introduction to simply know it was her. There was no doubt in my mind.

"My . . . Lady," I said hesitantly. The woman was seated with one leg crossed above the other. She wore a white lace gown that clung to her gaunt features. Nothing about her resembled the look of someone alive. Either her skin was so pale it was ashen or she was covered in a light layer of grave dirt. I suspected the latter.

Lady Kalma stretched out a long-fingered hand and pet a great black beast seated to the left side of her throne. The creature had the head of a dog or a wolf, but its body quickly became formless and melded into the deep shadows behind the throne. Whatever the beast was, it reacted pleasantly to the goddess's touch, and something about the natural, human-like interaction helped to set me somewhat at ease.

For a moment, I thought to stand. Then I thought better of breaking decorum. I had not been invited to stand. I had been brought to my knees, so there I would remain.

I waited a long moment before chancing to speak again. "Lady Kalma, t-thank you for inviting me to your . . . palace," I finally said.

The tension in the room felt like judgment day. I was standing before a god, my very soul being weighed on a divine scale slowly tipping in the wrong direction.

"Look upon my visage," she commanded. "Witness your end, Benjamin Andrew Hales. Be welcome in the presence of my sisters."

I looked up and straightened my back, still terrified at the prospect of standing. Behind the throne and the shadowy wolf beast were two more women. One of them, the one to Lady Kalma's right, was frail and timid with slumped, boney shoulders. She wore a white lace band around her eyes, and her stringy hair fell in uneven layers. Though she had pale skin to match Kalma's, her neck was red with a line of blood.

On the goddess's other side stood a tall and imposing woman, every bit the opposite of the frail sister. She wore unadorned steel armor blackened by fire and run through with metal spikes. Despite her dozens of impalements, the woman had a proud and invincible air about her that spoke volumes.

"These are my sisters, Benjamin," Lady Kalma continued. She indicated with a wave to her right. "My youngest sister, Lowyatar, the blind daughter of Tuoni, an old and wicked witch. She lives in fields of sin and sorrow, and her breath is the source of cold."

At the mention of her heraldry, Lowyatar seemed to straighten a bit, though her eyeless gaze was fixed on some random point close to the ceiling.

Next, Lady Kalma nodded toward the sister on her left. "My eldest sister, Vammatar, holder of oblivion, sower of void, and herald of sorrow."

Much like Lowyatar, Vammatar straightened with pride at her introduction. She shifted her weight, and the heavy armor hanging from her body clanged against the side of the bone throne. Her posture and overt arrogance reminded me a bit of Elyk.

"Thank you," I said, politely bowing my head. "I am truly in the presence of beings I cannot hope to ever comprehend. Please forgive my ignorance."

Lady Kalma let out a truncated chuckle. "Come here. Let me get a better look at you. My eyes have grown cloudy over the centuries."

I stood on wobbling knees and slowly approached the throne. Wearing only cloth pants, a pair of leather boots, and with a chest covered in blood, I felt unnecessarily exposed, like I was a pig being inspected at auction and about to be slaughtered. Again, I bowed my head.

The goddess reached out and took my hand, and her grip was like ice. It made my flesh crawl. A wave of shivers ran up and down my spine, making all the hairs on my body stand on end.

"You do not have the look of my previous servant, Benjamin. Why?" she asked.

I didn't know how to answer her question. Was she simply

talking about the difference in physical appearance between Xollmomath and me? Or was she—the coded AI controlling her—trying in vain to make some sort of meta comment about how I was a real player and not an AI like her? "I . . . am not like Xollmomath," I said. "He is a powerful necromancer. I am but a lowly servant."

The entire trio shared a brief laugh. At least if they were laughing they weren't killing me, so I figured I was doing well.

"Xollmomath was a faithful servant. He conquered much before the Great Sleep, and he brought the Stench of Corpses to millions. But you . . . *you* . . . brought an end to the Great Sleep. It was you who awakened us from our millennium of slumber. For that we owe you . . . our gratitude."

I was floored. All three goddesses offered me bows, and I felt like they were genuine. Perhaps wrecking the scripted quest in Whitechapel had brought back the code that ran the goddesses, and to them—to the insanely detailed artificial intelligence that had made Wonder such a popular game—it felt like waking up.

"I . . . uh, you're welcome," I said, basically tripping over my own words. I decided to try and get us a little more on track. "Xollmomath and I recovered the Founder's Stake. We rebuilt it together."

Lady Kalma cracked a smile, and some of the grave dirt around her mouth flaked off to the floor. "Ah, the Founder's Stake! Lowyatar made it herself many centuries before the Great Sleep. She used it to kill our father. When he died, Lowyatar used the Stake to cut out her eyes to pay the ferryman for the transport of our father's soul. It was a glorious day."

"Xollmomath said that sacrificing something with the stake would bring me power. There are enemies at Undercroft Citadel. An army that is stronger than our defenses. We need your help. I need it." I hoped my plea didn't sound too desperate, but the fact of the matter was that I *was* desperate. If Undercroft Citadel was going to survive, we needed a bit of divine intervention.

"I have been watching your battle, Benjamin Andrew Hales. You have done well, but you will not prevail," Lady Kalma stated. "You have already suffered great losses. You will suffer more."

Vammatar moved forward a single step, and Lady Kalma immediately reached out a hand to stop her. "My sister is eager to walk the mortal plane once more and come to your aid," the seated goddess said with a devilish smile.

For the first time, one of the sisters who was not Lady Kalma spoke. "Make them suffer!" Vammatar said, her words more like a hiss than human speech. Half of her face was obscured by a shattered steel helmet. Its broken and jagged edges were cutting into the sides of the woman's mouth and flaying her lips.

I thought of the possibility of taking one of the goddesses back to Undercroft Citadel. I had no doubt that we would conquer Resurrection with one of them helping. But would their influence be so strong that I would be usurped as the leader? And if I was overthrown by a goddess, did it really matter? Would I care?

"I have no doubt that any one of you would be able to crush our enemies. I would be honored to fight at your side for the glory of the Stench of Corpses!" I announced as confidently as I could.

Again, the sister clad in armor and bloody spikes was overtly eager while her blind counterpart remained unmoving and timid. In the center, Lady Kalma fixed me with her dead, grey eyes. "The Founder's Stake has provided me enough power to send one of my sisters back with you to your plane of existence, Benjamin. Which would you prefer to help you bring death to your enemies?"

It was hard both to fully comprehend and to believe what the goddess was saying. She was offering me one of her sisters, a divine entity within Wonder, as personal assistance. Whatever I had given up to the Founder's Stake, it was certainly turning out to be worth it. But there was still something more, wasn't there?

"Xollmomath led me to believe that the Founder's Stake would also make me stronger. Is there anything you can offer to enhance my own abilities?" I felt just as timid as the blind sister as I asked my question.

Luckily, Lady Kalma didn't seem to mind my greed. Perhaps being a goddess of death meant that she offered a little more leeway when it came to moral vices. Hell, she probably admired traits like greed and vanity a lot more than noble characteristics.

The death goddess smiled at me. "I have given you much already, Benjamin, though the well of your rewards has not yet run dry. When you return to Undercroft Citadel, I will grant you another floor on your glorious necropolis."

"Thank you, Lady Kalma," I replied, awkwardly bowing my head.

"Now, if you've made your decision—?"

I turned away from her, hoping to buy a little more time. "Just give me a few minutes to think it over," I said. In truth, I already knew which sister I was going to summon into the battle. I just wanted a few moments to myself to select some new talents and finish levelling. I wouldn't really get the chance in the midst of the fight, and now seemed like the perfect opportunity.

I summoned my character sheet to my vision to go over the changes.

Ben Hales, Level 17 Deathbringer, Defender of the Necropolis
Physical: 30
Cunning: 35

Influence: 26 (36)
Renown: 21
Investigation: 8
Trade: 10
Craftsmanship: 10
Fortune: 11
Infamy: 48
Status: unstable, feared, hated and feared by Echelon, hated by Imps (wild beasts)
Holdings: Undercroft Citadel (Dungeon), Riverside (Vassal), Tendershoot Mine
Allegiance: Lady Kalma, the Stench of Corpses

I had risen to level seventeen, and that meant I had talent selections waiting for both level sixteen and seventeen. I opened the first three to get started:

Powerful Tools (Physical): All production buildings under the deathbringer's command receive a one-time reward of mithril tools. The tools will not break so long as they remain in their respective workshops. In addition, any crafter under the deathbringer's command using a mithril tool receives a 4% chance to create an item of Masterwork quality when crafting. Passive.

Battle Room (Cunning): The deathbringer's necropolis is outfitted with a Battle Room. The room contains magical maps of the surrounding area which are updated with new information once per day. Passive.

Glyphs of Power (Influence): The deathbringer's necropolis spawns ten powerful runic glyphs in a ring around its perimeter. Whenever an ally stands upon one of the glyphs, their highest attribute is effectively doubled without effect on their level. Passive.

I read through the options a couple times—probably appearing insane to my NPC company who could not understand what it was I did. My initial thought was to take *Battle Room*, but the talent quickly lost its luster in my mind. If we survived the Resurrection attack, we wouldn't need it. Our only remaining enemy that could give us any threat would be Echelon itself, and we knew exactly where the city was located. In all honesty, the land surrounding Undercroft Citadel was flat and boring. Those two characteristics also made it easily defensible, so having some magical maps probably wouldn't be useful for very long.

I looked to *Powerful Tools* and unlocked it. The chance to craft masterwork items was just too promising to pass up, and the influence skill sounded extremely position dependent. A warlock standing on a glyph would certainly be a formidable defender, but they also wouldn't be able to move. I didn't like betting on our static defenses with our lives. And—I reminded myself again—if we survived, we wouldn't be defending too often in the future. We would go on the attack.

Satisfied with my first choice, I opened the new notification for my level seventeen talents:

Reap Honor (Physical): Whenever the deathbringer kills a target at least level 15 with 0 Infamy, the slain enemy will be raised as an undead to fight at the deathbringer's side. Passive.

Breath of the Dead (Cunning): The deathbringer no longer requires such trivial things as air to survive. Passive.

A Pack of Horrors (Influence): The deathbringer summons a Spawnsire into the world which spits forth untold horrors from its dripping maw. Only one Spawnsire may be summoned each day, and each beast requires a constant gift of lifeforce to maintain. Active. Consumes massive energy.

My last choice was an easy one. Despite the plain *cool* factor of summoning whatever a Spawnsire was, I knew I wouldn't be able to sustain it for long enough to be useful. And even if I could, I was a much bigger threat in the middle of a battle with my legendary gear than I would be channeling some demonic presence. As for acquiring unending breath, I just couldn't imagine it being terribly useful. My mind went to darker places, and I imagined all sorts of tortures I could be subjected to if a lack of oxygen no longer killed me. If I was hung, I would stay there forever. Being trapped underwater would have the same result.

I unlocked my second physical talent in a row and then returned to my position in front of Lady Kalma and her two sisters. "Alright. I'm ready to go back," I announced.

The shadowy dog thing beside the throne fixed me with its black gaze, and a shudder ran down my spine. Whatever the creature was, I felt like it wasn't happy that I was there. Perhaps I had overstayed my welcome.

Luckily, Lady Kalma did not share her pet's emotion. "Have you made your selection?" she asked.

"I have." With a solemn gesture, I pointed to the sister I would bring home with me.

CHAPTER 15

Vammatar reached out a hand, beckoning softly for me to take hold of her armored fingers. Of all the things she could have done, offering to hold hands was about as far from my mind as it could get. I extended my own hand to take hers, but I found myself hesitating. I was about to touch a death goddess. She had been introduced as some sort of champion of void and oblivion—touching her physical body didn't sound like a great idea. It sounded like it was going to hurt.

I steeled my mind as best I could and took hold of the death goddess's iron gauntlet.

The moment I touched her, I realized my mistake.

I knew at once that the goddess was the very embodiment of sorrow. She brought void and oblivion wherever she went, and all of that chaos was just a mere prelude to sorrow. As our fingers touched, she gave me a taste of her sorrow.

Vammatar showed me a glimpse of what I had given up just to be in her divine presence. She showed me my final moments as Xollmomath had sacrificed my memories to

Lady Kalma. All my memories of my wife—the good and the bad together—flew past my mind's eye.

Then they vanished.

"No . . ." I muttered. The only image of the woman I had loved for so long that still remained in my memory was from Ingrid's birth. I remembered the event, but only in bits and pieces. It was too disjointed to enjoy.

The world started slipping into utter darkness, and I felt Vammatar pulling me away from the throne room and back to Undercroft Citadel. The gentle sounds of torches flickering in sconces were slowly replaced with the sounds of war. Even the smells were changing.

As I slipped back into the closest thing to reality I had known for the past few months, I cursed myself. I was foolish. I had given up too much. Winning the battle against Resurrection wasn't worth what I had lost. Death would be a better fate.

Hard stone materialized beneath my feet, and I collapsed onto the top stair of my necropolis, tears streaming down my face once more. I barely had the concentration to notice that I was about fifteen feet too far up from the ground. All I wanted to do was wallow in self-pity and regret. Had I picked the blind goddess, I wouldn't have ever realized what I had given up. I would have kept my solitary memory and that would be it. Now . . . sorrow was all I knew.

I used my sorrow to fuel my rage. My adrenaline spiked, and all the muscles of my body were taught with anticipation. Lady Kalma had healed my physical wounds. I was primed for a fight.

But I had no armor. I had given everything to Elyk before going into the ossuary for my sacrifice. I stood and scanned the battle, and Elyk was easy to find. He was holding the front line right at the breach. At least I assumed it was him. A towering inferno of wrath was swinging my sword from side to side, smashing into defensive wards and steel armor alike.

If my assumption was correct, Elyk had activated the ability on Infernum that I had never ventured to try. He had summoned the mantle of Kagu, First to Walk Among the Flames of Righteousness. The harvester stood maybe twenty feet tall, and while his features were still somehow discernible, his entire body was shrouded in a billowing, smoking pillar of fire.

Helvegen and Xia were still holding at the wall on either side of the breach, frantically throwing their spells against the ten remaining attackers. Actually, once I was able to focus through the chaos and get a clearer picture of the battle, I realized that two of the Resurrection members had already fallen. We only had eight more left to kill.

An ice-cold hand on my shoulder ripped away my attention and made me jump. Vammatar was standing next to me in her bloody and ruined battle armor, looking more like the inside of an iron maiden than a death goddess. "With your leave, I shall enter the fray and drink their blood, Master," she said evenly. Her voice was muffled by the steel of her helmet covering her mouth. On the side of the visor, a steel rod had been rammed through the piece to pin it to her skull.

I pointed to the guild members on the other side of the breach. "Kill the Resurrection guild. But not all of them. If you can, leave the ranger alive. He's the strongest one. I have a new ability I'd like to try out on him."

The bloody, armored woman gave me a slow nod before starting her march down the steps. I still had no weapons or armor, and I couldn't get my usual set from Elyk, so all I could do was watch as it all unfolded.

Vammatar stood about six feet tall. She looked kind of small as she approached the breach, but she had an aura of command about her that suggested she was so much more.

As she moved, I could feel a force gathering around the woman's feet. It came from everywhere in Undercroft Citadel all at once, like a tide being pulled out to sea and leaving the shore dry.

Shadows gathered around Vammatar's feet. They pooled between her greaves, sloshing as she moved and splattering against her breastplate. On the other side of the wall, Resurrection was actively pulling back. They were afraid of her, and rightfully so. The guild's offensive focus quickly shifted from Elyk's tower of fire to the shadowy death goddess. Spell after spell rained down on her, and hundreds of magical arrows shot forth from Kevin's bow. The sheer amount of destruction poured out on her was nothing short of cataclysmic. What was left of the walls was blasted apart. Hel and Xia both ran for cover, and everyone except Xollmomath and Elyk was forced to retreat. The ancient necromancer had returned to his massive spellcasting, both hands laced through the dirt and mud at his feet. A horde of undead zombies rose from the battlefield to attack their former comrades.

Elyk didn't look like he would be able to stay in the fight much longer. His fiery, magical form was slumping over at the waist. He was going down, and there were still eight members of the guild left to kill.

Vammatar knocked Elyk in the back with an open palm and sent him sprawling thirty feet to the side. Infernum's magic instantly dissipated, and he returned to his human form in a crumpled, battered heap. The armor I had given him was so dented and charred it was almost unrecognizable. I had no idea if Geirr—assuming he survived the attack— would be able to fix it. He probably didn't have nearly enough craftsmanship to work on such exquisite, legendary armor.

Another huge explosion of magical force pulled my attention back to Vammatar. Resurrection was throwing everything they had at her—and it was not enough. The death goddess didn't even notice. Magic slammed into her jagged, shorn armor, and it simply dissipated. The woman, half of her body now obscured by a growing pool of shadows, tilted her head back. I couldn't hear if she was laughing, but that was certainly the impression she gave off. Everything about her conveyed arrogance.

Resurrection kept backing away, holding tight to their semi-circle formation, and then Vammatar charged. Shadows splashed in her wake like a boat cutting through a foamy spray. At the last possible moment, Vammatar drew her sword. The weapon she wore wasn't anything ornamented or extravagant as someone in the lofty station of a goddess might have. Instead, the weapon was a single piece of iron lacking a crossguard, and it held a slight curve, though it simply looked more like an unintentional bit of damage than a smith's design.

When Vammatar's unassuming sword connected with the first layer of defensive wards swirling around one of Resurrection's wizards, it sank straight through in a shower of sparks. The player, a fifty-fourth level wizard, was impaled where he stood.

Then I heard Vammatar's laugh. It echoed off the bones of my necropolis like a peal of thunder.

Resurrection broke ranks. Their offensive efforts came to an abrupt halt as they turned to run. "Chase them down!" I screamed at the top of my lungs. I ran down the citadel stairs as fast as my tired legs could take me. I had an extra flight to traverse, and though I desperately wanted to see what Lady Kalma had gifted me, there was no time. I had to rally everyone to flood through the breach and hunt down the guild before a single one of them could escape.

Xollmomath's zombie army was almost fully formed as well. The corpses were raw and terrible fighters individually, but as a horde, they would be effective enough.

Xia led the charge out of the breach. I was right on her heels, though I was still unarmed and unarmored. Luckily, there were so many dead and undead bodies within reach that finding a bit of gear was easy. I grabbed a hatchet and a kite shield from a nearby corpse and rejoined the fray. Helvegen was there as well, leading both Kingsley and Alyssa like a musher urging on her dogs. I fell into step at her side with a smile on my face.

"We'll kill them all," I said between breaths.

Helvegen looked enthusiastic, but she didn't quite share *all* of my optimism. "What the hell is that thing? That woman you brought with you?"

"Vammatar," I answered. "She's a death goddess. One of Lady Kalma's sisters."

A visible shudder ran through Helvegen. "How long is sh—"

We reached the first of the fleeing guild, and Helvegen had to roll to her side to avoid the last remnant of a paladin's holy magic. She slammed into the man at full speed and brought him to the ground, though all she had for a weapon was a small dagger against a paladin covered in steel from head to toe.

I grabbed Helvegen by the shoulder and ripped her aside, instantly throwing my whole weight behind the hatchet I held. The blade bit deep into the paladin's pauldron. A second strike nearly severed the player's arm from his shoulder, and I immediately adjusted my aim for the visor of his helmet. It took me two strikes before the paladin's visor caved in and sliced through the front of his brain.

A notification flashed across the bottom of my vision telling me that *Reap Honor* had activated and claimed the paladin's life. I shoved off the undead and scrambled to my feet, finding Helvegen's side in the process and rejoining the battle. Well, it wasn't much of a battle. With Vammatar leading the charge, we were cutting down Resurrection guild members as easily as we would a town full of peasants. Helvegen filled their heads with horrific visions, Xia blasted them with magic, and I cut off their heads with my salvaged hatchet.

We whittled them down until only two members of the guild remained. I had brought three players back from the dead. They stood arrayed behind me: the paladin, a rogue, and a warlord, each of them at least level forty.

The final two members of Resurrection had stopped fleeing. Kevin stood in front of a female player, a level fifty-one warden dressed in armor of living bark and leaves.

Vammatar took a step forward. Her bit of iron she used as a sword was even more bent and twisted than it had been at the start, and blood covered her hand from her fingertips to her elbow.

I motioned for Helvegen to stay back and then walked up to the death goddess's side. "I'll only give you one chance," I said to Kevin. "You *will* be joining me today. The only choice is whether you're alive or dead when you walk into Undercroft Citadel as my vassal." I nodded over my shoulder to the three Resurrection members standing idly behind Helvegen, their bodies full of ruin. "Make your choice quickly."

For the first time in my life, I saw a hint of fear on Kevin's face. I had watched a few hours of his streams online, and he had always been the absolute image of calm and collected, even when his raid group was failing and he knew he would die. Now, he looked terrified. His dark beard quivered beneath the bottom of his beautifully ornamented and winged szyszak.

"I don't . . . You don't have to—" Kevin's voice trailed off, and his eyes shifted from me to someone else.

Doctor Hubert Malbec—or Ministrel, according to the name floating above his head—had wandered into the semi-circle of combatants. The appearance of a deranged old man normally would not have given any one of us pause, but what he held made my own breath catch in my throat. He was carrying a face. A human face. It dangled from his fingers, bloody and dripping gore onto the dirt. The old man wore a small dagger in his belt, and the amount of blood staining both the blade and the man's clothes around it told me how he had procured his face. Then I noticed two more disembodied faces folded over the man's belt on his left hip.

"What the fuck . . ." I muttered. I had seen a lot of death and had brought about far more than my own share of it, but cutting faces off of bodies churned my stomach. It was having a similar effect on Kevin and the warden as well. The woman turned away and hid her face, stifling a cough, and Kevin took another step backward.

The only one who didn't seem put off by the gruesome display was Vammatar, and that made sense.

Then, to everyone's growing horror, Ministrel unfurled the crumpled upper edge of the face he was holding and began laying it out and flattening it over his own features. Blood and gore ran all over the old man's face, and all he did was whistle as he worked. He simply didn't care.

The warden let go of her staff. The weapon fell over, and she made no move to pick it back up again. She unfastened her helmet and let it fall to the ground as well. Tears streamed down her heavily tattooed face. "I submit. Just . . . Just get that *fucking monster* away from me," she said, trying her best to hold back sobs.

I held up a hand to make sure Ministrel wouldn't take any more steps forward, but the man wasn't even paying attention. He was busy with his mask, pulling it this way and that to make sure it fit just right.

"I accept your surrender," I said. I turned to Helvegen. "Take her weapons and armor and lead her back to Undercroft

Citadel. Put her in the ossuary, and get fifty or so zombies to guard her. If the orcs are still around, get them to help you as well. And take Kingsley. He's a nature kind of guy, or at least he used to be. Maybe the two of them will be friends."

The warden quickly followed Helvegen back toward Undercroft. She lifted a hand to her eyes to block her view of Ministrel as she went, and I could hear in her breathing the effort she had to put into not retching.

"Alright, Kevin. Last chance. You're vastly outnumbered. Vammatar is a death goddess. All your friends are dead. If you come with me, you'll live. You and the warden both. If you don't . . ." I pointed at Ministrel, though I honestly couldn't stomach looking at him for very long and had to avert my gaze. "If you don't . . . I'll let that lunatic take what parts of your body he wants. *Then* I'll kill you and raise your corpse to fight for me anyway."

Kevin visibly deflated. He lowered his magic bow, but he didn't release his grip on it. "I suppose I have no choice," he said quietly.

"That's right."

"And you'll personally guarantee my safety and that of Ellen's, the warden?"

I shook my head. "I can't guarantee anything. We have some pretty rough people living in Undercroft Citadel. You look at Elyk wrong, he'll probably cut you in half where you stand. And if the orcs get hungry and you're the first one they happen to see, consider yourself dead. But throw down your weapons and armor, and I'll escort you back to the walls and show you around. What do you say?"

Kevin rubbed a hand across through his beard. He looked once at Ministrel, then dismissed his magic bow. He reached behind his head and unhooked his helm as well. He continued removing his armor until he stood in just a pair of linen pants and a thin sleeveless shirt that accented the bulging muscles of his shoulders. "Alright," he finally said with a sigh. "I surrender. I'll go back with you."

A smile broke out across my face.

"Sorry, Vammatar. No more killing here," I told the death goddess.

The steel-clad woman gave me a slight bow. "Five more days, mortal," she stated, her voice betraying her disappointment. Then she stalked off back in the direction of the necropolis without a word further.

"Come on. The zombies will carry your gear. I know you can summon your bow whenever you want—just don't. I won't hesitate to kill you. I think you understand that now. Am I right?" I fell into line behind the man so I could watch his movements.

Kevin nodded. "I get it. I want to live as much as you do. I won't throw that away."

When he finished speaking, the color of Kevin's name floating above his head changed to that of Undercroft Citadel. He was one of us.

I watched the sunset from the top of Undercroft Citadel and basked in my victory. There were still a few loose ends, but we would start cleaning up all of that tomorrow. Rebuilding everything we had lost would take weeks. For now, we had an army of over a hundred undead milling around outside the shattered wall to keep us safe. Ellen was asleep—magically so as a form of sedation—in the barracks on the second floor, and Kevin was chained to the altar in the ossuary in the same fashion as Madrid had been.

The first floor of the necropolis was massive. The whole structure had grown outward as well as upward, and we now had all the trappings of a real military fortress. The lowest level contained an armory, the barracks with bunks and other living accommodations for the various people residing in Undercroft Citadel, a large stable with four undead horses, a vastly expanded workshop, a storehouse, and a small vault where we could lock away valuables.

On the second floor of the necropolis, the bone chapel had grown in size. It now contained about a dozen rows of benches facing two stone altars instead of just one. Above the altars hung a bone chandelier holding fifty candles made of black wax. We hadn't lit any of them yet, but I got the feeling that the light they would produce would be anything but ordinary. Next to the ossuary was another new room. It was built of black stone with the texture of basalt, and it was cool to the touch. Past the unadorned black door was only a single item: a pool of calm, reflective liquid that had the smell of the ocean. I had no clue what the room or the pool was supposed to be used for, though Vammatar was still here, so I planned on asking her in the morning.

For now, the victory celebration was in full swing. The hospitaler and Kingsley were the only two not partaking in the Dark Revelry. They still had some wounded orcs and gnomes to take care of, though judging by the screams I heard when I had checked on them earlier, our wounded weren't likely to make it through the night alive. All in all, we hadn't lost as many troops as I had initially feared. I summoned the holdings sections of my character sheet back to my vision to go over everything one last time.

Undercroft Citadel (Dungeon)

Commander: Ben Hales (Influence: 36)

Bosses: Xia (Warlock), Helvegen (Painter), Xollmomath (Necromancer), Elyk (Harvester), Ugg'chugg (Shaman), Vammatar (Goddess)

Resources: Moderate stockpiles of food and lumber, large stockpiles of weapons and armor, minor stockpiles of wealth (gems), minor stockpiles of exotic goods or artifacts, moderate stockpiles of crafting resources

Military Strength: 2 warlocks, 167 zombies, 11 orc raiders, 3 gnomes, 2 truthbreaker paladins, 1 fallen warlord, 1 bone thief, 1 ranger, 1 warden

Specialists: 1 engineer, 1 alchemist, 1 herbalist, 1 hospitaler, 1 inventor (unstable)

Defensive Structures: Partially destroyed wooden wall enhanced with fear glyphs (detonating corpses), minor defensive wards, minor physical traps (punji pits), small guard tower, necropolis, moat, 10 stone gargoyles, 8 stone pillar bugs

Active Production Facilities: 2 forges, 3 crafting benches, 1 engineering bench, 1 alchemy bench, 1 herbalist grove, 1 bone chapel, 1 reflecting pool

A lot had changed as a result of the battle. Kevin and the warden were both listed under my military strength—for now. I had realized a problem as soon as I had returned to the necropolis. Kevin had more influence than I did, and that meant he would become the new commander of Undercroft Citadel as soon as his status was elevated from a simple military member to a dungeon boss. I wasn't exactly sure when that would happen, but I got the feeling that it had something to do with his loyalty to the dungeon as a whole, so perhaps it wouldn't happen for some time. Still, I couldn't take any chances. I would deal with that problem tonight.

Going over my forces once more, I noticed that the charnel golem had also perished in the fighting. The creature had served me well since the beginning, and now it was gone. Xollmomath was out of energy after raising over a hundred and fifty new zombies, so he wouldn't be able to make a new golem either.

Ministrel had been added to the sheet under the 'inventor' label, and I didn't need to read the word 'unstable' next to his name to understand just how unhinged the man was.

He had, surprisingly, taken up residence with the orcs out-side the walls. Perhaps he felt like man-eating orcs would be a little less judgmental about his own gruesome habits. I had tried to ask the man what it was he claimed to be working on, but I hadn't gotten anything useful by way of a response.

I cleared my head of Ministrel and his abominable exper-iments and returned my gaze to the Dark Revelry going on below. Xia and the two remaining warlocks had brought up the last of our alcohol, and everyone with a pulse seemed to be hitting it hard. I smiled as I watched them. We had earned the celebration. Even Vammatar was sitting cross-legged—still wearing the bloody and dented armor pinned to her body—and enjoying a goblet of aged mead. She didn't laugh and carry on with the others, but she joined their celebra-tion nonetheless.

Looking down from my lofty perch, there was one per-son I did not find. Helvegen was missing from the others. I scanned all that I could see once more, but I still did not find her among the celebrants. I mentally commanded a stone gargoyle to fly me to the top of the stairs. I landed softly on the stone, missing the familiar clank of my greaves. Every-thing had been so damaged in the fight that I still had no idea if the armor would be usable in the future or not.

The door to my bedroom creaked open a few inches, and Helvegen's soft voice found me. "Hey . . . how are you doing?" she asked.

I could barely see her in the darkness. Moonlight graced the side of her face, illuminating her long brown hair and gentle features. "I'm alright," I answered. "Just tired and sore. How about you?"

She smiled and retreated a few inches deeper into the darkness. "I feel like all the tension and worry and stress is fi-nally gone. We're going to survive," she replied triumphantly.

I knew she was right. As soon as Kevin had submitted, I

had felt it as well. It was victory, and it felt great. "Why aren't you down with the others having a drink?" I asked.

Helvegen shook her head. "Last time I drank too much. I . . . don't feel like losing so much control again. Would you like me to go get you something?"

It still amazed me how eager the woman was to serve both Undercroft Citadel and me personally. She was a terrorist at least partly responsible for one of the largest disasters in human history, but she was genuinely a *nice* person. I liked that about her. She gave me a little reminder of what the normal world outside Wonder had once been. In fact, she reminded me of someone . . . but I couldn't quite place who it was. Perhaps a coworker at the Ministry of Public Health. All of that—my life before the game—felt so far away in my memory that it almost didn't seem real.

I shook my head and returned my thoughts to the present. There was a kind, beautiful woman standing in the entrance to my bedroom asking me if I'd like a drink. "You know what? That sounds nice. I'm not in the mood for a hangover, so just one. I only have one thing I need to take care of first, then I'll be back and we can share that drink. Give me a couple minutes."

Enjoying a bit of the Dark Revelry as it was meant to be enjoyed sounded like the best way to ease the soreness and pain of the battle. First, I needed to pay the ranger a visit, and I didn't want to spend any more time away from Helvegen than was absolutely necessary. I grabbed the hatchet from my belt, mentally summoned a handful of stone bugs and gargoyles, and scampered down the steps to the second floor. The creepy, twisted doors of the ossuary greeted me with their image of death, and I eased through them as quietly as I could. Luckily, Kevin was still asleep, likely exhausted from all the fighting and still waiting for both his physical stamina and his mana to regenerate. That meant his magical defenses wouldn't be nearly as effective. And without his impressive armor, killing him would be easy.

I crept forward on the balls of my feet. There wasn't much light coming in at all, and the stone defenders I had brought as a backup plan were blocking what little ambient light normally reached the altars.

The man's arms were chained above his head, and they had gone pale from blood loss. I swung the hatchet hard for the very center of the ranger's forehead. There was a brief flash of magic, a small shower of sparks spraying to either side of my blade, and then the sleeping man's breath came to a quick halt. *Reap Honor* flashed across my vision, and my character sheet changed once more. Kevin was dead, but he was mine. I didn't have the keys to his shackles, so I left him for the morning.

I needed to take care of the warden as well. I didn't know if her influence would be high enough to challenge mine, but she was so much higher level than I was that I couldn't take any chances. And she was close to Kevin, or at least she had been until a few seconds ago, and his death might incite her to rebellion. I couldn't take that risk.

I made my way through the darkness to the barracks and eased open the door. Without all my armor, I was basically silent. Inside, the woman was awake. Her feet were shackled together, and she was sitting on a cot just staring at the door almost as if she had been waiting for someone to come through.

"Uh, hello," I said awkwardly.

The woman didn't respond. She just stared at me from across the room.

"I need to know something. How high is your influence?" I asked. I didn't want to spend any more time away from Helvegen than I had to, so I figured getting right to the point was the best option.

The warden's face showed a bit of confusion, but she did well to hide it. "Kevin was our guild leader. None of the rest of us specialized in influence. If you intend to force me to lead dungeon raids or attacks on Echelon, he is the better choice."

It seemed like she had no idea what my true worry was. She probably didn't understand how dungeons operated and what a high influence score would mean. That was perfect. Even if I couldn't trust her, I didn't need to worry about her taking over my town.

I brushed off the gore from my hatchet and threw it to her feet. "I need to know that you're loyal to Undercroft Citadel. Perhaps you noticed Helvegen, my second in command, and her nine fingers. I'll be back tomorrow morning. If you have nine fingers like her, I'll know that you want to survive—that you'll do anything I ask of you in order to live. That's the kind of loyalty I need. And if not, well . . ." I let the rather obvious threat linger in the air and left, shutting the barracks door behind me and commanding the stone defenders to guard outside it. Everyone else would probably be sleeping under the stars in drunken heaps anyway. They wouldn't need the barracks tonight.

Going back to my room, I took the stairs two at a time. The door was open about a foot, showing only darkness within.

A trap? An ambush? My mind suddenly whirled with grim possibilities. I remembered the 'unstable' status line on my own character sheet, and I knew my worries were just an unwarranted attack from my own subconscious. In a brief moment of clarity, I knew I was insane.

Then I thought once more of Helvegen waiting inside with a goblet of honey wine and her long hair cascading down her chest—but damn . . . she reminded me of someone I couldn't get out of my head!—and all the thoughts of an ambush dissipated.

I slipped inside and closed the door behind me. I mentally ordered the door to lock, and a soft clicking sound answered my command. I thought about bringing up the lights a little, but decided against it.

Before I could think any further, a cool leather cup was pressed into my hand, and a warm, gentle breath landed on the side of my neck. Helvegen wrapped an arm around my waist and drew me close. She smelled like flowers, an odd juxtaposition compared to the death and bones my very necropolis was made of, but I didn't think anything of it.

I fell into her embrace, and she led me to the center of the room, to my bed. The room was cool, perhaps a little too chilly to be comfortable, but Helvegen's embrace lit a fire in my chest that I could not deny.

"What—" I started to speak, but a finger touched my lips telling me to be quiet. Then her finger was replaced with a kiss, and the leather cup fell from my hand, the mead inside it untouched.

CHAPTER 16

I woke up a few minutes before Helvegen and watched her sleep. The room was still pitch black with only a little sliver of light coming in under the door, and it was just enough to make out her features. She faced me, her right leg still resting across my hips where it had been most of the night, and she looked happy.

I didn't understand *why* she looked happy. It made no sense to me. All around us, the corpses of our enemies were guarding Undercroft Citadel. Their stench filled the air like clinging spores and wouldn't let go. More undead were housed in the barracks, and the image of death was so omnipresent that the very walls were practically made of it.

Yet the woman wrapped around my body was smiling in her sleep. She was happy.

I got the feeling that Helvegen had made peace with her imprisonment within Wonder far before I had, and now that Undercroft Citadel knew some semblance of peace and security, she had everything she needed. At some level, I was getting close to the same thing. The dagger that had taken Ingrid's life only had one charge left, and that meant there was only one person left to kill before my vengeance was complete.

Helvegen stirred awake and opened her eyes. I couldn't see their color in the darkness, but I knew their shade of brown so well that I didn't need the light. "Hey," she said softly.

I wasn't sure how to respond. "Hey."

"What time is it?" she asked.

"That's one of the few features my enchanted room apparently lacks. Not a clock to be seen. But I don't think the rest of the necropolis will be coming out of their hangovers anytime soon," I answered.

"Good," she said. She brushed a strand of her hair behind her ear and laid her head on my bare chest. The room was a little cool, but the two of us generated enough heat to be perfectly warm beneath only a single sheet.

Relaxing in the morning darkness with a beautiful woman wrapped around my body quieted my mind enough to let a few questions start bubbling to the surface. I didn't want to jeopardize the morning, so I tried to artfully word my curiosity. "We haven't really talked much about what's going on here in Undercroft Citadel. I know you're . . . hiding, I suppose. But you aren't an evil person. At least I don't think so."

She wiggled her body closer into the curves of my own and readjusted her pillow. "I've done horrible things," she whispered, closing her eyes and exhaling heavily.

"I know . . . but there's a pretty big difference between doing some bad things and *being* evil. You're not a bad person. I am." I remembered what Elyk had said after the first drunken celebration we held. Helvegen had looked for me and tried to tell me something. Had she only been trying to tell me she was attracted to me? Attached? Or was it something different and more sinister?

"You're wondering why someone like me would ever want to be with a guy like you, aren't you?"

So much for being tactful. "You can see right through me," I said, somewhat defeated.

Much to my relief, Hel laughed. She sounded like someone who was genuinely pleased by the prospect of someone else considering her out of their league. In a word, she was flattered. "The world's gone to hell. Everything is fucked. Even before the server crashed, there wasn't anything on the outside worth fighting for. Now I have you. I know you'll keep me safe, and that's all that matters."

"But before the crash it was just a game. Killing people didn't *mean* anything back then," I went on.

She shook her head. "No, I don't believe that," she said. "Even if we respawned back in the real world, killing other players was still *wrong*. We hurt them. They experienced real pain. Nothing about Wonder was ever really a *game*, not like you mean it. It was never like the virtual reality arcades our parents grew up with, it was just a different world. Maybe a different plane. And we still hurt people even then."

The woman had a point. "Maybe it is. Maybe you're right. It wouldn't surprise me if the portals just took us all to some other planet. I mean, has anyone ever explored the entire thing? How do we even trust anything the developers ever said about the size of the world or anything else?" Everything I knew about the game was starting to unravel. My understanding of Wonder had always been a little frayed, and now Hel had tugged on one of the loose strands and started to pull it all apart.

"So I think . . . I think I'm just as evil as you are. Maybe even more since I helped commit atrocities before ever stepping foot inside the game." She let out a heavy sigh and pulled a few inches away.

"Whatever we are, we have each other, right?" I knew deep down that I would protect her life with my own if it came to it. I only hoped that time wouldn't come until after I had found Vic and exacted my vengeance.

She hesitated for a moment. "There's just . . . I—" She rolled away from me and stopped speaking. Whatever it was, something weighed heavily on her conscience. I knew she wanted to get it out, but I wasn't going to push her.

"Hey, whatever it is, don't worry about it," I told her. I tried to wrap an arm around her waist and pull her back into my embrace, but she scooted away from me. Then I heard her feet touch the floor on the other side of the bed, and I knew our morning was at its end. It was time to go to work. We had gone too deep, and now the peacefulness of it all was behind us both.

"I'm sorry . . ." I muttered, but it was no use. I leaned up on my elbows and watched her gather up her clothes from the floor and leave. She didn't walk like she was angry, and for that I was thankful. She would come back to me in her own time—probably tonight—but for now, our conversation had run its course.

When I stepped out of my room about ten minutes later, the only player I saw up and walking around was Kulgun. The alchemist probably had some potent mixture he could drink to ward off the effects of a hangover.

"Congratulations!" he called to me when he finally noticed that I was standing on the steps.

I waved back to him. "Thanks, but it wasn't really me. All I did was manage to find us a savior. Speaking of which, have you seen Vammatar anywhere?"

Kulgun looked confused. "Who?"

Then I remembered the alchemist had likely not seen her in the battle, and he certainly wouldn't know her name.

"She's the one with armor pinned to her limbs with steel rods. Ring any bells?"

"Oh yeah," Kulgun said with a laugh. "She was drinking last night with everyone else. I think she and Xollmomath probably stayed together at his place. You might check for her there."

"No worries. I was just wondering where she might have gone. I don't plan on getting a whole lot done today, but we should start figuring out how to rebuild," I said. The two of us exchanged a few more pleasantries before parting ways.

My first stop was at the barracks. I needed to see what the warden had chosen. I found her almost exactly where I had left her sitting on a cot and facing the door. Much to my surprise, the hatchet I had given her was resting neatly a few feet away, not a spec of blood on the blade, yet the woman showed only nine fingers.

"I see you've decided to stay among the living," I said. I grabbed the hatchet by its head and offered her the handle.

She took the weapon and then extended a hand as though she needed my help to get up from her cot. I gladly pulled her to her feet, though she couldn't move far in shackles. Geirr had the key, and I hadn't seen him yet. "At your level, breaking your chains shouldn't be much of a problem," I stated. "Am I right?"

In response, a swift gust of magic swelled up from the ground. The whole room smelled like autumn, and then a grasping tangle of vines reached up from the stone floor to wrap around the woman's shackles. The iron holding her fast to the cot shattered. When the spell was done, the vines simply withered away and vanished as though they had never been there at all.

"Very impressive," I said. "But why didn't you escape last night when everyone was either partying or asleep?"

The woman's eyes found the floor beneath my feet. "I've

seen what you can do. I'm not stupid. If I escaped, where would I go? The Resurrection guildhall was my home, and that's in Echelon. I imagine the city won't be standing for much longer."

"Well I certainly appreciate your foresight and honesty. If you stay loyal to Undercroft Citadel, we'll keep you safe. The necropolis can be your home now. Feel free to claim a bunk in here; I don't think any actual houses are left after the battle." I shook the woman's hand and left, leaving the barracks door open behind me as both a literal and symbolic image of her freedom.

To my surprise, she followed me out right on my heels. "What should I do? I mean . . . what are your orders?" she asked.

It took a conscious effort to keep from laughing. The woman was incredibly high level and from one of the best guilds in the entire game. On top of that, I wasn't wearing any armor. She could kill me with a thought—she was just too scared to do it.

"Help rebuild the walls," I told her, thinking of something useful for her do. "We have a druid of sorts, Kingsley, who might be able to help augment your own warden abilities. He's undead, though, so he doesn't say much."

The woman slowed her pace a little, obviously unsure how to respond, and I kept walking toward the workshop entrance and left her behind.

No one was inside the workshop when I arrived, so I spent the next twenty or thirty minutes walking around the perimeter of Undercroft Citadel and assessing the damage while searching for our engineer. I finally found him sleeping under a tattered cloak behind one of our lumber stacks, a broken glass bottle resting in the dirt not far away.

I nudged the man awake, and after giving him about thirty minutes to get his bearings, rub the sleep from his eyes, and find some food to quiet the rumbling in his stomach, we made our way to the workshop.

"Our first priority will be rebuilding the walls," I started.

Geirr nodded over the edge of a water cup. "Honestly, the walls weren't much to begin with. Rebuilding shouldn't take long. Couple weeks."

"Good. I'll get the orcs to bring in more metal from the mine. I'd like to make the defenses better than they were before," I said. "Once the wall repair is underway, I have another project for you and however many gnomes are still alive. Kulgun will need to help as well."

A shadow fell over Geirr's countenance, though it could have just as easily been from his hangover as it was from the portent of bad news.

"We're building a flying machine," I told him.

The man nearly spat out his water. "Why on earth would you want to do something like that? Have you gone mad?"

"Almost certainly, but that's beside the point. We aren't going to use it ourselves. We'll fly it over Echelon. The city is too big to take it street by street, and we don't have that kind of army. Make sense?"

Geirr pondered for a moment as he sipped his water, and then his eyes lit up with recognition. "When the game spawns dragons or whatever other hell it will send, Echelon will get caught in the middle. Use the game to destroy the city. Risky, but it might work."

"Risky indeed, my friend. Risky indeed," I said.

Geirr shook his head and turned to keep his balance with the aid of a workbench. "If Kulgun can make enough gas, I can put together a frame that'll float. Then it will just be a matter of steering and propulsion. A simple propeller on the back should get us close to a zeppelin."

"Excellent. Draw up some plans and start getting it together once the walls are secure. If we find Vic's hideout by then, we can use the machine and the game to rain destruction on his raiders. If it takes too long to find him, we'll at least have an easy way of removing Echelon from the equation. The king still poses a threat despite Resurrection's defeat." I left Geirr in the workshop to overcome his hangover on his own, and I got the feeling he was glad to once more be in solitude.

My next stop was Xollmomath's small wooden house. Actually, there was barely anything left of the trio of houses where Undercroft Citadel had started. The necromancer was nowhere near the ruins where he had once lived, instead camped out for the night atop the gatehouse. Both Xia and Vammatar were with him, and their positions left no question in my mind about what had kept them up long enough for them to still be asleep only an hour or so before noon.

In similar fashion to rallying Geirr, I spent more time getting food and water—and a healing potion for Xia—before anyone was ready to be useful. Finally, the four of us sat in the shade with our backs against the side of the guard tower and started going over plans.

"Geirr says that rebuilding the walls will take a couple weeks. That should be plenty of time for us to find Vic. The only question is how." I looked to each of them, memories of my days running meetings in the Ministry of Public Health making me smile. All I needed was a nice big conference table and a box full of cheap donuts.

Xia was the first to offer a solution. "If we go at night, they'll be too disorganized to resist. We can take them house by house for interrogation. Someone knows something. We just have to make them talk."

"That would take far too long," Xollmomath said solemnly.

I shared the ancient necromancer's observation. Snagging handfuls of people every night would take months and months. And once the rumors of what we were after started to spread, anyone with the right knowledge would flee the city. "We need something faster. Some way to process people as quickly as possible. Hundreds a day if we can."

Vammatar clanked as she shifted positions against the guard tower wall. "We need to drive them from the city like pigs. Push the people out, and then offer a reward. They can all go back to their homes once you have the information you need," the death goddess explained.

I liked her strategy much better than Xia's. Vammatar was strong enough to make it work. "The only thing we have to worry about would be the city guards. There are still hundreds of them. And the king won't be too happy to see forces from Undercroft Citadel rampaging through his streets once more."

"Then kill the king first," Vammatar stated as though the solution was really that simple. Though, the more I thought about, it *was* that simple. With Resurrection gone, storming the castle and slaughtering everyone inside would be easy.

All three of us came to the same conclusion. "Let's move on the castle tomorrow," I said, getting to my feet. "We only have three days to pull it off." Once the death goddess returned to wherever it was she lived, our task would once more become impossibly difficult.

Vammatar seemed pleased that we were going to try her plan. I got the feeling that in the triumvirate of death goddesses, she didn't get too much authority. Here in Undercroft Citadel, she liked having respect. "Three days," she said solemnly. "Then I must return to my sisters. We cannot waste a single moment."

We concluded the war council, and by then Undercroft Citadel was starting to crawl with action. Orcs brought raw supplies to the repair sites, Geirr and Kulgun shouted orders at both the human and undead workers, and I caught the occasional glimpse of Helvegen running back and forth with a pad of notes in her hand.

I watched Undercroft Citadel come alive without much to do myself. My craftsmanship skill was still pretty lackluster. I could have joined one of the work crews to lend a hand with physical labor, hopefully gaining a stat increase or two in the process, but a more pressing need occupied my mind. If we were going to the castle tomorrow, I needed armor. I needed a weapon.

The legendary gear I had given to Elyk was too dinged and blasted to be worn. I showed it to Geirr after lunch, and he was confident he could fix everything, but that would take at least a week. Vammatar would be gone by then, so I had to come up with something else. At least I still had my cloak.

Since we hadn't yet conscripted a proper blacksmith to work our forges, I strapped Infernum to my side and went back to the battlefield in search of armor. Luckily, the zombies Xollmomath had raised had cast aside their armaments in favor of the natural defenses Kingsley could offer, so I had a decent selection left for the taking.

I was about a quarter of the way through the field of the dead with a handful of pieces under my arm when a bit of movement caught my eye. Ministrel was out in the field of the dead hunched over a corpse. Being so close to the crazed wizard sent a shiver down my spine. Still, the man was loyal to my forces, and I knew I needed to get better acquainted with him if I was ever going to trust him. I caught his attention when I was about twenty yards away, and he seemed thrilled that I was there.

"What brings you to the garden?" the old wizard started. Thankfully, he wasn't wearing anyone's face but his own.

"The garden? I don't see too many flowers," I called back.

The man laughed. "What you see is not always the truth!"

I had no idea what the man meant. If he was implying that the corpses surrounding us were not actually corpses but rather flowers in a garden, he was more insane than I was ready to admit. If he was simply speaking in a metaphor, I didn't understand it.

"Come across any useful bits of armor?" I asked, nodding toward the couple pieces I was still carrying.

Ministrel rubbed a hand under his beard. "Many pieces to dull a blade, but only if you know how to wear them."

His cryptic answer made me think he was referring to faces. The man had obviously seen me fight, so he had to know that wearing armor was well within my skill set. I decided to change the subject in hopes of getting more cogent responses. "What brings you out to the garden? I would have expected you to be back in Undercroft."

He held up a severed hand and waved it at me. Blood dripped from the stump and onto his shirt, but he didn't mind. "Everyone needs parts!" he happily answered.

Again, I found myself at a loss. Whatever he needed parts for, I was positive that I didn't want to know. Something about the way the old man acted kept bringing the word 'cannibal' to my mind.

Ministrel didn't seem too interested in carrying on any kind of conversation, so I let him get back to his macabre work as I returned to looting. There were so many bodies, and while a good chunk of them hadn't brought much in the way of magical loot to our doorstep, there was still far too much of interest for a single person to go through it all. I closed my eyes and called to the gargoyles flying patrol around the necropolis. After a minute, three of them flew out to meet me, thought they couldn't go very deep into the field of corpses. Still, I was able to hand them an armful of loot each, and they dutifully flew it back home.

By the time night fell, I estimated that I had collected about sixty percent of all the magical loot available to be scavenged. A few pieces had stood out from the others, though I hadn't yet gone through every single item. I sat with

Xia and the two warlocks going through all the gear in the armory. We sorted everything into three piles: immediately useful gear, things that might be repaired, and items fit to be consumed by Xollmomath.

It was sometime around midnight when we finally had it all sorted. Our two remaining cultists would go out into the field tomorrow and finish collecting gear. So much of it was damaged that I made a mental note to try and recruit or capture half a dozen blacksmiths as soon as I got the chance.

For my own gear, I was woefully lacking. It seemed that everyone who had come against Undercroft Citadel had either been much smaller than I was or else built like a high-level barbarian, and I was still thoroughly average as far as my musculature was concerned.

I sat on one of the few chairs in the armory and surveyed the small pile of gear I had assembled for myself. I had gauntlets with matching bracers, a rather ugly helm that only fit if I went without an arming cap, and a heavy chainmail dress that extended past my knees. There had been a dozen or more breastplates similar to the Masterwork Etched Pyreborn Plate I was accustomed to, but none of the ones that fit me had any enchantments worth carrying into battle. I opted instead to try wearing chain for the added mobility, though I knew that without my legendary greaves, anything I wore would slow me down sooner rather than later.

As I surveyed my equipment, I realized just how much of a true commander I would have to be when we raided the castle. I wouldn't be leading from the front and absorbing brutal hits that otherwise would cut me in half. I would have to lead from the rear, directing my forces without standing shoulder to shoulder with them.

I didn't feel confident. In the best-case scenario, we would crash through the halls of the castle with such an overwhelming force that my absence from the front lines wouldn't be noticed. In the worst-case scenario, our undead would be cut to ribbons and not a single member of our attack group would make it back alive. To make matters worse, we were still battered and bruised from the last fight.

But one thing still gave me hope: Vammatar.

No matter how powerful I was, the death goddess was still stronger. And she was covered in armor from head to toe, so she made a fine replacement for me at the front.

I placed my chosen set of armor on a wooden rack near the armory door and made my way back up to my room. I was exhausted, and I would need every ounce of my strength and endurance tomorrow. As I eased open the door to my bedroom, I saw Helvegen's outline standing by the side of the bed.

She was facing away from me, wearing only a simple pair of linen pants and no shirt. I entered and shut the door. "Hey," I said, mentally commanding the lights to come up just enough so that I didn't trip on anything.

She turned and smiled, then slipped under the covers with a playful purr.

I hesitated for a moment on my side of the bed. "So . . . is this going to become our regular thing?" I asked, not quite knowing the right words to use. It had been so long since I had been with a woman that I actually couldn't even remember if it had ever happened at all. There had been a couple inconsequential high school girlfriends, but after that, I had just focused on work.

But Ingrid . . .

I had raised a daughter, so I must have at least had someone.

Had Ingrid's mother been anyone special to me? All I remembered was that Ingrid had been born, and I had been present in the room. Maybe it all had been a fleeting tryst not worthy of any lasting memories. It must have been. But no . . . that wasn't my style. It wasn't like me. Or . . . was it? I had no idea. Figuring out my past life was a mystery for another day.

Helvegen was tugging on my hand. She pulled me out of my thoughts with a look of concern on her face. "Are you alright? You're a hundred miles away. I'll go if you want me to."

I peeled off my sweaty clothes and slid into bed next to her. "Sorry," I said. "I just kind of got lost there for a second. Sorry if I made it awkward."

"Did you hear my answer?" she asked. She planted a brief kiss on my forehead and wrapped an arm around my waist.

"No, I missed it," I answered. "Sorry."

She kissed the back of my hand. "Well then you'll just have to ask me again tomorrow. I'll be waiting for you."

CHAPTER 17

Helvegen shook me awake an hour before sunrise. I hadn't gotten nearly enough sleep to feel refreshed, but it would have to do. Everyone else on the raid team was already assembling by the front gate. The painter had asked to go along back to Echelon, and I felt bad commanding her to stay in Undercroft Citadel. I told her that I needed my manager to stay behind, but we both knew it was a lie. I wanted her safe. I had failed to keep Ingrid safe, and I was determined not to make the same mistake twice.

In the end, Hel had relented and agreed to stay back to manage the repairs while I was gone. If everything went well, I would be gone for about five days, maybe a week at the most. If things went poorly, I'd be home a lot sooner. Or I'd be dead.

The two of us said our goodbyes in private, and then Helvegen helped me carry my armor to the gate to join the others. We had a pretty large invasion group assembled. Xia would essentially be our leader, and she had forty zombies directly under her command. Each of the basic soldiers had been augmented by Kingsley's druidic magic making them far tougher than ordinary shambling undead.

While Xia would have direct control of the bulk of our army, I was going to command the small group of specialists that would do the more covert work. I had the truthbreaker paladin, our nine-fingered warden, Kevin's reanimated corpse, and our undead thief, a class the game listed on my sheet as a 'bone thief.' Despite having the most advanced group, the company wasn't all that interesting to be around. After all, only the warden could actually speak. The others just blindly followed my commands without any kind of verbal acknowledgement at all.

I felt a little uneasy leaving Elyk behind. He was more than a formidable fighter, but he had taken a hell of a beating in the siege and still needed more time to recover. On top of that, I wanted more human players staying behind in Undercroft Citadel while I was gone. Xollmomath would certainly be able to defend the place on his own, but he wouldn't always make the same decisions that a real person would. Having Elyk remaining behind to protect Helvegen helped ease my fears.

I strapped on my new gear and went over the stats, shaking my head at how utterly inferior it all was compared to the legendary armor I was leaving behind.

Silver-Lined Bracers: Worn about the wrists, these steel bracers grant the wearer +4 Fortune.

Tasgur's Chain Raiment: The long-forgotten fencing champion of the Emirid Kingdom, Tasgur the Wise, once wore this chain armor. When worn, the armor grants +1 Physical, +1 Cunning, and +2 Investigation.

Focusing Helm of Awe: The wearer's ability to think clearly in combat is greatly enhanced, though when facing opponents with exceedingly high cunning, the helm may have unintended negative consequences.

I went over my gear, and I knew it was garbage. There had been other pieces—with much better magical enhancements—but they had been made for people larger than myself. I had opted to take a better fitting outfit as opposed to the most powerful gear I could find, hoping that my own skill in combat would help make up for the magical deficit. And no matter what I decided to wear, I still had Infernum. The weapon had served me well, and I knew it would save my life another dozen or more times before I left Echelon.

On our journey to the city, the warden and I watched with some amusement as Xia occasionally struggled to keep the herd of undead together in a cohesive group. Other than a few moments of constrained laughter, the woman never really spoke, though I knew she enjoyed the relative comedy of the spectacle. I could also tell she was . . . unnerved by everything, and I got the distinct feeling that she and Kevin had been more than simple guild acquaintances. Perhaps they had been together. If that was the case, she would probably try to kill me as soon as she thought she could do it and escape without being seen. The thing was, wardens weren't really fighters. They were support classes. If she turned on me while I still held Infernum, she wouldn't have much of a chance. I smiled as I imagined how an eventual fight between us would go, then shook my head and continued onward to the city.

With such a huge army moving across the flat plain outside Echelon, we were spotted by the guards before we ever got close. There was no avoiding it. Alarm signals of all kinds went up at the sight of our horde. Banners were raised, signal fires were lit, and trumpet calls sounded from every battlement.

When we were about a hundred yards from the base of

the wall, a row of archers appeared with bows in their hands. They stood at attention on the uppermost battlement, their steel caps gleaming in the morning sun. At the end of their column stood a sergeant, the only player of the lot, with a thin black pennant. He waited for a moment and then dropped his arm.

A dozen arrows lifted into the sky and fell down on our ranks. Against the zombies, they didn't do much. A third of the missiles scored hits that would have easily killed regular soldiers—but I hadn't brought more than a handful of regular soldiers to Echelon. The arrows tore through rotten flesh and twisting vines to plant themselves in the ground, and my army continued unhampered.

"Vammatar!" I called. The death goddess at the head of the zombies glanced back over her shoulder but did not respond. I took that to mean she was at least listening. "We need to get through the walls. That's your job."

She gave a curt nod and turned back toward Echelon. Then she broke into a sprint with her head lowered and her arms bracing her chest. When she collided with the wall, it sounded like a bomb had gone off. Dust obscured the impact zone, but when it cleared a moment later, I could barely believe the damage Vammatar had wrought. A crumbling hole big enough to stoop through had appeared in the wall, and the death goddess was not finished. She threw her entire weight into the edges of the breach. Every blow brought more stones and mortar crashing down to the ground.

"Inside!" I yelled as loudly as I could.

The army took off for the entrance, though I knew our progress to the other side would be slow. All the while, arrows continued to rain down on us. One of the zombies—or at least only one that I could see—had gone down with an arrow in its head.

"Ellen!" I called to the warden, realizing that I had never

really considered her human enough to have a name despite knowing that she wasn't just another mindless undead.

She ran to my side, her staff in her hand and a shield of slowly rotating earth hovering in front of her like a pavise to keep the arrows from reaching her. "I can shield our passage," she said at once, basically reading my mind.

I slapped her armored shoulder and told her to do it. A moment later, more swirling disks of soil began rising from the ground to protect the zombies as they fought over each other to get through the breach. By the time the zombies had made it through, only three of them had been damaged enough to be rendered useless. The last zombie made it through, and it was time to take my small hit squad somewhere else. I waved to Ellen and the undead ranger who used to be her friend.

"Come on. We're going for the castle," I commanded. The five of us ran left, away from the crumbling breach, and found the sally door where I had previously gained entry into the castle. The gate had been sealed with stones, but that didn't matter. I had a different plan in mind.

"Kevin, use *Grappling Shot*. Eight of them." I pointed to the top of the battlement, and the undead ranger mindlessly obeyed my order. He drew a magical arrow from his quiver and fired it toward the parapet. When the missile hit stone, it buried itself to the fletching. A steel chain magically appeared in the air. It was stretched taught to an anchor point at the ranger's feet. Seven more *Grappling Shots* followed in rapid succession, making a temporary bridge from the ground to the top of the wall.

I didn't need to give a command for my underlings to understand what to do. The five of us scrambled up the chains and were standing on the top of the wall about thirty seconds later.

I had guessed correctly, and the section of wall we stood

upon was higher than all the others nearby. We could see the entire keep from where we stood. All hell had broken loose down below. Vammatar, Xia, and the zombies were fully engaged in the bailey against at least three dozen guards.

From our position, we had about a ten-foot drop to the roof of the castle's central hall. I turned to the bone thief. The undead was small and jittery, constantly shifting its weight from foot to foot and fiddling with a pair of curved daggers. "Go. Break through the roof." I pointed to the nearest patch of red shingles. "Bring me heads. Collect them on the throne."

The bone thief leapt from the parapet and landed softly on the roof. It began tearing up shingles, and I knew it would fulfill its mission without any more direction from me. Such a brutal distraction would give the rest of us time to find King Ahmose II and claim the city in the name of Undercroft Citadel.

I led from the front, charging away from the pitched battle in the bailey down below toward the deepest sections of the castle. We came across twenty or so guards, but none of them put up any real resistance, and we cut them down with impunity as we moved. Surprisingly, only two of the soldiers we slaughtered were affected by *Reap Honor* and joined our ranks. I immediately sent them off in the opposite direction from ours in the hope that they would simply cause more chaos and disrupt the king's defenses.

The four of us arrived at the point farthest from the city streets. The building was a private chapel only used by the royal family, and it had ten tall, beautiful stained-glass windows reaching from floor to ceiling. I used the hilt of my sword to shatter the nearest one, and we all dropped inside.

Three unarmed civilians were cowering behind a wooden altar. They were probably priests or acolytes—NPCs dedicated to Wonder's 'official' religion that vaguely mirrored a combination of polytheistic religions from Earth. The truth-breaker paladin killed all three in the span of a few seconds, and we were alone in the chapel.

"The king's personal quarters won't be far away," I said. "He's bound to have the best personal guards in the city, and the king himself is fairly high level. We need to move carefully and think things through."

None of the undead responded, but I knew they understood.

The truthbreaker was the most armored, so I let it open the door and peer into the hallway beyond. As soon as the door opened, I could hear the faint sounds of battle far below. There were screams closer to us as well, coming from both directions in the corridor. The truthbreaker paladin knew what we were after, and it made a decision to turn right after a few seconds of listening.

We scampered down a stone passageway lined with rich tapestries and expensive wall sconces. A large door towered at the end, and the lack of guards standing in front of it told me the king's chambers would not lie beyond. Unfortunately, the door was too thick to hear anything distinct coming from the other side. I tested the brass handle and found it unlocked. Motioning again for the truthbreaker to take point, I stood to the side as I eased open the door.

All hell broke loose almost immediately. No guards or soldiers were waiting behind the door to ambush us, but instead a horde of civilians began screaming and throwing all sorts of kitchen implements. A few rather burly men came at the paladin with knives, and the undead blasted them backward with dark, twisting magic from its chest. I poured in after the paladin, swinging Infernum and easily cutting down a pair of shrieking household servants.

It didn't take long for the unorganized and unarmed mob to give up their assault. Seven of them were dead at my feet, and the others realized that they would soon join them, so they began looking for a way out. There was a door in the back of the room, but something from the other side was blocking it, and only the smallest of the mob would be able to fit through.

"Stop!" I yelled, holding Infernum aloft to try and gain everyone's attention.

A clay pot came whirling for my head, though the throw was off and there wasn't much strength behind it in the first place.

"Stop! If you want to live, listen to me!" I waited for a long moment while the wails and sobs of various NPCs died down. Surveying the crowd, I figured they numbered about thirty or thirty-five, and only a handful of them were players.

One of the players had a bit more nerve than the others, and he stepped forward. He barely looked old enough to play the game. "What do you want?" he asked with a little more gusto than I had expected.

"Vic Fuentes," I answered. "Someone here has heard of him and his band of raiders. Tell me where he's hiding, and I'll let you live."

No one came forth with any information.

I nodded to Kevin, and the undead ranger launched a pair of arrows that blasted apart two more NPCs.

Finally, someone in the back spoke up. "We don't know who that is!" a man in an apron called.

I had to believe them. They had no reason to protect Vic, and if they were all just members of the king's household staff, their collective knowledge wouldn't be relevant. I looked back to Kevin. "Kill them all," I said evenly.

Again, the room exploded into violence and panic. People fought against each other to get out the back door, and without any coordination, the end result was only a single NPC escaping. Everyone else was cut down in a flurry of magical arrows. The full might of Kevin's gear and high-level talents made the whole scene look too easy to even be enjoyable. It was like watching a fisherman scooping a huge net through a tiny pond. No matter where the people ran, Kevin's arrows found them.

When the room was quiet, I tried to watch Ellen with my peripheral vision and judge her reaction. The woman was aghast, but she did not flee or lose the contents of her stomach. She simply stared at the corpses in horror, no doubt wondering if she should have opted for death rather than surrender when I had reached her.

A rocking explosion stole my attention, and I could hear glass shattering all around the castle. Vammatar was probably wrecking her way through every wall and guard tower in the whole castle complex.

"Come on, we might not have too much time," I said. I pointed to the partially obstructed door at the end of the room. "Kevin, blast it down."

The undead ranger complied, and the door flew from its hinges in a burst of splintered planks. We pushed aside a few obliterated corpses and made it into the next corridor. There were two pathways, one leading down to a turn and the other sloping up to a set of ornate double doors. "Almost there," I said.

Again, no guards were standing watch on the outside of the doors. I tried both handles, and they were both blocked. "Kevin, do your thing," I ordered, stepping back to stand behind the ranger. Being anywhere near the door when it exploded would likely be catastrophic.

The first four arrows sizzled when they hit the wood, and none of them even did enough damage to scratch the glazed surface. Powerful magic was nullifying Kevin's arrows from the other side.

"We might have found the royal family," I said to the others. "We just need to find a way inside."

To my surprise, the warden stepped up with her staff leveled at the door. "My magic isn't nearly powerful enough to break through a defensive enchantment, but I can speak to the wood. Perhaps I can convince it to open."

She closed her eyes, and a faint green glow emanated from the end of her staff. The magic coalesced into a tiny sprite that flitted through the air toward the door. After a few moments of what I presumed was Ellen 'speaking' to the wooden door through her sprite, the bottom-most panels of the door began to creak and groan. They moved outward, wrenching apart their iron banding and sending heavy bolts ricocheting all over the corridor. Soon enough, the double doors looked like they had been blasted open from the opposite side, and we had enough room to get through.

We hadn't yet found the king's private chamber, but we had made it to the common area that linked all the bedchambers together away from the castle's public places.

A dozen or more armed guards stood with their weapons ready in a practiced formation. They were fanned out in a half-circle, protecting each of the doors generally rather than specifically, giving me no indication of where the king himself might have gone. Every single guard was a player, and they all shared the same warrior class as well.

I had never heard of the king having any special regiment of elite personal guards. I scoured my memory as quickly as I could, and then the real answer crept up in my mind: the room was powerfully enchanted with dampening magic. Whatever had stopped Kevin's arrows from making a dent on the doors also prevented all other forms of magic. The warden's sprite had worked more or less by means of a loophole.

To test my theory, I mentally commanded Infernum to blaze with fire. Nothing happened. The sword didn't react.

The men across from us must have realized how magic dependent we were. They kept formation and started advancing, halberds leveled low like a giant threshing machine.

"We need to run," I said quietly so only my own party would hear. We didn't have any fully dedicated melee class—even the truthbreaker paladin was about half magical—and without my legendary armor, I couldn't hope to finish the fight on my own.

Kevin shot a handful of arrows in rapid succession. They all passed harmlessly through the guards, not even eliciting a single flinch.

"Come on, we're running! Now!" I yelled. I took off for the descending ramp in the previous corridor, grabbing Ellen by the shoulder and pulling her along in my wake.

I could hear a chorus of armored boots stomping steadily along behind us. They moved in unison, showing absolutely flawless training, but they stopped right at the edge of the ruined door. For whatever reason, the soldiers did not pursue us into the hallway. I thanked my lucky stars as I bolted around a turn and then shouldered through a low archway and into a deserted sleeping area.

"What's the plan?" the warden asked. She still looked just as terrified as she had before. I didn't blame her.

I tried to think of a strategy, but nothing creative came to mind. Without magic, the forces of Undercroft Citadel were woefully unprepared. The only reason we weren't already dead or at least running for our lives through the rest of the castle was because the guards had refused to follow us. "If the king is behind one of those doors upstairs, it'll take a lot to get through to him," I said, thinking aloud. "We need Vammatar. She's our only true melee class. Maybe she can get through the guards. How much nature magic do you think you could use up there?"

Ellen shook her head. "I told you before, my magic won't

kill anyone. Or at least I'm not very good at killing, anyway. I can keep summoning spirits, but the floor was all stone. Maybe if it were wood . . ."

"No, we need Vammatar. We have to find her. Save your mana." I climbed over a low cot to get to the nearest door and ripped it open. A small stone platform served as a terrace, and from the height I could see some of what was going on below.

Fires had sprung up at the front of the keep. I had no way to know who had set them or why, but it was clear that no one was making any kind of effort to put them out. The front sections facing Echelon were mostly wooden, and they would all burn. Then, if the fires kept going, the roofs above the stone structures would burn as well, leaving a ruined shell completely open to the elements. Maybe by then we would be able to breach the king's private chambers from above, but if the man was even remotely intelligent, he'd be long gone before the roof ever burned.

The bailey and stables were one contiguous mess of bodies. Hundreds of them littered the ground. I couldn't see who they were, nor could I see the current position of my army. All I could do was hope that my army was still intact and slaughtering.

A bit of motion caught my eye. We could see the audience hall in the main keep across about thirty feet of corpse-strewn bailey. The windows had been blown out, and though they weren't very wide, I made out the silhouette of the bone thief darting around inside. "Kevin, can you chain us across to the throne room?"

The ranger stepped to the edge of the cramped pavilion and began firing. He set up a dozen chains, each about three or four inches apart, effectively making a rather rickety bridge that promised a painful fall for any of us who would lose our step. We made it across somewhat slowly—making me worry about when the spell's effect would expire and drop us all to the ground—and we squeezed through the shattered windows into the throne room without incident.

The audience chamber was so chaotic it was hard to get my bearings and figure out what was happening. Guards in Echelon's colors were trying desperately to hold the front door against a handful of my zombies, though for what purpose I had no idea. The room behind them was gone. Standing their ground only meant they protected a pile of the dead. Kevin took aim down the long hallway and fired once, felling six castle guards with a single enchanted arrow. Around the throne itself, the bone thief had done some serious work. At least twenty disembodied heads were scattered across the beautiful marble tile. The floor was slick with blood, and the scent of it hung in the room like a thick mist. A door up ahead was wrenched open, and I watched the bone thief scamper inside. A chorus of screams came muffled through the door a moment later.

"Come on, out the front. We have to find Vammatar before the king can escape," I said to my companions.

We ran through the front doors and into the bailey where the last knots of zombies were scurrying over their fallen brethren toward the city streets. The vanguard of the army was already too far away to be seen. We had reached them too late. Our forces were fragmented.

I looked to the three others and tried to formulate a new plan as quickly as I could. "Vammatar will return," I said. "For now, we need to clear out the castle and remove every last defender. Once we have the main compound secured, we can settle in for a siege around the king's private chambers until the death goddess arrives. Understood?"

My underlings showed their acknowledgement, and we got to work. The outer sections of barracks, walls, guard houses, towers, and other battlements were the first to fall.

We swept across them like a plague of death, killing any who had been stupid enough to remain at their posts, until everything outside the inner keep was eerily quiet.

When the first stage was complete, I sent the truthbreaker into the kitchens and servants' quarters by himself. As heavily armored as he was, none of the civilians would stand a chance. Then I took Kevin and the warden back inside the throne room. By then the whole area was so saturated with blood that it looked like the walls had been painted red with it. We spent a few minutes thoroughly checking the first few doors until we came across a ladder at the back of a storage closet that led to the roof. I sent Kevin to the top with orders to shoot anyone not from Undercroft Citadel who tried to run.

The warden and I were alone among all the death, and we started exploring the council chambers and other rooms behind the audience hall. Our work was methodical, and we only managed to find a handful of cowering victims to add to the piles of death already decorating the keep. Within an hour, Echelon's mighty castle was ours—all but a single suite of rooms at the top of the innermost keep.

The bone thief was the first to return to the throne room for new orders. The undead creature had lost an arm and taken numerous other wounds that would have killed players, though it did not seem to understand or even care about its missing limb. All the mindless being understood was obedience and death. I told it to prowl the walls in case anyone tried to break in or out. The truthbreaker paladin arrived next, and I gave it an assignment at the front door. I left Kevin as our night lookout on the roof.

Ellen and I cleared out a section of the bailey in order to unpack our gear and settle in for the long haul. We would stay as long as the royal family still lived, however many nights it required, all the while figuring out a plan to find the king. At the same time, we had to begin the process of interrogating the citizens of Echelon. Someone would know where Vic was hiding. Once we found whoever it was, all we had to do was rip the secrets from their flesh.

CHAPTER 18

I slept on a soft collection of blankets stolen from the barracks, though not for very long. A hand shook me awake in the middle of the night. Since Kevin had no need for sleep and hadn't shot at the newcomer, I knew I wasn't in any danger before I opened my eyes.

Xia stood above me, her clothes splattered with blood. "Vammatar reached the end of the city," she said with a smile.

"Already?"

"At least half the population fled through the front gate. Maybe a quarter of everyone who was here when we arrived is already dead. But we have thousands of captives. Tens of thousands. We're holding them in a handful of civic buildings on the eastern side of the city that runs up against the wall. They aren't going anywhere," she explained.

"Excellent. Wait until morning to start questioning them, and begin with volunteers. Anyone who has info regarding Vic is to be sent to me as soon as they're identified. Understood?"

Xia nodded. "If no one volunteers?" she asked.

Out of all those people, someone else was bound to have

a grudge against Vic and freely give him up, though I had to at least entertain the possibility of no one coming forward. "Start with males my age or similar. Any raider or warlord classes move to the top of the list. Thieves as well." The difficulties of processing such a huge population immediately began swirling though my head, and I could feel the mounting stress threatening to transform into a headache that would keep me up the rest of the night. "Has there been any violent resistance yet?" I asked.

Again, the warlock nodded. "The captives resist at every turn. That is why I woke you. What do you want us to do with those who refuse to comply?"

I had a few different options. I remembered reading about the reeducation camps in China and Russia and other places around the world after the wars forty years ago. Dissenters were taken to camps and introduced to so much propaganda that they became complacent or at least quieted down. But that strategy took time. And it wasn't particularly effective. I needed a much more direct method.

"If anyone acts out, don't worry about it," I began. "If they attack anyone from Undercroft Citadel, remove them from the general population. Bring them here and lock them in the king's crypt. I'll deal with them in the morning. But don't let the others know where you're taking the dissidents."

Xia and I confirmed some of the details, and then she left to disseminate my commands to Vammatar and the others. I didn't know how we would control a population of thousands—if it was even possible—and hopefully we wouldn't have to subdue them for long.

By the time dawn arrived, I was already awake, having only slept in fits since Xia's visit. There was so much work to be done that sleep had been nearly impossible.

First on the list was dealing with the handful of violent resistors locked away in the king's crypt. Unfortunately,

Vammatar was still on the other side of the city helping keep the rest of the captives under control, so I still couldn't consult her on ways to penetrate the innermost rooms of the keep. That little project would have to wait until the afternoon or perhaps tomorrow. If the death goddess hadn't returned by then, I'd send someone out to find her.

As it went, figuring out which captives had information and which knew absolutely nothing proved to be a daunting task. I had read about various megalomaniacs and tyrants from history, and how they possibly controlled such a large number of disgruntled people all at once was something I did not understand in practice. Riots broke out by lunch, and Xia ended up killing more than a hundred captives when she lost her temper and loosed a fireball into a building with only a single exit. That settled down the others, but it was a tenuous peace at best.

By dusk, we hadn't made much progress. Our only real accomplishment was separating the raider classes from the others and bringing them to the keep. We built a camp of sorts in both the underground crypt and on the muddy bailey above. Only a few of the raiders claimed to have ever heard of Vic and his band. We had twenty-eight of them, and I knew at least a handful had to be lying. Two in particular had names in the same color font as Madrid—members of his crew.

The pair of raiders belonging to Vic were given special treatment. I had them taken to the top of the wall and stripped naked with their hands bound behind their backs. The raider captives in the bailey had been tied hand and foot, though I had allowed them to keep their clothes and other items as they were interrogated by my NPC underlings.

I questioned the two on top of the wall myself.

I had been at it for more than an hour without much progress. The naked prisoners were covered in bites and scratches delivered by a trio of my zombies. The wounds hurt more than their appearance would indicate, and they festered with rotten disease. Still, the two captives held to their stories. They claimed that they had left Vic's band when they learned who I was after, but they hadn't yet formally aligned themselves with Echelon.

It was a likely story, one that made some sense, but I knew they were holding back.

"Before you left the raider band, where did you meet? Where did all the other raiders get together to plan?" I demanded for the fourth or fifth time.

I was met by a familiar answer. "I never got deep enough in the organization to see the headquarters," the naked man to my right whimpered. It was the same line I had heard before, basically repeated word for word.

I prompted the man to my left with a look, and he only weakly nodded. He hadn't changed his answer at all.

"Why are you protecting him?" I asked, lowering my tone and trying to sound more conciliatory. "What do you stand to gain?"

The man on my right shook his head. "Nothing. I don't care if you kill them all. I don't *know* anything!"

The zombie supporting the man's shoulders looked to me for orders. "Throw him down to the bailey," I commanded.

At once, the man on the left broke into a renewed round of sobbing and pathetic begging, and the undead soldier obeyed my command, unceremoniously pushing the captive over the edge. The man fell thirty feet to the bailey, his legs audibly cracking as he landed. "Go put a gag in his mouth," I order the newly unoccupied zombie.

I turned my attention back to the final raider. Not surprisingly, the font on his name had gone to a dull grey indicating that he held no allegiance at all. "Has your memory been sufficiently jogged? Anything you'd like to say?" I asked.

The man swallowed hard. His name was Bert, and he probably hadn't been playing Wonder for very long before the server crashes since he was still only level fourteen. He wore a scraggly, patchy beard, and the tops of both of his thighs were covered in poor quality tattoos reminiscent of prison work.

I pointed to the tattoos. "You did some time in prison, didn't you?"

He nodded and avoided my gaze.

"For what?"

"Wire fraud," he finally said, his voice shaking.

"Great. So you're a professional liar."

The man started sputtering again and shaking his head. "No, no, not . . . not anymore," he began. "That was a long t-time ago."

"If you're such a changed man, Bert, why did you join up with Vic? Why pillage helpless players who can't defend themselves?" I paced in front of the man as I spoke, trying to invoke a mental image of a prison guard.

Bert was silent for a long time. When he finally did speak, his voice was level once more, though he didn't answer my question. "Whenever I met with anyone in Vic's group, it was always a woman. I think her name was Tess or Tessa or something like that, but I don't remember exactly. We would meet in alleys or bars, never the same place twice. And when she left, she always went north out of the city. I remember it because it was peculiar, you know?"

Finally I was getting somewhere. "Any identifying features? If I round up every woman with a similar name, how will I know which one is which?"

The man met my gaze. "I never got a great look at her, but she had an accent. Australian, I think. You'd know it if you heard it. The kind of voice you don't quickly forget."

"Anything else?"

He shook his head. "If you find her, I'd probably recognize her," he said.

If Bert was playing with me, gambling for a little extra time unharmed, he was doing it well. He had me pinned in a corner. "Alright, Bert. I'll make you a deal. I'm going to have every single woman whose name begins with a T brought here tomorrow. We'll go through them all together. If we find the one we need, I'll let you go. If not, you're going to die. How does that sound?"

Bert's eyes went back to the bloody stone at his feet. "Am I allowed to say no?"

"I'm afraid not, Bert. That's the only deal you get," I answered.

Torturing the other raiders was a full-time job. My NPC underlings—completely lacking any moral reservations—carried out my orders without complaint. We chained most of the raiders either to the wall around the bailey or to various monuments and other heavy objects inside the crypt. The zombies slowly ate bits and pieces off the prisoners in an effort to get useful information, and by midnight we had a couple leads. I dispatched troops to investigate them at once, but of course they turned up nothing. Inns which supposedly harbored Vic's goons had already been abandoned, and secret meeting places hidden behind bookshelves and fireplaces in unassuming taverns turned out not to exist at all.

Many players died before the next dawn. At least half of the raiders were gone. The other half were probably completely innocent, though that minor fact didn't save them from their share of inconveniences.

Much to my delight, Vammatar arrived right at dawn. She had a set of chains over one shoulder and was dragging a man by his ankles behind her. I counted the days since the death goddess had arrived, and I knew she wouldn't have much time before she returned to her sisters.

"Who's that?" I asked as the heavily armored woman stalked through the front gates.

"He knows what it is you seek," Vammatar stated flatly.

I glanced past her shoulder to see the man. He was so beaten and bloody that he only vaguely resembled a man in the crudest sense. He used to have feet, but now sported a pair of bloody, freshly cauterized stumps. His arms ended in similar fashion. Where his bottom jaw once fit into the shape of his face, his bloody and dirt-covered tongue lolled out of his skull like a drunken golden retriever. Every shred of his torn body was caked in a mixture of mud, sticks, and blood.

"How in the hell is he still alive?" I asked, clearly bewildered.

Vammatar smiled beneath her dented steel helmet. "Dark magic, young one. There is not much concerning death that remains beyond my reach."

Her cryptic answer only gave me a fuzzy notion of what she meant. I decided not to press the issue and simply to accept that the mangled sack of chained pulp groaning on the street was a living person.

I knelt down to the man's shattered head. "The sooner you tell me what you know, the sooner it all ends," I said. I made sure to speak slowly so he could understand. In all honesty, I wanted to be away from the breathing corpse just as surely as the corpse wanted to actually die.

He tried to answer, but I couldn't make sense of his words. His mouth was too mangled to be of use.

"Do you know what he said?" I asked. If the man couldn't effectively communicate, I was wasting my time.

"He is Michael Fuentes, or so he claims. That name means something to you, yes?" the death goddess said.

"You're Vic's brother?" The name floating above the man's

head was 'Azgore.' Slowly, the pulverized lump of flesh made a move that resembled nodding.

"Where does Vic live?" I demanded, again speaking slowly and clearly.

More mumbling. More blood fell out of the man's ruined mouth and onto the ground.

Vammatar translated again. "He says they have a hideout north of the city, west of Riverside. Does that name mean anything to you?"

"It means more than you think," I said, almost giddy with excitement. Then, looking back to the lump of meat, "Is it underground? How do I get inside?"

Again, a few seconds of incoherent mumbling served as my only response.

"He begs for death," Vammatar said nonchalantly. She held the chains with an easy posture that reminded me of how a high-brow kind of woman might watch her dog at a dog park.

"I'll give you death if you tell me how to get inside. That's all I need," I said.

More bloody incoherence.

"Underground, he says, in a cave. A symbol on a tree. I do not know what he is referring to. Perhaps it makes more sense to you." The death goddess was staring off toward the crypt entrance as though some of the torture taking place there held far more interest than translating the only important messages we had ever received.

I finally knew what to look for. A cave marked by a symbol on a tree. West of Riverside, my food-producing vassal.

"Kill him," I said sharply. "Let him die. We have what we need."

Vammatar released her grip on the chains, and the death that overtook the lump of man was so sudden and thorough that I could *feel* his soul leaving his body. A shudder ran through my spine, and the hairs on my arms and the back of my neck stood on end. Whatever the death goddess was truly capable of doing, I knew in that moment that I *never* wanted to be on the receiving end of it.

With her chains lying lifelessly on the ground, Vammatar turned her attention to a new subject. "I have the females you requested ready for interrogation. There are one hundred and sixty-one with names beginning with T. Where would you like me to bring them?"

That was a lot of prisoners. The bailey wouldn't hold them all at the same time. "I don't know yet. Just keep them segregated for now. I'll figure out how to deal with them tonight. But there's another issue I'd like you to handle. Come with me."

I summoned the truthbreaker paladin and the bone thief away from their duties and back into the inner workings of the keep. The four of us stalked through the hallways until we reached the heavy doors Ellen had opened two days ago.

"They have a dozen guards, all warriors, and there's a strong presence of anti-magic that blocks everything I can do," I explained to the death goddess.

Vammatar listened as I told her about our previous encounter with the royal guards, but she did not speak. I got the feeling that whatever magic was preventing me from using my abilities, it would not affect her. Or if did, she wouldn't care. Being without her magic was only a minor inconvenience.

We got into position with the armored goddess at the front and prepared to breach the door. When we were all ready, Vammatar shouldered through the door, blasting the heavy oak planks to splinters. At once, the guards we had seen before lowered their mighty weapons and began their slow, unstoppable march forward. It was all happening exactly as it had before.

Vammatar charged forward, a short piece of twisted scrap metal in her hand, and swung for the guard in the very center of the row.

Her weapon sailed right through the warrior. Still, the NPC marched onward. He didn't even flinch. "Did it work? What's happening?" I called, still too afraid to step into the chamber myself.

The death goddess looked back at us with a smile on her face. "They're illusions. Come. We will chase out any who remain."

Of course they were illusions. The encounter had happened *exactly* the same as the first time, meaning it was a scripted part of the AI—a spell or an enchanted rune left behind to deter followers. The magic would operate according to the same parameters no matter how many times it was triggered. The only confusing bit that remained was figuring out how it worked alongside such powerful anti-magic. That puzzle would have to wait for later.

Vammatar seemed to have some idea of where to go despite the presence of more than one door, and she blasted through her chosen portal with all the strength of a hurricane, once more sending splinters of wood and twisted metal all over the place. I had expected to hear a few shouts of distress as we breached one of the inner rooms of the keep, but no such noise found my ears. I walked through the illusory warriors and peered into the next room.

Empty.

There was a bed in the center of the room and a high, narrow window to the side along with the other standard accoutrements of a bedroom, but that was it. No royal family cowering against a far wall begging for their lives.

We checked all the other doors in rapid succession.

More emptiness. The royal family was gone.

"Tear the rooms apart!" I barked. "Check everything!

Every wall, every stone on every floor. Find their escape route!"

The truthbreaker and the bone thief instantly ran into the rooms to begin their frantic search, though Vammatar only stayed casually by my side.

"You know something, don't you?" I asked. She smirked like someone waiting to reveal their master plan, and her quiet confidence pissed me off.

"The magical dampening effect is only present in the entryway," she said slyly.

"What does that mean?"

"Get your warden. She should be able to detect magic within each of the private chambers."

I cursed myself for not testing the geographic limits of the magical deadzone myself. The first thing I should have done in each room was order the truthbreaker to cast a weak spell just to see if it would work. I shook my head and called for the bone thief, then gave the undead rogue orders to take over for the warden in the bailey and send her to me.

A few minutes later, Ellen joined our merry band, though she looked perplexed at the presence of a dozen imperial guards blocking her path.

"Just walk right through them," I said somewhat dejectedly. "They aren't actually real."

She glanced side to side before stepping through. "What do you need from me? The rogue doesn't speak, so all he conveyed was that I was needed," she said.

"You can detect magic, right? I think that's a fairly standard warden spell. Vammatar says the anti-magic field is only in the main room, not the individual bedchambers," I answered.

It took about five minutes for Ellen to discover how the royal family had escaped. Beneath one of the beds, the stone floor was another illusion. When I bent down and got close to the surface, I found that I could see right through it in certain places, though the magic still fully supported my weight. It took another hour or more for the two of us to find the correct angle needed move through the magic and not simply bounce off the floor as though the stones were tangible.

The passage below the bed was well lit and comfortable enough to accommodate the entire castle's population. From the entrance, I couldn't see far enough to tell where it was going. "Get some zombies in here. Map out the passages. I want to know where it leads, and I don't want to risk anything more than a handful of undead in case Ahmose rigged it with traps."

Ellen acknowledged my command and left to assemble the zombie exploration team. I stayed behind a few moments longer as my mind wandered. If the hidden passage extended very far—and I had absolutely no doubt that it would—our chances of capturing King Ahmose II would plummet to almost zero.

I didn't let my failure linger long in my mind. I had so much more left to finish before I could even think about getting back to Undercroft Citadel.

My task for the afternoon was much darker than exploring hidden tunnels and searching for runaway royals. I had the entire collection of females with T names to process, and I wasn't exactly sure how to begin. Xia decided that talking with them in groups of three at a time would be the most effective, and I didn't know any better strategy, so we went with hers.

The first three women proved absolutely useless. None of them had any accent whatsoever, and they didn't react in any discernible way to my questions. I had them taken to another area of the city with a handful of zombies to guard them. Despite the relatively low number of guards I had stationed to watch over all the captives, Vammatar had a very effective method of controlling everyone. Simply put, enough of Echelon's citizens had seen the death goddess up close that the aura of rumors surrounding her was strong. Everyone was rightfully terrified. Catching the ire of a death goddess was an easy way to earn a horrible death.

We found the first woman with a strong accent about half way through the group. There was a portal to Wonder in Australia, so finding an Australian woman near the Atlanta portal was certainly something that stuck out as memorable. Bert's story was starting to gain more credibility.

The Australian was an assassin, level thirty-four, and I immediately recognized that she'd be a tough woman to crack. I had Ellen walk her past Bert up on the wall on her way into the throne room. When the two women approached me behind the throne, Ellen nodded, indicating that we had the right person. Or, in a very different scenario, we had the woman Bert *wanted* us to have.

"So," I began, the bone thief clicking and rattling as it paced the room behind me, "I've been told that you worked for Vic Fuentes. I'm sure you're aware that he is the person I am after."

I watched the assassin intently, eager to judge any reaction she might have, but saw nothing. She out-leveled me, and from the way she carried herself, I got the impression that she thought herself my superior. I remembered my lack of legendary armor, and I knew there was a good chance the woman was right. But her hands were tied behind her back, and she wore only simple cloth pants and a matching sleeveless tunic. No weapons. No armor. No magic items.

I waited for a moment to let the woman respond. When she didn't, I had to press on. "You've seen what Undercroft

Citadel is capable of doing out there. Either you tell me the answers I need right here and right now, or you go down into the crypt where we pry your secrets away with knives and brands."

A flicker of a smile played at the edges of the woman's lips. "Thank you for telling me where you live," she said quietly, her accent strong.

I wanted to ask if the woman was insane. If anyone *didn't* know I was from Undercroft, they were either blind, deaf, or incapable of coherent thought. Hell, my own name floating above my head was in deep scarlet, the color of Undercroft Citadel. Instead of insulting the woman, I decided to play dumb. "What do mean?" I asked. "Do you not know who I am?"

She shook her head. "I never kill someone unless I've found the proof with my own eyes and ears that they deserve to die. You say you are from Undercroft, and I believe you."

Maybe she *was* insane. "You're . . . a strange kind of assassin," I remarked.

Again, she smirked. Mocked me even. "Thank you," was all she said.

"Alright, enough of your cryptic nonsense. Vic. You know him. You worked for him, right?" I demanded. The bone thief could sense my agitation, and it started pacing closer and closer to the woman, ready to pounce and add her head to its vast collection.

"Yes," she answered.

"Mind being a little more specific?"

"You only asked if I worked for him," she said.

The assassin's confusing non-answers were starting to grate on my nerves. I thought about taking her right down to the crypt to watch her die without another question, but I needed information. "*How* did you work for him? In what capacity?" I clarified.

She looked into my eyes and said, "He hired me for several contracts."

"What kinds of contracts?" I asked, though I felt like an assassin as high level as she was would only be hired for one kind of job.

"Procuring specific items and removing certain enemies," was her response.

Now we were getting somewhere. "What items? Which enemies?"

All she did was smile.

I asked the same question, thinking that somehow the assassin had failed to hear me the first time, though I knew it was impossible. Still, she did not answer.

"What are you hiding?" I demanded. I waved for the bone thief to grab her shoulders and push her forward, exposing her neck like a sheep ready for slaughter.

She offered another sly smile. "All the contracts I signed with Vic contained confidentiality clauses. If you would like the details, I suggest asking him yourself."

The sheer arrogance of the woman's blind loyalty to whatever sense of honor or contractual obligation she subscribed to was staggering. I drew my sword and held it against her throat. A little droplet of blood appeared on the side of her neck and dribbled down my blade. "The only thing that will save your life right now is if you start telling me the truth. Tell me everything about Vic and his compound. How many people does he have? What are his defenses? Has he fled his hideout since the server crashes? And what in the hell was someone like you doing with a nobody like Bert?" I had so many questions whirling through my mind that I wasn't sure where to begin.

"I haven't seen Vic in several months. I'm not sure anything I know can help you," the assassin answered with another round of vagueness.

Deep down, I knew she was right. If she was telling the truth, her old information wouldn't be useful. "And Bert?" I asked. "Why did you meet with him?"

"All I can say is that I signed a contract concerning Bert. Infer from that what you will," she said.

Perhaps my little war against Echelon had inadvertently saved Bert's life. I only had one more line of questioning that felt productive. "Vic's hideout. It is near Riverside, I know that much. How can I find it?"

Thankfully, the woman didn't have any reservations at all about telling me exactly where it was. I guessed she hadn't made any sort of agreement with Vic about keeping that particular secret safe. "Go west of the town. Look for a sycamore tree with a ring scratched into the bark around the base. It isn't far from Riverside. You'll still be able to see some farmhouses when you find the right tree. From there, go north ten paces and you should find a trapdoor under a bunch of leaves and other camouflage. If you reach a stream, you've gone too far."

Getting Vic's location was so easy that I immediately suspected a trap. The woman had, after all, already mentioned killing me. Why would she give up her former employer so easily? Was it all a web of lies? Or perhaps she hated Vic for the same reasons she hated me. Both of us were morally contemptible.

"Why give him up?" I asked out of genuine curiosity. In the long run, her answer wouldn't really matter. Whether she was leading me to a trap or not, the first thing my soldiers would do would involve checking for those traps. Her forthright answer didn't change my anticipated behavior at all.

Finally, she answered. "I owe no allegiance to that man. Whatever issue exists between you two is not relevant to my life."

"I feel like there's something more you're not telling me," I continued.

"And self-preservation," she said with a smile.

It made enough sense to me. I dropped my sword from her throat and nodded to the bone thief to let her go.

"And killing me? What about that?"

Her smile persisted. "By kidnapping me, you have done me harm. Almost everyone who has ever done me harm has died by my hand."

I didn't really know what to make of her answer. On one hand, I liked her style. She was remorseless. On the other hand, she was a huge liability. I also wondered how far her drive for self-preservation would take her. If I offered her a place in Undercroft Citadel, would she take it? Would she ever be truly loyal? Or should I slit her throat and have her body hauled back to Xollmomath to be converted into a mindless undead?

She must have guessed at the different possibilities being weighed in my mind and realized that one of those options would lead to her death. "I can lead you to Vic's lair if you like," she said.

"You'll help me kill him?" I asked. It didn't seem likely.

"No," she said, shaking her head at me like an insolent child. "I said I would help you find him. I owe him no death."

In my mind, bringing a killer directly to the prey was no different than holding the knife yourself. I didn't understand the assassin's strange morality at all. I also wasn't sure the woman understood her own morality, either.

"Alright, you'll live for now. Until we find Vic. If you try to escape or harm any of my people, I'll kill you," I told her.

She seemed outwardly agreeable to my plan, and that was good enough for now.

I knew where Vic was, or I would know soon. Step one was complete. Finding and deposing the royal family no lon-ger mattered that much. Enough of the city had been ruined that I was confident in Undercroft Citadel's ability to repel an attack. If I found Ahmose II, the only gain that would come from his death would be as repayment for allowing Vic to live so close to the city before the server crashes.

We waited until the next day to leave Echelon. I had the un-dead guarding all the captives at the other end of the city slowly leave their posts to hopefully prevent any rioting or all-out warfare in the streets. If the people knew we were get-ting ready to leave, they'd probably chase us out. I didn't want another fight, even if having Vammatar on our side meant we would ultimately win.

As I had feared, the hidden passage underneath the royal bedchambers was an escape route, and it had so many dif-ferent exits both inside and outside the city that pursuing them all would be fruitless. At the end of the day, I had all the dead bodies—and there were thousands—taken from wher-ever they had fallen and brought to the audience chamber. We packed the room full of corpses until no more would fit, and then we simply piled the rest outside the entrance to the keep. For the raiders left over in the crypt, I didn't bother or-dering their release. I simply built a fire on the staircase and then shut the only door.

We did manage to plunder the castle and the nearest buildings before our departure. When we left for Undercroft Citadel, I was on horseback at the head of a lengthy column. We had plenty of valuables and gold pieces, though we would have to eventually find a new city if we were going to trade any of it. But we also brought with us eight wagons of fresh corpses for Xollmomath to convert into soldiers. We had gear as well, more than we would ever actually need.

Sitting on a horse right behind me, her hands still tied be-hind her back and her weapon in one of my own saddlebags, was Titania, my newly acquired assassin. I had kept Bert alive as well, though I had concealed that fact from the assassin. A time would come for the two of them to resolve whatever it was between them. As long as their dispute didn't interfere with my own objectives, I didn't particularly care when they learned of each other's' existence.

My army arrived at Undercroft Citadel sometime in the afternoon of Vammatar's final day among us. Part of me wanted to set out at once for Riverside, but I knew better. We needed supplies, time to rest, and time to develop a strategy. On top of the more mundane preparations, I missed Helvegen. Being away from her for a few days had taught me how much I enjoyed her company. She offered a warm touch and a level head among so much death and chaos. She was the only piece of solid rock in the storm that raged through my mind.

My mind was full of blissful images—flitting between thoughts of Helvegen and visions of Vic's impending death—when the peaceful serenity of it all came crashing down. Elyk ran out of the gate to meet us. He was unarmed and unarmored, his hair matted with dirt, blood, and pieces of gore I couldn't easily identify. Something was wrong.

"What is it?" I demanded from horseback before he was even close enough to really answer.

"An illusionist," he yelled. "Someone from the guild—from Resurrection. They must have gotten through the wall during the fight. They were hiding when you left."

"And?" I shouted back, kicking my horse into a faster pace.

"Kulgun, half the orcs, the hospitaler—they're all dead!"

A shadow passed over the man's face. There was more he wasn't telling me. "What else?" I barked.

Deep down, I felt the answer before I heard it. "Helvegen, too," Elyk said.

CHAPTER 19

Tired and weary as we were, my whole army stormed back into Undercroft. We had more plunder and corpses than we could honestly carry, but none of it mattered in the face of an internal threat. I leapt from my horse once I was through the gate and landed in step with Elyk, my hand wrapped tight around the hilt of the sword hanging at my side.

"Follow me," the man said gravely. He led me to the side of the necropolis where our workshop had been partially destroyed by fire. Luckily, the last upgrade Lady Kalma had bestowed upon the structure had replaced the majority of the wood with stone. Only about half of the workshop would need repair. The problem would be a personnel one, not infrastructure. Replacing Kulgun would be difficult.

We went past the workshop and entered the barracks, and the smell of blood instantly hit my nostrils. The area had been set up as a triage, and a few orcs were laid out on cots and being patched together by Geirr.

Helvegen was on a cot against the far wall, her body unmoving. I went to her side at once. She wasn't drenched in blood as I had imagined the moment Elyk said her name, but a thin line of it snaked from her brow down to her collarbone. It looked like more blood had been cleaned off her chest at some point.

But there, under the red sheen that tainted her skin, was the steady cadence of her breath. "What happened?" I asked Elyk softly. I didn't know if Hel was asleep and recovering or . . . something else.

Elyk let out a heavy sigh and shook his head, his hands on his hips. "She was the first one out with the orcs to fight the illusionist. But none of us could tell exactly what was happening. It was chaotic. Xollmomath started launching magic, and I think some of it clipped Helvegen. Honestly, I don't really know exactly what hit her. Powerful magic, that much is certain."

"And her treatment?" I practically demanded. She was just lying there without any bandages at all. I wanted to draw my sword and gut Elyk where he stood, but I could barely move. Fear had wrapped its cold fingers around my muscles.

"We gave her all the healing potions we could," Elyk explained. "She was a lot worse off yesterday. The potions stabilized her, but we don't have a real healer. The hospitaler died in the first blast, I think. And with Kulgun dead, there's no one left to make potions. I don't know what to do."

I knew exactly what Elyk was hinting at, and it made my stomach churn. Before the server crashes, we would have killed someone so heavily injured and just waited for them to come waltzing back through the portal good as new. Respawning had meant that advanced or prolonged medical treatments didn't exist in Wonder. There was never any need to help someone recover from grievous wounds. Looking down at Helvegen's body, I wondered if she would prefer the same fate despite the lack of regeneration.

"How long has she been like that?" I asked.

"Stable? Since last night. I wanted to send a runner to Echelon, but we needed everyone we had in case there was another attack."

"You did the right thing, Elyk," I told him. "Defending the citadel is more important than anything. What happened to the illusionist?"

A visible shudder ran through the harvester. "The orcs were more than upset with her, as you can imagine. She ran out of mana before she could do too much damage—a suicide mission. Then Ugg'chugg picked her up by the ankle like she was just a stick or a piece of trash. She bashed the poor wretch against the wall until there was nothing left but a stain. They ate the bigger pieces raw, but there's still a red smear lingering on three or four of the posts. It was horrific, Ben. They made sure that woman suffered."

My grip on my hilt tightened even more, and I had to make a conscious effort to let go and relax the muscles in my hand. *Helvegen is still alive,* I told myself.

One of the orcs tending to their wounded comrades bumped into me from behind. "The orcs are our best nurses? And Geirr?" I asked. I was starting to fully realize how poorly we were staffed when it came to medical personnel.

"The best we have," Elyk said. "The orcs are at least decent with some low-level healing spells. If Kingsley was still a player, I think he would be better at it. But not anymore."

"Alright, they can figure it out. I need to talk to Vammatar before she leaves for good." I exited the barracks and took a deep breath of fresh air. All around me, Undercroft Citadel was in a state of disarray. Xollmomath stood with the new bodies we had brought back, though it looked like he planned on animating them one at a time, right in the middle of town. Xia had our assassin prisoner and looked somewhat lost. "If Hel were organizing it all, everyone would know what they were doing by now," I muttered under my breath.

The only person who seemed to have some direction was El-len, the warden. She was already at the damaged walls casting earth magic spells to augment the repairs with twisting vines and rapidly-growing trees.

I found Vammatar where I expected to: kneeling in front of the altar in the bone chapel.

"Hey, I have a question," I said, not waiting for her to ac-knowledge me at all.

She turned her head ever so slightly. I didn't know what the gesture meant. It could have been a warning that inter-rupting her in the chapel would result in death, or it could just as easily have been an indication that she was waiting for me to go on. I bet on the latter and continued. "My friend, the most important member of Undercroft Citadel, is hurt. Maybe dying. Maybe already brain-dead. Can you save her?" I asked. To an NPC who didn't understand death the same way as a player, the question made sense.

Vammatar stood up and stretched, her twisted metal ar-mor creaking. "Perhaps," was all she said.

"She's in the barracks, the only human there besides her brother. See what you can do," I ordered.

The death goddess shot me a sidelong glance before slowly leaving the chapel. Again, I didn't know how to inter-pret the woman's actions. Never one for prayer either inside or outside Wonder, I shook my head and left as well, heading up the steps toward my room.

There was so much work to be done, and all I wanted to do was sleep. I couldn't process it all. Managing every single aspect of a burgeoning empire was taxing. Beyond taxing.

My immediate goals, beyond seeing to Helvegen's rescue, all revolved around Vic's underground lair. I was so close to finding him, but I didn't feel like it. I felt a million miles away. Looking out at all the chaos and damage down below, I decided to take things one step at a time. The first thing I needed was information. To start, I summoned my character sheet to my vision and then clicked into the settlement tab to take stock of all we had lost.

Undercroft Citadel (Dungeon)

Commander: Ben Hales (Influence: 36)

Bosses: Xia (Warlock), Helvegen (Painter - incapacitated), Xollmomath (Necromancer), Elyk (Harvester), Ugg'chugg (Shaman), Vammatar (Goddess)

Resources: Moderate stockpiles of food and lumber, large stockpiles of weapons and armor, minor stockpiles of wealth (gems), minor stockpiles of exotic goods or artifacts, moderate stockpiles of crafting resources, moderate stockpiles of corpses

Military Strength: 2 warlocks, 153 zombies, 6 orc raiders, 2 gnomes, 2 truthbreaker paladins, 1 fallen warlord, 1 bone thief, 1 undead ranger, 1 warden

Specialists: 1 engineer, 1 herbalist, 1 inventor (unstable)

Defensive Structures: Partially destroyed wooden wall enhanced with fear glyphs (detonating corpses), minor defensive wards, minor physical traps (punji pits), small guard tower, necropolis, moat, 10 stone gargoyles, 8 stone pillar bugs

Active Production Facilities: 2 forges (offline), 3 crafting benches (offline), 1 engineering bench (offline), 1 alchemy bench (offline), 1 herbalist grove, 1 bone chapel, 1 reflecting pool

My fears were confirmed. Everything was too damaged to be used. We would burn through four or five days, maybe a week, just to get back to a solid baseline. I had to assume that Geirr hadn't finished working out the dents from my armor, either. That would take a couple days. No matter how I looked at it, there was just no possible way to raid Vic's lair with Vammatar still augmenting our ranks. She would leave tomorrow, and there was nothing I could do to stop it.

I went inside my room and stripped off my armor. Collapsing on the bed, I closed my eyes and tried not to think about anything. My relaxation was short-lived, though, when maybe twenty minutes later a knock sounded on my door.

"Yeah, come on in," I called.

To my surprise, Elyk opened the door with Vammatar in tow. "Figured you wanted to make the decision," he said.

"About what?" I propped myself up on my elbows and rubbed a hand across my face.

Vammatar stepped forward. "The woman's mind is gone," she stated. "I can bring her back, but she will not be the same. She will be more like me."

"What do mean?"

"Stronger, certainly," the death goddess said with a laugh. "Though perhaps more like my sister and myself. I cannot say with certainty."

I remembered my one and only encounter with Kalma's daughters quite vividly. Lowyatar was blind and feeble, shy to the point of being basically mute. Still, there was no doubt in my mind that either of Kalma's offspring were anything but incredibly powerful. A full-time death goddess on my side would be a welcome addition. But at what cost?

"What will remain of her personality?" I asked. I already dreaded the answer.

I couldn't read Vammatar's expression in the relative darkness. "Before Lady Kalma took me under her dark wing, I was a different person. I only remember bits and pieces, fleeting fragments of memory that barely feel my own. Does that answer your question?"

"It does," I said, my head drooping down to my chest. "Do it. Do whatever you have to do to bring her back. If it means she's changed, that's better than being dead, right?"

Curiously, Vammatar did not answer. Perhaps to a death goddess, death wasn't such a bad thing. Hell, the more I thought about it myself, the more I realized how my own feelings toward death had changed. Once I killed Vic, what would be the point? Live inside a game for the rest of my life?

But Wonder wasn't really a *game* in any traditional sense of the word. At least it didn't fit the definition of the games I had grown up playing and hearing about from friends. My parents had grown up with virtual reality arcades dominating the world's entertainment industry. *Those* had been games. Wonder was something different altogether. Wonder was a completely new world, a new planet. Was living inside Wonder for the rest of my days worth it?

I had no answer.

I laid my head down on the pillows and mentally commanded the room to darken and cool. We still had hours of useful time left, but I was too tired to deal with any of it. I just wanted to clear my head and wait until morning.

Sleep overtook me eventually, though it wasn't very restful. I tossed and turned between nightmares until dawn and awoke just as exhausted as when I had gone to bed.

At least Undercroft Citadel was relatively quiet when I emerged from my room about an hour after sunrise. The chaotic activity going on in front of the necropolis had calmed down for now.

I made my way to the workshop where I found Geirr asleep on a cot under a few thin sheets. I shook him awake and then gave him a few minutes to relieve himself and get his bearings. Sadly, there wasn't any coffee ready from the herbalist, so we had to clear our minds the more mundane way.

The two of us finally sat down on a pair of smoke-blackened chairs to go over Undercroft Citadel's status. "How much time will you need to repair everything?" I asked.

Geirr rubbed his chin. "Two weeks at least. But I can get your armor finished by tomorrow, I think. I was working on it before the attacker showed up, so I've already made progress hammering out all the dents you put in it."

My legendary armor was hanging on a set of pegs on one of the few walls that hadn't been destroyed by fire. It brought me a little bit of comfort to know that I'd have it back before long. Still, the best comfort I had was the simple knowledge that every enemy we had was now solely on the defensive. Echelon was crippled and terrified, Resurrection was gone, and Vic's band had never made a single attack attempt in the past, so there was no reason to expect one now.

"Any thoughts on the flying machine?" I asked. The idea still bounced around in my head. It would be an easy way to ensure the total destruction of a major city, and the bodies such a slaughter would produce would give me an army. An incredible army. Besides the zombies, I had other ideas as well. When the flying machine went into the sky, there was a good chance that whatever the game AI generated to come kill it would be biological. That meant Xollmomath could raise it from the dead.

Geirr pulled me out of my fantasy with a laugh and some bad news. "Now that Kulgun is dead, it'll take longer. He knew how to make the gas. I don't."

"Shit. That's not ideal. Well, it was a crazy plan in the first place. We can shelve it for now," I said. "Just work on the walls and repairing armor. We have a lot of new pieces from Echelon as well."

I left Geirr and the workshop to go and find his sister in the barracks. My feet moved slowly, my mind dreading all the horrible possibilities for what I would find.

Helvegen was right where I had left her. Her body was unmoving except for the steady rise and fall of her chest, and someone had cleaned all the blood from her forehead. She looked peaceful. At least she wasn't contorted in pain or fighting against a hospital's relentless plastic tubing and beeping monitors.

The closer I looked, the more I noticed that something

was different about her. She had changed. It was subtle, but I felt like I knew the topography of her body well enough to notice, and it wasn't just a trick of the low lighting.

Though it was easy to see that something was different, it was hard to pinpoint exactly what that change was. She looked . . . bigger. Like she had grown several inches and added layers of muscle as though she'd been lifting weights for a decade. And her brow was sharper, more defined, matching the harsh lines of her chin that I had never seen before.

She looked a lot more like Vammatar than she had before. Her face matched the jagged lines of the death goddess's twisted helmet, and I wondered how much of Vammatar's personality had seeped into Helvegen's mind as well. If the transformation of her personality was as dramatic as the one that had taken over her body, she wouldn't even be the same person.

At least she's alive, I reminded myself. Being alive and . . . changed . . . was still better than being turned into another mindless slave in my undead horde. I stayed with Helvegen for about an hour before giving up on the prospect of her awakening. There was nothing I could do to help her recover. Either she would wake up and live once more, or she would wither away and die in a couple days.

To take my mind off Helvegen's grim situation, I spent the afternoon and part of the night helping Xia go through all the items we had brought back from Echelon. We had a ton of gear, and sorting it by usefulness was no quick task. On top of everything we had brought back from the city, there was still a huge pile of gear waiting to be processed from the fight with Resurrection. It would take days to go through it all, and the mindless sorting was almost like meditation for me.

Helping Xia and me the entire time was Titania, our captive assassin. She knew a lot about magic weapons, and allowing her to handle them helped us all trust each other a little more. I didn't think she would be able to kill me quickly with Xia right by my side, but the fact that she never even tried was at least somewhat telling.

Another restless night of sleep met me when I lay down in my room. My mind was full of dark and unsettling dreams, though I couldn't remember anything more than a subtle feeling when I awoke sometime after dawn.

I opened my bedroom door, and a different sight met my eyes. Instead of a sleepy dungeon getting ready for the day, a mass of people stood at the foot of my necropolis. Something was happening, but the scene went quiet as soon as everyone saw me looking at them. "What's up?" I asked awkwardly.

Helvegen stepped forward from the knot of people, breaking free of Geirr's grasp. A circle formed around her like some sort of circus spectacle, but instead of cheering or laughing, everyone was deathly silent. Even Xollmomath was there, and his hairless face showed fear.

"You're awake," I stammered.

The woman I used to know so well looked alien to me. She stood closer to seven feet tall than six, and her physique was more reminiscent of a powerlifter than the dainty painter I had known. She walked with a confidence she had not previously displayed as well. The way she held her muscled shoulders spoke of strength and authority.

Suddenly realizing what might have happened, I quickly summoned my character sheet to my vision and jumped to the dungeon tab. A wave of relief spread through my body when I saw that I had not been usurped as the leader of Undercroft Citadel. For all of Helvegen's newfound physical stat, she hadn't accelerated that much in influence, and for that I was thankful.

The woman walked up a handful of steps and stopped. She didn't say anything.

"How . . . uh, how are you feeling?" I asked.

She stretched her limbs, flexed, and twisted her neck from side to side. "Alright," she finally answered. Even the quality of her voice was different. She was more commanding than she had been before.

"That's good," I replied. "Do . . . do you remember who I am? Where you are?"

I glanced above her head and made sure that the color of her name was still the same. Thankfully, it hadn't changed. She was still loyal to Undercroft Citadel.

"I know where I am," she snapped back at me, though her voice betrayed her lack of confidence.

"Where is that? What is it called?"

She hesitated for a moment. "Undercroft Citadel," she finally answered. "My home. I'm at home."

A wave of relief washed over my shoulders. At least she didn't view me as an enemy. "And what is our goal here?" I asked.

She thought for another moment before answering. Finally, she said, "Kill Vic Fuentes. Revenge."

So she wasn't *that* much different after all. She looked different, sure, but deep down, I could still trust her. "Alright, everyone," I announced, turning my attention back to the assembled mass. "Helvegen has returned to us. Vammatar gave her a gift, but she's still the same person deep down. You can trust her just like you did before." Then, once more speaking to Hel, "Are you ready to go back to work? Can you manage Undercroft Citadel for me once more?"

Helvegen nodded. She turned her back to me and stomped down the stairs, her footfalls somehow sounding far heavier than they should have been even for her enhanced frame.

Everything more or less went back to normal. The sounds of industry—basically just everyone trying to get repairs done to bring back a sense of safety—filled the air once more.

Helvegen was more violent and commanding when she ordered around the zombies throughout the day, but that was fine. The undead didn't seem to mind.

Geirr had my armor finished by nightfall, and he delivered it with a somber tone. I tried to comfort him and explain to him that at least his sister was still alive, but I don't think my words made much progress breaking through the wall of grief in his mind. Comforting people in their time of need had never been my strongest skill. Being responsible for the tragedy made it a lot worse. Geirr departed before I could stumble through any more awkward sentences, leaving me alone in my room.

I managed to get a decent bit of sleep despite the incessant spinning of my mind. Another day arrived, and we continued making progress. Crews rebuilt the walls and raised new timbers for the burnt workshop, and Xia and Titania finished sorting all the new equipment. We still had weeks of work left to do, but everything that had to be completed was getting attention.

I spent the day atop the necropolis watching Helvegen while everyone else worked. The woman spent a large amount of time at the edge of the rift, her hand falling by her side and brushing against the writhing tentacles as she walked. I didn't know what she was doing, and I didn't want to go down and ask her yet, so I contented myself with watching. By the end of the day, I hadn't learned anything. All I knew was that Helvegen had organized the work crews before I had awoken, and then she had gone for a rather lengthy walk.

The next day brought more of the same. I got out of bed early enough to witness Helvegen in her managerial role once more—a small reminder that her mind was somewhat intact—and then I watched her make her rounds.

An hour or so after the work crews finished their midday meal, I realized that I had not seen Helvegen eat since her transformation. I mentally commanded one of the gargoyles to fly me down to her side. I matched her step, though my stride was now a few inches shorter than hers, and I thought for a moment about how I wanted to begin my questions.

"You haven't eaten in a while," I casually observed. "Feeling alright?"

Helvegen shot me a sidelong glance. "Lady Kalma sustains."

So she had also unlocked a talent letting her go without food. It was good to know. "Do you—" I cut myself off as a new question arose in my mind. "Want to go fight?" I asked.

Her glance hinted at a grin. "Always," she answered.

"Perfect. We aren't doing much hanging around here right now. Let's go pay Riverside a little visit. And I'll be bringing Titania with us. We'll find Vic's lair and do a little poking around."

For a split second, it looked like Helvegen was trying to reach out and take my hand, but she pulled back before getting very far. Still, I couldn't deny the smile it brought to my face.

CHAPTER 20

Word of my trip to Riverside spread through Undercroft Citadel quickly. Xia tried to talk me into taking her, and Ellen offered council regarding the dangers of traveling with an enemy assassin. When it came time to leave, the only person who gave me more than a few words of advice or encouragement was Ministrel, or whatever his name actually was. He came outside the walls with a linen sack and handed it to me. I was almost too afraid to look inside. When I did, I didn't understand what I was seeing.

"Masks?" I asked. "What are these?" They looked like paper or cardboard masks that a young kid would make in school.

The old wizard laughed and slapped me on the shoulder. "The many faces of Doctor Hubert Malbec!" he cackled before abruptly leaving.

I pulled one of the masks out of the bag and held it in my hand. It had a thick black moustache and crooked eyebrows. The two eye holes were mismatched. There wasn't a string or anything to make wearing it practical, but as soon as I turned it over, I saw the telltale gleam of magic on the item. The description appeared in my vision:

The Third Face of Doctor Hubert Malbec: Wearing one of Doctor Malbec's many faces completely disguises the wearer for an indefinite amount of time. The image granted to the wearer will be chosen by Doctor Malbec. Wearing a face for an extended period of time is not advised.

The item was unlike anything I had seen before. If it modified my appearance, I didn't know what kind of benefit that would confer. It might only be useful when tricking NPCs. As long as I had a name floating above my head, tricking a player with a disguise would be impossible.

I returned the mask to the bag and tied it shut, looping the end of it through my belt to keep it in place. If the need arose, I would be more than happy to give one of the masks a shot.

"That guy creeps me out," Titania said when Ministrel was out of earshot.

I nodded. "You have no idea," I replied. "He's certainly the strangest member of Undercroft Citadel."

"Then why do you keep him around?" The assassin fell into step beside me, her hands never far from the daggers at her sides. It was disconcerting seeing her without restraints, but in my legendary armor once more, I didn't fear her weapons.

When I thought about Ministrel's presence, I didn't come up with a great reason for letting him stay. "I guess he hasn't done any harm yet, and he came with some gnomes, though most of them are dead by now."

The two of us made idle small talk as we walked to Riverside. We opted to leave our newly acquired horses behind since the trip wasn't that far and we didn't want to carry any food for them. The whole time, Helvegen didn't say anything. She marched to my left about ten paces, staying close but never close *enough*.

We made excellent time and arrived at Riverside before

noon. Walking right through the center of the village, we drew more than a handful of nervous stares, but we weren't there to burn the place to the ground. We could probably go door to door capturing people, dragging them into the street, and interrogating them, but that would take time. I didn't want to be gone for more than a day or two at most, so we carried on through the town to the woods on the opposite side.

"Alright, lead on, Titania. Show me the entrance to Vic's hideout," I commanded.

The assassin took point, and Helvegen and I followed her into the forest. In her new body, Hel still hadn't practiced walking enough to be skillful at it, and she routinely ran into tree branches and had to brush cobwebs from her face.

For armor, the painter was attired more similarly to Vammatar than I had expected. She wore a chainmail tunic and steel helmet with hardened leather greaves and gauntlets. The outfit didn't match—her choice of items had been limited on account of her size—but she looked capable in it. She looked terrifying.

Our jaunt through the woods lasted about an hour before Titania found a tree that matched the description Bert had given. I had no idea if it was a sycamore or not, but it had a ring carved into the bottom right above the dirt. We walked north ten paces and started stomping around until Titania's boots found the hidden trapdoor.

"Well, here it is," she said, brushing some of the debris from the top of a large square plank.

It was kind of hard to believe. I felt like I was getting so close to killing Vic—but something wasn't right. It was too easy. Vic's hideout had been one or two hundred yards from Riverside the entire time.

"Open it," I commanded. I took a few steps back and drew Infernum from my belt.

Surprisingly, Titania didn't hesitate. If there was a trap on the other side, she either didn't know about it or didn't care. The assassin felt around the edge of the wood until she came to a spot where her fingers found purchase. The trapdoor came up and revealed dark passage below.

There wasn't much room. The passage was about three or four feet in diameter and at such a steep angle downward that I couldn't see anything but darkness.

"What's at the bottom of the hole?" I asked.

Titania answered with a smile. "It goes about twenty feet deep until you reach a door. There isn't enough room to stand, and the other side of the door is always guarded. There's no safe way to get inside."

"Shit." Vic's defenses were better than I had expected.

Helvegen stepped up next to me, her towering physique casting a shadow across my face. "Smoke them out," she stated. "We can fill the tunnel with wood and oil and burn it."

"They have to have escape routes. Where can find them?" I asked the assassin.

She shook her head. "I never needed to use any of them, so I do not know. Perhaps you could find them if you searched."

If I had brought a hundred undead with me, finding escape tunnels would likely be a decent option. Though if those paths were equally well guarded, it would still be risky.

"Do they have a password or something to get inside?" I asked.

"They do. And I know it," Titania answered.

I pulled the trio of masks from my bag and handed one to each of the women. "Let's try a little disguise," I said.

I slipped my own mask on first, and my appearance instantly changed. My hands felt bigger, older, and I had a bushy beard on my chin that looked like it hadn't been washed in weeks. Beneath my helmet, I felt all the hair on the top of my head missing. I had transformed into someone much, much older than myself.

Titania put her mask on second. Instantly, the name floating above her head disappeared. She had taken on the appearance of an NPC. "Hey, do I still have a name?" I asked.

"No, we're all NPCs now," Titania answered breathlessly. "If I had known things like this existed . . . Talk about the best item in all of Wonder for an assassin."

Helvegen had her own mask firmly in place, and her name had also vanished. And not only had we successfully hidden our identities, but we didn't even look like fighters. We were just civilians. I could feel all my legendary armor still weighing down on my shoulders, but I couldn't see it. Instead, my body looked clothed in peasant's garb.

"Alright, let's move quickly. I don't want to wear the masks too long," I said. "Titania, you're taking point. Lead us to the door and get us through."

"How?" she asked.

"The password?"

She laughed as though I was an idiot. "That only works for members of Vic's band or his contacts, not random civilian NPCs from Riverside."

I had to think for a moment. "Alright, take off your mask and lead us down. They'll recognize you. Say we're your captives."

The assassin removed her mask and at once reverted to her normal image, name and all. She also gasped for breath and stumbled, catching herself on a tree to keep from falling. "What the hell . . ." she muttered. "I . . . feel like I've been out of breath for hours. Drowning."

"Good to know. When we take off the masks, we need to be somewhere safe." We waited a minute or two for a Titania to catch her breath and then started the descent. The tunnel was too tight to stand or even stoop, so the three of us crawled forward on our hands and knees until we reached a metal door shrouded by absolute darkness. We were at least fifteen feet below the surface. The only indication that we had reached the door at all came when Titania banged her head against it. I tried to look back and see Helvegen behind me, but all I could detect was the steady rhythm of her breathing. For as large as she had become, it was a wonder that she fit in the tunnel at all.

An answering bang came on the door from the other side.

"Where, then, the voice of the unheard melody?" Titania said softly toward the door.

A response followed quickly from the other side: "And the voice of the unheard language?"

"Hildegard spoke it thus," Titania concluded.

A few long seconds passed in darkness, and then a sliver of light appeared up ahead. The sliver grew into a square as the door was removed from its place. The room beyond—what I could see of it around Titania's body—was somewhat small. A single armed and armored woman stood to the side of the door. She had a small stool and a table with a few candles and a book upon it, and the rest of the room was completely bare. I figured the room was something of a sterile chamber used to evaluate newcomers before they entered the rest of the complex.

Much to my surprise, the woman guarding the door was not a raider. She was a rogue, and she was level forty-one, making her far more powerful than I had expected for someone in such a mundane position.

Titania fulfilled her role as our pretend captor immediately. "I found these trespassers outside," she announced. "A pair of bumbling idiots from Riverside, no doubt. I'm taking them to Vic."

The guard scoffed. Clearly, she didn't think a couple NPCs from Riverside were worth her time. "Should've just slit their throats and thrown their bodies in the river," she said.

I tried to look as scared as possible to play my part. "No, please, we were just minding our own business in the forest, that's all," I begged.

"Vic won't want to be bothered with useless rabble," the rogue said. As she spoke, she pulled a jagged black knife from her belt. She moved to slit my throat, but I caught her off guard with a quick punch to her stomach. My hand crunched against her armor. It seemed that the mask transfiguring my appearance also hid my armor, and a sting of pain shot through my knuckles. The mask also meant drawing Infernum was impossible. And if I took it off, I'd be too winded to fight.

Perhaps I made a mistake.

I rolled to my side and cast *Pull from the Darkness* and *A Feast of Spores* as quickly as I could. My shadow pet launched for the rogue's face, and the woman staggered backward in a haze of spores.

My victory was short-lived. The woman was used to a brawl, and her gear far outclassed the basic sackcloth clothing the three of us were wearing. A sharp kick landed in the center of my chest before I could react to it, and I sprawled backward onto the hard ground. In the low candlelight, it was hard to follow the rogue's movements.

The woman regained her balance and awareness with lightning speed. She lashed out toward Helvegen with her jagged black dagger, and her arm became a blur. At once, I knew we were doomed. Without our gear, the rogue was simply too strong. There was nothing we could do. I ripped my mask from my face. Helvegen apparently came to the same realization at the same time, and she tossed hers aside with a yell.

Helvegen collapsed on the ground next to me. She was gasping for breath, her eyes a thousand miles away, and I wasn't much better. I looked to Titania as a savior . . . and my heart sank in my chest.

Titania had betrayed us. She had a dagger in each hand and was coming right at me while the rogue fell on Helvegen.

A pair of sharp daggers crashed into my breastplate. Fire blasted out of my armor in response. Luckily, Titania's physical stat wasn't nearly high enough to pierce my breast-plate with her straightforward attack, and I grinned as she wheeled away. I mentally commanded my shadow pet to switch targets as it was doing basically nothing against the high-level rogue. It leapt onto the assassin's face and began clawing at the woman, eliciting a chorus of screams in the small, dimly-lit room.

I didn't have time to see how Helvegen was faring. I knew she was tough, beyond tough, and that would have to suffice. All I could think about was myself.

Struggling for breath, I barely got to my feet before an-other two-bladed attack came soaring toward me. Titania's daggers crashed into either side of my head, and the only thing that saved me from a quick death was the sheer strength of the metal encasing my face. The assassin had never seen my legendary armor in action, so she had no idea just how strong it was.

Her ignorance would be her undoing.

She attacked with relentless fury. Her blades smashed against my armor, but they didn't penetrate. The woman ac-tivated talent after talent—her body was practically a light show with the number of buffs and aura affecting her—and none of them did more than increase the speed at which she uselessly fought against me.

I regained my balance and drew Infernum. When I willed it to life, Titania's eyes went wide. She hadn't seen the sword, either. She was so unprepared that I almost laughed.

Swinging Infernum in a wide arc, I advanced on the as-sassin with a grin on my face. She backed up, but she didn't have anywhere to run. Her back was against the wall, and no matter how fast she tried to maneuver her weapons, her skills were simply inadequate compared to the strength of my legendary sword.

She backed into a corner, her back hit the wall, and she tried to use a talent to magically skip forward and past me. It was the exact move I had expected since it was her only viable option of escape, and I held Infernum out to my right with a tight grip on the hilt. When Titania attempted to magically sprint by, she was cut in half at the waist. Her torso fell in a bloody mess against the wall while her legs continued a single step onward to fall behind me.

Now fully focused for the first time since taking off my mask, I turned my attention to the rogue wailing on Helvegen. The rogue had made significant progress. Hel's armor wasn't nearly as good as mine, and in her dazed state she hadn't been able to fend off the attacks. Her upper arms and chest were both covered in blood. I couldn't tell if she had landed any strikes herself, though trading blows with swords wasn't exactly her style in the first place.

I moved to the rogue's back to cleave through her from behind when Helvegen loosed a stream of yellow and red magic that smashed into the rogue's face as solidly as any weapon. The magic overtook the woman, clearly stupefying her. Her eyes were so wide they looked like they would fall from her head.

Helvegen stalked forward and wrapped the rogue in a giant, oppressive bear hug.

"Want me to kill her?" I asked, still holding Infernum in a way that decapitating the rogue would be easy.

Helvegen shook her head. She wore a devious, brutal smile. She was downright terrifying—no doubt a result of her recent transformation at the hands of Vammatar.

I stood behind the struggling rogue with my weapon

ready. Helvegen simply squeezed, and I could hear the rogue's spine popping.

. . . then the screams began. The woman bellowed in pain at the top of her lungs. Helvegen was snapping her back, laughing the whole time.

Finally, the slaughter concluded, and the rogue slumped to the ground broken in half. I realized that the tip of my sword was no longer on fire, and when I pulled it back closer to my body, the flames returned. I tested my theory once more only to confirm that Helvegen now had an anti-magic aura about her that she had not possessed before.

Your Physical skill has increased to 31!

Your Cunning skill has increased to 36!

Congratulations! You have increased to level 18!

"You stopped her from teleporting away," I said in awe. I pushed the level notification out of my vision and decided to spend time picking a new talent later.

Helvegen gave a curt laugh. "An insect crushed beneath my boot heel. I am so much more . . . a goddess . . ."

The power in Helvegen's voice was enough to make my hair stand on end. Her transformation was so profound that I barely recognized her. She was so much more than she had been before. If she wanted to kill me, I knew she could. The rogue had been a high-level player, not some hapless NPC without a clue how to fight. Helvegen had killed her as easily as a wolf would kill a squirrel.

"Alright, let's scout some of the complex. We need to know what we're up against before we come back with an army," I said.

Helvegen didn't acknowledge that I had spoken. Instead, she picked up the broken rogue in her arms and then threw the corpse into the tunnel where we had entered. Once she had shut the door with the corpse on the outside, she finally looked to me and nodded. "Let's go," she said.

I slowly opened the door leading out of the entryway and peered into the next passageway. Though we were underground, the complex we were in was far from a cave. Everything had been mined out and reinforced with wooden and metal supports. The floor was a mix of hard-packed dirt and thick, square paving stones like the crew that had built it all had only finished bits and pieces. Torches burned every few paces, and the smoke was all funneled out through small holes drilled into the stone above at regular intervals. The whole complex spoke of craftsmanship and planning. I wondered if Vic had been the one to build it or if he had conquered some ancient dwarven stronghold and claimed it for himself much like I had done with Whitechapel.

Multiple passages extended from the entryway in a trio of directions. Each of them looked just as promising as the others. I had no idea which path to take.

"Which way should we go?" I asked, though I knew Helvegen would only know as much as I did.

The painter investigated each of the passages for a few moments before selecting the one all the way on the right. "Here. There's sound coming from this one," she said with confidence.

I tried to listen as closely as I could, but I heard nothing. To me, all of the tunnels were silent.

I followed Helvegen down the tunnel she had selected. It wound to the right a while before coming to a large hall with a handful of occupants. From what I could see and smell, the open room was a commissary or cafeteria. "Too many in there. We don't want an all-out war," I whispered.

We doubled back the way we had come and had to duck into an uneven alcove to hide from someone running the opposite direction with a tightly rolled scroll in their hand. Luckily, we remained undetected. From the central confluence of passages, we instead chose the middle path. It was

tighter and steeper than the previous tunnel, and I got an uneasy feeling about it as we went.

The tunnel quickly ended in a heavy banded door. No
sounds came from behind it that either of us could hear.
Helvegen tested the knob and found it locked. "I can break
it," she stated flatly.

I nodded and glanced behind, making sure that no one was
coming from the opposite direction. When we were certain the
coast was clear, Helvegen gripped the knob with all her considerable strength and simply began to turn. The gears and mech-
anisms inside the lock squealed in protest before shattering.
Hel shook out her fingers and smiled. "We're in," she said.

The next room was someone's personal quarters. There
were multiple beds with matching chests of drawers arrayed
in a line across the far wall. Ventilation holes had been drilled
into the ceiling every few feet. The only light source in the
room other than some of the torchlight coming from the
hall was produced by a single pair of candles to my left. In the
farthest bed, someone was asleep. They were a raider, and I
didn't recognize their name.

"Come on, we need to keep investigating," I said, turning
to head back to the final pathway from the entrance.

Helvegen wasn't quick to follow me. She took a few long
strides into the sleeping chamber and then brought her
sword down on the raider's neck, beheading him in one
quick motion. "Fewer enemies when we return," the woman
said quietly when she rejoined me at the door.

We ran down the tunnel on the balls of our feet trying to
make as little noise as possible. Before we returned to the entryway, we basically collided with a pair of low-level thieves
heading toward the bedrooms and talking loudly with each
other. Helvegen and I dispatched them both in the span of a
few seconds and then tossed the corpses to the side. "We're
running out of time," I said. "Someone is going to find the

bodies, and then the whole place will go on high alert. We don't want to have to fight our way out."

Helvegen shared my concern and quickened her pace. We found the third chamber and took it at once. Ahead of us, someone was running in the same direction. They had probably seen the dead door guard and were racing to spread the word. Time continued to run out. We reached another confluence of pathways and came to a stop. There were too many options to check them all. I made a quick decision and picked the room on my immediate right. I burst through the wooden door, and a raider on the other side jumped with fear and surprise. I didn't hesitate to ram Infernum through his chest. As my blade cackled and smoked, charring the meat now surrounding its steel, I realized where I was. The room wasn't quite a library, but there were certainly plenty of books. I pushed the dead raider clinging to my weapon until his back hit a rack of scrolls. Infernum's fire instantly leapt to the dried parchment and started climbing up the walls.

"We have to run!" I yelled. I pushed back toward the door, my armor crashing into a shelf and bringing it down at the same time. I had no idea if the fire would spread from the small storage room to the rest of the underground complex, but I knew the smoke would at least cause some problems. At the very least, Vic's gang would be forced to go above ground for some time. If I could rally the rest of Undercroft Citadel quickly, we could catch Vic in the open.

My investigation skill ticked up a point as we fled back toward the tunnel that would lead us to the surface. The two of us arrived before anyone else could cut us off, and we scrambled past the door and the corpse we had left. Helvegen went first, and her powerful clawing threw clods of dirt into my face so much that I had to shield my eyes. Luckily, there was only one path back to the surface.

"Back to the necropolis?" she asked once we emerged on the surface.

"Exactly." We took off back toward Riverside and reached the village in no time. "Come on, let's steal some horses," I said.

It didn't take long to find a stable with a pair of poorly trained colts, kill the owner when he came out to protest, and we were riding toward Undercroft Citadel.

As I rode through the gate into my domain, my goal was more clear than it had ever been before. I had Vic's hide-out, and he would be scrambling to put out a fire. My army would descend on the disorganized raiders like an unstoppable plague. Vic's death was inevitable.

CHAPTER 21

We spent a day getting ready. Though more time would have made us even more prepared, I couldn't afford to waste time. A single day was all we had.

Everyone assembled in front of the gates, and I surveyed the army from horseback. We were only leaving behind a minimal skeleton crew to essentially defend the walls, but no one was after us, so I had every confidence that they wouldn't be needed. Besides, Xollmomath could not venture all the way to Riverside, so he had no other choice than to stay behind. I laughed when I thought of some hapless band of raiders trying to sack Undercroft Citadel thinking I was not home and the whole place was therefore undefended. Any would-be attackers would face a dozen or so mindless undead, a few of the support personnel, and the untold might of one of the world's strongest necromancers. It wouldn't be pretty.

Everyone was anxious to get going, and I had no final words of inspiration to offer. I thought perhaps it would be fitting to give a rousing speech, something to get everyone's blood moving, but three quarters of my army was undead.

They wouldn't be motivated by simple words and an inspiring tone. Instead, I turned my stolen horse toward Riverside and urged the beast forward. My army was quick to follow.

Helvegen rode at my side, her huge form somewhat comical atop a small-ish horse. The rest of the players rode behind the two of us, and a massive train of herbally augmented undead shambled along behind them.

I used the time in the saddle to go over my new options from reaching level eighteen. I had three talents available, of course, though they were more powerful and unique than all the other abilities I had seen before. It felt like level eighteen was something of a benchmark offering rewards beyond what would otherwise be available. I hadn't heard of such benchmark levels before, but deathbringer was an unknown class, so anything was possible. I pulled up the talents and read through them:

Borne Beyond Realms (Physical): The deathbringer calls upon the very fabric of the universe, shredding it and bringing forth a small fragment of another plane into existence. The fragment can be used for a variety of purposes including self-augmentation, extreme temporary magical enhancement, and summoning. Other uses may yet be discovered. Only one shard may be produced every week. Active, consumes massive energy.

Walking Dissipation (Cunning): The void obeys no one, though Lady Kalma's most faithful servants have been known to occasionally bend it to their will. The deathbringer partially melds into the void, becoming one with nothing and impossible to see or touch for a short period of time. Active, consumes moderate energy.

Host of Blasphemies (Influence): A gentle voice beckons in the darkness. Mysteries untold for generations roil in the abyss. Cosmic horror emerges, and transmogrification begins. With needle in hand, Lady Kalma begins her foul work, grafting and stitching, suturing and removing until all that remains is blessed perfection. Active, consumes everything.

I spent the better part of an hour contemplating my options. All three talents were so far beyond anything I had even heard of in Wonder that I had no idea where to begin. I guessed that the skills were at least part of the reason why the deathbringer class had never made it into the real version of the game. Some developer working on the earliest versions of Wonder must have come up with the talents, and when they tested the game, I had the suspicion that the class was simply too strong to compete fairly with anything else. Or maybe the alpha and beta versions of Wonder had been full of extravagantly powerful abilities that had brought too much chaos. There was no way to know.

We reached the half-way point to Riverside, and I was still no closer to making a decision. The physical ability would probably yield the most sheer power over the longest period of time, but without a few days to sit down with Xollmomath and research the otherworldly fragment I would produce, I would essentially be rolling the dice. I wanted something that would be immediately useful, and *Borne Beyond Realms* was not it.

Walking Dissipation was much the opposite. It would be immediately useful, *and* it would come in handy when I finally met Vic in his underground lair. I tried to think of more creative uses for it, and one in particular came to my mind. If I held onto someone and activated the talent, stepping into another realm only described as the void, could I then let go and leave that person there? I didn't know if it would work that way, and the skill's description didn't make it clear. Still, the possibilities were more than intriguing.

My final option, *Host of Blasphemies*, was the most enigmatic of them all. Every line was more shrouded in the unknown than the last. When my eyes read the final two words—no matter how many times I read them—a shudder ran through my body that made the hair on my neck stand on end. *Consumes everything* . . . Was it suicide? Some sort of death-pact sacrifice that would only work if the game's regeneration capabilities were functioning properly? I saw the first farmhouse on the outskirts of Riverside and knew that I needed to make my decision soon. I longed for more time to ponder, but time felt like the only thing I never had enough of.

I thought of all I had lost, all I had gained, and the twisted path that had led me to Riverside with an army of the dead at my back. Echelon, one of the greatest cities in the entire world, was practically in ruins. A royal family wielding power I had once thought unattainable had run rather than face the might of Undercroft Citadel.

A smile spread across my face. I couldn't help but laugh as I unlocked *Host of Blasphemies* and added it to my character sheet. The talent blinked into existence, and I almost activated it right there without waiting. But no, the time would come. I would find the perfect moment to transform myself into . . . whatever I would become. The promise of that much power—of *blessed perfection*—was downright intoxicating. For a few seconds, I felt as insane as Ministrel, and I absolutely loved it.

As more and more of Riverside came into view, I let go of my wild anticipation and calmed my mind. The time would come, but now I had to prepare for battle. Vic's lair awaited, and I would not keep him in suspense much longer.

We rode past the outlying farms and cottages and into the village proper.

Everything was quiet. Though it was around noon, the sleepy town had not yet awakened, and no one was going through the streets about their business.

Circumventing the town would have been easily possible, but I chose to march right through the middle for expediency. And if anyone from Riverside reported our position to Vic's gang? So be it. His death was inevitable.

Moving through the web of streets separated the army into several small groups, and I waited for them with the other mounted players toward the far edge of the village in front of a bakery. As I watched my advancing horde, I started to recognize something about the quietness of the place that I should have noticed earlier.

No smoke billowed up from the bakery's chimney. It didn't smell like baking bread or other sweets. I crouched down on my horse to get a look through the only window, and I saw no light or motion inside. I started paying more attention to the other nearby houses and businesses and found more of the same. I held up a clenched fist to tell my zombies to stop. They came to a halt at once, operating with a flawless unity that could only come from AI control.

"What is it?" the warden next to me asked. Her voice betrayed her sudden nervousness.

I shook my head. "Something isn't right. There's no one here. They aren't just hiding."

"Wha—"

A loud noise interrupted the warden. Coinciding with the crash came a shift in two of the buildings across the street from me. It was as if their supports had been magically removed, and they toppled over on top of my scurrying undead. Dozens of soldiers were crushed to death before they could escape the falling stone blocks.

"To the center of the street!" I yelled, kicking my horse into action.

The two-story building behind me started collapsing, fire licking up toward the sky from the eaves of its roof. We were caught in an ambush, but the losses were at least initially minimal. I yelled for the zombies to get to the widest boulevard of the city where they would be immune to falling buildings and burning debris. As I watched them move, I saw more fires springing up around Riverside. Whoever was orchestrating the ambush—Vic, no doubt—was trying to trap us in a ring of fire.

In a few minutes, my undead horde was safe, though we were split into two roughly equal positions with a row of un-burned houses between us. I circled my horse around Helve-gen and Ellen, constantly searching the buildings for some kind of movement.

Thirty seconds went by before I saw something. A little bit of movement farther down the street caught my eye. I pointed to the building and was about to command the other players to follow me there when a door on a second-story veranda opened. We were about a hundred yards apart from each other, but I could see him clear as day. Vic Fuentes was standing in full battle armor, his hands on his hips.

My heart sank through my chest. I wasn't afraid or even worried that he would get away and somehow elude me, but the prospect of coming face to face with him after *so much* was simply overwhelming. A rush of emotion pounded through my body. I swallowed hard and took off my helmet.

Helvegen said something as I started trotting forward, but I didn't listen. I continued onward until I was close enough to the veranda to get a good look at the man who had taken so much from me.

I stopped about thirty feet from the house and exhaled a long breath to help steady my mind.

Vic spoke first. "I . . . I have you surrounded," he said some-what quietly. His voice wavered and his hands were gripping the wooden railing so hard that his knuckles were already white. I couldn't imagine what was going through his head.

I made a little show of looking side to side as though I was just now noticing the burning buildings. "I owe you a death," I said, tapping the hilt of the poisoned dagger tucked into my belt.

I could see Vic's Adam's apple moving up and down. He

started to speak but cut himself off before getting out a single syllable. He waited a few moments before beginning again: "There's no way out. I know you have a lot of . . . troops . . . but so do I. A lot of people in Echelon really hate you, and I don't blame them. You might not understand how many allies I have."

Was he threatening me? If he was, he didn't really paint a great picture.

"If you have any care at all for the lives of your people, come down now. Let me kill you in front of them," I stated, though it was a blatant lie. I would never just kill Vic. No, his end would be so much more than a simple dagger running across his throat.

He shook his head. "Don't throw away everything you have just for a chance at me," he said.

From my peripheral vision, I saw someone quickly duck beneath a windowsill. The glass was such poor quality that I couldn't tell if they were one of Vic's troops or just a cowering civilian who hadn't been able to flee quickly enough. "Xia," I called, and the warlock moved her own mount up beside mine. I pointed to the building where I had seen movement. "Burn the building to the ground. Leave nothing left."

"That's not—"

Vic's voice was lost in the conflagration that erupted from Xia's hands. She rained destructive fire down on the small wooden house, and the structure collapsed into a heap of charred beams and shattered furniture within moments. I smiled as the drifting sounds of dying screams reached my ears.

"Those weren't even my people," Vic said, his eyes wide. "Riverside is your *vassal*. You'd sacrifice their lives as well as your own? Are you really so blind?"

I couldn't help but laugh. The man in front of me knew nothing. He understood nothing of what I had become.

"I kill them all!" I bellowed into the sky. I turned toward Xia whose own bloodlust was evident in her eyes. She was just as hungry for death as I was. "Burn it all! *Kill everything!*"

I leapt from my horse as the chaotic battle erupted all around me. My undead began swarming through the buildings on every side, ripping Vic's waiting soldiers and helpless civilians into the street, where they were torn limb from limb in indiscriminate slaughter.

At the same time, more ambushers appeared on rooftops with bows, crossbows, and magic. They launched devastation into the undead ranks of my army.

None of it mattered to me.

Vic ran back inside his building, and that was where I had to follow.

Arrows and bolts clattered off my legendary armor as I ran for the front door of Vic's building. One of them was angled perfectly for my head and probably would have found the narrow gap in my helmet's faceguard, but I activated *Forsaken Barrier* before it reached and magically jaunted forward a pace, leaving the bolt to shatter on the cobblestone street.

I shouldered through a wooden door and was instantly met with two raiders waiting with maces held high. One weapon crashed into my pauldron—I barely felt more than a mild sting—while the second clanked off my breastplate and elicited a gout of fire in response. Neither of the raiders had activated any magic yet, so their attacks were beyond weak.

Infernum still at my side, I whirled to my right and landed a fist on the side of one attacker's face. He crumpled beneath my extraordinary physical stat, yelling in pain and bracing himself on the wall to keep from falling. The second raider came in again swinging for my head, and I easily dodged to the side of his heavy mace. Overbalanced, the raider fell too far forward, and his weapon crashed into the lightly armored chest of his compatriot.

The two idiots were nearly out of the fight before I had even drawn my sword. I wheeled back with another punch and landed it on the center of the nearest raider's spine, and down he went. I could have easily killed him a number of different ways, but I decided to save my energy and simply let him scream on top of the ally he had crippled.

The building I was in was some kind of business, likely a general store from the looks of the shelves, though there was barely any inventory left. I guessed Vic's raiders had probably looted most of Riverside as they had set up their ambush.

I found a staircase leading up to the second floor in the back of the shop and made for it. I hesitated a moment at the bottom of the stairs, trying to listen for what might meet me at the top, but there was too much chaos to hear anything. Between the full-scale battle raging in the streets, the numerous fires burning all over Riverside, and the wailing man with a broken back behind me, all I could do was climb the stairs and hope for the best.

A trio of crossbow bolts slammed into the bottom of my breastplate right above my tassets. One of them was strong enough to break through, and the shimmer of red magic surrounding me indicated an enemy actually worth my time. Pain shot through my abdomen in hot waves, but it wasn't enough to really slow me down.

The three crossbowmen were kneeling in front of a locked door across the tight space. When I didn't collapse and immediately die, their eyes went wide. I gritted my teeth through the pain and charged, easily clearing the small span in two strides. The first crossbowman died before he really had a chance to even figure out what was going on, and the second fell not long after the first. I was a tornado of death and fiery steel, and two screaming sacks of meat and blood would do nothing to stop me.

The third crossbowman was far beyond the skills of the

first pair. He was a player, and the level floating above his head read nineteen. Without my legendary gear, perhaps we would have been somewhat evenly matched. As it was, the man didn't stand a chance, though he *could* slow me down, and wasting time wasn't something I wanted to do.

I spun to my left as the crossbowman's short sword came hurtling in at my waist. The weapon bit into a wooden beam, and the man was quick to rip it free and keep up his assault.

I parried a pair of strikes before pushing into the crossbowman's space with an attack of my own. Infernum swinging from overhead, I stepped forward with considerable strength. In response, the man activated a talent and rolled to his side faster than I could follow—where he came to an abrupt halt as his body connected with the fallen corpse of one of his comrades. There simply wasn't enough space in the cramped upper room of the building. I imagined the man's talents would make him adept at creating distance and quickly reloading his primary weapon, but in close quarters, Infernum's reach was unmatched. I swung again, and he tried to scramble away once more. My sword took both of his feet off at the ankles.

With a chorus of screams at my back, I slammed my weight into the barred door the crossbowmen had been protecting and shattered through it. The next room looked like a ransacked bedroom with one door directly ahead of me leading to the veranda and one to my right going somewhere else. I immediately turned to my right and blasted through the door like a heavy tree ruining a house in a storm.

Finally, I was out of the building. The chase was on. Narrow boards and other bits of household refuse had been strung together in a makeshift series of catwalks that Vic had used to escape. They led from one balcony to the next, crossing rooftops where the houses and businesses of Riverside were only a single story. Judging by the number of fallen planks in the alleys below, there had been more paths than the singular one remaining before me. Vic had escaped along the boardwalks and then destroyed some of them, very likely leaving a specific path for me to follow and nothing else.

I was quite literally walking into a trap. If Vic and his band were smart, the ambush awaiting me would be so overwhelming that I wouldn't have any possible hope of survival. On the other hand, I hadn't given him much time to prepare. Whatever was waiting for me at the end of the boardwalks would be less than perfect. Still, I couldn't take the risk.

In the streets to my left, seven or eight of my undead soldiers were shambling along the cobblestone and fighting over what appeared to be the remains of a civilian woman. Ellen was behind them, a scared expression on her face and blood staining her armor. I waved and called to them, and the warden was standing by my side about thirty seconds later.

"Send three zombies out on the boards!" I commanded.

It didn't take long for her to figure out my intention, though I silently counted every single second that went by. Vic was getting farther and farther from my grasp.

A trio of zombies ran out onto the first series of precariously balanced boards. When they didn't fall to the ground, I followed quickly behind with Ellen and the rest of the undead group bringing up the rear. We made it over the first four catwalks without incident until the fifth broke away under the weight of the undead and sent two of them plummeting to the street.

"I can reinforce it," Ellen said quickly, already diving into her magic. She summoned a burst of vines and rapidly growing saplings to lift the fallen planks back into position, and we were off again.

More traps met us on the next rooftop. They weren't extravagant, but we lost another zombie to a loose patch of shingles revealing a burning brazier below. Down to only four undead, we quickened our pace. I ordered Ellen to pre-emptively reinforce each boardwalk before we took it. Casting so many spells drained her mana, but it was a sacrifice I was more than willing to make.

Finally, after what felt like an eternity, I caught a glimpse of Vic. Or rather, I didn't *see* the man myself, but I saw Helvegen's outline in one of the buildings below thanks to the magic imbued in my helmet. When I called to her, she fired back an almost imperceptible amount of her painter's magic that showed me a crude image of Vic, and I knew she was also pursuing him and was closer than I was.

"Drop us down!" I basically yelled at Ellen.

Winded, the warden only nodded before starting up with her spells once more. She crafted a ramp of twisting vines and leafy branches, and we charged down it with our four remaining zombies in tow.

We stormed into Helvegen's building with all the tact and stealth of a drunken brawl. Pots and pans went flying from the nearest wall, and Ellen stomped right through a poorly made chair as we made our entrance.

"Where is he?" I yelled.

Helvegen's devious smile told me I was going to like the answer. "I changed what he sees, and he didn't notice the magic. I moved him to the wrong room. He's waiting for an ambush—but it isn't there." She pointed to two different buildings across the narrow alley from where we stood. "His trap is rigged *there*, but I moved him to the room diagonal from it. He has no idea."

"What kind of trap?" I asked.

"The floor gives out over spikes," the painter answered. "The spikes might be enchanted as well. I can't exactly tell, but I feel magic coming from them."

Perfect. I imagined getting behind Vic and pushing him

toward his own trap, slaughtering him on the spikes he had laid for me.

"Let's go," I commanded.

I led our small army out a door that would take us behind the building where Vic was hiding. We moved slower than before, taking extra care to muffle our footsteps. "One more bridge," I said to Ellen. Her eyes were bleary and cast down at the ground. If I pushed her much more, she'd be completely spent.

Tired as she was, the woman still didn't hesitate a single second. She reached down to the flagstones beneath our feet and began chanting softly under her breath. The rocks and stones started to rise until she was holding a large plate of street under her palm. Her expression soured, and she looked at me with sadness on her face. "I'm not strong enough," she said. "Not enough mana."

With a smile, I activated the enchantment in my cloak. *The Black Goblin's Restless Vengeance* instantly came to life, and a stout, shadowy goblin shimmered into existence at my side.

As far as I knew, shaman and wardens were fairly similar in the types of magic they employed, so using one to augment the other would probably work. "Finish the bridge!" I commanded the goblin. "But do it quietly, if you can."

The translucent goblin recognized Ellen's magic and began pulling more and more of the street into the air. He manipulated the floating stones and other debris with his hands, never touching anything, but rather conducting the pieces like a symphony. In less than a minute, we had a graduated staircase leading from the street to the base of the building's second story. It was wide enough for three of us to stand abreast with a little room.

I took point, and my goblin companion stayed right next to me. "Blast us through," I stated flatly.

The goblin shaman summoned a blast of swirling rock and

brilliant lava to his fingertips. When he had so much that he couldn't hold it all without it slipping through his incorporeal fingers, he shoved it forward where it collided with the wooden wall, blasting apart the entire back side of the building.

Through the rocketing shrapnel, I saw Vic facing the wrong direction. He shrieked and jumped forward, away from the blast, where he hit the closed door that he expected me to walk through. He only had one lieutenant with him, a warlord decked out in fairly high-tier armor that I recognized from some of the streams online. It was a set made by a blacksmith, and all the pieces together usually cost more than my entire year's salary.

In such a small space, I held every advantage: superior numbers, superior firepower, and superior defenses. At once, I launched my shadow pet at Vic's face while commanding both the goblin shaman and my four undead to charge forward with everything they could muster.

When Vic turned around to face the oncoming storm of devastation, I could see the fear in his eyes. He knew he was trapped. Helvegen's magic must have worn off, because he didn't immediately try to flee through the room's only door. He must have known exactly where he was and exactly what would meet him on the other side.

The goblin launched more and more fire into the room, filling the small space with choking smoke and brilliant tongues of flame. We wouldn't have more than a minute or two before the whole place would crumble. My undead soldiers—completely ignorant of the fire charring their already rotten bodies—attacked first. They ran toward Vic and his lieutenant with arms outstretched.

"Finally, something worth fucking killing!" the level thirty warlord bellowed. His name was Edgar, and he held a two-handed sword much like my own between his meaty hands. For armor, he wore studded leather glimmering with pale blue light. A single swing cut two of my zombies in half at the waist. Before I could recall the second pair of zombies, they met a similar fate, ending as splatters on the burning wall to my left.

My shadow pet managed to latch itself onto Vic's face without being summarily killed, but I only let it stay there for a single pulse of my lifeforce before dismissing it, opting to save as much as I could for when I needed it. The goblin shaman had much better luck. He threw wave after wave of elements into the crumbling, smoke-filled room. Vic turned and shielded his eyes from the elemental torrent. Edgar, much to my surprise, only laughed. The man was completely unaffected. He stomped forward—his left foot broke through the floor to the room below as he went—and then swung his sword overhead with both hands like a strongman trying to ring a bell with a mallet.

Edgar's weapon didn't slow as it passed through the goblin's body. It bit into the ground, sending up an explosion of smoking wood, but the shaman dissipated all the same. Whatever enchantments were on the warlord's weapon, they were extremely powerful.

The warlord roared into the sky, and more of the building's roof collapsed. Some of it landed on his shoulders, though he didn't even bother knocking it off.

Finally, Vic had endured enough of the smoke and the flames, and he fled through the only door, leaping as far over the deteriorating floorboards as he could. The supports on the other side of the room gave way, and all I could hear was a muffled, clipped scream as he fell through the rubble and out of view. That left Edgar standing between Vic and me. Honestly, facing Edgar alone wasn't something I really wanted to do.

"Hel, can you take him?" I asked, keeping my voice quiet enough that Edgar couldn't hear it.

The hulking woman shouldered past me without saying a word. She hefted her weapon up around her torso, and then all hell broke loose faster than I could comprehend.

Whatever talent build the warlord was utilizing, it was one I had never seen before. He fought with insane ferocity, countering even the heaviest of Helvegen's enhanced attacks seemingly with ease. Nothing the painter managed to put together—no combination of magic and brute strength—broke through Edgar's defenses.

The insane confluence of destruction quickly began to take down the whole building. All of the fire thrown inside by the shadow goblin accelerated the process, and I had to run back down the magically raised stairs after only a few seconds of fighting to avoid being hit by the collapsing roof. The whole structure toppled in on itself, throwing a huge wave of hot, smoky dust into my eyes. About ten feet away, I saw Ellen leaning against another structure trying to catch her breath, and it looked like her own chosen refuge was going to collapse any minute. Everywhere I looked, Riverside burned.

When the smoke cleared enough to see, both Helvegen and Edgar were still standing. It felt like watching two primordial titans slamming into each other at the creation of the world. The whole display was beyond awe-inspiring, but there was a distinct problem—Helvegen was losing. She didn't have enough physical combat experience to hold her own. There was only so much that her physical augmentation could compensate for, and the warlord was clearly an extremely talented fighter. I suspected the man had spent his entire life as Vic's personal bodyguard, and it showed. I checked my own stats, and I knew Edgar's physical stat would be so far beyond mine that I could never face him directly. At level thirty, assuming he had focused on physical which felt like a safe bet, he had sixty points in the stat. I only had thirty-one, and my gauntlets added thirty, meaning that we would essentially be tied. Against lesser opponents, my effective sixty-one would be devastating. Against someone who had spent their entire life fighting . . .

I needed another answer. For a moment, I thought of abandoning Helvegen and Ellen—perhaps my entire army— and just trying to grab Vic and make it back to Undercroft Citadel. Tempting as it was, I knew I couldn't. Edgar would come for his master one way or another, and I would not be adequately prepared.

More than anything, I thought of Ingrid. I didn't want to die. Death would mean the loss of her memory, and that was something I could never accept.

I flew through all my abilities searching for an answer.

Only one held any promise at all: *Host of Blasphemies*.

Riverside burned, my army was mindlessly slaughtering through untold numbers of civilians and Vic's raiders, and two unequaled fighters squared off amidst a pile of blazing ruins. The only members of Undercroft Citadel who might have offered any semblance of hope were Xollmomath and Kevin. As my luck would have it, neither of them was close at hand. Xollmomath still couldn't travel far enough from his summoning circle to go on a campaign, and my undead ranger was somewhere in the middle of the battle. Finding him would take time, and Helvegen would be dead by then.

I watched for another few seconds as Helvegen was forced back on her heels in a wild series of parries that left her unbalanced and out of form.

A shudder ran through my spine.

I activated *Host of Blasphemies*.

CHAPTER 22

I blinked.

When I opened my eyes, the world was different. I wasn't standing in Riverside. I was back in Lady Kalma's hall once more, though that wasn't exactly as I remembered either. Instead of a marble floor cool beneath my feet, I stood in about ten inches of swampy, fetid water. Reeds were growing up through patches of missing stone on the walls. I got the feeling that I was in a different time, either far in the future or far in the past, and the hall was little more than a ruin.

At the front of the chamber, Lady Kalma reclined on her throne, her unclothed feet making small circles in the water. Her black dog sat at her side as well. Neither of them seemed to mind the morass in the least.

"Hello?" I asked. I looked for the death goddess's two sisters, but I saw neither of them. Much to my surprise, I could see outside the room through the gaps in the walls. The last time I was in Lady Kalma's presence, I hadn't seen anything beyond the goddess and her sisters.

Lady Kalma reached out a hand and beckoned me forward. I took a few cautious steps, and the ground beneath my feet squished and sloshed. A swarm of small, annoying insects flew around the surface of the water, darting back and forth in seemingly random patterns.

"I . . . I'm here to serve," I stated, my head bowed in reverence.

"I know." A cold hand touched the top of my forehead. I didn't think I was close enough to her to be within arm's reach, but apparently I was wrong.

"You have served me well, Ben Hales," the goddess whispered. "You have spread the Stench of Corpses through all of Echelon. One of the great capitals of the world has fallen beneath your feet."

Somehow I got the uneasy feeling that I was about to be rewarded for my victory like an ancient Aztec athlete, and my celebration would end with my own death. "There is still much work to be done," I said. "Echelon is not entirely mine, not yet."

Lady Kalma laughed. Her dog gave a snort as well, as though it understood perfectly the words being exchanged. "Minor details," she said.

I wasn't sure what to say next. I had to measure my words and step carefully if I ever wanted to get back to Wonder with my life. "With your support, I know I will prevail."

Lady Kalma's hand moved from the top of my head to my cheek. Her touch was ice-cold, and it sent a cascade of shivers down my spine. "What would you have of me?" I dared to ask.

Her fingers tapped out a gentle pattern on my cheek and jaw like she was contemplating what to say next. "It has been many centuries—millennia, perhaps—since I have conducted such a ritual as you ask of me in this very moment."

I swallowed hard. Sounds started coming through the water behind me. People were approaching. Many of them.

"How long is it going to take?" I asked.

Lady Kalma tsked. "You cannot rush the old gods," she answered quietly. "Perfection takes time."

A tentacle reached around my legs. It came from below and behind me all at once. More grasping appendages wrapped around the rest of my body, and they slowly pulled me down toward the murky water. It wasn't a violent action—more like a loving pull, but it terrified me nonetheless.

I sank to my knees, and then the worm-like tentacles kept pulling me until I was entirely underwater. The swampy water flooded into my lungs. It stung my eyes and sinuses. I could barely see beyond the top of the water, and it looked like someone—maybe Lady Kalma—was kneeling on top of me.

One of her hands reached below the water. I was running out of air and my lungs were burning. The tentacles held me down so strongly that I could barely even move my shoulders.

Lady Kalma's hand came into view, and she was holding a thin white needle. She pressed it into the side of my neck, and a bolt of pain rocketed through my entire body.

I closed my eyes, coughing and sputtering underwater as the relentless swamp filled my lungs, and everything went black.

I awoke exactly where I had been when I activated the talent. I felt like I had just come awake from a long sleep—thousands of years—and I immediately noticed something was wrong. My perspective was different. My senses were enhanced, of that there was no doubt, but something was also . . . *different*. It took me a few seconds to fully realize what it was. I was taller than I had been before. It wasn't an extreme difference, maybe six or eight inches, but that was more than enough to be significant.

My armor was also gone. The legendary gear sat in a pile to my side. It wouldn't fit again without modification, but Lady Kalma had seen fit to at least let me keep it. If I could get Elyk into the armor and whirling through Riverside, nothing would ever stop us. By then, I thought with a sigh, the battle would be over.

Another difference caught my attention as I exhaled. My breath was different. It was deeper and more resonant—and then I realized I didn't actually *need* to breathe. I only sighed because my human experiences had made the action second nature. When I held my lips closed and refused to let any air escape through my nose, my lungs did not burn. Perhaps I didn't even have lungs.

I quickly summoned my character sheet and ran through my stats, scanning over all the radical changes:

Bentalÿk, Level 20 Blight of Deep Waters, Defender of the Necropolis, Host of Blasphemies, Scourge of Echelon

Physical: 38

Cunning: 40

Influence: 37

Renown: 55

Investigation: 9

Trade: 10

Craftsmanship: 10

Fortune: 13

Infamy: 413

Status: unstable, feared, hated and feared by Echelon, hated by Imps (wild beasts), blessed by Lady Kalma

Holdings: Undercroft Citadel (Dungeon), Riverside (Vassal - destroyed), Tendershoot Mine

Allegiance: Lady Kalma, the Stench of Corpses

Everything had changed. My class was different, my stats were elevated, and Riverside was already listed as destroyed. Perhaps the most profound change of all was in my name. I was no longer Ben Hales. When I thought about it, I realized that perhaps I hadn't actually *been* that person with that name for quite some time. I was something different.

My class was also different. I had completely dropped the 'deathbringer' label in favor of something altogether insidious: Blight of Deep Waters. I loved the new moniker. It had a devious ring to it that evoked images of great sorrow and drowning and disease.

The name made me think of humanity's extinction.

Somehow, like the low rumble that indicates hunger, I *felt* like I knew my true purpose as Lady Kalma's servant. Visions of destruction flashed before my eyes. In the space of a single, isolated moment in time, I saw the whole of Wonder. The world burned and crumbled. Legions of the dead swarmed over buildings and through streets littered with corpses. My lieutenants stood on raised plinths and commanded the horde, bringing forth destruction in every possible way. Behind it all, I stood as motionless as time itself, radiating pure terror and sanity-breaking unreality into everything that was not quickly slaughtered.

As quickly as the vision came, so too did it vanish. The extinction of humanity could wait a moment longer. For now, I only had one task.

I took a step forward and saw that the changes which had overcome my body were just as profound as those affecting my character sheet. Not only was I taller, but I was barely even *human*.

No, I thought, shaking my head. *I'm not human. I'm so much more than that. What was the term Lady Kalma had used in the Host of Blasphemies talent? Ah, yes. Blessed perfection.* That *was my form.*

My lower half seemed to be composed more of cephalid parts than mammal, a trio of powerful tentacles extending from my torso to the street. I felt every sensation through them as well. The rough stone that normally would have been hidden from my sense of touch by my boots now felt detailed and alive. My waist and torso, while not cephalid, were certainly aquatic in nature. My upper body was made from something hard, perhaps similar to insect chitin or a crustacean's scalloped carapace. The plates that composed my body were certainly organic, and they were held together by heavy bands of a dark cloth material that looked like leather but felt hard as steel.

I touched the bands of thread holding me together, and I marvelled at my hands. I was no longer bound by weak human limitations. Where four fingers and a thumb had been, I now had eight digits, each completely flexible in any direction and intricately possessed of sensory capabilities. My new arms were also longer than they had been before, extending well beyond their original lengths. I tested them, moving my fingers in all directions to form different shapes that might be useful. I grabbed Infernum from my pile of gear and tested it in my hands. Somehow, the sword simply felt weak. It felt less than myself, like I could do so much more without the limitations of humanity's inventions, effective as the sword might actually be. I tossed it aside and formed the digits on my right arm into something resembling a cone or a drill.

I slammed my tentacle arm into the street, and the stone shattered. I wasn't *that* much physically stronger than before— my physical stat had only increased by a marginal amount— but my flexible digits were so much more precise, and the rigidity they possessed was unparalleled. I formed a fist, and my own fingers felt like a hammerhead at the end of my arm.

With so many dramatic changes, I was eager to find a mirror. When the dust of Riverside settled, I would search the ruins for one.

But a mirror could wait.

For the second time since my transformation, I committed myself to Vic's death.

System Administration, Incoming Message, All Players . . .

Alert!

My cephalid feet froze in place. All of Wonder came to a quiet halt.

This is a personal message from Samira Koinos, Director of Player Relations and Gameplay Experience.

The text scrolled slowly through my vision, taking a painstakingly long amount of time to reach the top. I got the feeling that Wonder was making sure they had everyone's undivided attention before allowing the rest of the message to be transmitted. Finally, more text came:

Progress concerning server repair has been delayed. After the initial attack, it took our technicians several weeks to detect a subtle bug, a glitch in the code, that accidentally allowed an earlier alpha version of the game, one of the first patches created by the development team, to be reconnected to the primary server modules. The patch in question was written during the game's infancy, and certain key decisions regarding gameplay had not yet been made. One of those decisions deals with player reconstitution and resurrection outside the game.

In the first version of Wonder, players reconstituted within the game world itself, coming back to life at central resurrection hubs near each capital city. Obviously, decisions were made during testing that changed that system.

Another long pause. The text floated all the way to the top of my vision and disappeared. After what felt like at least five minutes, the message continued.

Finally, some good news. It is with great pleasure that I am able to inform you that due to the old patch attaching itself to the primary servers, player revival within the game world should be operational upon the conclusion of this message. Players who die inside the game will be resurrected at the hub located on their continent.

Unfortunately, the addition of the old patch has brought other difficulties. The alpha version of Wonder included certain NPCs, deities, mythos, and storylines that were not included in the retail version of the game. One such deity from the original version of the game was scripted to be the only NPC capable of passing through a city portal into the real world, supported by dedicated servers integral to sustaining the game itself. Events had been planned surrounding the NPC's arrival in the real world, but those plans were cancelled when the patch was discarded. As you know, no real-world crossover events have ever taken place.

It is with a heavy heart that I now inform you of the return of the deity known as Hastalÿk. Since the character was never fully scripted by the development team, little is known about it other than its sole ability to cross the barrier between the game and reality. Hastalÿk is a cruel and evil deity, powerful beyond reason, and will likely wreak untold havoc on Earth.

Wonder Technologies, Inc. has created a projected timeline for external player reconstitution. Right now, it is the estimate of the server repair team that Wonder should return to normal function in approximately ten months. When that happens, all city portals will also return to normal function, and players will be encouraged to leave the game.

When the portals return to their functioning state, the delays to cross back into reality will be massive. In order to prioritize such crossings, Wonder Technologies, Inc. has authorized me to offer a bounty. Whichever player or guild or other coalition of players is responsible for the death of Hastalÿk will receive priority departure from the game when the portals come back online.

More updates will come as they are made available.

Thank you for your patience in this trying time.

The world returned to normal speed, and my mind reeled. *I* was Hastalÿk. My name wasn't *exactly* the same, but it was close enough to remove any doubt from my mind. *I* was the old god awakened from a since-deleted patch. I was supposed to be an NPC, but that felt like a minor detail.

Still about ten feet in front of me, Helvegen and Vic's warlord bodyguard continued to fight, but it was obvious that their hearts weren't in it like before. Death no longer held much sting. They would both regenerate at wherever the new spawn location happened to be.

I could feel everything I had worked for slipping through my fingers. With death no longer permanent and a bounty on my head that would be attractive to every single player in the game, I was failing. I wouldn't be able to hold Undercroft Citadel together for more than a few weeks at best. Armies of high-level players would come looking to collect, and from the tone of the message, I didn't think I would be able to respawn. I would be the only one still affected by death.

One of Vic's raiders, a lightly armored thief wielding a dagger in each hand, came hurtling at my side, pulling my attention back to the battle still raging through all of Riverside. I quickly formed my tentacle arms into a shield of sorts and deflected the attack. My rapid parry added to the thief's momentum and slammed him to the side where he landed in a skid on the broken street. I slithered to him as quickly as I could—which turned out to be much faster than I was previously capable of—and melded both my tentacles into one solid, drill-like point. When my arms connected with the thief's armor, they went straight through him. The man's chest was blasted apart, and he died with a quiet whimper and a spray of internal organs.

It didn't matter. He would come back in a few moments ready to fight again. Unless I destroyed the resurrection module outside Echelon, the man would keep coming back life after life.

Unless I destroyed the resurrection module . . .

I knew what I needed to do. I would destroy the resurrection nodes around each city, bringing back the wonderful gift of real death, and then I would walk through a portal. Then I could bring that same gift to everyone else. Humanity's light would extinguish, and I would be free to remake both worlds. Lady Kalma and I would create a new reality.

But my grand plans had to wait. The resurrection point outside Echelon had become my new, immediate priority.

I propelled myself toward Helvegen on my new cephalid legs. She was still essentially holding a neutral position against the warlord, though she had taken a beating before, and the wounds covering her upper arms were numerous. I tried to push her out of my way and succeeded in throwing her roughly to the ground, but I didn't care. The warlord was coming on all the same, swinging his weapon with both hands and all the weight he could muster. Instead of deflecting the blow, I used my quick speed to jolt to the side. My tentacle arms shot out with digits splayed, wrapping the man's face and neck in my strong grasp. He struggled and fought to free himself, but he was too off-balance to get any purchase and really fight back.

Holding the warlord in place, I slithered behind him where I would have the most leverage. He started screaming as I pulled his body backward, bracing his shorter legs with my own muscular, dripping lower half. His back popped, and I pulled farther. When his neck broke a few seconds later, he stopped screaming, and I tossed his body into the burning rubble nearby.

"Vic!" I yelled, hearing my new voice for the first time. Aloud, I sounded the same as before, but inside my skull, it sounded like a handful of voices were all calling out the same thing at the same time. Perhaps I was possessed. It would make sense. Or maybe the true NPC entity I had accidentally become was trapped somewhere in my consciousness. Either way, the extra voices were unnerving.

Not surprisingly, I didn't get any response from the rubble and ruins. Fires burned all around, and though I could tell my sense of hearing had been enhanced, I didn't detect any sounds of a human struggling to escape.

I yelled a few more times, and still nothing.

"Helvegen, help me find Vic," I commanded.

The two of us tore through the fallen rubble. Vic had been in the middle between two collapsing buildings, so there was no possible way he could have gotten very far. But . . . he had seen the same message I had. He could have killed himself after the message went through, and that would mean he was totally healed somewhere outside Echelon, effectively out of my grasp.

I dug with more and more frenzy, ignoring the burns that bubbled up on my pallid, squid-like flesh.

Finally, I found him. He was alive, still conscious, and pinned beneath a slowly smoldering square of fallen roof. Both his legs were hopelessly shattered. In his left hand he held a small crescent of leaded glass, and his right wrist was bleeding, though not too badly.

"Don't have the balls for suicide?" I taunted, grabbing him by his shattered ankles and pulling him out of the wreckage so that his chest and face were brutally scraped by the underside of the fallen roof.

His head rolled to the side, and he spat a glob of blood and dirt from his mouth. "Fuck you," he grunted.

"Hel, grab a healing potion. Feed it to him." I used my considerable height and strength to hold Vic up from behind while Helvegen forced a potent healing potion down his throat. His body stiffened a bit as the healing magic ran its course, and before long, he was no longer in any imminent danger of death.

"You have him," the painter said with a bit of relief in her voice. "What now?"

A short wave of relief ran through my body. "Get my sword and armor. Find Elyk and the others, rally whatever is left of the zombies, and meet me back at Undercroft Citadel as soon as you can."

"And Riverside?" she asked.

"Round up any civilian survivors you can. If they try to run, I don't honestly care. Kill them, let them run, it does not matter. Anyone with a useful skill is welcome back home, though we won't be able to feed them to Xollmomath until I destroy the regeneration beacon," I answered.

Judging by Helvegen's expression, she had not considered the destruction of the regeneration points a likely course of action. The entire concept probably hadn't crossed her mind. Soon her surprise gave way to understanding, and she leapt into her tasks with all the haste she always brought to the job.

I made sure to collect my poisoned dagger before heading back to Undercroft Citadel, Vic slung over my left shoulder like a sheep being carried to a slaughterhouse.

Finally, I mused. *I have him.*

By nightfall, Riverside had been so thoroughly destroyed that it didn't even show up on my stat sheet anymore. The town was razed, and what was left of my army had returned to Undercroft Citadel to regroup and recover.

The sight that greeted my army was one of morbid splendor. Lady Kalma had seen fit to enhance my necropolis once more, and the entire structure had at least tripled in size. Made of bone columns banded with steel, carved marble tentacles, detailed relief etchings showing all manner of horrific underwater displays, and extensive spiraling staircases more fitting for a grand ballroom than a palace of evil, the necropolis towered over a hundred feet into the sky. There were so many rooms that I didn't have time to explore them all.

I found the ossuary, the dark and death-filled chamber Lady Kalma used as her church, and brought Vic there. I took some chains from the workshop and used them to tie him to the altar, then brought Ellen and as many potions as she could find.

I started by removing Vic's legs and genitalia at his waist. With enough magic, he couldn't bleed out or even lose consciousness, but he felt enough of the pain to keep up a steady, wallowing scream all the way until dawn. With the sun warming my back, I used Infernum to cut off both of Vic's arms. We ran out of healing potions then, and we had to resort to more conventional methods of healing as Ellen was out of mana as well. I fashioned a tourniquet for each of Vic's newest stumps, then began working with a small knife on his eyelids, lips, tongue, ears, nose, and nipples. I took it all. The refuse contained nearly as much mass as what was left, and I had the pile of gore thrown into a fire in the central courtyard.

When Vic had been reduced to nothing more than a bloody torso attached to an even bloodier head, I took one of his eyes. I left one just so he could see what was coming, and then left him in the ossuary for the night.

Walking back to my room at the highest point in the towering necropolis, I only felt *slightly* satisfied.

Torturing Vic felt too easy. It didn't give me nearly as much pleasure as I had thought it would. No matter how many cuts I made—and I made *thousands*—none of them would bring Ingrid back to me. The motions felt hollow and lifeless.

I didn't bother fighting back any tears as I collapsed into my sheets. Helvegen must have heard, and she knocked on my door only a couple minutes later.

"Come in," I said, brushing my eyes and sitting up to calm my breathing.

She entered the door and shut it behind her, then came to sit by my side. With my new height, I was close enough to equaling her stature that we could look each other in the eye while sitting without making it awkward.

"I've separated the useful civilians from Riverside. The ones too old or too weak to be of service have been killed. They'll just respawn now, but that was easier than letting them go right outside the gate," she began.

"I know, I caught a glimpse of it earlier," I said. "There's so much work to do. But we can start handling it in the morning." I hadn't even finished going through my own character sheet and selecting new abilities, so consumed was I with Vic's torture.

Helvegen nodded and got up to leave, but I caught her wrist with my own hand, forcing my long digits to resemble something like a human touch. She didn't immediately pull away from me, so I figured that whatever sensation she felt wasn't too unnerving.

"Hey," I whispered. "Before your . . . transformation, do you remember much? About us?"

She looked down at me, and instead of disgust or trepidation, I saw the same Helvegen I had seen before.

"Yes, I remember," she answered.

I pulled her down closer, and she let herself be guided by my touch.

I tried to think of something else to say, but she cut me off before I could. "I didn't think you would want me any more . . ."

I couldn't help but laugh. "Look at me," I said. "We're both . . . different." I had almost said 'monsters,' but that label didn't necessarily apply to her, just me. I was the freak, not her. It was my turn to move away, suddenly ashamed of my appearance despite still not having seen my own face. Perhaps I was hideous. Perhaps I wasn't. I didn't know.

Helvegen wrapped an arm around my shoulder and pushed her body close to mine. I felt so empty inside after torturing Vic that all I wanted was some kind of positive human contact. I mentally commanded the lights to dim, and again, Helvegen did not retreat from my closeness.

Before I knew exactly what was happening, the two of us were kissing, and my breathless lungs added a strange feeling of death to the whole experience that I think we both equally enjoyed. It made our kiss exotic, unusual, *invigorating*.

We spent the night together much as we had in the past, and though Helvegen's personality had changed quite drastically since her transformation, we still shared an undeniable connection. Most interestingly, the two of us discovered that my new, terrifying body still worked in the traditional human sense despite my altered anatomy.

When I awoke in the morning, the tall, imposing woman was still in my room, though she had left my bed. She stood near the doorway barely clothed, wearing only her undergarments and holding a tin cup. We didn't have anyone left to make coffee, so I figured she was drinking either water or wine.

I felt so much better, so much more full of life than I had the previous day, that the smile I wore must have looked stupid. The two of us spent the better half of the morning bantering back and forth, trying desperately to move things back to the way they used to be.

Things were starting to feel normal. I still had a monumental amount of work waiting for me with the resurrection points, killing Vic, and then . . . carrying Lady Kalma's message of death to the rest of humanity. I thought about going through the portal in Echelon right away, but there was no way it would work. If they thought I was truly a threat, there would be military soldiers with modern equipment waiting on the other side of every single portal. I had to wait and build up strength.

There was so much to do, and all I wanted was another couple hours of normalcy with Helvegen. She came over once more and ran a hand along the new, elongated line of my chin, then offered me her glass. It was half-full of syrupy white wine that smelled like mead. I finished the cup and set it down on the small nightstand to my side.

"Hey," I said, gently pulling her close once more. "I've been meaning to ask you something."

"Oh?"

"A while back, back in the beginning of all this, after we got our first big win and everyone got drunk, Elyk told me you looked for me. He said you had something to say, some-thing to tell me."

She pulled a few inches away, and her expression clouded. Perhaps it was the change in her demeanor, her emboldened confidence, but I got the distinct feeling that she was about to tell me something horrible and had only the barest of reser-vations about saying it.

Her eyes met mine. "Remember the organization I joined back on Earth? The whole reason why I ran to Wonder to hide in the first place?"

I nodded. The sinking feeling in my gut deepened.

"The next plan," she went on, "was to attack the servers. Af-ter the nuclear site, everyone wanted to take down the game. That was the second target. I don't know for sure, but I think my group is responsible for the server shutdown. They're the reason Ingrid is dead."

All the emptiness I had finally filled returned tenfold. Helvegen stood still, staring me in the eyes and still letting my squid-like digits rest on her hand. Her expression showed no remorse.

The old Helvegen would have never told me, not even when she was drunk. And there was good reason, too. She knew I would kill her, that I wouldn't hesitate, and her death would not be pleasant.

The long digits of my right hand curled around with an iron grip on her forearm, and my left tentacle formed into a sharp point. I ripped her in close at the same time I jabbed with my spike, and Helvegen was impaled where she stood.

She died in my arms, and I mentally summoned a gargoyle to come and take her corpse from my sight. Her dead body dissipated in a greyish swirl of pixels before the gargoyle could even scoop her off the bloody floor. Resurrection was back, and that meant Helvegen was still alive.

I cursed my fucking luck and grabbed a simple shirt from my small wardrobe. Vic could wait—now he would *have* to wait—until the Echelon resurrection node was completely destroyed. I ordered a group of four of my pill bug guardians to roll to the ossuary to stand guard over the limbless lump of flesh that used to be Vic Fuentes. I told them to do whatever it would take to keep him alive and in as much pain as possible, and I received the mental feeling indicating that they understood.

I went next to a large marble veranda below my bedroom that overlooked the main grounds of Undercroft Citadel. Xia and Xollmomath were down below sorting some of the spoils from Riverside—not that we had really captured much—and the handful of civilian NPCs we had spared were lined up against a wall.

"Get everyone together," I commanded. I didn't particularly care who followed my order so long as someone went to get the rest of the players and NPCs. Xia did, and she had everyone assembled within a few minutes.

I surveyed my domain, both hands on the marble banister like a dictator in a history textbook. "I know we just got back from war. You're tired, and we need to reassess our strength before we move again. I know that. Unfortunately, we don't have time. We campaign tomorrow for the resurrection module outside Echelon. I don't know what it looks like, but it will be easy to find. When we destroy it, everyone on this continent will once more be subject to true death. Then we'll find the next and the next. Seven nodes, six cities full of players who will be protecting their nodes with their lives, and we'll destroy them all."

Xollmomath fixed me with dark red eyes and smiled.

ABOUT THE AUTHOR

Stuart Thaman is the international best-selling author of almost twenty novels. He writes epic fantasy and LitRPG, trying to find unique plots and bring them to readers everywhere. He holds degrees in politics, classical philosophy, German, and law.

He spends his days playing with his cats, going to metal shows, smoking cigars, collecting tattoos, and trying to learn card tricks.

Check out all the latest books at stuartthamanbooks.com where you can grab a free download just for signing up on the email list.

THE ADVENTURE CONTINUES IN
FORSAKEN TALENTS: A RUINED WORLD

Get a free copy of *The Minotaur King*
by joining the mailing list!

https://dl.bookfunnel.com/lt2mw0eidx